HOSTILE CHARMS

The Possession Chronicles #5

By

Carrie Dalby

For Sandra Buford,

one of my biggest cheerleaders,

and

Jeremy Northam,

for bringing so much charm to numerous Edwardian Era films

One

Frederick Davenport walked the floor of his bedroom in the midnight hour, swinging a teething Bethany in his arms as she sucked a wet washcloth. The fifteen-month-old settled against his shoulder, her cloth leaving a wet spot near the buttons on his pajamas. He switched to swaying, hoping to lull her to sleep.

"You get those molars through and everything will be better," he promised, sealing it with a kiss on her brunette hair. "Happy Valentine's Day, Little Princess."

It was a night for romance, but he'd spent the evening with his daughters, allowing them chocolate after supper. When he'd picked up Phoebe and Bethany from Lucy's house after work, he tried not to allow the vision of Alexander's arm around his ex-wife's waist pain him. But on a day like that—when desks were crowded with flowers and men took meals with their women—he couldn't stop the loneliness from creeping in.

After transferring Bethany to her crib in the corner of the girls' room, he paused to lay a hand on his four-year-old's blonde locks. Phoebe's little mouth curled into a slight smile, every bit her mother's daughter. Frederick prayed his oldest had enough of him in her to keep grounded.

The next morning, Frederick missed his shave because Bethany clung to him. He ate breakfast with her in his lap and the three rode in his automobile for the cross-town drive. Letting themselves in the front door of the Eastons' old home, Phoebe ran to her bedroom upstairs with her favorite doll and bunny in her arms.

Lucy, wrapped in her silk kimono, kissed Frederick's cheek and took Bethany from him. "Freddy, you look positively exhausted. Help yourself to some coffee in the kitchen."

"Her molars are about through." He smoothed Bethany's blue dress and tried not to think why Lucy's hair was tousled. "I'll gladly stop for coffee. I didn't get a chance to make any."

Bethany settled against Lucy's shoulder, taking a fistful of her mother's hair into her little hand. Lucy moved to follow Frederick into the kitchen.

"I've got it, Goosy. Relax while you can. You'll get quite a workout holding Beth today."

"Darla is supposed to be here this afternoon, so that will give me a break. Let me know if you want me to keep the girls for the weekend. I'm sure you could use a respite."

He looked away from her tender green eyes. "I'll let you know when I get them this evening."

Upstairs, feet stomped and Phoebe's battle cry rang out. "Kingdom Davenport is here to battle Melling Militia!"

"No!" Alexander's voice was high and playful. "Send anyone but Knight Rummy! Retreat, retreat!"

Frederick imagined Phoebe attacking her stepfather with her stuffed rabbit in one hand and a play sword in the other. He met Lucy's bright countenance with a smile.

"They play together like you and Edmund used to," she remarked.

In his sleep-deprived state, his guard dropped and a hand went to her cheek. "Are you Alex's fair maiden now?"

She nuzzled into his hand, kissing his palm. "You'll always be my knight."

Frederick hid himself in the breakfast nook off the kitchen in an attempt to fight his weakness for Lucy. Halfway through his coffee, Alexander sauntered in. His unshaven face looked fresh, his gray suit unrumpled because he hadn't handled children all morning.

"I didn't know you were still here." Alexander poured himself coffee and sat at the table. His discolored hand held the dainty china with the grace of a gentleman.

"Lucy took pity on me and suggested coffee before I head to work."

"She told me she offered to keep the girls over the weekend. It would be no trouble. We have no plans as we attended a masquerade last weekend and enjoyed time together last night and this morn—"

"I appreciate being friends with you, but there are some things I don't wish to hear."

Alexander laughed, looking like his old self with the mischievous smile. The Alexander who claimed victory in getting to Lucy first. The one who boasted in having prowess in bed that made Lucy come back for more even after he mistreated her when they were first engaged.

"Freddy, you know I'd only say something like that to you. You're the only one who understands what it's like to share her passion. I no longer tell stories of my conquests and there is only one with whom I—"

"Spare me the details." Frederick unclenched his fist and rubbed a hand over his stubbly jaw.

"Why don't you take Susan up on her offer of hosting you for the long Mardi Gras weekend? Go meet some of those Grand Bay beauties she's forever telling you about."

"Because being matched by your ex-sister-in-law isn't completely awkward."

Alexander grinned. "Those Easton girls are something else. I'm surprised Lucy hasn't tried to play matchmaker herself."

"She has, in a way. She's told me who she will in no way share me or her daughters with. Too bad she didn't listen to me in those regards. But I'm glad you turned out decent." Frederick slapped Alexander's shoulder in parting.

Ten minutes later, Frederick walked into Davenport Allied Accountants and was besieged by Judith Smith. The young widow had her eyes on him since she first came to the office for accounting help while he was still married to Lucy. Her brunette hair was piled high and her neckline cut provocatively low for a day dress.

"Mr. Davenport, you poor thing. Did you have a difficult night with your girls?"

"Thank you for your concern, Mrs. Smith. My youngest is getting some teeth in and it makes her uncomfortable much of the time. I needed to hold her more often than not."

"That's a lucky girl to be in your arms." She fingered the pearls at her neck and smiled. "You pull off the sleepless look well enough, but it's been over a year now. When will you settle with a new wife? You need someone to help you during the night."

Frederick smiled, knowing Judith was at the top of Lucy's list of women she didn't wish to see him with, but she was also someone he would never settle for—even if her body was pleasing to look upon. "When the time is right, but it's nothing for you to worry over."

"There's a performance of 'The Old Town' this weekend at Mobile Theater. I've thought of going but Mr. Peabody doesn't think

I have room in the budget for another outing during carnival season. I was hoping someone would ask me."

"Good luck, Mrs. Smith. I'm certain Mr. Peabody knows best." He hurried to his office and slammed the door.

Two

Melissa Stone stood on the top deck of the swaying ship, sea legs well established from her world travels. Rather than holding the railing, she touched the brooch she was gifted in Jamaica as she gazed across the mouth of Mobile Bay. When she'd received the telegram from Mr. Noble about an assignment in Alabama, she didn't relish the thought of babysitting a novelist, even though her publisher had thrown in a nonfiction piece for her as well. He flattered her through a series of telegrams sent to her hotel, including phrases like "you are the only one I trust" and "your readership will expand once you tie in with the Southern novel set."

So Melissa reluctantly agreed, leaving her last assignment in Kingston to steam across the Gulf of Mexico. On the voyage, she completed her travel bit on the local customs and wonders of Jamaica for *Noble Travels* magazine, and also an essay for her collection of travel writing she hoped she could talk her boss into publishing as a book when she returned to New York. Beyond padding her own portfolio on her Mobile stop, she believed obliging Mr. Noble would soften him toward her pitch of the marketability of stories from a single woman traveling the world—just the thing for suffragettes and career-minded women, as well as adventurous wives fantasizing about getting away from it all.

Her journey to the port city took a day less than expected. Rather than going to the home of Olive Kent, she secured a driver to bring her to a hotel the first of March. After re-pinning her red hair and freshening her clothes, she telephoned the publishing company.

"Ms. Stone, I'm glad you've arrived state-side." Mr. Noble's voice came through the wire. "I hope everything was satisfactory."

"Yes, and I'll mail my article first thing Monday morning. I'm a day early so I checked into a hotel. I'll send word to Ms. Kent—"

"Not Ms. Kent, it's Mrs. Davenport—no Melling. She remarried last year."

"I thought I was to assist the author of *Winter of My Heart*."

"And you shall, Ms. Stone. Olive Kent is her pen name. She was Miss Easton when I first met her, but she's on her second husband now."

Melissa wrote the names on her notepad. A frown settled as she thought of keeping a novelist on task when she couldn't focus on one husband during her short career. She was certain she'd have nothing in common with the woman who wrote romances. True, she'd seen love expressed on five continents and in dozens of countries—a few of the instances involving herself—but how a Southern Belle might fit into her life's collection of the human experience she didn't know.

"I mailed Mrs. Melling a new contract with the extension date of May third," he continued.

Melissa inwardly sighed at the mention of her thirtieth birthday.

"That's six months after the last one and a year from the original. I wish everyone was as punctual as you when it comes to deadlines, Ms. Stone. I also reminded our star novelist that the longer she waits to publish the next book, the more she will have to work to keep her readers. We'll rush through edits to get it published by November, but that's still a two year wait from her last novel."

"I'll do all I can, Mr. Noble."

Upon finishing her conversation, she asked the concierge for directions to the nearest jeweler. Walking a few blocks, she enjoyed the architecture and the public square edged with pink blooms—the famed azaleas of the southern town. Though she enjoyed traveling, it was always good to be back in her home country, especially in a quaint city like Mobile. Under her parasol, the same emerald of the stones on the gold brooch, she strolled to Hofstedder's Jewelry.

Mr. Hofstedder himself promptly waited on Melissa. "Welcome to my establishment, Miss. I can see you have exquisite taste."

"Thank you. The concierge at The Battle House recommended you. I'd like to get this appraised, please." She slipped off the pin and handed it across the counter.

Melissa browsed the displays, spending most of her time near the cameos in an attempt to feel closer to her departed grandmother. The jeweler double and triple checked with multiple eye pieces and polished the gold front and back.

"Miss?"

"It's Ms. Stone." She returned to the counter nearest his workspace, tucking her parasol further under her arm.

"Ms. Stone, where did you acquire such an amazing piece of history?" He rubbed his balding head.

"On my travels to Jamaica."

A knowing smile lined his face. "Then it's pirate treasure, I'd say."

Her pulse quickened as she thought back to the fantastical story the old woman outside the hotel had told her about Anne Bonny and Captain Calico Jack, who were captured, tried, and hung in Port Royal in 1720. "Why do you think it's pirate treasure?"

"It's Spanish from about seventeen hundred. If you purchased it in Jamaica, there's a good chance it was pirate loot.

Many ships from Spain were lost in that era to piracy. Would you be interested in selling it?"

"No, thank you." She smiled. "How much do I owe you for the appraisal?"

"It was a blessing to see such workmanship. No charge, but do come to me if you decide to sell or have any other jewelry needs on your stay."

"I will. Thank you, again."

Melissa felt odd pinning on a treasure when she'd thought it a clever copy, but calmly stopped at a restaurant on the way back and took an early supper.

At the hotel, she looked up the telephone number she was given for her assignment.

"Mellings' residence," a kind voice answered as the sound of children twittered in the background.

"This is Ms. Stone from Noble Publishing. I'm trying to reach Mrs. Melling."

"Yes, Ms. Stone. She's expecting you. Just a moment."

The sounds of rowdiness ensued, followed by a "Go get your momma!"

A minute later, a new line clicked on and the noisy one went silent. "Sorry about that. My husband recently arrived and the girls were excited to play. And who's this?" Her voice was youthful and more open than Melissa expected.

"This is Ms. Stone from Noble—"

"Melissa Stone! Mr. Noble speaks so highly of you and I've enjoyed your travel articles. I look forward to you coming tomorrow. I must say, this connection is quite clear."

"I arrived this afternoon and checked into a hotel for the night."

"Oh, but you could have come straight here! Your room is ready and everything."

"Thank you, Mrs. Melling, but—"

"Please call me Lucy," her voice was rushed, breathless.

"Very well, Lucy. I'm already settled at the hotel and it would be best if I rested fully before coming."

Lucy's laughter sounded like zills worn by belly dancers in Turkey. "Traveling can be exhausting, and if you'd happened in on this excitement with the girls here, it might scare you back to New York. Things will be quieter tomorrow. What time should we collect you?"

"I have a trunk and several suitcases. It would be easier for me to hire a driver who could help carry the luggage."

"If you think that's best. Will you be here in time to take dinner at one?"

"Yes, thank you. I'll plan to arrive the hour before."

"That's perfect, Ms. Stone. I look forward to seeing you tomorrow."

Three

After leaving the office the first day of March, Frederick went to the gym as he did three afternoons a week—taking exercise time and grabbing supper with bachelor friends before picking up the girls from Lucy. Often Henry Adams joined him, but he'd left work early to travel with his fiancée for a weekend with his parents in Chatom.

Frederick changed into his boxing clothes and warmed his muscles on the rowing machine before meeting Chuck Brady, the head of advertising for Gayfer's department store, in the ring.

"Are you joining the tournament on the sixteenth?" Chuck asked as Thomas Charles, another regular, tightened his gloves. "You'd have as good a chance of winning as anyone else in our division."

"It's on a Saturday. I'd have my girls." Frederick circled his opponent and made a few jabs.

"No excuses this time." Chuck shook back the wave of black hair that fell across his eyes. "You've turned down all invitations lately and I've heard you say Lucy is more than willing to watch the girls as she did last month when you went to the cinema like a bachelor should."

Frederick ducked a swing and countered. "I'm not a bachelor. I'm a twice-married man approaching thirty with two daughters to raise."

"And a beautiful ex-wife you see a dozen times a week and she's ready with a kiss for each greeting."

Frederick punched recklessly, earning him a laugh from the men watching.

"Come on, Davenport. I've seen how she is with you and the way you still look at her. You need to get over Lucy. She's happy with Alex. I doubt she'd ever come back to you."

"I wouldn't take her back." Frederick landed a strike to Chuck's gut. "Well, maybe for the girls' sakes."

Chuck got Frederick on the side. "Like hell it would be for the girls! Lucy's—"

"I'm ready to move on." He circled, guarding his face.

"Good. I invited a couple ladies to join us tonight." Frederick's fists dropped a few inches and Chuck took the opening to win the match. "Two out of three. Loser pays for supper!"

Frederick took out his frustration over the unexpected dinner date on the younger man and walked to the showers as winner. They arrived at the quick service restaurant and Frederick almost ran for his automobile when he saw who waited inside.

"Judith Smith! Are you crazy?"

Chuck slapped him on the back, gripping Frederick's jacket so he couldn't get away. "Sorry, Freddy. I invited Rachel and told her to bring a friend. One meal won't kill you."

It was difficult for Frederick to remain pleasant in his office when approached by Judith, but he found when he didn't have his business persona to rally him, he had trouble mustering a smile.

"Mr. Davenport, don't you have a handsome post-workout glow about you this evening." She went right for the lapel of his suit jacket, brushing off an invisible piece of lint. "I don't normally dine so casually for super, but when Rachel told me it would be with you, I was more than happy to make an exception."

"How good of you, Mrs. Smith." Frederick stepped back. "I was unaware I was dining with anyone other than Chuck until a few minutes ago. You look well, Ms. Wiseman."

"Enough with the formalities, Freddy. I insist everyone calls each other by their Christian names while we eat." Chuck offered his arm to his date. "Come on, Rachel."

Frederick reluctantly offered his arm to Judith and they followed the couple to a table in the corner.

Judith took the opportunity to feel his biceps and sighed. "You're the most athletic man I know, Frederick. I'd love to see you in the ring sometime."

"I'm trying to talk him into signing up for the tournament."

"You should." Rachel smiled across the table. "I'd like to see Chuck get what he has coming to him for once."

Chuck laughed and kissed her cheek spontaneously. "You would, wouldn't you?"

Rachel gave Chuck a flirty shrug, looking not a mite over twenty. Frederick felt himself growing gray hairs just looking at their young love. He glanced at Judith. She was around Lucy's age, but her games were more in line with the younger set than he was interested in. Still, he missed a woman's touch and enjoyed the smell of her perfume. By the time their food came, he'd grown to appreciate Judith's profile and was willing to chance a few glances her way to experience the view she was more than happy to afford him in her tight dress.

Halfway through the meal, Frederick set down his glass. "I think I will sign up for the tournament."

"I'll hold you to that," Chuck replied.

"I'm more than happy to sit with your daughters." Judith brushed a hand across his knee under the table. "I do *love* children."

In that flash of her sickly-sweet smile, Frederick remembered why he despised Judith Smith. "That won't be necessary. I'm sure Lucy would prefer to see to our girls. She and Alex will probably want to bring them and sit as a family."

"*Family?*" Judith mocked. "I wouldn't use the term in conjunction with that trollop."

Frederick was up in a flash, throwing his napkin onto his plate. "Thank you for dinner, Chuck, but I must go."

He stormed back to the gym, dropped his jacket on the floor, and pounded a bag for quarter of an hour before going to his automobile partially calmed. Seeing Chuck leaned against the Owen Touring made his sore knuckles whiten.

"Davenport, I swear I didn't know Rachel would bring Judith."

"I'd rather dine alone than be setup with any of these judgmental women. Why can't they leave Lucy alone?" Frederick kicked the forty-two-inch front tire. "Never mind. I know they're jealous. They can't get over themselves for shunning a famous novelist and it eats them up."

Chuck laughed, but when he saw Frederick's fist moving toward him, he held up his hands in defense. "Let her go, Davenport. She's dropped your name and you need to drop the protective act. It amazes me all these women are willing to fight for a taste of your affection when they know they'll have to share it with the previous Mrs. Davenport. Maybe it's a sport to them. Who can turn Freddy against his ex?"

"It'll never happen," he said through clenched teeth. "No matter how much she hurt me, I'll not disrespect the mother of my girls. Whoever wishes my affection cannot slander Lucy."

"She was your childhood infatuation. It's time for you to find a woman for your adult years."

Frederick shoved him aside and went for his door. "I'll see you Monday."

"And you better put your name on the sign-up sheet!" Chuck shouted as Frederick pulled away.

On Lucy's porch, he looked in the parlor window. Alexander was on the floor with the girls, Pinky the doll strapped to his back like he was a horse, while Phoebe showed Bethany how to hold her paper sword. Frederick let himself inside, leaving his jacket in the foyer. He needed Lucy's soft touch before seeing to the girls and peeked in the kitchen.

"Good evening, Mr. Frederick. You doing okay?"

"Yes, Naomi. Thank you."

"The girls ate supper real good and had dessert. Don't let them spoiled things talk you into more sweets. I did up a carrot cake to help Miss Lucy feel better."

"Is she unwell?"

Naomi shrugged. "One of her moods. She's got that woman coming from her publisher tomorrow, and though she puts on a brave face, she's scared."

"Where is she?"

"Walled up in her study with her third piece of cake."

Frederick knocked softly on the closed door to not draw attention from the parlor. When there was no response, he entered. Lucy was curled on the blue chaise crying.

"Goosy, what's wrong?" He dropped beside her and she immediately reached around him, pulling herself into his lap.

"It's no use." The metallic neckline of her red dress hung provocatively low.

He ran his hand over her loose hair, trying not to appreciate its silkiness, and kissed her forehead. "Tell me about it."

"Ms. Stone arrived in town today. She called me before supper and sounded nice enough, but what am I to do with her? Mr. Noble sent the new contract for the book, and the deadline is in two months. I told him she was welcome to stay in our guest room, but what if he's told her to stay until I complete the manuscript? How will I work if I'm expected to entertain a guest until May?"

He passed her one of his handkerchiefs. "You'll have to talk over all that when she comes. You said she's a writer. She'll understand your concerns."

"Freddy, she's a *nonfiction* writer." Her voice held disgust. "She'll understand nothing!"

"Still, it's putting words on paper into coherent sentences to tell a story."

"You're an insufferable numbers man!" She backhanded him on the arm and he fought the urge to plant a kiss on her lips.

"I love you too, Goosy." Frederick smiled at her until he saw the mood on her face soften. Then he needed her out of his arms. "It's good to be with you after my unpleasant supper."

She fingered his collar. "What happened?"

He used the words he knew would mortify to chase Lucy from his embrace. "Chuck wanted to take supper with Rachel and told her to invite a friend along so I wouldn't be the odd man out. When we got to the diner, Judith—"

"Oh no it wasn't!" Lucy bolted upright and stomped to her desk. She plopped in her chair, shoved a bite of cake into her mouth, and glared.

He stretched his legs and exhaled deeply. "I was livid with Chuck and let him know it. I had to walk out halfway through the meal."

Lucy scoffed. "I'm surprised you made it that long."

"She offered a pleasant view."

"Frederick Lionel Davenport, get out of my room!"

Alexander burst in, the doll flopping off his back from its saddle. He looked between the two and then went for his wife. "What is it, my queen?"

Lucy pointed at Frederick with a sneer. "He appreciated Judith Smith's figure over supper. I'll not have him in my house if he consorts with the likes of her!"

"Phoebe," Frederick called out the open door, "your horsey got away."

"Daddy!" She ran in and jumped into his arms. Bethany toddled in on her chubby legs. He lifted her to his other knee and kissed them both.

"If your lips have been—"

"Give me some credit, Goosy." He stared at her until she looked away. "Be sure to write down March sixteenth on your calendar. I'm signing up for the boxing tournament and I'll need you to watch the girls."

Lucy folded her arms and huffed. "What if I already have plans?"

"Then I'll have to take Judith's offer to sit with—"

Alexander intercepted Lucy's flight. He scooped her into his arms and planted a firm kiss on her mouth like Frederick had wanted to before carrying her out.

"Go on, girls. Help clean up the front room and collect your dolls." When they were gone, Frederick settled himself at Lucy's desk and ate the rest of her cake. If there had been any alcohol in the house, he would have poured himself a glass to go with it.

Alexander returned staring in disbelief over Frederick's bold seating choice. "What's going on with you today?"

Frederick came around the desk, looking down at Alexander from his three-inch advantage. "It's been a rough few weeks and then I was unknowingly set up with a hideous date for supper."

He smirked. "Judith Smith?"

"I can't stand her, but she smelled nice and it felt good to have a lady on my arm."

"You're human, Freddy."

"But then she was back to her obnoxious self, claiming to love children and offering to sit with the girls at the boxing match. All I could think of was Lucy's face at the thought of Judith even speaking of our daughters. Then she called Lucy an unforgivable name and I walked out."

Alexander held Frederick's stare. "Why did you come in here rather than to the girls when you arrived?"

"I wanted Lucy's touch but ended up comforting her. She was crying when I came in. She's scared about the visit from the publisher lady. Hit me if you want Alex, but when she was crying in my arms I knew I needed to go. I got her mad about Judith to get her away from me."

"She's stubborn." His smile was genuine, his blue eyes merry. "And a glorious sight when upset, but nothing compares to her when she's—"

Frederick shouldered for the door. "I can't listen to it today."

"Your standards are high. Call me biased, but you'll never find a woman that compares to Lucy."

"Thanks for your vote of confidence."

Frederick joined the girls picking up books in the parlor, pacing near the doorway while they finished. The lavender scent of the woman he was once devoted to move behind him. When he turned, Alexander's face was at Lucy's plunging neckline. He turned away, but it did little to soften the blow.

"Come say goodnight to Momma." She dropped to her knees before the girls, her red gown fanned out becomingly.

Frederick knew Alexander stood beside him, but he couldn't remove his attention from the sight of his daughters loving their mother. When Lucy came for the door, she brought her left hand to her chest and brushed aside the neckline to expose a fresh passion mark. Frederick gripped her wrist and stared down at her with disdain.

"Don't cheapen yourself to play these games with me, Lucille." He released her and trailed a finger over her cheek. "I've loved you. That's proof I have better taste than for the likes of Judith Smith."

The hard set of her mouth softened, but she left without a word.

He took Bethany into his arms while she clutched her rag doll. "All done, Phoebe?"

"Yes, Daddy. Let me say good night to Mr. Alex." She skipped ahead and hugged Alexander around his knees, squishing Pinky and Rummy between them in the process. "See you for battle on Monday!"

He saluted her when she stepped away and clapped Frederick on the shoulder. "Hang in there, Freddy."

Four

The hired car pulled in front of a gray, picturesque Queen Anne home trimmed to the gills with white fret work along the massive porch. Melissa asked the driver to wait a moment while she checked to see if it was the correct house. A sensible enclosed automobile was parked in the porte-cochere and azalea bushes ringing the home were covered in buds.

As she climbed the front steps, the bell-like laughter from her telephone conversation the day before spilled out the open windows. Curious, Melissa leaned toward the window to the left of the door. Within the Victorian-styled parlor, a blonde in a white tea dress was enjoying the attentions of a man with roaming hands as they both lounged on the settee. *Leave it to a romance novelist to be caught in the middle of the day engaged as such!*

Melissa rushed back to the automobile, clutching the brooch at her neck. "Could you sound the horn, please?" She took her smaller bag and parasol from the backseat. "Thank you."

She made heavy footsteps across the porch, but the horn seemed to have done the trick. The man stood behind the screen door, slipping on a suit jacket.

"Your tie, Alex!" The woman rushed into the foyer waving the blue silk. Upon seeing Melissa through the screen door, she laughed. "There goes trying to look respectable. Forgive us, Ms. Stone. I'm afraid we're a bit Bohemian about the house."

The man opened the door for her and Melissa found herself staring at his discolored hand on the latch as she entered. His unshaven face was handsome and blue eyes full of life, though the shadow of something dark hovered beyond the surface.

"I've seen cultures and people around the world in various stages of dress. Don't feel you need to wear a jacket or tie about your house if you aren't accustomed to it. Mr. Melling, isn't it?" She offered her hand.

"Exactly right, Ms. Stone." He offered a firm handshake despite his skin's texture. "But call me Alex. I'll go help the driver, excuse me."

Melissa stepped to the side as he rehung his jacket.

"And Lucy, Miss Olive Kent herself. You're much younger than I expected. You've done well for yourself these past years."

Lucy's flushed face redden more and she smoothed the tiers of her white lace gown. A classic, poetic style perfect for the woman with eyes the exact shade of green in the Norwegian aurora borealis.

"Thank you. *Azalea Blossom* published before I turned twenty-two, six years ago this month. Do you wish to see your bedroom so you might decide where you want your luggage?"

"That would be fine, thank you."

Melissa followed Lucy up the stairs and was shown to a room in the back corner of the house. She placed her small suitcase on the foot of the bed and leaned her parasol in the corner by the dresser. "It's a lovely room, thank you."

Lucy smiled. "I grew up here and bought the house from my father last January after I went through a divorce. This was the boys' room most of the time. My daughters use my old room across the hall and I keep the other room free for company as well. We host friends once a month and you'll need to share the bath when there's company or my girls are with us."

"They live with their father? How unconventional."

"Yes, well—"

Alex and the driver hoisted the trunk into the room.

"Under the window, please." Melissa stepped toward Lucy to get out of their way, noting the way the woman's eyes followed her husband. When the men were gone, she tried to bring back the topic of conversation. "Your previous husband lives nearby?"

"A few miles from here, north of downtown. You'll see him often. He brings the girls every work day to stay and then picks them up in the evenings. They stay some nights and weekends as well. It's an open situation for all of us, but yes, unconventional. It worked best for the situation we were in at the time. The courts wouldn't have allowed me the children, so Frederick claimed full custody."

When the last of the luggage was brought, Lucy offered her a few minutes to settle down, but Melissa preferred to get to know them. They gathered in the parlor after the driver was paid.

"Would you like tea or coffee?"

"I'm fine, thank you." Melissa looked at the way the Mellings sat snug against each other as he caressed her knee. "You're newlyweds?"

"A year ago January." Alex kissed Lucy's neck. "The best year of my life."

"We were sweethearts and engaged to be married but we had a falling out seven years ago. A year and a half later, I married Frederick, my best friend." Her fingers played across Alex's burned hands. "But Alex came back for me after *Winter of My Heart* was published."

Melissa had tried to read all of Lucy's books because Mr. Noble raved about them, but that was the only one she could get through. "That was your ode to your young relationship?"

"A tame version." Alex's eyes were intense. "Things were much more wonderful and horrific at times, but I recognized the passion behind her words and could no longer stay away."

"I should see to dinner." Lucy stood, Alex rising beside her.

"Could I be of help?" Melissa asked.

"No, thank you. We keep things simple for midday but I have a cook who comes in for supper. I'll holler when it's ready."

Alex kissed her on the lips and followed her every move as she left. Then he turned back to Melissa. "Lucy puts on a brave face, but she's terrified of why you're here. Mr. Noble told her you're to make sure she stays on task and meets the deadline, but he gave no specifics."

"Alex," she said as she adjusted her posture to project authority, "I can see you love your wife, but in the world of publishing, a first year of marriage—even for lovers reunited—isn't grounds for breaking contracts. I was sent as a final attempt to keep Olive Kent as one of Noble Publishing's top authors. If she fails to meet this deadline Mr. Noble will drop her. His lawyers have already encouraged him to sue for breach of contract. He has, if you've noticed, listed a forthcoming Olive Kent in the last four publishing catalogs. Revenue is being lost each time she fails to deliver."

"I've worried about that, but haven't voiced the concerns to Lucy. She has enough stress to deal with and I didn't wish to burden her with legal matters when it could stifle her artistic side."

"What's your profession?"

With his smile, Melissa couldn't fault Lucy for being distracted by her husband. "I'm a lawyer, as was my father and grandfather."

"Then you know that sometimes you need to be brutally honest with your client. I have no problem being the bearer of bad news so you needn't be the one to bring harsh reality to your wife. She's younger than I expected, but she's by no means too young to understand the gravity of her situation or the importance of being professional. Writing is an art, but she needs to be better in tune with the business side if she wishes to continue."

"Do what you must, Melissa. I'll be there to scrape her off the floor when you're done." Alex's smirk was just as challenging as his words, endowing her with more respect for him. She'd do what was in her power and he would clean up the aftermath.

***

After pleasant conversation about Melissa's travels over their meal, Lucy brought her into the study to talk business and Alex settled in the parlor. When the sounds of Tchaikovsky's "Swan Lake" drifted through the open doors, Lucy smiled and excused herself.

Tired of waiting, Melissa stepped toward the hall a minute later. Alex waltzed his wife around the parlor, pressing close with one hand low on her hip, the other caressing her arm. Despite her annoyance, she couldn't deny that Alex, in his socks and with the top two buttons of his shirt open, and barefoot Lucy in a simple dress were by far one of the most beautiful couples she'd witnessed in the world. The song ended and Alex was upon her lips. Not wishing to spy, Melissa returned to the study and looked over the books on the shelves until Lucy returned.

"We have more in our bedroom," Lucy remarked. "We keep the poetry and some of our favorites up there."

After witnessing the couple's relationship on the ground floor, Melissa didn't wish to imagine the happenings in their private room. "That's lovely, but we need to stay on task. Mr. Noble sent me to help you make your deadline. I'm to do whatever you need to help you work. I can be an assistant, typist, anything."

"Shall I need to give you a salary?"

"Room and board is plenty. Mr. Noble is seeing to the rest."

"I already employ Naomi. She's my cook and housekeeper. And Darla. She used to come five days a week when I was with Freddy, but she's down to twice a week and special occasions as she's working with Dr. Hughes now."

"What does Darla do? And is it a hardship for you that she's not here often?"

"She entertained Phoebe when I wrote while Frederick was at work. And she was my midwife with Bethany and helped me those first weeks after she was born. My doctor was so impressed he hired Darla out from under me."

"I could watch the girls for certain hours during the day for you to get regular writing time in, but I have an assignment here as well."

"The girls are picky about who they like and Freddy is even more particular about who they associate with."

Melissa threw her hands into the air. "Is there anything typical in your life or is it all as complicated as an over-worked Gothic plotline?"

Lucy looked like a reprimanded child, eyes filling with tears. "I don't expect you to realize the dynamics of everything in one afternoon. I live a quiet life and do the best I can."

Taking a calming breath as she'd learned in a Buddhist temple, Melissa asked a more straightforward question. "Show me your system. Do you do long-hand first? Type?"

"I used to write long-hand, but the last book and what I'm working on now I've exclusively typed. I have journals for notes and ideas. When I get stuck, I sit in the gazebo or on the porch with my journal and write nonsense."

"Then what purpose is that?" She pointed to the blue chaise with a velvet blanket tossed over the edge of it.

"That's for Alex." Lucy kept her chin high.

"Does he often watch you work?"

"Several times a week."

"And do you expect me to believe after witnessing you both this afternoon that he sits placidly here"—she pointed to the chaise as she spoke—"while you're over there?"

The smile on her lips said it all. Melissa moved around the chaise to shove it toward the door in an attempt to rid the space of distractions.

"You cannot come into my house and rearrange my things!"

"I believe you've mixed too much pleasure into the business of writing."

"That was a present for my husband! Alex has every right to be in here and we have every right to enjoy each other. I'm finally married to my muse and there's no shame with what we share."

"The purpose of a muse is to inspire you to work, not take time away from your creations."

"You have no idea what I aim to create!"

Alex rushed in, arms closing around Lucy. "Would you please give us a minute, Ms. Stone?"

He didn't have the decency to wait until she'd left the room before he kissed Lucy. As he hadn't waited for proper privacy, Melissa didn't feel the need to give it to him. She leaned against the wall outside the door and listened.

"It's no business of hers if we lie together here! She speaks of my creations, but I'm more concerned about creating a family with you than writing another book for Mr. Noble."

"Lucy, my queen, we have a lifetime together. You need to honor this contract with Mr. Noble. You have two months to complete this story you've been working on since before I came back. I hate to think I had something to do with your work slowing down."

"You are my work, Alex. I want nothing more than to give you a child."

"You need to focus your energy on the book while Ms. Stone is here."

"I'll not deny you, not deny myself!"

"My queen, I'd never ask that of you. We just might need to delay."

"Delaying gratification never worked well between us." The bitter tone was soon followed by giggles and other pleasurable sounds.

"Hours rather than weeks or days will be much easier, Lucy. And it can't hurt to try."

"I'll not remove your sofa."

"Nor would I want you to. Meet your daily writing goals and I'll convene with you here or anywhere else. Type two new pages this afternoon and you may do with me as you wish."

Melissa backed down the hall and shut herself in the half-bathroom. She washed her face with cold water and tried to forget everything she'd just heard. Never would she have expected a romance novelist to live a life more tantalizing than her books. The thought of living among such passion for several weeks caused her knees to weaken—which she couldn't stand for.

After looking at Lucy, Melissa's own reflection appeared weathered from her explorations in the outdoors. She plucked a gray hair from her temple and sighed over the creases beside her eyes.

When she returned to the hallway, Alex waited for her—the study closed. "Lucy would like an hour alone to write before discussing anything further with you. You're welcome to join me in the parlor or roam about."

Melissa reached for the door.

"She's locked herself in. You'll come to see she's very stubborn, even if she looks as meek as a kitten."

"I'd never mistake her for being meek. She has a fire burning in her eyes and—"

"Yes?" Alex's tone was challenging.

"And, excuse my bluntness, but I think it would take a feisty woman to hold your attention."

Alex guffawed. "You'll get along fine with her, just like Darla."

"I don't need to get along with her. I'm here to do my job."

"That's Darla's attitude as well, though there's mutual respect involved and a friendship of a sort. You'll come to understand her, Ms. Stone."

"If you wish to make me feel a part of your eccentric household, please call me Melissa."

"All right, Melissa. You look like you have more questions. Let's go to the parlor."

He waited until she took her previous chair before sitting.

"From what I gathered, beside the marriage, Lucy also lost her weekday helper after her second child was born."

He nodded.

"I'm sure that all contributed to the declining production. It sounds like Lucy would be able to work during the day if someone was to entertain the children, but she said her ex-husband is particular about who's in charge of his girls."

"Naturally. He's a protective father."

"When might he meet me to decide if I'm fit for the responsibility?"

Alex draped an arm across the back of the settee. "He'll bring them Monday morning, about seven-thirty."

As much as she disliked the idea of meeting Lucy's ex-husband—probably another man with a flashing smile and a craving for playfulness—it needed to happen. "And we should expect him to make a rash decision on the spot? Is there no way we could arrange a meeting this weekend and allow him time to consider me?"

"I'll ring him now."

Alex returned a few minutes later. "No answer. He sometimes takes the girls for ice cream on Saturday afternoons."

She rubbed her eyes, not looking forward to the possibility of being a nanny to spoiled children. "Very well, why don't you tell me about them in the meantime."

Five

Frederick trudged behind his daughters across Lucy's yard from their parked automobile. Phoebe held Bethany's hand and sang a snatch of a song she'd picked up from Alexander. By the time they reached the front porch, Alexander stood in the parlor window and waved them in. The girls climbed onto the settee with him, but Frederick stopped in the doorway hoping he wouldn't have to socialize after the fight he had with Lucy the night before.

"Where's Momma?" Phoebe kept a bag of peanuts behind her back as she knelt next to Alexander.

"She's locked in her room and we can't disturb her until she's done writing." He dropped his voice. "I bet if you press your ear to the door you'll hear the *clickity-clackity* of the keys as she creates a new story."

Phoebe ran past Frederick into the hall. The miniature-Lucy smile brightened her face and her finger went to her lips. "Momma's working."

Frederick followed Phoebe into the parlor where she gave her stepfather the bag. "You protect this until Momma's done."

"I'd be honored to, Phoebe. Miss Naomi's in the kitchen if you want to get some milk or lemonade."

"Bring Beth along with you," Frederick told her.

Alexander set the peanuts on the side table and looked to Frederick. "I tried to call you an hour ago."

"We were at Monroe Park." Frederick dropped in the nearest armchair. "Phoebe insisted on buying Lucy peanuts and bringing them to her on the way home. How is she? Did you call because something's wrong?"

"Melissa from the publisher is here and she wanted you to meet her to see if she passes your test."

"My test?"

"For being able to help with the girls. She thinks if she watches them a few hours a day it will help Lucy write more. And I need your help with something as well."

"How long is the woman staying here?"

"Until Lucy hands over a completed manuscript, which I hope is before the May third deadline because I'd rather spend my birthday in New York City with my friends."

Frederick stood at the firm, feminine voice and turned toward the door. Surprise registered on the woman's tanned face—a striking sight against her copper hair.

Alexander jumped between the two. "Melissa Stone, Frederick Davenport. Freddy, Melissa. Come join us."

The woman took a seat in the corner of the settee closest to Frederick's chair and touched the gold and emerald brooch at the neck of her blouse. After they all settled, Frederick laid in with questioning.

"Why would Mr. Noble send someone to watch our children?"

"He sent me to do whatever is in my power to see Lucy meets this deadline. His lawyers will force him to sue if she breaks another contract and he doesn't wish to lose his favorite novelist. Mr. Noble's been charmed with Lucy since he met her on his travels here. There's never an office party that the story of 'The Southern Rose' isn't mentioned."

Frederick huffed. "I hope you didn't tell her that bit."

"Of course not. But he did love having Lucy to parade around to the literary circles last year."

Alexander gave a cocky grin. "That's *my* beautiful wife."

Frederick could have punched the smirk off Alexander's face. He saw Melissa look to his fists and made the effort to relax them.

"I'm here to complete a magazine piece about the Southern charms of Mobile in conjunction with Lucy's books and do whatever I can to be sure she stays on task to meet her deadline."

Frederick laughed and pointed to Alexander. "You might want to ship him out for a month."

"That's an option I've already considered."

Frederick appreciated the spark in her brown eyes.

"If this is going to turn into a conversation on how I'm not right for Lucy, I think I'll get a glass of lemonade. Would anyone else like one?"

They both declined.

When Alexander passed his chair, Frederick put his arm out to stop him. "What is it you need my help with?"

"If Lucy begins to balk about writing or seems stuck, say something to get her upset."

"Like what and why?"

"Something to spur her on to prove herself valid as a writer. Mention that Judith or Kate think she can't top her last book because now that she has me she doesn't need to create love stories."

Frederick shoved him away. "Come off yourself, Melling."

Alexander left the room laughing but rushed back to grab the bag of peanuts because he knew better than to appear before Phoebe without safeguarding the treasure.

When they were alone, Frederick met Melissa's warm gaze. "I hope Mr. Noble prepared you for Lucy's situation."

Her smile was broad and friendly, nothing like Lucy's suggestive, subtle one. "It wasn't until I called him when I arrived in town yesterday that I found out her real name."

Frederick adjusted his tie. "I'm afraid I'm part of the baggage that goes along with Olive Kent."

"I admit after meeting Alex I was worried, but you seem level-headed. It appears Alex counts on you to nudge Lucy along, which he's putting me in charge of on this end because he doesn't want to be the bad guy."

"I doubt he could do anything that would tarnish himself in her eyes. If that were possible, their relationship would have corroded long ago."

She raised an eyebrow. "You don't approve of the man your ex-wife left you for?"

"I didn't approve when I first saw them walking down the street together in '04, but that's beside the point." He stood and removed his jacket, laying it over the back of his chair. "What is it you expect from me?"

She didn't speak as she took in the span of his shoulders and arms. "Has anyone told you you're built like James Jeffries?"

He laughed. "The men at the gym remark upon the similarities."

"You're a boxer then?"

"As a hobby."

"I thought you might have been because of how quick with your fists you were when Alex got pompous. What's your profession?"

"Accountant."

It was her turn to laugh.

"Lucy and I were doomed from the start." Frederick stared at his hands. "I nurtured her creative side, but Alex always possessed her heart. I was only the fill-in when he was gone."

"Then she's even sillier than I imagined." As though realizing how he could take her remark, she cleared her throat and changed the subject. "What do you wish to ask me to decide if I'm a fit companion to your daughters?"

"I see nothing wrong with you watching the girls while Lucy's working." He stood. "Now if you will excuse me, I'd rather get them home before Lucy emerges."

"Why's that? She thinks you're wonderful, in case you're curious." Melissa's confident smile and shine of her copper hair caused Frederick to grin in return.

"I upset her last night and would rather wait another day or two before seeing her, for both our sakes." He collected his jacket and offered his hand. "It was good to meet you, Melissa. If you'd like to come with me to get the girls, I'll introduce them on our way out."

"Yes, please."

She followed him into the kitchen where the bag of peanuts sat on the empty table.

Naomi turned to him. "Mr. Alex has them running like heathens in the backyard."

"It doesn't take much encouragement for Phoebe to let loose. Have you met Melissa Stone?"

"I surely have. She'll be both a blessing and a curse here the next few weeks."

Frederick laughed. "Yes, depending on whom you ask. I'm going to collect the girls and be on our way. I'll see you next week, Naomi." He turned to Melissa. "Shall we?"

She nodded and went through the door he held open for her onto the screened porch.

Just as they reached the door to the back stoop, Phoebe ran by with a stick raised like a sword. "Death to the militia!"

"That's my big princess, Phoebe. She's four and a half and plays as I did at her age. The militia is Alex, formally called Melling Militia. Phoebe is Kingdom Davenport. Those are two terms you need to be aware of in this household."

"And it doesn't bother you that your daughter runs about screaming for her stepfather's death?"

Frederick felt the grin before it culminated with a laugh. "Not in the least, but it's pure fantasy, mind you. She already creates stories for her playtimes, much like Lucy did."

"You knew her as a child?"

"I was best friends with her brother. She tagged along most of the time when we were little. Most of Eddie's friends were all eyes for the twins, Cora and Emma. They were older, giggling beauties. Lucy was either like one of the boys or had her nose in a book." Frederick sighed and turned back to Melissa. "You might think Lucy a flighty, self-centered, overly passionate woman, but she's much more than that. I've known her practically her whole life, but I don't think even I've seen all she has to offer the world. She hides behind layers of pain and plays flippant around those she doesn't know well, but she feels everything. Deeply."

Phoebe ran toward him. Frederick caught her with one arm and swung her onto his back. She hooked an arm around his neck and brandished her weapon with the other.

"Quick, Daddy! Melling Militia has the princess in the castle!"

He ran for the gazebo and deposited Phoebe at the door. Frederick took the handle of the wagon where Bethany sat and pulled her to safety as his oldest attacked the stronghold. Melissa was on the flagstone path halfway to the house. Lifting Bethany into his arms, he smoothed her disheveled hair beneath the brim of her sunbonnet.

"Bethany Iris, this is Momma's new friend, Miss Melissa. She'll be staying here for a while."

She waved her pudgy hand and then buried her face on her father's shoulder.

"She's precious. How old is she?"

"Sixteen months. She was born on Thanksgiving two years back."

"I think it's darling how you each have one that favors you."

"It's funny how things work out." He kissed Bethany's cheek and stood her on the path. "It's time we went home, Little Princess. Stay here and I'll get Phoebe."

Phoebe and Alexander still knocked sticks together.

"Time to call a truce. We need to get home before Miss Sharon thinks we've abandoned the kingdom."

"Don't forget Momma's peanuts," Phoebe told Alexander as the three walked toward the back of the house.

"Do you think she'll share them with me?"

"Only if you say please and are nice," she replied, arms crossed to show her seriousness.

Alexander's impetuous smile returned. "I'm always polite and *very* nice to your momma. I take care of all her needs several times a day."

Frederick punched him on the shoulder. "Innuendos aren't necessary."

"But they come naturally to me." Alexander ducked out of range from the next strike. "You're going to play like that in front of company? What will Melissa think?"

"She's probably wishing she could have struck you herself by now."

They both looked to Melissa. She rocked back on her heels and looked up at the magnolia tree, feigning innocence.

Frederick laughed. "I'm sure it will come in handy to have an ally here."

Phoebe stopped directly before Melissa and stared. "I'm Phoebe Camellia Davenport, protector of the kingdom. Are you here for training?"

Melissa looked to Frederick and he nodded. "Yes," she said, "I am."

Alexander stepped beside Melissa. "But not until Monday. Remember your daddy needs to take you home."

Phoebe didn't heed her stepfather. "What's your name?"

"Melissa Stone."

"That's a beautiful treasure you wear. What are the green things?"

"Emeralds. I got it on my last adventure, in Jamaica."

"Where's Jamaica?"

"She can show you on Monday, Phoebe," Alexander said. "You'll see lots of her in the days ahead. She's staying in the big guest room for weeks."

"Weeks? Where do you live?"

"New York City, but I travel a lot."

"Momma and Mr. Alex went there last year. They brought home all sorts of pretty things. May I touch your emeralds?"

"Of course." Melissa leaned over and Phoebe reached a finger toward the largest gem that hung from the gold brooch.

"Ouch!" Phoebe jumped back and stuck her finger in her mouth. "It bit me!"

"Emeralds don't bite, Princess." Eager to get away, Frederick patted her head and picked up Bethany.

"There was something sharp!"

Melissa straightened and felt the pendant for herself. "I'm sorry about that, but I don't know what it could have been."

Frederick shrugged and urged Phoebe toward the front yard. "No worries. We'll see you all Monday."

Six

Melissa settled in a chair near the parlor window with her notebook. Glancing outside as the Davenports pulled away, she smiled at the oddness of the situation.

"I told you he was wonderful," Lucy said from the doorway. "He's the finest catch in town, but he can't stand any of the women."

Alex's hands went around Lucy's waist as he leaned over her shoulder from behind. "That's because you've spoiled him, my queen. I do feel sorry for him to have lost you. The pain is vast." He kissed her neck. "Did you write two pages?"

Lucy smiled at Melissa before turning in her husband's arms, her hands trailing down his chest. "No, Alexander Melling, I wrote three."

He held her close and whispered in her ear. Melissa could have imagined what he said, but she didn't allow herself to dwell on their behavior. She could only think of Freddy's words, how earnest he sounded as he told of Lucy being more than frivolous. If she appeared like a love-struck fool on the surface, her passion for Alex must be unfathomable. Enough to leave her beautiful children to Freddy and live a life of desire across town.

The Mellings retired to the study and Melissa turned to her journal page with the notes she'd made when talking on the phone with Mr. Noble. Beside Davenport she wrote

Freddy: Pleasant ex-husband. Boxer. Accountant.

Caring, protective of girls and Lucy.

Two daughters live with him in the city.

Phoebe: highly imaginative, bright, gorgeous girl.

Bethany: shy, classic beauty, dark features.

The notes next to the Melling name were:

Old lovers. Passion without limits. Lawyer.

Plays with the children like a brother/uncle.

Phoebe calls him "Mr. Alex."

Protective of Lucy but a <u>major</u> distraction.

Eyes, hands, music, innuendos.

Chaise in study—bad idea.

When she reread the page, she admitted she was leaving much unsaid in the Davenport column. Freddy was more than pleasant, but she didn't know how to describe him without it sounding like some drivel Olive Kent would have written in *Azalea Blossom*. He was the type of man Grandmother Stone spoke of— honorable, courageous, and kind—but Melissa never expected to meet.

Quarter of an hour later, the telephone rang in the hallway. On the third ring, Naomi answered it. She looked in the parlor and Melissa pointed across the hall. Naomi boldly knocked on the door.

"Mr. Alex, Father De Fiore is on the telephone. I wouldn't bother you, but it sounds urgent."

Melissa was too far away to hear the muffled reply, but Naomi retreated. Alex stepped out of the room shirtless. His pale torso was tarnished with scars and the discoloration on his hands reached both elbows. He was out of sight in a moment, but the image of him burned in Melissa's mind. Her quandary in understanding the novelist widened with each bit of information she collected. Lucy appeared to be the type to chase after beautiful things and handsome men, but Alex's wounds cast a shadow on his attractiveness. Melissa noticed when they were in the yard the sunlight showed what appeared to be more marks on his unshaven face. Yet Lucy looked upon him as though he fulfilled her every craving in one perfect man.

"Naomi," Alex called out, "can you handle one more for supper?"

"If it's for Father De Fiore, yes!"

Alex laughed, and not long after the telephone hung up. Melissa watched the hallway to observe him when he returned to the study. He caught her looking and unabashedly leaned an arm on the parlor doorframe.

"There'll be company for supper, but we don't dress too formal."

"Or even at all, it appears." She lifted an eyebrow at him.

His boyish smile lit his dimpled face as he laughed. "As you've said, you've seen people all over the world in varying shades of dress, and undress, I'd imagine. I'm sure I'm not too much of a shock."

"You remind me of my time with the Karo tribe in Ethiopia. The men scar their chests to signify killing enemies. But that doesn't explain your arms or face."

"But it does." He ran a hand over his chest and then held out his arms. "They symbolize killing my demons, the most terrible of all enemies."

The darkness she'd noticed when she first met him overtook his gaze. Alex appeared to grip the doorframe to stay upright, as his thoughts took him back to a time and place he didn't wish to be. He closed his eyes for several seconds and then disappeared into the study.

***

Melissa pulled on a purple silk dress with red and gold art deco details for supper. It was a faux wrap-around, reminiscent of a kimono that she'd picked up in London. The bold colors cheered her and the shiny flats were comfortable without being fussy. Leaving the brooch in her dresser, she pulled her hair into a bun and returned to the main floor. When she entered the parlor, she was glad she opted to change.

Lucy paced the room in a gauzy, burgundy gown with a black skirt that accented her curves exquisitely. "There you are, Ms. Stone. I'm sorry we left you earlier but you did seem involved in your work."

"Yes, and you in yours." They stared at each other a moment. Not wishing to seem too cold, Melissa continued. "Three pages is a good place to start, but you'll need to do more than that each day if you wish to be rid of me."

"Those pages put me over one-hundred and thirty total. I'm halfway through, though some things will require adjusting by the time I'm done."

"Naturally. No one writes a perfect first draft."

"This one will be more imperfect than others, but I'm making notes as I go. The story is a mystery and I'm still learning about what clues to place where."

"No more romances? Do you think that will upset your readers?"

"I don't think of my readers when writing, but there is some romance because what's life without love?"

"A dark and dreary place," Alex said as he joined them. He swept Lucy into his arms and waltzed her around the room before pulling her to his side as they fell upon the settee. Alex kissed her and she trailed her fingers along his jaw. "We've been apart more than we've been together, but you're the reason I made it this far."

Alex was an artist, painting with caresses and punctuating with kisses. While nothing they did was lewd, the display was intimate and Melissa retreated to the front porch swing.

As the sky faded to an orange-violet, a man in black walked up the driveway. When he drew closer to the ambient light of the house, she saw his collar and the cross hanging around his neck and knew he was the dinner guest.

"Unless I am mistaken," he said with a Tuscan accent, "you are neither family nor friend—yet."

She smiled, liking him instantly. "And unless I'm mistaken, you were raised in Florence, or there about."

"*Sí, signorina.* I have been in this country for seven years but have not lost the sound of my youth. My family has lived outside Florence for centuries. Have you traveled there?"

"All over Italy, but I love the people, sights, and food of Tuscany best. I'm Melissa Stone, here on assignment from Noble Publishing."

"Lucy has been much worried about your arrival. I am Father De Fiore, but call me—"

"Claudio!" Alex stepped out and the men embraced with back slaps and a kiss on each cheek. "Melissa, meet my best friend, Claudio."

"You're best friends with a priest?" To her embarrassment, her voice sounded incredulous.

Alex laughed. "It makes it handy for all the things I find myself needing to confess."

"*Sí*, I have helped Alexander many times. Welcome to the fold." He kissed both Melissa's cheeks. "No day is ever dull with a Melling nearby."

"Come inside." Alex held the door open. "Lucy and I might have caused Melissa to seek fresh air, but we've settled down."

"How long have you been here?" Claudio asked her.

"About six hours."

"And they have already let down their guards?"

Melissa laughed as she stepped into the house. "I don't think they ever had any up."

"We would sooner stop breathing than hide our love."

Claudio patted his friend's cheek. "You have the heart and passion of an Italian." When the priest crossed the threshold, he clutched his rosary. "What have you done, *amico*?"

"What do you mean?" Alex let the screen slam.

"It feels like Seacliff Cottage."

Alex's eyes went wide and he laid a hand on his chest. "I've done nothing, Claudio! I swear to you, I've—"

Claudio rushed to the parlor calling for Lucy. Melissa followed and found the priest pressing his cross against Lucy's forehead. The woman looked ready to cry as he prattled in Italian.

"Stop it, you're scaring her!" Alex pulled Lucy into his arms.

"A little fright from the unexpected is nothing to the horrors of an infestation. Allow me to finish my blessing. We cannot be too careful."

Alex smoothed Lucy's hair. After pressing his lips to her cheek, he gazed into her startled eyes. "He didn't hurt you, did he?"

"It just frightened me for Claudio to come in like that."

"He'd like to finish his blessing if that's all right?"

Lucy nodded, and he handed her back to the priest.

Never having spent much time in church, Melissa watched with interest as the friends switched rolls from joking to spiritual matters without thought of offense. When he was done with Lucy, Claudio turned to Alex.

"It's not in me! I've lived my life the same as I have for over five years. I would never ruin what I have with Lucy. Nothing is worth the risk of losing her again!"

"But something is here. Allow me to bless you."

When he finished with Alex, all eyes turned to Melissa.

"She's the only thing new," Lucy whispered. "If she's brought evil into our home I'll—"

"Hush, Lucy." Alex tucked her under his arm. "Allow Claudio to do what he can."

Melissa found the priest before her, studying her with his dark eyes that shone amid his olive countenance. His face under the full light of the parlor brought her back to her summer in Italy where she spent many weeks at a vineyard in Tuscany, both tasting wine and the lips of a certain local.

"Will you allow me to bless you, Melissa? It is only a safeguard."

Not trusting her voice, she nodded. She held her breath as the cross was pressed to her forehead and his fingertips brushed her skin. With his words came a warmth and peace she didn't realize she lacked—nor did she know she craved—until her soul was filled with light.

"Thank you," she whispered when he was done. "I haven't felt like this since I visited the Buddhist mediation temple in Indonesia."

Claudio's smile was as handsome as any she'd ever seen. "You get around the world. Is it for pleasure or business?"

"Both." Melissa went to finger the brooch, but touched her bare neck instead.

"And in all your travels have you not yet found what you are seeking?"

She was quiet a moment, reading between the unspoken words and into his friendly gaze. "No, not yet."

Naomi collected them for supper and they gathered at the massive dining room table. The place settings had two on either side of the center of the table with the platters of food on the edges. Alex sat Lucy in the nearest chair and Claudio walked Melissa to the other side, settling next to her. The lack of wine was surprising, but Melissa accepted both water and hot tea.

Halfway through the meal, Claudio pushed his chair back. "Something is off in here, but it is not coming from any of you. May I come after Mass tomorrow to bless the house?"

"Of course, Claudio." Lucy tucked a lose strand of hair behind her ear. "We need to make sure it's safe before the girls come."

"Do you all go to the same church?" Melissa asked.

"No, I am here to help at St. Joseph's through Easter. My parish is in Monroe, Louisiana. Alex and Lucy attend St. Mary's just up the road."

"But we were raised in the cathedral downtown." Alex trailed his hand along Lucy's arm and linked their fingers together. "We started fresh when we were married last year."

"How did you meet Claudio?" Melissa held Alex's gaze.

"Seven years ago, on the bay ferry. Claudio was going to report for training to the Italian congregation in Daphne and I was headed to my family's weekend cottage on Ecor Rouge. Which reminds me, Lucy, when I took lunch with my mother yesterday she offered me the property if we'd like to build a new cottage there. Apparently the Watts have kept the carriage house and stable in usable condition, as well as tame the forest around the sepulcher, but Mother hasn't been back nor does she wish to go."

Claudio crossed himself and muttered something in Italian.

"I wouldn't build on the exact site, but I thought it might be good to have a place for us to escape town from time to time."

Lucy looked across the table at the others and back to Alex. "I'd rather discuss it later."

He squeezed her hand and kissed her. "All right, my queen."

"Have you not gone back either?" Claudio asked Alex.

He shook his head. "I don't wish to go alone and Lucy…well, I've only asked her once."

"It was poor timing," she whispered.

"I would go with you before I return to Monroe." Claudio gestured to Lucy. "Maybe going on a Saturday would give Lucy more time to focus on writing for a day when she doesn't have the children."

"I never said I didn't wish to go."

Alex brought her hand to his lips. "Sometimes not saying something says a lot."

Lucy stood and the men rose to their feet as well. "I'm going to check on dessert."

"Allow me to help." Alex's hand went around her waist and slipped lower once they were in the hall.

Melissa looked to Claudio. "Are they always like that?"

"I met Alexander a week after his engagement to Lucy was broken. Though he spoke of her often, I did not meet her until he came back to Mobile. When I laid eyes on her, I knew she was his perfect match, though she was married to another. They are both deep and with troubled pasts, but they are two of the truest people I know. They have been through hell but finally found happiness together." Claudio placed his hand on hers. "Consider yourself lucky if Lucy ever shares their full story with you. Not many people know, but everyone has heard different versions."

"I take it there was a scandal involved."

Claudio nodded. "*Sí*, each time they joined or parted. And this last time corresponded with the news of Lucy being Olive Kent and Alexander being back from the grave. The local headlines were sensational and reached as far as Louisiana because he was working as a lawyer under a false name in Monroe. He is no longer allowed to practice law in Louisiana, but his home state has proven more forgiving. I am sure his father's name and connections had something to do with that, though Alexander would never want to admit to his father helping him posthumously."

Melissa opened her mouth to question further, but the Mellings returned. Alex brought a pot of coffee and Lucy carried a glazed lemon cake that smelled wonderful.

"I hope you'll find Naomi's suppers worth suffering through my mediocre dinners."

"The chicken salad this afternoon was wonderful."

Lucy laughed. "It's Naomi's recipe, I just compiled the ingredients she prepared for me."

Alex whispered something into Lucy's ear that made her blush.

After several minutes of enjoying dessert, Lucy spoke. "How long can you stay tonight, Claudio?"

"Are you already planning the time you can disappear with Alexander?" The priest's eyes were merry.

"Always," she whispered as the rose on her cheeks further bloomed.

The spark in Alex nearly lit the room afire. Melissa expected him to take Lucy on the table. Instead, he rushed from the room. Soon the sounds of Tchaikovsky floated in from the parlor, followed by Alex's return. He offered his hand to Lucy and they waltzed out of the room leaving a trail of yearning in their wake.

Claudio laughed. "Like I said before, no day is ever dull with a Melling. Now that Lucy has his name, they are unrelenting."

"Why do they not serve wine or other drinks?"

"Communion wine is all they partake of. Alex suffered much from drunkenness. He hurt himself and many others, but the worst casualty was Lucy."

Claudio offered his arm and brought Melissa into the parlor.

"Dance, you must dance!" Alex said as he led Lucy across the room.

The priest looked to Melissa with a dashing smile before addressing Alex. "You know it is not proper for me to dance with a single woman, but with your lovely wife it would be well."

"Everything is good when my queen is involved." Alex stopped before them. "Treat her well and don't step on her bare toes."

Claudio kicked off his shoes and Lucy's laughter pealed as the priest danced her away. Alex watched them several seconds before turning to Melissa. Standing so close to him, she was surprised to notice she was taller.

"You won't turn me away, will you?" His pale blue eyes were bright with mischief.

"I'm sure I'm not as lovely a dancer as Lucy."

"Freddy taught her to dance. Next time he's over he could give you some pointers."

Melissa felt her face warm at the suggestion of dancing with Freddy Davenport but accepted Alex's arm. With the slightest touch of his fingers at her waist, he guided her through the steps while the scarred hand that held hers felt as light as a butterfly. Thirty seconds in Alex's arms and she knew she'd never had such a skilled dance partner.

"You may be sure I'm a perfect gentleman. My days of leading the hearts of women astray are long gone. I possess the only heart I wish to claim."

"I wouldn't have accepted your arm if I feared for my virtue, Alex."

"Then you're smarter than my Lucy was when I first presented myself to her."

"With a decade more experience under my belt from what I gather, so don't be too hard on her."

"Do I detect a touch of understanding in that business mind of yours?" His dimples peeked over the stubble on his cheeks and it made her dizzy at the close range. Being under the spell of Alex's dancing skills and charming grin would be distraction for most women.

"Everyone's protectiveness of Lucy has had an effect on me. It says something when a woman's ex-husband and a priest do nothing but speak of her true heart and deep emotions. There's no question that she's loved, I just need to decide how many enemies I'm willing to make to push her to succeed."

"I told you, push and shove her all you want. I'll see that she doesn't collapse."

"She'll need to do more than two or three pages a day, Alex," she whispered.

"I'm working on it." His puckish smile said it all.

Before Melissa went to bed that night, she turned down the lights and opened a window to allow the sun to wake her in the morning. Out of the corner of her eye she saw movement on the lawn. Lucy and Alex ran across the backyard for the gazebo. They were still in their supper clothes and he had a blanket thrown over his shoulder. Wishing she had not experienced the dance with Alex—for she could now imagine what those caresses he gave Lucy felt like—Melissa knew what type of magic they would find within the night surrounded by azaleas.

Seven

Frederick woke early Sunday morning and took a few minutes to drink the last of his coffee in the backyard for a moment of solitude. From the Beauchamps' house next door the sweet, lonely sound of Alice playing "Nearer, My God, to Thee" on her violin wafted through the spring morning. It had been weeks since he caught part of her playing. Frederick smiled, remembering how he used to dance with Lucy when Alice played a tune that moved them. Then he thought of the horrific weekend sixteen months before that forever changed his life, made possible by Tchaikovsky violin solos and Valentino De Fiore. He could have blamed Lucy for writing *Winter of My Heart*, but he didn't think Alexander would have returned for Lucy as quickly if Claudio wasn't coming to town to see his cousin perform.

Rather than thinking ill of Alexander and Claudio, Frederick's mind settled on meeting Melissa Stone. He'd dreamt of her cinnamon hair and exotic scent the night before. She was beautiful, grounded, and smart—but completely out of reach as Lucy's houseguest. Already there was an air of battle about the Eastons' old house. Frederick didn't want to choose sides, but after their brief encounter, he was certain he'd side with Melissa.

Monday morning, Frederick had to force Phoebe to dress.

"Don't you want to find out if Momma enjoyed her peanuts?" He handed her clothes for the third time.

She shook her head and crossed her arms, refusing to take the dress.

"What about learning about Jamaica? Miss Melissa was going to show you where she traveled."

"Her treasure bit me. I'll stay with Doff."

"Doff isn't big enough to watch you. He couldn't even pour milk. Besides, it's Monday. Doesn't that mean Miss Darla is coming?"

"Yes! Can I go next door and ride the streetcar with her?"

"That's something we have to set up beforehand. Maybe we can try that for Thursday."

Placated, Phoebe accepted her clothes. Frederick turned to Bethany's crib to dress her. When finished, she snuggled on his shoulder a minute.

"Dada. Momma. Go."

"Yes, Beth. You're going to Momma's today. I'm sure she's missed you." He kissed her head, enjoying the clean smell of his daughter. Some days it hurt to hold Bethany when he brought her home because Lucy's lavender scent was all about her.

Breakfast was prepared and consumed at a faster pace, making up for the time Frederick spent convincing Phoebe to dress. After a final check, bows were added to the girls' hair, and Frederick donned his tie and jacket on the way out the door.

When they pulled to a stop, Phoebe let herself out the passenger side and dashed to the house with Pinky and Rummy in her arms. Frederick set Bethany on the grass to walk but carried her doll. Lucy stood in the doorway with a smile. He was glad she was fully dressed—for her standards—rather than still in her robe.

Bethany clutched her father's finger as she climbed the front steps, eyes only on her mother, who bent down with open arms. Their youngest was soon settled against the breast of Lucy's royal blue gown.

"Ever since she cut those teeth last month, I spend the first hour holding her. I'll be sad when these days are gone." There was love in her eyes but Frederick didn't deceive himself by thinking it was for him, though she rested a hand on his forearm and kissed his cheek. "I'm sorry I yelled at you Friday night."

"And I'm sorry I ate the rest of your cake, Goosy."

"That was you? I thought it was Alex."

"And he was forgiven?"

"Naturally." Her smile did its best to sway him to old cravings but he remained unmoved.

"I suppose I'll need to bring you a new treat today."

"Something decadent to make up for it."

"I might be a bit later than usual with the gym and buying dessert."

Lucy kissed his cheek once more and then turned for the parlor. "I'll only complain if you return empty-handed."

"What's this?" Alexander said as he came down the stairs, fixing his necktie. "You only allow Freddy entrance if he brings gifts? First it's children, next it's chocolate."

"I wouldn't turn down chocolate."

Alexander looked between them. "So you two have kissed and made up, have you?"

Lucy's chin went high. "Only if he brings me dessert."

"I thought I was in charge of dessert." Alexander pressed against Lucy's hip opposite from where she held Bethany and nibbled her ear until she squirmed away with a laugh.

"Bye, Beth." Frederick waved at his daughter and went for the door. "I'll be back by seven-thirty."

Frederick frowned on his way to the automobile, realizing he was looking forward to seeing Melissa. Not wanting to begin the week depressed, he gazed up at the wisteria vines tangled in the trees that lined the side yard in an attempt to clear his mind before getting behind the wheel.

"Are you a birdwatcher?"

Frederick found himself smiling as he turned toward the voice. Melissa stood at the edge of the property, a closed parasol used as a walking stick in her hand and her copper hair shining in the morning sun. Her smiling face glowed against her white blouse and the black lace trim set off the brooch she wore at her neck.

"I do seem to have a penchant for things that fly away from me."

"Surely one wife—"

"Lucy was my second."

The truth was out and the startled look on her face spoke volumes. It was better to scare her away because Frederick couldn't handle her kindness while he longed for more.

"That's quite a feat. You don't look like you could be over thirty."

"I'll be thirty in August." He crossed his arms and watched for clues to her thoughts.

Her smile returned. "I'm thirty in May."

"And how many husbands have been lucky enough to call you their wife?"

"My achievement is having made it thirty years without the benefit of a man's name." The tip of her parasol dug into the dirt.

"Are you opposed to the idea of marriage? Does it sicken you to be around a man who was married twice in his twenties?" His tone was too intense, but he decided he didn't need the hope of a woman who would be returning to New York in a few weeks.

"I find it intriguing. This whole situation is much more than I expected when Mr. Noble asked me to come." Her warm brown eyes studied him. "And is the first Mrs. Davenport's story similar to the second's?"

He shook his head. "I'm not one to repeat the same mistakes, though I consider my time with Lucy worth the heartache because my daughters came from our union. Nor do I regret my six months with the first for the comfort it gave our families. It's only what I left undone in between the two that I would change, but I'm not one to dwell on those things."

Melissa's eyebrows came together with concern and she tapped a finger on the handle of her umbrella. "Freddy, you're the most complex man I've ever met. I'd like to get to know you and try to understand your life, experiences, and passions."

"Please don't speak to me of passion." He opened the automobile door. "I must get to the office. Good luck with the girls today."

"Wait, there's something I think you should know."

He stopped, one foot on the running board, and turned to her.

"A priest, Claudio, came for supper Saturday evening."

"He's done that often enough while he's in town. I've even taken supper here with the girls when he's visiting."

"When he arrived, he said something was off and he insisted on blessing everyone in the house. Alex looked frightened because Claudio said it felt like…Seacliff, I think he said."

Frederick gripped the door. "Seacliff Cottage?"

"That was it. He came back yesterday afternoon and blessed the house with salts and incense, but wasn't satisfied because he couldn't find the source of trouble."

"And they didn't think to tell me?" His hands were in fists before he realized. "If something is going on, I don't want my daughters here."

He stepped for the house, but Melissa put a hand on his arm. "It could be nothing, but I'll watch out for the girls. I won't let anything happen to them."

"Did they tell you about what happened at Seacliff Cottage?"

She shook her head.

"Then you can't possibly understand the danger."

"But I think Alex does. He asked Claudio to come back today to bless the girls."

"Yet Lucy mentioned nothing of this to me?" The anger in his voice tumbled out and his knuckles strained further. "I won't forgive so easily when it comes to my daughters."

"I'll keep watch today." Her soothing voice and steady gaze calmed him.

Frederick hesitated before taking the driver's seat. "One day. But don't be surprised if I check in. And call me if anything's amiss. The office number is by the telephone. Tell the secretary it's about my daughters and she'll put you through even if I'm in a meeting."

"I will, Freddy. I promise."

He tucked Melissa's words beside his love for his daughters as his white knuckles strained around the steering wheel.

Eight

Melissa didn't like sending Freddy to work upset. Feeling defeated, she entered the parlor and Phoebe immediately ran behind the settee.

"Come now, Phoebe"—Lucy's voice was soft as she held Bethany in her arms—"you should say 'hello' or 'good morning' to Miss Melissa."

Phoebe popped her head over the back of the seat. "Hello, Miss Melissa." And then she was gone.

"Lucy, might I bring the globe from your study in here?"

"Of course."

It felt strange to be in the room now that she knew Lucy and Alex were intimate in there, but after seeing them necking on the settee when she arrived—as well as running for the gazebo in the night—she figured there was little of the property the amorous couple had yet to consecrate as their own.

Melissa sat in the middle of the parlor floor with the globe before her, slowly spinning it. "I wonder if there are any pirates in Kingdom Davenport. Jamaica and many of the other islands in the Caribbean were home to pirates."

"Jamaica is an island?" Phoebe asked from behind the settee.

"Yes, surrounded by beautiful blue water and colorful fish."

"I have friends that live on an island. Kade and Tabitha and their mama and papa. And the Walkers, but I don't like Abraham." She crawled around the side of the settee and peeked out. "Miss Darla grew up on the island."

"A far away island?" Melissa asked.

"No, an Alabama island. Dolphin Island."

"Dauphin Island, Phoebe." Lucy corrected her with a smile. "Dauphine was the title of the heir to the throne of France."

"It's a royal island?" Phoebe smiled when her mother nodded. "Kingdom Davenport will conquer it!"

"It has been conquered many times before, but I don't think President Taft would take kindly to Kingdom Davenport rallying her forces against it."

Phoebe crawled toward the globe. "Could I take Jamaica?"

"I'm not sure," Melissa said. "They have a huge fort with lots of cannons."

"I must have an island!"

Melissa put her finger on the globe. "There's Jamaica. What makes an island, Phoebe?"

"Water!"

"Yes, it's surrounded by water. When you play, you can turn anything surrounded by something else into an island. The settee, your bed, and even the house because it's surrounded by grass."

"This is Melling Militia's island and I shall conquer it when Mr. Alex returns!" She scooped her doll and rabbit into her arms and ran for the stairs.

"Those battle plans should keep her busy most of the day." Lucy looked at Melissa as she stood. "I feel sorry for Alex when he returns. If he calls, I'll have to warn him."

"Let her get in a surprise attack."

Lucy pursed her lips and raised her chin. "It's clear to see which side you're on."

"I'm not here to take sides."

"I saw you talking with Freddy for several minutes."

Melissa spun the globe. "He was leaving when I came back from my walk."

"And what could you possibly have to talk about with Frederick?" Lucy's voice was insufferably condescending.

"The girls, for one thing."

"And for another?"

She seemed to dare her to say that they had spoken of her, but Melissa refused to reward her with that information. "He asked my opinion on marriage."

Melissa returned the globe to the study. On the way back, she looked in at Lucy murmuring over her youngest. Continuing upstairs, she checked in the girls' bedroom—all pink and flounces. Phoebe sat on the Oriental rug between the bed and crib, a pile of newspapers before her. She folded one into the shape of a sword.

"Preparations are in order?"

Phoebe looked up with a devilish smile, much like the one her stepfather often wore. "I'm making your sword. Training begins today and the island siege will be your test. Melling Militia usually reports at half-past four on Mondays, so be ready."

Melissa crouched by the girl. "I'll do my best. Where and when do we meet for training?"

"The front porch at eight-thirty. And no treasure." She pointed the tip of the paper sword at the brooch.

Melissa placed the emerald pin in her top dresser drawer before returning to the parlor. Lucy still held Bethany, both looking drowsy.

"I have an eight-thirty training date with Phoebe. I can bring Bethany with me so you can get to work."

"How often have you watched more than one child?"

"Today will be my first attempt."

"Phoebe is demanding. I'd rather you not try to keep an eye on Bethany the first day."

"I believe I can handle playing with both."

In response Lucy stood, bringing Bethany onto her shoulder. She appeared to breathe deeply of her daughter's hair, a slight smile finding her lips. "Phoebe is intense. It's not play to her, it's her life's mission."

"So all her shouting for the death of Alex is reality?"

Lucy didn't take the joke as well as Freddy. "She loves Alex, both girls do! And he loves them." Moisture welled in her eyes. "We're a family as much as possible in our situation."

"I was trying to be funny."

"Don't attempt to tease me about my husband. You know nothing!" Lucy's voice was as hard as anything Melissa had ever heard directed at her, causing her to take a step back. "I met my writing goals the last two days, that's all you need to be concerned about."

"And today you need to double the three pages you've done."

"I already told Alex I'd complete seven."

How Lucy managed to look down her nose at her though she was shorter Melissa attributed to the woman's Southern breeding. She glared back at Lucy—the romance writer willing to write for intimacies with her husband. The thought of asking Alex if he *could* hold back for a day if Lucy missed her goal flashed through her mind, causing her to smirk.

Lucy scowled. "I doubt you've ever written anything more than five pages in length for your articles."

"But I've never missed a deadline and write hundreds of pages each year. Now I insist you get some fresh air for a few minutes and then set to work."

The two stared at each other, Lucy clutching her youngest to her chest like a shield. Half a minute later, she stepped to Melissa and handed her Bethany. "I'll be back for her."

Bethany snuggled against Melissa's shoulder, tucking her head against her neck. Melissa knew in an instant why Lucy smelled her daughter's hair and smiled. Freddy's scent was all about her—masculine and fresh. If she closed her eyes, she could have imagined Freddy nestled against her. The sweet girl spent the weekend at her father's house and he had surely held her often. But it wasn't Melissa's place to fancy such things, nor was it Lucy's. Disgust over knowing Lucy still had feelings for her ex-husband while she was rapturous over Alex stormed within like a typhoon.

To calm herself, Melissa took Bethany to the swing on the front porch and sat the girl on her lap. Her pale blue dress was all ruffles and lace, her black buckle shoes shiny at the end of her pudgy legs.

"Bethany, remember me? I'm Melissa and I'm going to be here for a while. Do you like swinging?"

"Yes." Her voice was quiet, much different from Phoebe's shrill one.

Melissa pushed off to get the swing moving and then settled back. With Bethany in her arms, Melissa absorbed the surprising comfort of holding a child.

Phoebe exited the screen door, arms full of newspaper swords, a wooden one, a small wooden shield, and several paper hats. She carefully arranged her supplies in front of the rocking chairs. "Training in five minutes, Miss Melissa."

"We might have to wait an extra minute or two until your mother comes for Bethany."

"Beth is a knight!" Phoebe lifted the shortest paper sword and brought one of the hats. She crowned her sister's head with a newspaper bicorn like British naval officers would have worn a century ago. Then she held the sword before her sister. "Knight Bethany Iris Davenport, your sword."

To Melissa's surprise, Bethany snatched the hilt and climbed off her lap. Phoebe took her own wooden sword and carefully parried her little sister's strikes as not to damage her inferior weapon.

The two were involved in the battle when Lucy came around the driveway from the backyard. A wistful smile found her pretty face and she leaned against the bottom post of the steps to watch. Phoebe and Bethany parried their way to the far corner of the porch.

"If Bethany gets too antsy, bring her to me." Lucy kicked off her shoes inside the door and disappeared.

***

If she'd expected a kind word over keeping the two girls entertained all morning, Melissa would have been disappointed. Lucy emerged from the study at a quarter to twelve and set about preparing their lunch without a word. At noon, she called to the girls to get washed up so Melissa assisted them and followed Phoebe's lead to the kitchen porch.

The only thing Lucy said to Melissa during the whole meal was "Three pages so far." But she doted on her daughters every moment.

Lucy took a handful of dishes to the kitchen, and as Melissa stood to help clear the table, a striking young woman let herself in the door from the back yard. Her hair was so dark it was almost black, her skin ivory, and her eyes sapphires.

"Miss Darla!" Phoebe leapt into the lady's arms without asking to be excused from the table.

"How were the battles Friday?" Darla kissed the girl's forehead and set her back on her chair.

"Melling Militia is on the run and this house is their private island. We attack at four-thirty. Can you help?"

"I'm afraid not. Dr. Hughes is picking me up at four to see a new client. He wanted to bring me at one, but I told him I couldn't miss my appointment with Kingdom Davenport." Darla kissed Bethany's chubby cheek and then smiled at Melissa, offering a hand. "You must be the lady from the publishing company. I'm Darla Beauchamp, a part-time knight for the kingdom."

She set down the stack of plates she'd gathered to shake Darla's hand. "Melissa Stone, temporary knight."

Lucy returned in time to witness the friendly handshake. Melissa saw the frown before she gathered a smile.

"Darla, how was your visit with Henry's family? I hope it went as well as last time."

"Yes, and the horses seemed to remember me. I was afraid Henry would have given me up if I failed to stay upright for an entire ride on my fourth visit, but it's all fair play because he turns green on a boat." Darla's round face was merry. She looked to Melissa to explain. "Henry's my fiancé. We're to be married the Wednesday after Easter."

"Congratulations."

"Now that Darla's here, Ms. Stone, you're free to do as you wish. I should be finished by the time she leaves, so you're officially off-duty the rest of the day as far as I'm concerned." She looked to

Darla. "If I'm not out of the study, knock on my door before you leave. Now girls, hugs for Momma and take a good nap. You'll need your strength for the siege this evening."

When Lucy took Bethany out of her high chair, the girl clung to her mother's neck. "Momma love."

"Phoebe, please get Bethany's blanket and pillow and bring them to my study."

"Yes, Momma." Phoebe ran ahead and Lucy followed, carrying Bethany.

"Beth often naps in the study," Darla remarked. "Phoebe, too."

"That chaise is sabotage to her workspace. Alex—" Melissa paused and looked at the younger woman. "When he's home, it's nothing but a distraction."

A blush crept to Darla's cheeks. "I'm not often here when he is. I might have made that decision deliberately."

"You aren't keen on the lawyer with a charming smile who can't keep his hands off his wife?" Melissa carried the plates into the kitchen and Darla followed with the silverware.

"Nor could he keep them off her when she was Mr. Davenport's wife." She sighed and looked upward after depositing her load into the sink. "I begged him not to go to her, but he wouldn't listen to reason."

Intrigued, Melissa turned to her. "You were there for his fateful return?"

"I was at the hotel with the Campbells when he made himself known to them. Claudio was the only one who knew he was still alive. Claudio is—"

"Alex's best friend and a priest. He was over twice this weekend. I found him fascinating. But who are the Campbells?"

"My friends from the island. Before they were married, they were employed by Alex's parents at their home across the bay. They were the last ones to see Alex and his father before the fire."

"At Seacliff Cottage?"

Darla's eyes went large. "It isn't something frequently spoken of."

"The name was mentioned while Claudio was here. All I know is that something awful happened and it's been destroyed." Melissa began to put the tidbits of information together. "Is that how Alex was burned?"

"Yes, he wanted it to look like he died, but he escaped." Phoebe returned from her errand and slipped her hand into Darla's. "Let's get you ready for quiet time."

"Story first. Can you read me more about the Pepper family, please?"

"Fetch the book and I'll meet you in your room." Phoebe left and Darla focused back on Melissa as she opened the buttons on the pinstriped jacket that matched her skirt. "I'll be in the parlor when I'm done. Phoebe doesn't always sleep, but she'll stay in bed at least thirty minutes if you'd like to talk more. I get the feeling you're not getting much socialization from Lucy."

Melissa laughed. "I'm afraid she hasn't liked me since I tried to remove the chaise from her study, but joking about Phoebe wanting to kill her stepfather this morning didn't help my standing."

Darla's hand went to her mouth to muffle a laugh.

"I said something similar to Freddy and he thought it was funny."

"Mr. Davenport often thinks the same thing. He's a good man who happened to love the wrong woman. At first I thought Lucy was making a terrible choice leaving him, but then I realized he deserves more from a wife."

"I can see you think highly of him."

Darla hung her jacket and purse in the foyer. "The highest possible for a mortal man, though I'd have to place Henry slightly above Mr. Davenport on the ladder of perfection because I've never seen him punch a hole in a wall."

Nine

Frederick left the office an hour and a half early, though he had to reschedule two appointments. Rescuing his daughters from the Mellings took top priority, but he knew he needed to expel some angst before seeing Alexander.

Upon signing the list for the boxing tournament, he told the trainers to be sure to tell Chuck when he arrived. While he rowed on the machine, he congratulated himself for not breaking down and telephoning Lucy's house to check on things. Something in Melissa's steady gaze made Frederick trust her.

"Davenport, you've got a sappy smile today," Thomas Charles remarked. "Let the smile take over for a change. It looks like it has a lady behind it and I heard you went out Friday."

Frederick grimaced as he pulled himself through his final minute. "You can be sure it's in no way related to that experience."

Thomas laughed. "I had to poke you about that. Chuck said you left halfway through the meal. You should have held out for dessert. I bet Judith would have made it memorable."

Frederick remembered the feel of her hand on his knee under the table and knew any advances he made would be well accepted.

"You're probably right, but she's not my type and I'm not one to take advantage of a woman to fuel my needs."

"Saint Frederick."

He stood from the machine, grabbed a towel to wipe the perspiration from his face, and continued to the punching bag, then weights. Being joked over in the boxing ring spurred Frederick to win. After showering, he walked down the block to purchase chocolates and buy a sandwich for himself before driving west.

It was five-thirty when he pulled to a stop before the house. He immediately smiled at seeing Melissa on the front porch swing. She looked as natural there as Lucy, though he wouldn't have mentioned that to either woman. Placing a small box of chocolates on top the other, he heated noticing Melissa watching his approach. Frederick paused to peek in the parlor window. Lucy lay on the settee, her legs across Alex's lap and Bethany curled on her chest while Phoebe played on the floor.

He stepped to Melissa. "How were things today? The girls look fine."

Her immediate smile helped him relax. "Everything was good. I watched them all morning and then Darla came in time to put them down for a nap but I stayed nearby. When Darla had to leave, Lucy was done writing for the day."

He exhaled and took hold of the small box. "I don't know if you like chocolate, but I brought you a little sampler. If you don't care for them, there are others in the house that would be happy to take them off your hands."

"Thank you. I do enjoy chocolate but I feel odd accepting it."

"Think of it as a token of my appreciation for you watching the girls. I owe Lucy a box and she's not one to share."

"You bring your ex-wife gifts often?" Her smile was light, teasing.

He held her gaze without shame. "It's not a gift, but a replacement. I ate her last piece of cake Friday night and she requested chocolate in its place."

His gaze might have turned into a stare. Melissa looked at the box in her lap.

Frederick cleared his throat. "How was Claudio's visit?"

"He hasn't come yet."

Pacing between the swing and the front door, Frederick stopped before Melissa, his voice low. "I'm torn between rushing them from here and waiting to speak with him. My faith is different from the others, but I know Claudio is experienced with evil spirits—demons he calls them—and I won't turn him away from trying to help."

"Darla gave me a quick version of the events at Seacliff Cottage while the girls napped."

The screen opened behind Frederick and he turned as Lucy stepped onto the porch. "I thought I heard someone out here."

"I brought your chocolate, Goosy."

He didn't step as close as he normally did and she frowned at the slight—though it wasn't meant to be one. Lucy filled the void and leaned in for the kiss she liked to plant on his cheek as she took the box. Frederick instinctively brushed a finger against her hand.

"I'm glad you remembered. I told Naomi we didn't need dessert today."

"I'm officially on the list for the boxing tournament, so keep March sixteenth free."

"I wouldn't miss it." Lucy put a hand on his shoulder and ran it slowly down to his elbow. "You appear stronger than ever. Are you lifting weights more often?"

"Yes." He stepped away. "I'll get the girls now."

"Don't rush. They were expected to take supper here. Claudio is—"

"When were you going to tell me?"

"Tell you what?" Her lips pursed.

"You know what, but I'd rather discuss this with Alex. Send him out."

"Freddy, I don't know what you've heard, but Alex is innocent." Her voice sounded frightened, then she looked to Melissa and it turned sardonic. "I can't imagine where you've heard about what went on with Claudio, but nothing's happened beyond him feeling something was off."

Frederick crossed his arms. "Get Alex or I'll come in and retrieve him myself."

Lucy's free hand went to her shapely hip. After a glare to him and Melissa, she brought her chocolates inside. Alexander soon stepped out in his typical sock-clad feet. Frederick grabbed him by his open collar and shoved him against the wall by the dining room window.

"What gives you the right to allow my daughters here when Claudio declared the house felt like Seacliff Cottage?" Frederick stood back, shaking the tension from his limbs.

"I haven't felt a difference in the house. Either has Lucy."

"No, you two are too busy feeling each other up."

Alexander retrieved a silver cigarette case from his pocket and flipped it in his scarred hand. "Jealousy isn't your style."

"This is about the safety of my daughters!"

"They're as safe and well as any other time. Go see for yourself."

"Then why was a blessing for them sought from Claudio?"

"Precautionary. He blessed all of us, even Melissa." Alexander managed to keep a spark of mischief burning in his cold eyes.

"When is he expected?" Frederick demanded.

"Before six."

"You can't keep things like this from me. Even if you think there's no danger, I have the right to know."

"That's all up to Lucy." Alexander pocketed the case. "This is her house and though I love the girls, I have no claim to them."

"But she listens to you. If the house begins to harbor evil you'll not see my daughters here and you know what that would do to Lucy. Make this your priority, even more so than her finishing that book because family is more important than a novel."

"Do you think I've forgotten the horrors of what happened at Seacliff when I wear the reminders every minute of my life? You only heard the stories, I lived it." He held a discolored hand in front of Frederick's face until it was knocked aside. "Don't come to our home and tell us we're failing to meet your expectations on something you don't understand!"

"*Calmati, amico,*" Claudio called as he crossed the yard.

All eyes turned to the priest as he boldly stepped between Alexander and Frederick. He said something in Italian to Alexander, followed by "*Capisci?*"

"*Sì,* Claudio. I understand." He took a step back then looked to Frederick. "I'm sorry for my anger. You're right to be worried for your daughters. I know how precious they are to you."

Frederick gave a dry laugh. "You can't begin to understand until you're a father."

Alexander caught Frederick off guard with a shove that sent him tumbling against the porch railing. "And you'll never understand the pain of wanting something out of your reach!"

Melissa noisily sucked in her breath, causing Frederick to glance her way. Her brown eyes were dewy, but her face remained calm. Claudio took Alexander by the shoulders and spoke to him in a whisper before sending him inside.

"Frederick, I trust that you will remain out here until you calm down. I will not bless your daughters until you are in attendance." Claudio looked to Melissa. "I hope you are well today."

"Yes, thank you, Claudio."

Frederick paced several minutes after Claudio entered the house. He was grateful Melissa stayed on the swing for he didn't feel like being alone on the threshold of a home where he was once welcomed. With each passing week the old Easton house turned more Melling and Claudio's declaration of evil went right along with the transformation. Lucy was lost to him, but he needed to save his girls from the Melling taint.

"I don't understand why he got upset with me," he muttered.

"I do," Melissa whispered.

Frederick plopped onto the swing beside her. He realized too late how intimate their seating was when his knee brushed against hers.

"I overheard Alex and Lucy talking this weekend," she continued. "It appears they're desperate to have a child. Lucy is more concerned with producing a baby than writing. What you said struck a sour note with him because he wants to be a father."

"Once they do have a baby, they won't have half the opportunity for all the lovemaking they're fond of."

A rosy glow heated behind Melissa's bronzed skin. "I think that's why they're focused on it. Lucy not being pregnant isn't for a lack of trying, that's for sure. In all my travels I've never seen a couple more devoted to...*it*."

Frederick laughed. "Excuse me for leading us in to this obviously uncomfortable topic of conversation, Melissa. I think I've had enough of discussing the Mellings' bedroom practices."

"If only they kept it in the bedroom." Melissa covered her mouth. "I'm sorry, I—"

He laughed again and patted her hand. "Believe me, I know what you mean."

She looked down at his hand.

"I'm sorry." He stood and stepped away. "What must you think of me, speaking of my ex-wife's intimacies?"

"I hold nothing against you, Freddy. It's a topsy-turvy household," she said with a smile.

In an attempt to cover his embarrassment, he offered his arm. "Would you like to return to the circus with me?"

"Gladly."

They parted ways at the foot of the stairs. Frederick entered the parlor alone but was soon set upon by Phoebe. Lucy was back to lounging on the settee, this time upright against Alexander with Bethany sleeping in her lap. He had a hand on Bethany's arm but removed it. Frederick saw the pain in his eyes, reminding him of how Alexander looked after the times he'd hurt Lucy. Remorseful.

"It's nice you could finally tear yourself away from Ms. Stone to join your daughters. For one worried over their welfare you sure took your time coming."

"I'm not the enemy, Lucy."

"No," Claudio said as he stood, "I am here to protect against the greatest enemy. Precious angels sometimes need extra blessings. Come, *principessa*. I will endow the knights of Kingdom Davenport with the protection of Heaven."

With an eager smile, Phoebe raced to Claudio. He knelt before her and pulled a wood and metal crucifix from his pocket, asking her to hold it. The priest led her through the sign of the cross before drawing a cross on her forehead with his finger tip and laying his hands on her head. As he prayed in Latin, Frederick studied his daughter for any signs of discomfort. The only thing that alarmed him was Alex wiping the corner of his eye when it was over.

"Melling Militia will have no chance now," she whispered in her father's ear.

Frederick gazed around the room. With a slight nod, he acknowledged Melissa standing in the doorway as he wrapped Phoebe in a hug. Then Claudio started on Bethany. From Frederick's angle, he couldn't see her face, but Lucy looked peaceful as she held her. Just as it was over, Naomi was in the room to announce supper.

"Are you staying to eat, Mr. Frederick? I'll set you a place right quick."

Finding it humorous to be invited to stay by the cook rather than the man or woman of the house, he smiled back. "I ate on my way here, but thank you."

"You're welcome to," Lucy said.

"I've already eaten. If this little princess stays asleep, I'll hold her while you dine." He took Bethany from Lucy and claimed the armchair facing the window.

Ten

Not wanting to sit around listening to the Mellings after supper, Melissa excused herself to retire for the night. It turned out watching children, even delightful girls like the Davenports, was exhausting work. Halfway up the stairs, she remembered her journal in the parlor. One dim lamp in the corner near the piano cast Freddy's face in shadow. She passed him without word to retrieve her book from the far table. When she approached him on her way out, a light snore came from his chair. Thinking Bethany was deep asleep, she gently laid her hand on his sleeve.

"She's about to slip out of your arms," she whispered.

He tugged Bethany up his torso. "Thank you. I guess I needed a nap as well."

"A pleasant dream, too?" She couldn't see his eyes clearly, but there was no mistaking his smile. Wanting to say more, but knowing it wouldn't be proper, she took a step away. "I hope to see you tomorrow."

"Melissa?"

"Yes?" It sounded like her heartbeat was louder than the word.

"Thank you for staying on the porch with me. And for explaining about Alex. I don't know how to make amends over what I said."

"I'm sure it will come to you." She rested a hand on his broad shoulder a moment in what she hoped was a comforting touch rather than a forward one. His muscles tensed beneath her fingers and she stepped away.

"Enjoy your chocolates," he said on her way out.

With a sigh, she closed her bedroom door and went for the sampler on top of the dresser. She indulged in a truffle and readied for bed.

By the time the Mellings came up, she'd read a few dozen pages of *Ivanhoe* she'd borrowed from downstairs. Her light was off and she lay on her side, looking out the window at the magnolia tree moving in the wind.

"Seven pages, was it?" Alex's voice came from the hall. "I'll be sure you're rewarded for each one, my queen."

Lucy's laughter squeezed under the closed door, raking Melissa because she found herself vested in the Mellings' marriage without wanting to be. Did Alex play the part of lover to please his wife or was he really as sensual as he appeared to be? Was Lucy so desperate for attention that she acted like a love-starved fool? Did she feign sexual cravings to satisfy him? Were they both so in love that they were still making up for their years apart? Did their longing for a baby have them trying for one as often as possible? Or was it some combination of things?

Only the thought of her book proposal kept Melissa from running for the station to beg passage on the next North-bound train—that and the honorable character of Frederick Davenport. She could tell he had just as much passion as Alex but he channeled it differently. And the tenderness he had for his daughters was breathtaking. Flipping her pillow to the cold side, she resettled on her back and tried to sleep.

***

After a restless night, Melissa woke with the dawn, quietly dressed, and let herself out the front door for her morning stroll. She explored a bit too far and returned after the girls arrived and Alex had left for work.

Lucy spent the first hour in the parlor with her daughters and Melissa journaled on the swing about the flora and fauna she'd seen on her walk, as well as the locals she'd engaged with in conversations. Everyone who introduced themselves to her was extra chatty when they heard she was staying with Alex and Lucy Melling.

Melissa watched the girls nearly three hours both before and after lunch. She spent their nap hour in her room, skimming through Lucy's books to find places mentioned so she could plan outings to them. Monroe Park, Bienville Square, The Cathedral of the Immaculate Conception, and The Battle House Hotel made the list. She'd stayed at the hotel and there was a square near the jewelers she'd seen, but she needed to return to the places with her camera.

As the hands on the clock approached five, Melissa looked across the parlor at Lucy, in awe of how at ease she appeared in her red tea gown with her daughters curled on either side of her as she read aloud to them.

Without speaking, she collected her parasol and headed south. The last two mornings she went toward Dauphin Street, so she headed for the other main road, Government Street. Turning toward downtown, she strolled the well-kept sidewalks and gazed into the yards of the mansions as the streetcars, automobiles, and wagons rolled by. The oaks provided plenty of shade with the setting sun so she folded her parasol, using it as a walking stick.

After several blocks, a woman slightly her senior smiled in greeting.

"There seems to be a plethora of new faces about today," the woman remarked. "Good evening."

"Good evening." Melissa smiled. "It's my first time in Alabama and I've enjoyed what I've seen of the town."

She appraised Melissa's suit and nodded her approval. "You look like a Northern lady to me. I'm Ms. Verbena Moore. Are you visiting relatives?"

"It's good to meet you. I'm Melissa Stone, here on business. I'm staying with another client from the publishing company I work for."

"Oh, to be young and adventurous. Anyone I might know?"

"Most likely. Everyone seems to know Lucy Melling."

"Bless your heart." Ms. Moore's hand went to her bosom. "She was such a quiet girl growing up. No one guessed she'd go on to scandal and publishing novels under a false name like she was ashamed of herself—and for good reason!"

Melissa nodded and pressed her tongue to the top of her mouth to keep from speaking.

"And then the shock of Alexander Melling returning from the grave. His poor mother, but she's happy to have one member of her family back after losing both children and her husband in one year. She keeps on by herself in that massive house a few blocks from here, still throwing the best parties in town."

Curious to see the house Alex had forsaken, Melissa questioned Ms. Moore. "I find the architecture of this city fascinating. Are there any interesting details on Mrs. Melling's home?"

"Why of course! Mr. Rogers designed it. Look for it beyond Georgia Street on the south side, but you'll have a better view if you keep on this side of the road. It has paired columns across the veranda, quite striking."

"Thank you."

"But watch out now." Ms. Moore waved a finger at her. "I just came from that way and there was a strange man hanging about that corner. That's the other reason to keep to this side. Be sure you return before dark."

"Thank you for your information and concern, Ms. Moore."

"Any time, dear. I live around the next corner if you need anything."

Happy to have a purpose to her walk, Melissa increased her speed. The thought of the unknown man didn't alarm her. She lived in New York City and had wandered places like the market in Morocco alone. The supposed dangers in a small city were no concern.

When the Melling mansion came into view, Melissa caught her breath. In size and style it was one of the finest houses she'd passed on her walks. She took in the unique column placement and the curve of the east and west wings. Her impression of Alex being a spoiled rich boy appeared to be true. With a smile, she tapped her parasol twice on the sidewalk and turned back.

Across the road, movement between traffic caught her eye. Melissa stared at the dark man in a suit with a hat pulled low over his eyes. She took a few steps as he raised a cigarette to his lips nonchalantly. Out of the corner of her eye, she watched him blow out his smoke and walk parallel to her.

Along the next stretch of block, an automobile approached from behind, slowing along the curb. Her grip tightened on the handle of her umbrella.

"Melissa," Freddy's kind voice called. "Isn't it late for a walk?"

She realized her heart had quickened with the unknown situation, but Freddy caused it to race in a good way.

"Time got away from me. I hope to make it back before nightfall."

"Would you accept a ride?"

Melissa glanced across the street. The man leaned against a street lamp, watching. "Yes, I think I would."

Freddy set the brake and ran around to open the door for her, holding her elbow as she climbed in. She glanced behind them as they pulled away and the man stared after her.

"I missed you this morning," she said. "My morning walk took me further than I expected. Seems to be the story of my day."

"Did you need to see me for something?" Freddy glanced at her.

"Oh, I didn't mean…the chocolate is delightful. Thank you, again."

He smiled. "Anytime you'd like more or need something else, I'd be happy to pick it up for you." The smile faded, but Melissa kept watching him. "I know Lucy's house is a bit out of the way and it'd be no trouble to pick up things for you in town."

Was it out of politeness that he offered? A Southern gentleman, but at times it appeared to be more. Part of her yearned that his kindness was driven by feelings beyond chivalry, but the other part reminded her she was here temporarily and none of her other romantic liaisons on her travels ended happily. She guarded herself against being too sentimental when men were more than willing to share a few days without commitment.

"I've compiled a list of places I need to visit for my assignment."

"You're assignment, beyond being Lucy's nursemaid?"

Melissa laughed, pleased to see Freddy's smile return. "I'm a travel writer and essayist, not a governess for novelists. This is the first time Mr. Noble asked me to do anything relating to another writer and I hope it's the last."

"Are things as bad as that at the house?"

"I'm sure it could be worse, but it's not ideal." She sighed. "I'll give it another week, and then I might need to move into a hotel for all of our sanity."

"Let me know if there's anything I can do."

"I appreciate it."

"And what of the places you need to visit? The girls and I would be happy to bring you around on the weekends."

"I'd hate to impose."

"We love our adventures. They aren't as grand as yours, but they satisfy Phoebe for the time being."

"I'm to compose an article about the charms of Mobile in conjunction with Olive Kent novels. I need to visit the places Lucy mentions, like Bienville Square and Monroe Park, so I can take photographs and write about them."

"Monroe Park is one of the girls' favorite places. We'd be more than happy to show you all the amusements there and any other places along the way."

"I might need to take you up on that."

"And as for photography, Erik Overbey is one of my clients. He's the best there is with a camera around here. If you have any questions he could help you with, I will get you in touch with him."

"Thank you, Freddy. Knowing where to take my film for developing would be a great start."

He smiled. "I know just the place."

Alex's automobile was parked under the porte-cochere when they pulled into the driveway. Melissa hung back as Freddy went for the porch. He took her elbow with a gentle touch.

"There's nothing to worry over, Melissa. Yes, we are arriving together, but there's no harm in that. You were on a walk and I offered you a ride to make sure you returned before dark."

His brown eyes were sincere as she wrapped her arm around his, reflexively bringing a hand to his biceps as she felt the definition beneath his suit jacket.

"There needn't be so much touching involved."

Cheeks heating, she immediately dropped her arms.

His chuckle was as endearing as his own blush. "I was teasing. I don't mind, not even half what I should." He searched her gaze as though looking for a clue to her feelings.

Melissa closed the window to her heart, but she thought he discovered all before it locked.

"I don't mean to be forward, I'm used to being curious about the world. I investigate new environments through all the senses. Exploring things I'm interested in is part of my job." Her hand went to her mouth as she sucked in her breath. "That came out all wrong!"

Freddy's head tilted to the side as a playful grin found his perfect lips. He was too much of a gentleman to say it out right, but the statement was there on his face, though soft rather than with the commanding air he could have taken with the knowledge of her feelings: *That means you're interested in me and want to explore my body.*

Without speaking to further embarrass herself, Melissa went for the stairs to put away her parasol.

"Goosy, I'm here," Freddy called.

Melissa didn't like the jab in her chest when he called Lucy by her nickname—it felt too intimate for a man to call his ex-wife. She took a moment to collect herself in her room before joining the others.

When she entered the parlor, Freddy was in an armchair with Phoebe on his lap, listening to Lucy. Bethany was on her mother's shoulder, a fistful of her blonde hair held to the girls' little cheek like a comforting talisman.

"Could we try it tomorrow night?" Lucy asked. "Phoebe said she wanted to ride the streetcar with Darla, so Thursday morning would be perfect for that. It would save you a trip here."

"I want to ride with Miss Darla!" Phoebe bounced on her father's knee.

Freddy looked concerned. "They've never been apart overnight."

"They're getting older and I think some one-on-one time with each of us would be good for them. We could do it the other way one day as well." Lucy's gaze was earnest.

The desperation in her eyes must have been felt by Freddy as well. "All right, we'll try it. Do you need me to bring anything extra for Beth tomorrow?"

"Maybe a change of clothes and a few more diapers. They each have a nightgown here." Lucy raised Bethany to her face and kissed her cheek. "Momma will hold you all night tomorrow, Bethany Iris, but for now go home with Daddy."

Lucy set her on the ground and Bethany toddled to Freddy. Alex's hand went to Lucy's back, rubbing across the lace in a circular motion.

Freddy stood, taking each girl by a hand. "We'll see you all in the morning."

As the Davenports left, Melissa couldn't help but feel the emptiness in the house. It would prove to be another long night.

Eleven

The next morning, Frederick carried a suitcase and dress into Lucy's house, the girls running ahead to the parlor. Not seeing anyone, his daughters settled by the basket of blocks. He set Bethany's luggage at the bottom stairs and hung Phoebe's dress in the foyer.

"Goosy?" he called.

Melissa descended the stairs. "They were in the kitchen when I left on my walk, but it sounds like they're in their bedroom now." She paused. "Not like *that*. I heard talking when I put my umbrella away."

He couldn't help smiling at how she fumbled over words when she said something that could be taken the wrong way. Frederick remembered the delicious feeling of her hand on his arm the evening before and felt his grin widen with the memory of her exploration.

"Good morning, Melissa."

"Hello, Freddy." She stopped before him, slightly closer than would typically be comfortable. "I can watch the girls until Lucy comes down if you need to leave."

He shifted toward her. "You want me to go?"

"Not at all." Her words gave him too much hope for one in his situation.

"That's good to know." He held her gaze before lowering it to her lips. "But I do need to leave. I'll be back for Phoebe at six. I have a supper reservation for us at the Trellis Room at six-thirty. I would appreciate it if she was dressed and ready to go."

"I'll tell Lucy but see to it myself if needed. Phoebe will look exquisite in pink with her blonde hair."

Freddy looked to Melissa's beige suit, the straight skirt accentuating her height. "I bet you look lovely in green."

"I'll show you tomorrow."

"And now I wish I had a reason to come in the morning."

Melissa moved like she was going to close what little distance separated them and he decided he needed to leave lest he do something he might regret. "I'll see you this evening, I hope. Have a good day."

"You too, Freddy."

The way she said his name hung with a flavor of longing, more so than he ever heard from Lucy, or the too-eager-to-please way it clipped from Judith's tongue. True, he didn't want any of the women in Mobile, but did he have to fall for one from across the country?

At work, Frederick stayed in his office as often as possible. He found solace in remedial paperwork when he wasn't in meetings. At noon, he stepped to the coffee pot. Henry caught his eye and shook his head, holding up a hand. Wrapped in his thoughts, it took Frederick a moment to register the warning. In the meantime, he took another step toward the corner.

"Mr. Davenport," Judith simpered.

Too late.

"Good afternoon, Mrs. Smith." He looked to Henry's sandy blond head. "Thank you for the memo, Mr. Adams. I'm sorry I was too late to reply."

Henry smiled. "No problem, Mr. Davenport. I do have an urgent document that needs your trained eyes if I could bring it by your office."

"I'm just getting coffee, but meet me there in a minute."

Judith Smith held her position near the pot. Frederick had to brush past her, his arm grazing hers. He didn't frown, nor did he smile in return to her brazen one. It took all his control to not lash out.

"Ms. Neves," he said to the secretary as he turned back with his full cup, "remind me to see about a new layout over here. This corner is much too confining for my liking."

Judith huffed her displeasure and shuffled back a step. He returned to his office and Henry's firm knock sounded not a half a minute after he'd shut the door.

"Come in," he called. Henry stepped inside. "And shut the door fast."

Henry's good-natured laugh lightened Frederick's mood. "I gave you ample warning."

"I appreciate it, but with my mind elsewhere I'd forgotten she was here today for Mr. Peabody. Have a seat." He motioned to the upholstered chair before his desk as he opened his sandwich wrapper. "I'd assumed you had a fictitious document, but it appears you've brought me something after all."

Henry undid the buttons on his suit jacket and got comfortable. "I had to in case Mrs. Smith watched. This is the guest list for wedding invitations. They're being mailed next week."

"Darla seemed happy with the weekend trip when I stopped by the Beauchamps'." He took a bite of his lunch.

"We had a great time with my family, but more so with the horses. Darla did well on a ride to a nearby creek. We let the horses graze while we—we…"

Freddy smiled at the young man's stammering.

"I had to claim a bee was buzzing me and jumped away because I didn't trust myself to stay beside her another moment."

"Short engagements can be a blessing."

"Her silly aunt wouldn't allow a wedding until after Easter and it's getting more difficult to stay my desires." Henry's fists clenched in a way Frederick was all too familiar with. "We were together a year before I decided not rushing her was the bigger mistake. Sure, we needed time to settle into our careers, but blast it all! I can hardly think of anything besides being with her. Really *being* with her for the first time."

"A five month engagement isn't for weaklings."

"It's for idiots." Henry leaned back in the chair, sighing.

Frederick chewed more of his lunch, trying not to think about his three week engagement with Lucy. If it hadn't have been post-hurricane, they would have married even sooner. Of course, now he understood her eagerness for the wedding was an attempt to heal from the shock of Alexander's supposed death.

"I've got a supper reservation with Phoebe, so I'm leaving at four to get my gym time. Come along if you don't have any late appointments. It will be good for you to let off some steam and I'm tired of sparring with Chuck."

Henry looked at his watch. "My last appointment is at three. I'll go as soon as I can."

Henry proved a more focused partner, so he took a few good licks from the twenty-one-year-old. A hot shower helped soothe his muscles, and then Frederick changed into his tuxedo.

Chuck sauntered into the changing room. "I heard you're running scared from me, Davenport. Switching your gym time to avoid the humiliation of being whipped by a man five years younger."

"Then why would I spar Henry and have someone almost a decade younger nearly best me?"

Chuck laughed. "All right, fine. You came early because you have a date tonight. Who's the lucky lady: widow or bud?"

"I'm taking the prettiest blonde in town to the Trellis Room."

"And does Alex know you're stepping out with his wife?"

Frederick went for the door, punching Chuck in the shoulder on his way. "I'm taking Phoebe."

"You need a real date, Davenport," Chuck called after him.

Frederick drove across town with a smile, remembering his recent exchanges with Melissa. Knowing she found him interesting and that she would wear green to please him gave him a rush, but his head was quick to remind him she was temporary. He found himself craving more of her touch, and when he saw her in the parlor window with Alexander and the girls, he had to remind himself he was there for his daughter—not her. After letting himself in the front door, Lucy stepped out of her study and immediately wrapped her arms about his waist, tucking herself against his chest.

"I forgot how handsome you are dressed for a night out. I'm sure it's improper of me to say, but I'm glad it's Phoebe you're taking and not some woman."

"You're right," he said as he pried her arms off him, "it *is* improper. You made your choice and it wasn't me."

"I feel you slipping away. I don't know if I'll be able to tolerate it when there's a steady woman on your arm."

"You and your double standards. At least you've had over a year to consider the idea. You thrust Alex at me with no warning."

"You've been cruel to me lately, Frederick Lionel Davenport."

"Maybe I'm tired of wearing kid gloves around you, Lucille." He continued to the parlor.

Upon seeing Phoebe sitting like a little lady in one of the armchairs—complete with Lucy's silver masquerade tiara—he dropped to a knee and bowed his head. "Princess Phoebe, are you ready for your humble servant to take you to supper?"

The layers of pink ruffles flounced around her as she raced to him. She placed an azalea in his lapel and then squeezed him in a hug that nearly flattened it. Her little hands went to his cheeks. "You're a handsome king, Daddy!"

He kissed her forehead and stood. "Let me say goodbye to the little princess."

Bethany snuggled on Alexander's shoulder as he sat on the settee. Frederick passed Melissa on his way, making eye contact with her for the first time. His body warmed under her appreciative gaze. Then Bethany reached to him.

"You look swell, Freddy," Alexander said as he handed him his daughter.

"Thank you." He hugged Bethany to his chest and kissed her cheek. "You get to stay with Momma and Mr. Alex tonight. I'll see you tomorrow evening, Little Princess."

"Daddy love."

He kissed her forehead and handed her back. "I love you too, Beth."

Phoebe was quick to claim his empty hand.

"You two look like a postcard for fathers and daughters," Melissa said with a smile. "Would you allow me to take your photograph with my Kodak?"

"Would you like a portrait taken, Phoebe?" he asked.

"Yes, yes, yes!" She bounced.

Melissa laughed. "I'll be right back."

Lucy took a seat beside her husband. Bethany immediately reached for her. Taking her daughter, she kissed her cheeks and smiled as Alexander wrapped an arm around her.

"I think the light in the foyer would be good if you both stood in front of the door," Melissa said when she returned. "That would give the vignette of you two going out for the evening."

"All right." Freddy stepped toward the hall.

"Come say good night to me, Phoebe," Lucy said.

"Night, Momma!" She kissed her and then her sister before going to her stepfather. "Goodnight, Mr. Alex. I get to ride the streetcar with Darla in the morning like a big girl."

"I'm sure all the neighborhoods between Kingdom Davenport and here will be well patrolled."

In the foyer, Melissa situated her subjects. "Freddy on the right. I didn't think you'd be able to look finer than you do every day, but you've surpassed everything I imagined."

"Do you clean up even nicer in an evening gown?" he countered, relishing the news that she thought of him. Her cheeks glowed, and before he knew what he was doing, he spoke. "I'll have to see for myself sometime by asking you out."

Seeing the surprise on her face, he quickly added, "That is, if you'd like that."

Her cheery eyes met his. She bit her lip and nodded before refocusing on her task. "Now Phoebe, stand where you are and keep holding his hand. Good."

She stepped back to be able to get a full-length portrait, unclasping the camera to allow the lens to telescope. Seeing her standing smartly in her beige suit, Frederick realized he trapped himself into asking her on a date and now there would be no living with himself if he didn't follow through. But he was pleased Melissa wished to go out with him.

"Daddy, you look happy."

He gazed down at Phoebe, still smiling as she looked up at him. "I am, Princess."

He heard the shutter click and Phoebe's eyes went wide as a giggle erupted.

"I'd like a forward facing one now, too," Melissa said.

It took a minute more, and then Frederick helped Phoebe into her white fur wrap.

Melissa approached them. "Thank you for indulging me."

"We were happy to." His hand took hers. "Keep Saturday afternoon open for Monroe Park with the girls, but that will be just every day clothes."

He stepped onto the porch and remembered he wanted to talk to Alexander. "Could you watch Phoebe a moment?"

"Of course." She joined the girl on the porch.

Frederick went to the parlor door. Lucy's eyes were closed as she rested her head against Bethany's. Alexander looked up from gazing at them and Frederick motioned him over as he stepped into the hall.

"What is it?" Alexander crossed his arms.

"This might sound odd, but does Naomi have a beau?"

"Not that I know of. Why?"

"The last two evenings there's been a man at the corner on Catherine Street, just beyond the tree line. He's standing around smoking, like he's waiting for something."

"Just on the other side of our trees?" Alexander looked concerned.

"Yes. And he doesn't look familiar, though it's difficult to see his face in the twilight when he's standing in the shadows."

"I'll ask Lucy if she knows anything about Naomi. Thank you for telling me."

Frederick nodded. "Be sure you keep things locked, just in case."

Twelve

When Melissa came inside, Alex paced the hall.

"What's the matter?" she asked.

"Freddy just told me there's been a man around the corner the past two evenings. He asked if Naomi had a suitor, but I haven't heard mention of one. I told him I'd ask Lucy, but I'd rather not worry her. What if it's a reporter or something?"

She frowned. "If it's too improper for you to ask, why don't I ask for you?"

He smiled in a way Melissa was sure had led more than Lucy astray in his lifetime. "Would you?"

"Come on." She placed her camera on the bench in the hall and Alex followed her into the kitchen. Naomi loaded serving platters onto the trays to bring to the dining room.

"Naomi," Melissa said, "please excuse my impertinence, but do you have a special man in your life?"

She laughed. "If Mr. Alex decided to declare his love for me, I'd take a private audience with him."

"You know me too well." He winked.

"I've never had a man, Miss Melissa. Most don't care for my blind eye."

"Do you have an admirer, perhaps?" Melissa asked.

Naomi set down the final platter. "What's this about? Valentine's Day was last month."

Alex stepped closer, touching her caramel-toned hand. "Freddy says the last two evenings there's been a man standing on the other side of the trees. He thought it might be a beau of yours waiting for you."

"Mr. Frederick is sweet, but I don't have an admirer."

"Then I need to go speak to him and see what's going on."

"Not alone, you're not." Naomi untied her apron.

"I can't ask you to come," Alex said.

"You didn't—I'm telling you I am. If he's from my side of town, I might have a better chance of finding out who he is."

Alex looked to Melissa for input.

"I'll keep an eye out here."

"Lock the door behind us, and then the front."

After locking the entrances, Melissa checked on Lucy. She still held Bethany in her arms, eyes closed. Several agonizing minutes went by as she paced the kitchen before the knock sounded. She opened the door to a paler than usual Alex and a frowning Naomi.

"That man's up to no good," the cook said. "He's a handsome devil, but he's got a Voodoo vibe."

Alex grabbed Naomi's arm. "What do you mean?"

"Black magic, hexes. You need to keep him away from here, Mr. Alex."

"I'll telephone the police and give them a description." He rushed to the study.

Naomi looked to Melissa. "He had an island accent, but he wouldn't tell us where he was from. I wonder if it's someone you met on your travels."

Melissa's hands went clammy. "Why would someone follow me?"

"You never know with voodoo." Naomi lifted the tray and Melissa, not wanting to be left alone, followed her to the dining room. "Go get Miss Lucy and the baby. The food isn't getting any hotter."

"What about Alex?"

"He'll be along in no time."

Lucy, wrapped in her own concerns over Bethany, failed to recognize anything amiss during supper. For once she didn't flirt with her husband throughout the meal. As long as he smiled when she looked his way, she returned her attention to her youngest.

"Time for your bath, Bethany Iris. Alex, would you bring her to me in a minute so I can get it started?"

He trailed his fingers down her arm when she stood. "Of course, my queen."

Lucy stopped behind his chair and leaned over his shoulder, hands sinuous as they traveled down Alex's torso. Whatever she whispered in his ear caused the stress to fade from his features as a playful grin found his lips seconds before Lucy did. She shifted around the chair to get at him fully and his blemished hands caressed her back as he tugged her to him.

Melissa looked to Bethany as Lucy initiated more by climbing into Alex's lap. The girl happily played with the last half of her cookie, oblivious to her mother's antics. But Melissa feared clothing would soon be removed.

"Alex," she said with firmness.

The Mellings' lips came apart with a smacking sound.

"I'll see that Bethany finishes eating if you want to help Lucy ready the bath."

"Thank you, Melissa." He smiled in appreciation and carried his wife out of the room.

***

The long night finally behind her, Melissa stumbled out of bed with the sun. The Mellings' impassioned time revived once Bethany was asleep, and the sounds drifted into Melissa's dreams—dreams of Freddy, dappled with sensations she didn't think she was ready for. She was glad he wasn't coming that morning because she wouldn't be able to hide a blush from him if she recalled the visions.

Her most feminine day dress was her wardrobe choice that morning, a sage green that showcased an ivory camisole underneath. With her hair down to brush, it hung a few inches above the sash at her waist in unruly red-brown waves that tended to tangle. She wrapped it into a high pompadour to tame the wildness.

Her morning walk took her down the south side of Government Street. When she came in front of Mrs. Melling's house, she was surprised to see a black limousine pulling out of the driveway. The rear door opened and Claudio jumped out, kissing both her cheeks.

"*Signorina*, you are out early."

"Claudio, how are you?"

"I had a hearty breakfast and am happily engaged in the Lord's work."

She tried not to stare. It must be a sin to find a priest attractive, but Melissa wasn't one to shy away from beautiful things, wherever they were found. "You took breakfast with Mrs. Melling today?"

"She is still sleeping. I dine alone every morning." As though noticing her confusion, he continued. "I am her guest while in town, but I only take supper with her a few times a week. We rarely see each other."

"And Alex doesn't mind?"

"*Signora* does not affect me like she does him and Lucy. She respects my station and there is no need for her to try to impress people by showcasing me to her friends."

"You got along with the whole family when you lived across the bay?" she asked.

His smile was troubled. "I never cared for Mr. Melling and almost killed him once. But have no fear, it was in defense of Magdalene."

"Magdalene?"

"*Sí*, she is coming with her family soon. You will meet her. She was at Seacliff Cottage when it all happened. She and her husband are old friends with me and Alex."

"I look forward to it, but when will you visit? I think you need to check the house again. Things are unsettled and Freddy's seen a stranger around."

"I come for supper tomorrow, but I must report to St. Joseph now." He did the sign of the cross over her. "Give my greetings and love to all until then."

Melissa walked back to Lucy's house with a lighter heart and met a surprise in the kitchen. Wearing an apron over his trousers and white shirt, Alex toasted bread and scrambled eggs. She couldn't contain the laugh that blurted out.

"If you had told me six years ago that I would be fully domestic in a kitchen, I would have thought you daft. I didn't even know how to make my own coffee. Living alone for several years forces one to become self-reliant."

"I'm proud of you, Alex."

"I did take the luxury of having a woman come in once a week to collect laundry and clean my apartment."

"It's good to know one's limits."

"Yes, it is." His face turned serious as he refocused on the skillet. "Lucy's resting with Bethany. She had me bring the darling to our bed when I woke. It does her good to mother the girls extra hours. She should be ready to write today, especially with you and Darla both here."

"I'd like to see her complete ten pages."

"I challenged her to a dozen while we prepared the bath last night." He winked. "I owe you for that time, Melissa. Something about the way she touched me on her way out stirred me to life."

"So I noticed."

He caught her gaze. "We're often alone in the evenings and I had forgotten you and Bethany were there. I was ready to—"

"I'm well aware of what you were ready to do. That's why I interrupted."

"I was worried over the man outside and her touch melted my fears. Every time we're together it's like those years apart never existed." He turned off the stove's heat but fire smoldered in his eyes as he buttered the toast. "Each moment with Lucy is a gift. She's my everything. I'm sorry if our relationship makes you uncomfortable, but you're here temporarily and our love is everlasting."

"I wouldn't ask you to change anything. This is your home."

Alex wiped his hands on the apron and stood back. "Take what you'd like and I'll bring the rest upstairs. Breakfast in bed for my loves."

Curiosity got the better of her. "How is it to part-time father someone else's children?"

"I don't try to father the girls. Freddy's too good of a dad for that. I love them as though my own, but there's still a wedge between us. Phoebe and I are good teammates, but she remembers I wasn't always here. Bethany will be different. I was at her birth and take pride with her as she'll never know life without me. And seeing as how nothing has come to fruition despite our valiant efforts, Bethany might be the closest I get to fatherhood."

Melissa accepted the plate Alex offered. "Don't give up hope. I've seen couples married as many as ten years before their bundle of joy comes to them."

He laughed, blue eyes crinkling at the edges. "Are you saying I should better pace myself?"

She felt her cheeks heat. "I'm sure that's not my business, Alex, but thank you for breakfast."

After eating alone, Melissa collected her journal and settled on the front porch to prove she enjoyed the location, not just the chance of seeing Freddy in the mornings. Alex found her there a few minutes later, a look of desperation on his face and Bethany in his arms.

"Pacing be damned, Melissa. Could you watch her a few minutes?"

She stared at him, caught between demanding he take himself to his office so Lucy could focus on writing and wanting to tactfully remind him she was there for Lucy's work, not their sexual appetites. Neither thoughts formed into audible words before he set Bethany in her lap and rushed back inside.

Bethany smiled.

"It appears you take after your father in looks and temperament. Don't worry, Miss Melissa will take care of you."

She poked Melissa's cheek. "Sissa."

"Sissa will do." She smiled and fingered Bethany's nightdress. "I don't want to go in there, but you need to be dressed for the day. Then we can play outside."

Ignoring the noises that came from the study, Melissa took Bethany to the girls' room and found a two-piece sailor set to change her into. After pulling on the girl's socks and buckling her shoes, Melissa set Bethany on the floor and offered her hand. They made it to the porch when Darla and Phoebe arrived.

The girls scampered across the lawn and Darla joined Melissa on the front steps.

"I was hoping I'd miss Alex by coming later."

Melissa raised an eyebrow and Darla rolled her eyes.

"Right now, when they have Bethany? Did she not sleep well last night?"

Melissa snorted back a laugh. "She was fine, and let's just say I was painfully aware of two instances after supper, one of which I offered to keep Bethany because I was afraid I'd be subjected to viewing much more of the Mellings than I ever wish to at the dining table."

Darla shook her head, sunlight glinting off her chocolate brown hair. "And this morning?"

"Alex asked me if I'd watch her and put her in my lap before I could respond."

She huffed and crossed her arms. "I'll talk to him for you."

"You?" She looked at the younger woman.

"I'm not intimidated by him."

"Nor am I. I've developed a good rapport with Alex but to discuss—"

"It's not like *they* keep it to themselves, asking their house guest to babysit while they make all kinds of noise in the next room. Believe me, I know. It happened once on my watch. *Only once.* I gave him such a tongue lashing the angels in heaven sounded in triumph."

When Alex stepped onto the porch a few minutes later, briefcase in his gloved hand, Darla wasted no time.

"You have some nerve, Mr. Melling." She practically went nose-to-nose with him. "In case you didn't realize, Mr. Noble sent Melissa here to make sure Lucy finishes her book. He didn't send her hundreds of miles out of her way for you to have your way with your wife whenever you wish."

"These days it's often Lucy's way, not mine." He challenged Darla with his waggish smile. "And it does help her work."

"Why can't you keep it private as it should be? You needn't flaunt it around, especially as parents. Phoebe's at the age she'll want to know what those noises are and it's no way to treat your friends. Yes, we get that you're not ashamed of your zealous attraction for each other, but you need to draw a line for propriety's sake."

Alex looked to Melissa. "Do you mind so terribly?"

She knew it might be her only chance to speak freely. "I've thought about moving to the hotel for the remainder of my stay."

His cheeks colored. "I know Lucy needs you here and I don't wish to chase you off."

"Then never have her watch the girls for you two to go at it, especially when it's extra time Lucy asked for. That's wrong in so many ways."

"Yes, Darla." He gazed at her face with a hint of whimsy.

Her eyes narrowed. "Don't you dare say it!"

"You're nothing like Eliza!" He dashed for his automobile as Darla huffed her annoyance.

"Who—"

"His dead sister," Darla snapped. "She died nine months before he supposedly did."

Melissa had to ask. "And is *she* really dead?"

One hollow laugh escaped. "Yes, Claudio swears to it. Maggie, too."

"Claudio's Magdalene?"

"Most people call her Maggie now. That's the nickname her husband gave her."

"Is there anything else I should know?"

Darla laughed. "I fear you've not learned the half of it."

Thirteen

During his lunch break, Frederick called Lucy.

"Mellings' residence," Lucy's soft voice came over the wire.

"Do you have a minute?"

"Always for you, Freddy." She sounded breathy and he could picture her twisting her finger around the telephone cord.

"I wanted to check on how the girls did, in case I'm not able to get a private word this evening. How was Beth last night?"

"A little angel. It was nice to see her to sleep and hold her this morning. Alex made breakfast and the three of us ate in bed."

"And Phoebe? Did Darla say she did well on the streetcar?"

"I don't know." There was hesitation in her voice.

"Why not? She made it over, didn't she?" Frederick's fingers drummed his desk while he waited for a response.

"Yes, I've heard them through the door. I've been working. I didn't realize the time until you rang. I need to see to dinner now."

"How could you close yourself in your study before seeing to your daughters?" Anger colored the edge of his voice.

"I did see to Bethany. Melissa was here and Darla was coming. After breakfast, Alex brought me to the study. My muse in the study is always stimulating."

He was sure she could hear his fist strike the desk. "Don't tell me you're using Melissa to watch the children while you and Alex—"

"It isn't your concern what goes on in my house." Her voice held a defensive tightness.

"It is when my daughters are over there! If you're too busy making love to tell Phoebe good morning, maybe I should get a nanny to come to my house every day rather than sending them across town to be ignored."

"It was just one time I've missed greeting her arrival. And Bethany did receive my attentions before Alex."

"Can you at least leave your room to see that they eat?" His breathing came heavy.

"I'm going now. Please don't be mad."

"I'm not mad, I'm furious!"

"Freddy, it was one morning." Papers shuffled on her side of the line. "And I have eight pages to show for it. Everything will work out, you'll see."

He hung the telephone on its cradle, snatched his suit jacket off the coat rack, and rushed into the spring sunshine. It took Frederick five blocks to calm, and another two to decide what he was going to do now that he was in the lunchtime crowd. He wasn't sure how many people he'd unintentionally ignored, but he began to acknowledge passersby with nods because he couldn't smile.

"Freddy Davenport!" Maxwell Easton's unmistakable cadence called to him.

Frederick greeted his ex-brother-in-law with a firm handshake. "Good afternoon, Maxwell."

"You on your way to or from lunch?" he asked.

"To, once I figure out where I'm going."

"Come with me, I insist. You look like you could use a listening ear." Maxwell steered him to a nearby diner.

They removed their jackets and settled in a corner booth.

"How much are you lifting now?" Maxwell asked.

"Two-fifty."

"And what woman are you going to carry into the sunset with those muscles?"

"No one at the moment," Frederick grumbled.

"Then why do I see a flicker of interest on the corner of your forced frown?"

"It's complicated."

"Come on, Freddy. Tell big brother Max all about it."

After they put in their orders and had their coffee cups filled, Frederick gave into Maxwell's nudges. "I have my eye on a lady, but she's a doomed prospect. I'm trying to keep my distance."

"Something to do with the failed dinner with Judith Smith last week?"

Frederick groaned. "Does everyone in town know I ran out during supper?"

Maxwell laughed. "You ran out because you feared admitting your attraction to Judith was being unfaithful to the first Mrs. Davenport."

"The first?" Frederick gave a dry guffaw. "I ran out because she called Lucy a trollop."

Maxwell's jaw tightened. "Lucy's a lot of things, but that's not one of them."

"Precisely. I wasn't going to sit there and have the mother of my children discussed that way." He burned his tongue on a hasty mouthful of coffee.

The waitress came by with their sandwiches. After she left, Maxwell dug in for the meat of the story. "Who's the new interest and what can be so complicated? Is she already married?"

"She's a single career woman, my age, smart, witty, good with the girls, and I'm almost certain she likes me as well."

"Then what's the problem?" Maxwell spread mustard onto his sandwich. "Sounds like a perfect match."

"She's the woman sent from Noble Publishing to make sure Lucy meets her deadline."

Maxwell laughed. "And Lucy hates her?"

"They aren't fond of each other, that's for sure, but she's only here for a few weeks, two months at the most. What good will that do me when she heads back to New York?"

"That's plenty of time for you to show her how good life could be here with you. Next Saturday's the tournament, right? Make sure she has a front row seat. I'm sure once she sees you in your boxing shorts it'll be a done deal."

Frederick wished the table were six inches narrower so he could pop him.

"There's high interest from the female population for the tournament," Maxwell continued. "Lottie said every gathering in the past week has included a recap of which men are signed up. Your name caused quite the flutter the other day from what I hear."

"Shove it, Max. Tell me about your children. How are they doing these days? I miss the Easton gatherings."

"You're always welcome to join us," he reminded Frederick. "Mother says she telephones you about them."

"It's depressing to see how Eddie's let himself go. He looks like an over-stuffed turkey. I never cared for Mary Margaret, but I think she's a saint for putting up with him."

"Not everyone is lucky enough to be like you, Freddy."

***

Phoebe ran for Frederick's automobile when he pulled into the driveway. "Daddy, I was a big girl for Darla on the streetcar!"

"Excellent, Princess." He dropped to a knee on the lawn to embrace her and ran a hand over her unruly locks. When he straightened, Frederick waved to Darla, who was on the porch swing with Bethany.

Once up the steps, Bethany came for a hug. "Daddy."

Her voice wasn't as excitable as Phoebe's but it held just as much love. Frederick kissed her glossy hair. Rather than smelling like lavender, Bethany captured Melissa's citrusy fragrance, which caused him to smile. "Are you ready to go home?"

"Home." She burrowed into his neck, hugging him tight with her chubby arms.

"Is her suitcase ready or should I pick it up tomorrow?" he asked Darla.

"I'm not sure. Let me ask Melissa. Bethany's been her shadow today." Darla hurried inside, her black skirt nearly catching in the door.

A moment later, Henry's automobile pulled in. He joined Frederick on the porch and opened his arms to Bethany.

"Hey, Beth. Let me see those big-girl teeth I've been hearing about."

Once in his arms, her mouth went wide to showcase the new molars, and he tickled her. Bethany's laughter was the only thing loud about her. She was always unbridled in her joy.

Darla returned and rescued her from Henry's tickling, leaving him with a kiss on his cheek as she spun toward the swing. "Did that mean old Henry Monster get you?"

Frederick's attention went to the opening screen. His eyes widened to take in the sight of Melissa in a sage green dress. The cut accented her figure—perfect proportions, not too showy—and the shade of the fabric brought out the fiery highlights in her hair, which she wore with only the sides pulled back with gold combs. He went to speak, but his mouth was too busy smiling to form words.

"Does the green meet your satisfaction?"

Before he could respond, Darla pulled Henry over.

"Melissa, this is Henry Adams. Henry, meet Melissa, newest knight for Kingdom Davenport, though she resides with Melling Militia."

Henry laughed and offered his hand. "My condolences on your temporary location."

"Thank you, and congratulations on the upcoming wedding. Phoebe is excited about it, as well as Darla, of course."

Darla squeezed Henry's arm. "Could we bring Melissa with us to the boxing tournament?"

"Certainly. The men love a good crowd of women in the audience."

"Let me say goodbye to Lucy and then we're off." Darla went back inside.

Bethany pulled on Melissa's dress. "Sissa."

Seeing his youngest in Melissa's arms sent a spark through Frederick. If Henry hadn't been there, he would have reached out to her. "She says your name now?"

"Close enough." Melissa smiled. "I think it's sweet."

"It is." He looked away and cleared his throat.

Darla returned. "I'm ready. See you next week, Melissa. It was good to see you, Mr. Davenport."

When the young couple was gone, Frederick instinctively stepped closer to Melissa. His gaze was soft—possibly too tender. "You look even more beautiful in green. Thank you for showing me."

Melissa returned his smile. "It's no trouble."

Frederick's hand went for Melissa's arm and Bethany reached for him. He stepped closer to take his daughter, staying focused on the moment with Melissa. He cradled her elbow as he took Bethany from her with his other arm. The lace wasn't an enjoyable texture, so he trailed a finger to her bare forearm before stepping away.

When the front door opened, he turned to the yard and called for Phoebe. "Come say goodbye to your mother, Princess."

Lucy met his gaze, pain in her green eyes. "Claudio is coming for supper tomorrow. We could hold off eating for you to join us."

"That's all right, but thank you for the invitation."

"Then could I have a word with you now? There's something we need to discuss. Alex can come out and watch the girls so we don't bother Melissa."

"I don't mind," Melissa was quick to say. "I'm already here."

"Give Daddy and me a moment, girls."

Frederick turned back to Melissa. "Thank you for helping."

As he passed his youngest back to Melissa, his fingers skimmed up her forearm. A hint of pleasure spread to her broad smile as they held each other's gaze several seconds. When he stepped into the house, the memory of Melissa's skin under his fingertips surged into the need for more. He followed Lucy to her study, glancing into the parlor at Alex reading the newspaper.

By the time Lucy locked the door behind them, gone was the memory of his anger toward her from earlier in the day, as well as the feel of Melissa's skin. Only the heavenly form of his first love pressing against him occupied his thoughts.

"I need your help, Freddy. Desperately." Her hands went around his middle as she curled against his chest.

Reflexively, he put his arms around her and tugged her closer. He thought it would fulfill his needs, but her nearness made him want more. "Anything for you, Goosy."

The heat of her breath moved from his chest to his neck as she looked up at him. "Promise me you won't get mad."

The fear in her eyes brought out his protectiveness. "I'd never be mad at my fair maiden, at least not for long."

Her smile entwined him in its sensual curves and Lucy shifted against his side, tucking under his arm as her body pressed against him. She tilted her head to his ear. "I need a baby."

Frederick's breath caught in his throat as Lucy trailed a hand up his chest.

"The week after I asked for a divorce, you told me you wanted me once more, knowing it would be the last so you could commit it all to memory, but I was under doctor's orders so you abstained." She arched back, showcasing her décolletage. "I'm offering myself, Freddy. Lie with me once more that I might bring another child into this world. A baby for Alex, and you'll have the memory of me fresh in your mind."

The wrongness of the proposition was buried beneath a year and a half of denying the natural man. Frederick's body tingled with sensations he'd long ignored and found himself returning Lucy's affectionate caresses as his mouth lowered to her throat. With hands circling her waist and dropping to her hips, he nudged her toward the chaise.

"You want me to take you here?" His lips were against her cheek, whispering the words. "You want the Davenport seed to enter you where you were with your husband this morning?"

"Not here, not now." She nipped his mouth with a kiss. "Allow me to return to our wedding bed tomorrow."

"But you've awoken my needs." His hands traveled her silky dress, yearning to bring heat to her skin.

"I'll come to you at noon. Promise me you'll receive me as you want to right now."

"Why wouldn't I?" He kissed her neck below her right ear. "You've awakened my craving like never before."

"Promise me."

"I promise." He took her stubborn Easton chin in his hand and left a whisper of a kiss on her lips. "And I promise you'll want me more than once."

Fourteen

Lucy saw Freddy to the porch. The possessive way she watched her ex-husband through the screen door triggered bitterness within Melissa. Lucy didn't have the right to look so smug when five minutes before he'd touched Melissa and looked at her the way he did.

Freddy turned back to Lucy. "I'll see you tomorrow." His voice was lower than usual as he took Phoebe's hand.

Melissa held her breath when he paused before her. Frederick looked at her as though he couldn't remember how he came to that moment in time.

"Have fun with your daddy, Bethany." She handed her to Frederick.

His stride was slow as he descended the front steps. Then he abruptly set Bethany on the ground and twisted toward the door, resentment burning in his eyes.

Lucy stumbled out the door. "You promised! You promised me, Freddy!"

Appearing resigned, he lifted a daughter in each arm and stalked to his automobile. Melissa watched until the car turned the corner, surprised Lucy did the same.

"What did you do to him?"

"We sometimes have to discuss important matters pertaining to the welfare of our girls." Lucy's stare bore into Melissa in a way that made her feel completely unattractive in her fine dress. "Don't think you can usurp me in his life because he's given you a few kind glances."

"The self-centeredness you project is amazing in its scope." Melissa shouldered past Lucy and into the house.

"Good evening, Naomi," Melissa said as she entered the kitchen. "Do you need help with anything?"

"Not at all, Miss Melissa." The cook stirred a pot of sauce on the stove. "I'm used to working alone, but thank you."

"Would it be okay to take my supper in here?"

"What's Miss Lucy done to upset you? No, I don't need to know. Just realize that she sometimes speaks out of pain. Don't take it personally."

Melissa shook her head. "I'm sure the Mellings would appreciate a private meal, especially since they're entertaining tomorrow."

"It's your choice. Supper will be ready at six."

Lucy still stood on the porch when Melissa came out of the kitchen. She went to the parlor, finding the prospect of speaking to Alex easier than confronting Lucy. A shoeless foot was propped on one knee and his discolored hands held the paper in front of him.

"Alex, I'm taking supper in the kitchen today."

He looked at his wristwatch as he lowered the newspaper. "Were we really that poorly behaved last night?"

"Yes"—she smiled with the admission—"but it's not that. I'm sure it's tiresome to take supper with me every day. You two need your privacy and I could use the break. I'm used to living and traveling alone. I'll probably begin taking a meal or two out each week as I get to know the city. I'm going out Saturday afternoon for one thing."

Alex nodded. "I'm sure the breaks will be good for both of you. Are the girls gone?"

"Yes, just a few minutes ago. Darla before that. I got to meet Henry when he picked her up. They're a sweet couple."

"So they are. Where's Lucy then? She said she had a good report for me today but wanted to wait until the girls left to tell me."

Melissa suppressed a shiver, thankful for not having to sit through the Mellings' meal as they prepared for Lucy's reward. "You might want to catch her before supper to find out. She's on the porch."

With a boyish glint in his eye, Alex dashed for the foyer, sliding in his socks on the polished wood.

"Lucy, what's the report?" His arms went about her as Melissa turned for the stairs. "Fifteen! You're brilliant, my queen. Come, we have twenty minutes before supper."

Melissa shut the door to her room and focused on choosing clothes for the next two days so she'd know what to wear without over-thinking things in the mornings. During supper, Melissa was pleased to have Naomi as company, though they didn't talk much. Lucy and Alex were in the closed dining room with instructions not to disturb them. When the telephone in the hallway rang, the cook answered it.

"Telephone for you, Miss Melissa." Naomi returned to her seat. "It's Mr. Frederick."

Certain the smile on her face was telling, she didn't try to hide her eagerness to reach the telephone. Feeling like a young girl rather than a grown woman, she held back a giggle as she put the receiver to her ear.

"Hello, Freddy."

"Melissa, I need your help." His anxious tone chased away all giddiness.

"What is it?"

"I hate to involve you, but you need to know so you're prepared for what happens. You might want to plan an outing for yourself tomorrow, to get away from Lucy's mood."

"Does this have something to do with you looking upset when you left?"

"Yes." The pause gave opportunity for the slight buzzing sound in the wire to overtake the conversation. "The house—something isn't right. Lucy isn't herself, and God knows I wasn't in my right mind when she spoke to me. I'll not have my girls there—or go in myself—until Claudio cleanses it. I'm calling him next."

A touch of hope sprung to her chest. "You called me first?"

"No, second. I had to secure someone to take the girls tomorrow. I'd rather Lucy not know where they are, but no one needs to lie about it if asked. They'll be with her parents. Should something happen, you can call James Easton's house."

"But what could happen?" Melissa ran her finger along the telephone box.

"I don't know, especially after what I witnessed of myself. I hope to catch Claudio this evening and have him stop here to bless the girls—and me."

"What happened between you and Lucy?"

"I'd rather not say, but I wanted to let you know about the morning. I'll call once I get to my office to tell Lucy the girls aren't coming. Don't feel like you have to comfort her. She'll be upset and possibly lash out."

"She already did after you left. I asked her what she did to you."

Freddy groaned. "Please don't speak to her about me. I'll talk to Alex tomorrow."

"I'm worried about you."

He was silent several seconds. "It does me a world of good to hear you say that. I truly appreciate your concern. I'm sorry I won't see you tomorrow, but I look forward to Saturday. If you can be ready at one-thirty, we'll pick you up then."

"I'll be ready."

"Until then, I'll keep the vision of you in the lovely green dress in the forefront of my mind. Thank you for your help."

"You haven't asked much."

His laugh was soft, but held a tinge of bitterness. "You haven't seen Lucy upset before. Call me tomorrow if you need me, Melissa."

"Take care of yourself and the girls."

"Always."

***

Friday morning, Melissa sat on the porch swing with her journal, going back over the notes of location settings for Lucy's novels. She wore a functional green sailor-style straight skirt and jacket set and sensible walking shoes. Heeding Freddy's warning, her camera, parasol, and purse were in the foyer.

"There you are," Alex said as he stepped out. "I hope you enjoyed your solitude last night."

"Yes, thank you. You look sharp this morning." She nodded to his navy suit and red tie.

"Thank you." His genuine smile let her know he wasn't receiving as many compliments as he did once upon a time. His gloved hand tightened around the briefcase handle. "I have a court appointment late morning. I've yet to resume my original skills, but I'm getting closer with each case. It's odd how some things you lose over time but others stick with you forever, whether you want them to or not."

Melissa nodded. "Truer words were never spoken."

"You're joining us tonight, aren't you? Claudio will be here."

"Yes, I plan on it." She held his gaze, noticing the vulnerability in it. "I'm sure you'll do fine today. You possess an air of respect and sincerity. It should serve you well."

He leaned a hand on the railing. "I woke Lucy before coming down. She's not very talkative when she first wakes, and a kind word is always welcome. Thank you, again."

"All the best, Alex. I'll see you this evening." She watched him walk across the yard. He was different than Freddy in looks, manners, and spirit. They were both handsome in their own ways, but it was Freddy's compassion and giving nature that drew her to him. She craved his calming presence as opposed to Alex's stimulating one.

Quarter of an hour later, Lucy opened the door. She wore her kimono, hair braided rather than loose. Somehow it made her look younger, prettier. "They aren't here yet?"

"No."

"Alex let me sleep in. Maybe Freddy overslept himself. Or more likely Phoebe's giving him trouble this morning. She sounded rowdy yesterday. Was she?"

"No more than usual. She's a spirited girl."

"It's good to hear the laughter and games about the house. Frederick wanted to fill it with children as my parents did, but things are different with Alex."

"You're happy, aren't you?"

"I could never be happy without Alex." Her gaze was miles away. "Having him fulfills my every need, but it's his needs I'm concerned about. If he's hurting, I hurt. But I see relief in our future."

Something in the way Lucy spoke the words caused Melissa's heart to tremble. In the depths of her soul, she knew what Lucy referenced was what upset Freddy. When she put what she knew of the situation between Lucy and Alex coupled with Freddy's distress and Lucy's hopeful plan, a boulder of fear settled in her stomach.

"Lucy, some things take time. Enjoy your days with Alex. Don't be in such a rush."

Anger flared in her pale green eyes. "Alex and I have been waiting seven years for a family together. If our baby had survived, we might have been married all this time. God must be punishing us for not waiting for marriage. He took Alex's baby before she was ready to be born, and then Alex was stolen from me. Now we're together but we have to share my family with Freddy."

The phone rang and Lucy rushed for it. Knowing the news of Freddy withholding the girls would be even more difficult for Lucy to bear in her already-agitated state, Melissa stepped inside. Lucy admitting to her that she'd become pregnant before marriage showed that she was opening up toward Melissa—even if shared in anger.

"Frederick Lionel Davenport, you promised you'd never keep the girls from me!" She clutched the telephone box for support as she listened for a moment. "I don't care if it's just for the day! I want to see my daughters!"

Lucy wrapped an arm around herself and tremored as she listened to his reply.

"Claudio is coming for supper. He can bless—" Her flush of anger turned pale. "You planned this! You knew last night you wouldn't bring them yet you didn't have the decency to call me!"

She took a few moments to catch the sobs from escaping before speaking. "This doesn't change what we talked about. It makes it all the more necessary, and I'll hold you to your word."

Lucy hung the receiver on the cradle of the telephone box and looked to Melissa. "You're free to do as you wish for the day. Supper with Claudio will be at six."

Lucy ascended the stairs without a backward glance and Melissa gathered her things, heading for Dauphin Street.

Fifteen

Frederick wiped his sweaty palms on his pant legs and paced his office. Lucy took the news slightly better than he expected, but the lack of asking where the girls were surprised him. Maybe she anticipated seeing them when she came to the house at noon. It sounded as though she still wanted to come. While the idea had nauseated him last night, he now thought meeting at his home would afford them a quiet moment to discuss her irrational ideas away from whatever evil had hold of her house.

At eleven-thirty, he finished his rounds and stopped by his secretary's desk. "I might take a long lunch today, but I'll be back by two at the latest."

Ms. Neves looked to the calendar. "Your final appointment isn't until two-thirty. Enjoy yourself, Mr. Davenport."

He did his best to keep a blush from his face as he thought of the ways he used to enjoy his time with Lucy. "Thank you, Ms. Neves."

At home, he walked the empty rooms, seeing that everything was in its place while he heated water. He decided to offer Lucy coffee in the kitchen. A sensible plan—nothing unsavory for parents to sit and discuss things, even if they were divorced.

The knock sounded from the back stoop as the kettle whistled. He turned off the stove before opening the door.

"Freddy, it smells just like I remember! Coffee, fresh bread, and your aftershave." Lucy removed her large black hat and handbag, setting them on the kitchen table. Then she kicked off her shoes as if she was home before hugging him.

"Would you like some coffee? We could sit and tal—"

"We talked last night." Lucy looked up from the embrace, pink blouse straining against her chest with each deep breath. Wearing the color he liked to see her in best, her soft pompadour with a few blonde tendrils begging to be fingered, and her pouty lips in need of kissing—he knew she'd come to seduce him.

"Lucy, there's something wrong in your house. You know I would never agree to that under normal circumstances." He stepped out of her arms. "Would you like some coffee?"

"I want to see our bedroom." She ran to the hall.

"Goosy!" He had no choice but to follow. Hypnotized by the way her hips moved in the slim, dark skirt, he wanted to place his hands on them as she climbed the stairs. *To feel her body beneath my hands once more!*

"You bought a new spread." She fingered the emerald embroidered blanket and pulled back the corner to feel the white sheets. "Satin! You prepped it all wonderfully for our reunion."

"I prepared nothing but water for coffee because I didn't expect you to come up here."

Lucy closed the distance between them, hands teasing around his belt. "And all this is for you? You've shared this space with no one but me?"

"You know the answer to that. Not even Harriet came in this room when we were married. I had to make some changes after you left because everywhere I looked I was reminded of our years together."

"You miss me." She rested her cheek on his chest.

"I did, but I've gotten over it. I'm ready to move on with my life and can't allow you to stay here and infect my space with your memories."

"I'm not a disease, Frederick. I have a perfect bill of health from Dr. Hughes. There's no reason why I shouldn't be pregnant by now. Rather than putting Alex through possible humiliation, I've come to you. You can give me another baby and Alex will have peace."

"Do you hear yourself?" Frederick took her by the shoulders. "You speak of saving him humiliation from being told his body can't produce offspring, but how much greater would his pain be if you give birth to *my* child?"

"It would be our secret." She undid his tie, pulling it off with a deliberate tug.

"There's no secret where babies are concerned. The child could be born looking exactly like Bethany."

"But Phoebe hasn't a hint of Davenport."

"Are you trying to tell me something?" His voice was hard.

"I was physically faithful to you. I only thought of Alex, no one else. Never!" She kissed his neck before he could flinch away. "I'm only saying that there's the chance of the baby being all Easton and Alex would never suspect."

Her lavender scent made him light-headed and he closed his eyes. Only then did he notice her rhythmic swaying against him. The slow motion of her hands as she undid his shirt buttons. A thrill went up his spine as her fingers brushed against his skin. He cursed himself for not wearing an undershirt. *Did part of me expect this to happen? Do I want this to happen? Am I to become a man like I hated Alex for being all those years?*

"This goes against everything I've ever stood for." His hands gripped her upper arms. "You shouldn't have asked me to do this."

She stopped moving and looked to him, sultry eyes begging. "Please Freddy. Take your fair maiden once more."

As it was the evening before, his control was gone. He tossed her onto his bed. "You're not my maiden. I'm a knight in the heat of battle from the enemy kingdom, taking his spoils of war."

He crawled over the bed, looking down on his ex-wife and seeing only the woman he'd craved for years. The woman he was lucky enough to finally marry. The woman he devoted his life to and created two beautiful daughters with.

And he wanted her once more.

Her alluring smile teased as she finished opening his shirt. Frederick shuddered at the touch of her cold hands on his torso as he knelt over her. His lips went to her neck as a hand traveled down from her shoulder. Lucy's sweet flavor on his tongue brought back all their moments together like no time had passed. Dropping upon her, his mouth went to hers, seeking more of her taste—his first love.

Lucy went along with it for half a minute, and then started to push away. "You're much stronger now, Freddy. I can hardly breathe."

He propped on one arm and smiled down at her. "But I'm the powerful knight, coming to take what belongs to me."

"There's always a part of my heart waiting for you, Frederick." She ran a hand along his chest, pushing his shirt off his shoulders to expose his biceps. "You must have a lot on your mind to spend that much effort at the gym."

"I've been trying to clear my head this past year. Rowing, lifting, and punching Lucille Amelia Easton out of my mind." He kissed her forehead, then her lips. "Now that I'm conquering my maiden once more, I'll have to start over again."

Frederick fell upon her for several seconds before wrapping his arms around her and turning their positions.

Lucy hiked her skirt above her knees and trailed her hands over his arms. Frederick caressed her back as he held her closer.

"It feels like you could crush me if you wanted, Frederick. I'm sure you'll do great next week at the tournament. I can't wait to see you in the ring."

He wanted more, but settled for kissing her jaw as his hands shifted lower on her voluptuous body. Lucy moaned in pleasure. She was always vocal and it aroused him to know she was still the same.

"I'll imagine you're fighting for my hand as you're boxing Chuck or any of the other men."

Remembering Chuck's words about Lucy—that she was the love of his youth but belonged to another—gave him pause. He stared as she unbuttoned her blouse.

It was all fantasy, wasn't it?

A daydream.

He was a knight taking what he'd rightfully won. Lucy pulled her shirt free and smiled down at him, her body more pleasing than when they were last together from her efforts mothering their second child. He allowed one finger to play across the low neckline of her shapewear she was spilling over.

But he wasn't a knight.

He was an adulterer in bed with another man's wife.

Even if they had been married four wondrous years, she was no longer his.

He had no right to claim her, war or no war.

"Goosy, you're as gorgeous as ever, but I love you too much to do this."

"I need you, Freddy." She shifted on top of him, knowing how close they were to seeing her wish fulfilled. "You said you'd always be my protector and there's never regret with our actions. I need you to keep your promises, all of them."

"I'll protect you more by not following through with this because there would be regret this time."

"But Alex needs—"

"What Alex needs is a faithful wife." Frederick sat up, holding Lucy to his chest. "If we go through with this we'll become what you feared and despised in Alex when you left him. You're better than this, Lucy. Don't cheapen what we had together. Don't ruin your marriage with Alex over this baby obsession."

Her eyes widened and fear crept into her voice. "But it's *his* obsession. I'm trying to do my part to save him more heartache."

"This isn't the way, Goosy. You need to confess to Claudio and have him cleanse the house and bless you once more."

Her tears fell and Frederick tried not to focus on the swell of her breast against his with each sob. Giving in to one last indulgence, Frederick kissed the tears off each cheek before going for one on her lips. She opened to him and he deepened it as his hands went around her curves.

"Promise me you won't seek this from me again. Promise me you'll only share moments like these with Alex. Don't break his heart. Knowing how that feels, I wouldn't wish that upon another man."

"I promise. And I'm sorry, Freddy."

He handed her the handkerchief from his pant pocket and retrieved their shirts. They turned their backs on each other as they righted their clothing.

"I'll warm the water again so you can have a cup of coffee before you go," he said over his shoulder.

"I should go home before I do more damage."

"Would you like a ride so you don't have to take the streetcar?"

"And how would that look?"

"Pick out something of the girls to bring home so it can be said you came over to gather clothes."

She gasped. "Where are the girls?"

"They're having a Nana and Papa adventure day. I don't want them at your house until Claudio sees to things there."

She breathed a sigh of relief and kissed his cheek. "Thank you for watching over us, Freddy."

While Lucy gathered dresses in the girls' room, Frederick reheated the water and made himself a sandwich.

"I'm sorry I ruined your lunch hour. I think I will take a coffee. Do you have something I could eat with it?"

"Roast beef?"

"No, maybe a cookie or something."

"A slice of chocolate cake?" He went for the icebox to retrieve it before she answered.

"Yes, please."

Lucy finished the coffee-making while he brought their plates to the table. He studied her as he chewed his first bite. Green eyes downcast and a slight frown.

His hand folded over hers. "You'll feel better after talking with Claudio tonight. Trust in God to forgive our actions and see whatever the disturbance is at your home set to rights."

"I always make a mess of things." She sniffed and wiped a napkin under her nose. "Alex will hate me if he finds out."

"Goosy, he will find out. He needs to understand the level of evil manifesting itself in your home. He's been through this before. Last night, I told Claudio what you asked of me and Alex needs to know too. You heard the stories of what happened within Seacliff Cottage. He'll understand it's beyond your control."

"But I came here! I pursued the sin outside the walls of the house. What if it's in me? What if I claw it from me as Alex did?"

"I'm sure Alex would be upset if you marred your perfect breasts, Goosy." He gave her a teasing smile and squeezed her hand.

She hiccupped a laugh. "You still know what to say to lift my mood."

"I'll be here for you as long as I can be your friend. But let it be known if you try to seduce me again, I'll deal with Alex instead of you when it comes to the girls."

"Seduce the noble Frederick Davenport?" Her free hand went to her heart in mock surprise. "Wouldn't that put a bee in Judith Smith's bonnet?"

He released his hold on her other hand. "You were a temptress. A nearly successful one."

"I couldn't allow us last night—not on Alex's chaise." She looked him over and smiled. "But after seeing you with your shirt off, I almost wish I would have let you. Such virility should be a crime."

"You're incorrigible." He tried to sound gruff but his grin gave him away.

They ate in silence, and then Frederick collected his jacket and tie while Lucy gathered the girls' clothes.

"They'll need Easter dresses soon," Frederick remarked as he locked the front door.

Lucy sighed. "I don't see how I can fit in a shopping trip with this deadline looming."

"I'll take care of it. I just didn't want us both buying them new dresses."

He held the door to his automobile open for her and put the clothes into the backseat. Before he opened his door, he looked to the Beauchamps' house and saw Darla standing in the front window. He waved in greeting and then she was gone.

Sixteen

Melissa walked around Bienville Square, stopping to take a few photographs of the fountain and bandstand. She'd already been to the hotel for pictures and eaten lunch. When she straightened from looking through the viewfinder, she caught a movement in the corner of her eye. She turned toward the azalea bushes on her left and found herself staring at the man who had tried following her when she first walked by Mrs. Melling's house.

Not wanting to showcase fear, she managed a half-smile and turned away. She took a seat on a bench and carefully latched her camera shut. Gazing at the buildings around her, she noticed one office with the sign "Lyons, Melling, & Associates Law Firm." If she hadn't known Alex was in court, she would have stopped in to say hello. Instead, Melissa decided she'd keep to her plan and head to the cathedral.

When she paused under the pretense of window shopping, Melissa noticed the stranger a dozen feet back. Knowing it could be no coincidence that he'd followed her twice, her mind began to search possible scenarios for his behavior—but came up with nothing. If he wanted to speak with her, she'd give him the opportunity in public.

She took several pictures of The Cathedral of the Immaculate Conception from across the street before sitting on a bench facing the impressive church. The Greek-inspired portico dwarfed the people between the massive columns, and the twin-domed towers on the front corners oversaw the happenings below like gleaming eyes.

Every time she looked to the man, he was slightly closer. He wore his hat tilted back and his gaze pierced. Not wanting to prolong the inevitable, she walked until she was just out of arm's reach, closed parasol resting on her shoulder like a baseball bat.

"Is there something I can help you with?"

"I've come for my power." His deep voice held the musicality of Jamaica.

He must be the one Naomi said had Voodoo. Knowing he knew where she stayed sent a shiver up her spine. The other pedestrians parted around them. Would one of the Mobilians come to her aid should the man have ill intentions?

"I have nothing of yours. I don't even know you."

"Hepzibah," he whispered the name like a curse.

The image of the wrinkled woman she'd met outside Constant Springs Hotel flashed through her mind. "I don't understand."

His thin mustache drew attention to his grim smile. "I need it back. You may give it to me or I will take it."

"I don't under—"

"My power," he snarled as he reached for her arm.

Melissa brought her umbrella down but he recoiled. She took the opportunity to enter the cathedral property. The man waited at the gate. The point of her parasol stabbed each step as she climbed. She sought refuge in the shadows of the portico. Fingering the grooves on the column she leaned against, Melissa tried to roll the fright off her tense body. Just as she decided to enter the cathedral, someone laid a hand on her shoulder.

She swung around with the umbrella raised. "Alex!"

His gloved hand went to her elbow. "My God, Melissa, what has you so jumpy? This is the safest spot in the city."

She had to catch her breath before answering. "Is there still a man at the front gate?"

"I came through the side garden. Let me look." He leaned around the column. "It's the man that was at our house! He's turned into the crowd now."

"He followed me on a walk several days ago and shadowed me here, at least from Bienville Square."

Alex set his briefcase down and stared at Melissa. "What does he want?"

"I hardly understand. He said he wanted his power and said the name 'Hepzibah.' That was an old woman I met once outside my hotel in Jamaica."

"But his power?" Alex rubbed his stubbly chin.

"Naomi said he was a Voodoo man. He said it twice and the second time he reached for me."

"Come with me as I pray. Then I'll bring you home in case he lies in wait." He started for the entry, stopped, and pulled a silk handkerchief from the breast pocket of his jacket. "Place it on your head."

Melissa looked at it with narrowed eyes.

Alex laughed. "It's clean, I assure you. Women have to have their head covered to enter the sanctuary. Don't worry. It will only take a few minutes."

"But don't you attend Saint Mary's?"

"With Lucy. I stop in here before and after court appearances to pray for guidance and give thanks because this building will always be my spiritual home. Come, the windows are spectacular this time of day."

Melissa placed the handkerchief on top her head and Alex led her by the elbow through the enormous wood doors. She marveled over the soaring expanse of space under the arched ceiling. Alex was right about the windows. The stained-glass art depicting Biblical scenes cast rainbow fragments across the pews and marble floor. She was too busy soaking in the details of the Corinthian columns in the nave and the reverence of the space to watch Alex's routine by the candles. Vaguely, she was aware of him crossing himself and moving to a back pew to kneel. She wandered with awe near the doors, feeling unworthy to enter such a beautiful place while several people were in fervent prayer. A few minutes later, Alex joined her.

"I'm ready. Now let's find an officer to assist us."

Melissa accepted his offered arm, relieved that someone else witnessed the man stalking her.

"And so you don't get any ideas about me being too perfect, I spent many hours kneeling in that confessional over there." He pointed to the curtained space and winked.

"Alexander, my son."

They both turned at the whispered greeting. Alex stepped away from Melissa to embrace the gray-headed priest. "Father Quinn."

"I take it you had a case today."

"Yes, and then I came across our house guest out front and brought her to see inside. This is Melissa Stone. She's from the publishing company and is helping Lucy. Melissa, Father Quinn, a servant of the Lord who knows almost as much about me as Claudio."

"Pleasure to meet you, Ms. Stone. And is Father De Fiore still enjoying his work with St. Joseph's?"

"Yes, and it's wonderful to have him here. He takes supper with us a few times a week."

"Good." The priest looked over Alex and then Melissa. "And do either of you require a special meeting today?"

Melissa opened her mouth to question what type of meeting when Alex rushed a response.

"No, Father. All is respectable in my life. You know I'm devoted to Lucy." Alex took Melissa's arm and walked her to the door.

Alex caught the falling handkerchief as they stepped onto the portico and tucked it back into his pocket. "I told you Father Quinn knows much of my past. He wants me to stay the course of righteousness and his remarks are often meant to spur me to remembrance of my imperfections so I may safeguard myself against temptation. It was in no way a reflection of you, Melissa. I'll be cursed the rest of my life that anyone seeing me with a pretty woman will think me pursuing her."

She stared at his lean form as he paused at the top of the steps and searched the crowded sidewalk. Never would she contemplate a relationship with Alex Melling. Yes, she'd admired his dancing skills and charm, but he wasn't a temptation. But the fact that he called her pretty gave her hope. Hope that Freddy found her so as well.

"He didn't come back." With the sunlight on him, the burn marks on Alex's face were more pronounced. "But let's get home and I'll send word to the police."

"But don't you need to return to work?"

"I have no other appointments today, but I should drop in to report how the case went. The automobile is parked by the office anyway. We'll surprise Lucy when I come home early."

"Did she telephone you this morning?" Melissa asked as they descended the side steps and exited through the cathedral garden.

"No. Was something wrong? She didn't kick you out, did she?"

Melissa smiled. "She gave me the day off because Freddy called and told her he wasn't sending the girls over until Claudio blessed the house again. She was upset when he told her and I thought she might telephone you."

They headed toward Government Street. "I saw your office on Bienville Square."

"It was, years ago. From the window over-looking the park is where I fell in love with Lucy. I'd seen her at church and with her family, but it wasn't until I saw her there one day that she captured my full attention."

"What was she doing?"

"Dancing barefoot in the fountain in the middle of a summer storm." His smile said it all—admiration and love with a hint of lust. "She was glorious. She still is."

"But why aren't you still there? The office has your name on it."

"When my father and I died in the fire, Mother sold our practice to Rupert Lyons with part of the deal being that he had to keep the Melling name on the business until she passed away. It's a sense of pride for her."

Melissa stared at his profile as they walked and stumbled over an uneven patch of ground. Alex shifted the arm she held to give her better support.

"Why did you say you died when you stand here breathing?"

"My father died and I feigned my death because it was easier than committing to a lie. I was broken when Lucy left me. The next year, Mother sent me east with cousins for the summer. I met Beatrice Kirkpatrick in Newport and found her the least offensive of the young women within my circle, so I proposed to her."

Melissa gasped. "I remember that story from the papers! There was the hurricane and a mysterious fire that claimed the life of her fiancé. That was you?" He nodded. She twisted the handle of her parasol. "But life with a Kirkpatrick would have opened the doors of the world to you."

"I still loved Lucy. And when I got to Seacliff Cottage and saw Magdalene again I knew she was a closer match for me than Beatrice. Magdalene was artistic, naïve, and sensual like Lucy. I knew Mother would never allow me to walk away from my engagement the week before the wedding, so I did what I could to escape my hollow life."

"You disfigured your body and went to live in a strange city?"

"I needed to be cleansed by fire to atone for all I'd done. I lived in poverty several months before securing a humble living. I did it all to rebuild myself into a man that was worthy of Lucy. When I found peace—as much as possible without her in my life—I longed to return for her. And when I read *Winter of My Heart*, I knew she was ready for me."

"That's her best work."

"Her best novel, yes. But you haven't read her poems." His mischievous smile was back. "Her passion shines even brighter in those."

***

Melissa and Alex returned to the house at three and found Naomi in the driveway with a small crate of groceries. Alex took the purchases from her while Melissa gathered their things from the automobile. After the two disappeared around the corner of the house, Naomi shrieked.

Dashing to the backyard, Melissa found the others at the stoop, Naomi hiding her face on Alex's shoulder. At their feet was a dead rooster—its blood creating a rivulet on the cement step. Alex set down the crate, crossed himself, and turned Naomi over to Melissa.

"Lucy!" He banged through the screen to the locked kitchen door and fumbled with his key. "Lucy!"

The fear in his voice turned Melissa cold. What if the man had come for whatever power he thought she had and found Lucy alone? The hardness in his eyes showed he was capable of all manner of evil. She knew in that instance that Freddy was right to keep the girls away.

"Let's get inside, Naomi."

"I'm not crossing this doorway."

"Then we'll go through the front. If you can get Alex's briefcase, I'll get the rest." She tucked her parasol under her arm and put her camera on the top of the crate.

Relieved to see no ill omens hanging about the main entrance, they entered. Naomi set the briefcase in the foyer and relieved Melissa of the groceries. Melissa put her things on the bench and followed Alex's voice to the hall outside Lucy's study.

"Are you okay, Lucy?" he asked through the door. "I don't wish to disturb you, but please allow me to see you a moment before you continue working."

The door opened and Melissa instinctively took a step back. Lucy was dressed in the most functional outfit she had seen her wear—a simple skirt and pink blouse. Alex seemed to find the outfit a shock as well.

"Did you go out today?" he asked.

She nodded, threw her arms about him, kissing him hard and quick. Then Lucy put an envelope into his gloved hand. "I'll understand if you don't wish to see me."

The door locked in his face. Alex looked from the envelope to the door, brow furrowed.

"Alex," Melissa said, "Naomi's worried about the bird. I think we should remove it to help put her at ease."

"But Lucy—"

"She's here and safe."

"But something's terribly wrong."

"You don't want her to see the dead bird and whatever omen it means, do you?"

Alex shook his head and removed his suit jacket and fine gloves, trading them for work gloves and a shovel. He recited prayers while moving the fowl to a grave beneath a far hydrangea bush just coming to life from its dormant state. Melissa used a watering can to rinse the blood from the steps.

He solemnly finished. "That's not the first grave I've dug, but the fact that it was for an animal rather than human made it easier."

The shock must have been evident on her face because he came forward with a comforting touch. "Don't worry, that time it wasn't by my hand that a life was lost."

Chilled from his words, Melissa took a chair across from him in the parlor. His blue eyes studied what looked to be a poem from the envelope Lucy gave him. He leaned forward, tears dripping down his face as he shuffled to the next page. A minute later the pages fell to the floor as Alex closed his eyes.

"God bless Freddy," he muttered under his breath as he wiped his eyes.

Then Alex was in the hall, knocking on the study door. "Lucy, let me in."

Melissa couldn't hear the muffled response, but Alex pounded more. "Allow me to speak with you without a piece of oak between us!"

Quiet, then Alex's fervent voice. "Don't hide from me! When Claudio comes, we can repair what ails you!"

"I won't cause any more pain this day!" Lucy shouted.

Alex trudged up the stairs. Melissa waited a minute before retrieving the papers from the floor. She sunk to the settee as she read.

Broken Hearts

I failed you

Though I meant to bring you peace

Seeking your righteous desire

For if we don't have family

What do we have

Beyond each other?

Driven by love

Pursued by passion

I wanted nothing more than to see you happy

To give you what you yearn for

Flesh and blood

To carry on your name

The name we share in love and light.

I sought the one I knew could help

Willing to cleave to him

Though what we had is in my past

My body is now yours

But it was for you

That I went to another

My mistake

My folly

My sin

For which we all are wounded.

But my protector

Is always stronger than me

He foresaw the pain

And knew when to stop

Before it was

Too late

There will be no more broken hearts

On his watch.

Forgive me

My angel

My love

"Damn you, Lucy," Melissa whispered as she wiped her own eyes.

Whether she cried for Lucy, Alex, Freddy, or herself she didn't know. After witnessing the words and actions of the tangled group for a week, it didn't shock her, but it was still a jolt of reality. Melissa knew Lucy loved Alex more than anything, and if she was willing to be unfaithful, that proved there was evil in the house. And Alex's reaction to the news was testament to what he himself had experienced in Seacliff Cottage under the so-called demons.

Melissa thought back on the way Freddy's face changed when he stepped out of the house yesterday evening. He left with a pleased smile at Lucy, but the veil of darkness lifted from him when he reached the fresh air, like he knew what Lucy had spoken to him was wrong. But what had they done today? She shuddered to think of Lucy still having sway over Freddy. It wasn't right for her to possess the heart of more than one man.

Footsteps in the hall pulled her back to the present. The telephone picked up and numbers were given to the operator.

"Davenport, please. It's Melling."

Melissa dropped the papers onto the settee and moved back to her previous seat as Alex waited on the line.

"Then give me Henry Adams."

Seconds ticked by. "Henry, it's Alex. Did you see Freddy when he got back after lunch?"

A sigh. "Did he say anything to you about the girls or Lucy today?"

"The secretary said he's in a meeting. Can you tell him to call me at home. It's extremely important I talk to him before he goes to the gym." Another pause. "Thanks, Henry. I appreciate it."

The front door opened. Out the window, Melissa watched Alex pace the porch as he smoked. His shirt was opened at the neck and rolled to his elbows—his scars on full display. A few minutes later, he ground the cigarette butt in an ashtray on the table between the rocking chairs. Then he knocked at Lucy's door once more.

"Lucy, please don't shut me out! I love you and I understand." He rattled the door. "Lucy, talk to me so I know you're safe!"

A minute later he walked into the parlor, hands in his hair like he was ready to pull it out. He gestured to the poem. "Didn't I tell you her passion shines in her poetry?"

Melissa stared, not knowing if she should remark.

"I assume you would have read it. I won't be upset if you did. Denying curiosity isn't in line with a writer."

"Yes," Melissa said, "I picked it up and started reading without meaning to. It moved me to tears as well."

"Don't think less of her. Something sinister drove her to it. She'd never do anything to hurt me if she was in her right mind." He pivoted in his socks and paused in front of the window to stare up at the sky. "God in Heaven, let it be an evil spirit and nothing like what plagues Opal."

Seventeen

When Frederick's two-thirty appointment finally ended at a quarter to four, he found Henry waiting in the hallway for him. He saw his client to the front of the building and came back, arms crossed.

"What is it, Henry?"

"Two things. First, Darla telephoned and mentioned she saw you and Lucy leaving your house this afternoon. It's not my business what she was doing there—"

"No, it's not, but if Darla had looked closer she might have noticed us carrying clothes. Lucy needed more changes for the girls at her house and came to get them while I was on lunch. I offered to bring her home to save her trying to handle the clothing on the streetcar." He stared straight at Henry, thinking him more employee than friend at the moment. "And what's next?"

"Alex called. When the secretary couldn't put you on he asked for me. I'm supposed to tell you to call him at home before you go to the gym. And if you don't, he sounded worried enough to come looking for you. You might want to get it out of the way unless you want scrawny Melling showing up in the ring tonight."

Frederick gave a hollow laugh. "He wouldn't be an issue, but thank you."

He turned for his door, but Henry nudged his shoulder.

"You all right, Davenport?"

"No, but I will be after I get my girls home."

"Do you need Darla or me this weekend so you can get out?"

"No, thank you. The girls and I are taking a lady friend to Monroe Park tomorrow."

Henry raised his eyebrows in interest. "Anyone I know?"

"I believe you made her acquaintance." Frederick paused, knowing Henry expected more but unsure if he wanted to share. "Melissa. Melissa Stone."

"The redhead at Lucy's?"

Frederick nodded.

"Good match, Davenport." He lightly punched his arm before walking away. "I'll see you at the gym later."

Frederick settled at his desk and stared at the telephone. Alexander calling meant he knew about the girls not being at the house or he knew what happened between him and Lucy. Either way, it was best to get the conversation over. The receiver tried to slip out of his sweaty hand while he waited on the line for the call to be answered.

After the hum of the wires switched, the voice came. "Melling."

"Alex."

"Is there something you need to tell me, Freddy?"

Frederick's pulse quickened. "Why don't you tell me what you know so I don't waste time explaining things?"

"The girls aren't here for one thing."

"They're with the Eastons for the day. I told Lucy and she was fine with it once she understood I meant to protect them, not punish her. Did you not ask her about that?"

"She won't speak to me! There's evil about the house and a man's following Melis—"

"What?"

"The man you saw around the corner from our house. He's Jamaican and Naomi thinks he's a Voodoo man. He's followed Melissa around downtown this afternoon. I came across her at the cathedral and saw her home."

A burst of jealousy momentarily blinded Frederick. "That was good of you."

"When we got home, there was a dead rooster on the back step. I rushed in to check Lucy. She was locked in her study and only opened the door long enough to hand me an envelope."

"An envelope?"

"Damn it all, Freddy! Lucy wrote me a poem to tell me what happened between the two of you and now she won't open the door."

Frederick ran a hand over his forehead and exhaled sharply. "I'm sorry, Alex. I don't know what—"

"I know what it is! I'm about to bust down the door to get to her, afraid she'll hurt herself!"

"Have you contacted Claudio?" Frederick gripped the receiver tighter.

"No, I've been going out of my head with worry." Alexander sounded frantic.

"Telephone Saint Joseph's to ask for help. I'll pick Claudio up and bring him to you."

"Thanks, Freddy."

Frederick sat back, flexing his hands to keep from punching something. Alexander had asked about the girls and told about the poem and the stranger, but it surprised him he hadn't said more about what happened between him and Lucy. Fear ruled Alexander more than anger. The man who broke Rupert Lyon's nose for speaking of Lucy with ill intentions cast no anger on the man who almost took his wife in passion—another example of how far the Melling had matured.

By the time he pulled in front of St. Joseph's castle-like tower on Spring Hill Avenue, Frederick's patience was thin. Claudio climbed in with his black bag and put a hand on his arm before Frederick could drive away from the curb.

"Did Lucy come to you today, Frederick?"

"Yes." He gripped the steering wheel until his knuckles turned white. "I planned to talk with her to make her see the error of her thinking, but she ran for the bedroom. Like a fool, I followed."

Claudio fingered the cross around his neck. "Did you take advantage—"

"*She* took advantage of me! She knows I'd help her until my dying breath and used the evil in her house to ensnare me."

"But she came to your home." Claudio's measured voice grated him. "Take me there first. I must bless the space."

"But Lucy—"

"Lucy is stubborn and will be in the study no matter when we arrive."

Not able to protest that fact, Frederick turned on the next road and doubled back to State Street. Doff greeted them on the front porch and he reached down to rub behind the cat's ears before entering. Claudio removed a large wood and lead crucifix from his bag.

"Our bodies didn't join. I put a stop to it before our clothing was all removed, and it was Lucy who took off our shirts, not me. I shouldn't have allowed her entrance to my home after knowing what she had her heart set on. I shouldn't have followed her to the bedroom. And God knows I shouldn't have touched her when she approached me. For all that I repent, but I didn't let it go further. I know if I had looked upon her bare flesh, there would have been no stopping me."

Claudio pressed the crucifix to Frederick's forehead and prayed over him.

Frederick's pulse evened. Before he realized it, a tear ran down his cheek. "I thought I was over her, but I caved like a weakling. How do I move toward a relationship with another woman if Lucy still has hold of me?"

"Frederick, you are strong. When Alex called me, he said you did what he thought impossible—you turned away from Lucy when she offered herself to you."

"She did more than offered, she seduced!"

Claudio's hand settled on Frederick's shoulder. "But you held to your morals. That is what counts. Take me to the room where it happened."

Frederick trudged up the stairs, embarrassment sinking into his soul where he recently felt the cleansing warmth. He quickened his pace when he reached the doorway and smoothed the coverlet on his bed, trying to ignore the lavender odor permeating the room.

"I feel no lingering disturbance, except from you, but I will bless the space. Then my friend, I will seek to ease your worries."

Unable to tolerate the scent of Lucy in his room, he opened the window and paced the hall while Claudio prayed in his native tongue. Alexander didn't appear to be upset with him, but the thought of facing Lucy beside her husband—and Melissa—caused Frederick to break into a cold sweat.

"Let us go to the Mellings' house." Claudio put an arm around Frederick's shoulders. "You will feel better once you apologize, though Alexander does not blame you."

Frederick shrugged him off and started down the stairs. "I'd be furious if another man went so far with my wife."

"He understands. He did much worse when besieged by demons. I do not speak of it to many, but I was victim to temptation within Seacliff Cottage too and did not do half as well as you by walking away from sin."

Frederick paused at the front door, looking at the priest's earnest face. "I was inches away from complete adultery. You couldn't possibly understand."

Claudio tilted his head, an amused smile on his face. "Did you know Eliza Melling?"

"We shared a few dances at a couple masquerades. She was a beautiful girl, but it was Eddie that had an eye for her."

"She and I were lovers. For months, we met in and around Seacliff Cottage. She called me her muse and filled a sketchbook with our intimate times together. We planned to run away, me leaving the priesthood and Eliza abandoning her parents and fiancé. She was killed the night we were to catch a train together. I was in the forest by Jackson's Oak when Flora reared. I heard Eliza's head crack on the roots of the giant tree and had to pretend I happened to hear her scream for help, but she went down silent and graceful as she always moved. I was haunted, too ashamed to confess my sins. Magdalene helped me understand I needed to use the atonement and forsake my past. And then the demons tried using Magdalene as temptress—the one who helped me find peace." Claudio sighed. "*Sí*, I do understand, Frederick. And God will forgive you as he forgave me."

Silence filled the room after Claudio's confession.

"Maggie is a good woman," Frederick finally said.

"One of the finest I have ever known, and Douglas is her equal. I was pleased when they married, but within Seacliff their marriage did not stop the evil from besieging them. Alex pursued her many times, and I set my lust upon her several instances too. So you see, I do understand your pain."

Frederick nodded and allowed the priest to step out first. The cross-town drive was void of conversation. Claudio appeared to be praying while Frederick found visions of Melissa being chased by the stranger flashing through his mind—the terror on her face replaced with gratitude and longing for Alexander when he rescued her on the portico. Then the image turned to a memory of leading a broken Lucy up the steps of the cathedral after her agonizing night with Alexander at his worst.

Must Hell find itself on the doorstep of Heaven with the women I care for?

When Frederick parked, Alexander rushed out the front door. Claudio embraced his friend and spoke in Italian to him. The priest continued to the house and Alexander stood in Frederick's path.

Forced to confront him, he swallowed hard. "Alex, I—"

"I failed you both. I didn't notice the evil in the house or the obsession plaguing Lucy. I knew something troubled her last night, but I didn't relate the two until the facts were before me."

"I'm the one that allowed her into my home—the one who embraced her when I knew seconds before how wrong it was." Frederick's hands were balled into fists. "I stopped us, but if you need to strike me for what I did do with her, I'll not defend myself."

Alex smiled. "Says the boxer who looks like he's ready to punch something. I'm a lover, not a fighter, Freddy."

He forced his hands to relax and envisioned Alexander on the day he was last with Lucy that hellish winter, arms outstretched in the kitchen of his duplex as he proclaimed his prowess in bed before Lucy's fearful eyes. "You've done plenty of violent things in your life."

A shadow crossed Alexander's marred face. "But alcohol was always involved. Sober Alex never lifted a finger against anyone accept his father."

Not knowing how to handle the subdued reaction, Frederick tried to rile him. "But do you know what we did? Where my hands were on your wife? If you knew where I kissed—"

"Spare me the details, Freddy, like you always ask of me." A discolored hand touched Frederick's shoulder. "Lucy's poem said enough. The details aren't important. The only thing that matters is how it ended. You stopped before you went too far. For that, I thank you."

"I don't wish to go in, but may I see the poem? I want to know what you were told."

"The truth in Lucy's heart—that's all that matters to me." Alexander disappeared inside.

Frederick made his way to the porch, acutely aware of each footstep across the lawn. He settled on the swing as he waited for Alexander to return. When the screen opened, it was Melissa. She looked shy and the sound of her shoes on the floorboards comforted him—so unlike the silent steps of barefooted Lucy. She looked lovely in green, the sailor style of the outfit perfect for her day about town.

"Claudio was able to get Lucy to open the door and wanted Alex to stay in the hall so he'd be there when she's ready to see him. I'm supposed to give you this." She held out the papers professing Frederick's shame.

"Thank you, Melissa." He purposely kept his hand away from hers when he took the poem, though he wanted to caress her sun-kissed skin. "I'm glad she opened to Claudio. Hopefully she'll see Alex soon."

She nodded and silently went to the top of the steps, gazing across the oyster shell lane.

Wanting to get his misery out of the way, he unfolded the pages and set to reading "Broken Hearts." She had captured her truth, as Alex said. No details into their liaison were needed, though the references were horrifying to read. It was a crime of the heart, a sin of the flesh. Shame heated his face as he looked to Melissa.

"Did you read it?" he asked.

She turned at his voice and nodded, sadness in her brown eyes.

"People like to think of me as this righteous example of chivalry and nobleness, but I'm just a man."

Melissa came to him, a slight smile on her lips. "In all my travels, I've never met someone like you, Freddy."

Lightness began to fill his chest. *Hope.* He'd figured Melissa would have recoiled from him when learning about his mistake, but she seemed to hold him in the same regard.

"Lucy is beautiful and sensual." Melissa's voice conveyed her understanding. "Any man would have weakened before her, but it takes someone special to regain control after letting go."

Frederick leaned his head back and closed his eyes, not trusting himself to keep looking upon Melissa's earthy goodness. "I was ready to move on, and then she strikes."

"Like a disease or a snake?" The teasing lift of her voice captured Frederick's heart.

"A diseased snake, but I still care for her. I always will. She's the mother of my children, my first love, though I waited for her more years than I should have." He rubbed his forehead. "No, I can't say that. To not have waited for her would mean no Phoebe, no Beth. I would endure all the heartache again to have my girls. That's something the women in this town can't understand. They want to speak ill of Lucy as though they're commiserating with me. But there were glorious times, and in the end, it was all worth it."

Eighteen

Melissa wanted to kiss Freddy as he sat on the swing looking every bit the nobleman he claimed he wasn't. Though she didn't like Lucy, she respected his devotion to her. *"Melissa,"* Grandmother Stone had said when she turned sixteen, *"find a man that's true blue and your worries will be less."* It took her half her life to find one, but there was no hope for a future with him—the ex-husband of the woman she was staying with on business, a man a thousand miles from her home. She realized she'd been staring and broke eye contact for several seconds. When she looked back, his gaze was softer.

"I respect you even more for your conviction to your family, but I hope you keep the past where it belongs. I'm certain you have a bright future."

"Yes, tomorrow I get to show a pretty New Yorker around Monroe Park with my girls. That is, if she still wants me to after my behavior today."

"Freddy," she whispered his name as she reached out to touch his hand, "what is it I've been telling you?"

His thumb caressed the inside of her wrist. "That you find me intriguing and you don't blame me for my actions with Lucy."

Melissa smiled and Freddy's answering grin was so perfect it made her stomach puddle in her knees. Self-consciousness began to seep into her skin, but the sensation of his touch was stronger.

"I like you, Freddy. I'm honored to go out with you and your daughters tomorrow."

He stood, his impressive form filling the space before her with little breathing room. He brought the hand he still held to his lips and kissed the back of it without looking away.

"Until tomorrow." He released her. "One-thirty sharp—if Phoebe cooperates."

Melissa laughed and fought the urge to throw her arms around him. "I look forward to it."

Freddy returned the poem. "I'm sure Alex will want to add this to his collection."

"She writes him a lot of poems?"

"I don't know how often, but she started doing that when they were dating. And to answer your unasked question, she never gave me a poem. I suppose that should have been a sign during what I thought were our happy years together. The most she ever wrote me was a goodbye letter after Alex returned."

She held the poem behind her back to remove it from his sight. "I'm sure a woman in your future will be moved to pen many words for you."

"I don't need poems. I only need my commitment and passion returned as fervently as I give it." His brown eyes looked upon her a moment longer than necessary. "Excuse me, but I'm afraid if I miss my gym time, I'll be an unfit father tonight and poor company tomorrow."

"We can't have that."

"Tell the others I'm only a telephone call away."

"I do have one question I hope you'll answer."

Freddy stopped at the front steps and turned back.

"Who's Opal?"

He blew out a long breath. "When did you hear her name?"

"After Alex read the poem and Lucy wouldn't let him in. He prayed aloud for it to be an evil spirit and not what plagued Opal."

"Opal is Lucy's youngest sister. She's been in an asylum since she was ten. When Lucy acts erratically, those around her fear the worst."

"Did you ever—"

"Our last several months of marriage spiraled down, but it was because of her obsession over Alex. When he came back, she improved. Her moods leveled because she had the one she loved. I've noticed that same fervor in her the past few months. It must be over her wanting a baby."

Melissa nodded. "I've seen her anger over it."

"Whatever you do, don't mention Opal to her. If Lucy brings her up, that's one thing, but don't spring her sister's name into a conversation. Opal tried to kill her. Lucy was in the hospital days after the attack. When she's this upset, the memory might push her too far."

Melissa caught her breath then agreed to keep silent.

"She grew up in this fairy kingdom, but her life hasn't been easy." He shoved his hands into his pockets. "Thank you for understanding, Melissa. I was afraid I'd ruined any camaraderie we've developed this week."

She nodded without speaking because she knew better than to place the full blame on Lucy in his presence. Rather than watch him walk to his automobile, she slipped back inside. Alex was still in

the hallway. She patted his shoulder—frail compared to Freddy's—
and handed him the poem.

He slipped it into his shirt pocket. "Thank you, Melissa. Is he
still here?"

"He's off to the gym but said to telephone if anyone needs
him."

"There's no one more reliable than Frederick Davenport."

The way he said it was sincere, but the words were almost
bitter.

"I'll be on the porch if you need me."

Melissa settled in one of the chairs outside the parlor with her
journal so she could observe inside and better hear through the open
window. Alex paced the hall. Half an hour passed before Claudio
called for him.

Several minutes later, Claudio sat in the adjacent chair. "They
are making up."

She snorted a laugh.

"Not like that, *signorina*. At least, not while I was in the
room."

"After living here a week, I can only assume that's how they
do everything."

Claudio grinned. "They love much. You cannot fault them
for that. If you are jealous, I remind you your time will come."

"It might be upon me already, but it could be the wrong time,
the wrong person."

"Love is not wrong. Only what we do with it can be." He laid
a hand on her knee as he leaned closer. "And denying love is the
worst thing we can do."

"Even if you deny feelings to protect those around you?" she countered.

He straightened. "Is it truly to protect others or is it to shelter yourself?"

The sting of the truth smarted, but a smile found her lips. "In another culture, you'd be called a wise man and people would pilgrimage days through rugged terrain to speak five minutes with you."

He raised his eyebrows, his smile still bright. "Yet I come to you and you do not wish to hear my words."

"I do, I just don't wish to heed the advice because I'm afraid."

"You may talk to me. Help me understand your reluctance for opening yourself to love."

She knew with his intuitive gaze that he would understand. *I have feelings for Freddy!* She wanted to shout. *Any respect Lucy might have for me would be gone, my job more difficult. I esteem him too much to wish to break his heart by opening to him only to return home in a few weeks. It's better to deny love than to upset this family even more.*

After her thoughts quieted, Claudio nodded. "Sometimes you need to be willing to express yourself and allow the other person the choice to accept you or not."

"Can you read thoughts?" she asked.

Claudio laughed. "I hear the promptings of the spirit."

Naomi stepped out the front door. "Is supper still wanted at six, or should I push it back half an hour?"

Claudio rose, looking at his watch. "Is Alex—"

"The study is closed and I'll not knock upon the door."

"Six-fifteen should be good. And allow me to bless you before you leave tonight."

***

When Claudio walked Melissa into the dining room, her eyes fell upon Lucy in a stunning purple gown with a high lace camisole that elongated her graceful neck. Her coordinating fingerless black lace gloves had the same effect on her lithe arms. Alex stood behind his wife's chair, face bent over her shoulder as he held a clutch of loose hair while he whispered in her ear. The spark was back in the novelist's eyes and she used the sharpness to look disdainfully at Melissa's walking suit.

"With all the commotion this afternoon, I forgot to change," Melissa said.

Though the comment was directed at Lucy, she stayed quiet. Alex kissed Lucy's jaw and straightened, giving Melissa an appreciative smile. He was still jacketless in the clothes he'd worn to work, but his sleeves were down and gold cufflinks fastened them closed. His hand trailed Lucy's arm until it nestled in her grip as he took his seat beside her.

A hint of unease still darkened his blue eyes, but he smiled. "You look fine, Melissa."

"Thank you, Alex."

Naomi brought in the first tray and fussed over Lucy. "You should wear that dress out someday, it's lovely."

Throughout supper, Alex heaped compliments upon his wife. When the meal was over, Lucy could be hung in the night sky and outshine the moon. Melissa tried not to feel less than but it couldn't be helped in her plain dress and functional up-do.

When Naomi returned, Alex met her in the doorway. "We'll wait on dessert tonight. Claudio wants to see to cleansing the house first."

"*Sí*, and remember not to leave until I bless you, Naomi."

Naomi nodded and took a handful of dishes back to the kitchen while the group stood. Alex's arm went about Lucy. Her tendrils curled at the narrowest point of her waist and a veil of wavy hair fell over his arm. Melissa could only think of Freddy's arms around Lucy as they made their way to the parlor. *How much had Freddy rediscovered of his ex-wife before stopping? Could he ever be satisfied with me after being with golden Lucy?*

Claudio placed a hand on hers that rested on his arm. "You have traveled the world, yet an evening driving out evil from the Mellings' house causes concern."

She motioned to the couple before them as they entered the parlor. "They're quite daunting."

Alex and Lucy settled on the couch. She curled against him but still managed to look refined.

"Claudio, what do you need me to do?" There was inkling of fear in Lucy's voice.

"For now, continue to soak in your husband's arms. I shall bring Melissa with me as I bless the house. It will be good research for your articles, no?"

Melissa startled at the idea. "Yes, if you'd like my help."

Alex's hand began to roam Lucy's waist. "So I'll need to keep Lucy occupied while you two see to the house?"

"You may do as you wish, so long as you don't lock yourselves in a room. All doors must be open. I will not knock while about the Lord's business."

A hungry look overtook Alex and he nuzzled into Lucy's neck, murmuring about having his dessert.

Claudio laughed and went to his bag on the piano bench. He motioned Melissa over and she tried to ignore the Mellings necking behind them. The priest took a purple stole from his bag and hung it around his neck before handing her a large crucifix and a copy of the *Holy Bible* in Latin. Then he filled an aspergillum with Holy water, and his pockets with salt and oil containers.

"We shall walk the outside first. I like to seal the entrances before beginning."

"Will Naomi be able to get out if you do?"

"They are sealed spiritually so no unclean thing may enter. Come, I will show you."

Melissa followed him onto the front porch. With twilight settled beyond the trees, the lighted parlor was a beacon for moths and eyes. Lucy climbed in Alex's lap, his hand going under her skirt. Melissa looked away as her face heated.

"Perhaps I should have told them something other than keeping the doors open." Claudio grinned.

"If their clothing is removed, I'll hold you responsible."

He laughed before sobering. "They need this after the day they had. To see the pain on their faces when they are usually filled with love was difficult to witness. They have been happy since Alex returned. Happy and in love, with only one worry."

"One personal worry, but there is a big business worry on Lucy's part."

"The contract! I have forgotten that is why you are here because you are family now. Anyone who survives exorcising demons with the Mellings is adopted into their fold."

"Whether they want to be or not," Melissa muttered.

"*Sí*, but I believe at some point on your stay you will find yourself happy here."

Claudio turned to the closed front door sprinkling salt across the threshold, then he slung water from the aspergillum onto the entrance while praying in Latin. He walked down the steps, tossing water every few paces while reciting. Melissa followed behind him around the house.

When they passed through the porte-cochere, something in the tree caught Melissa's eyes. She closed the distance between her and Claudio, tugging his sleeve. He did not stop his incantations, but followed her pointing finger to what dangled from a magnolia branch. The feathered mass swayed eerily in the night breeze.

Another warning.

Claudio's voice rose with the intensity of trepidation. He flicked the aspergillum at the omen as his words rose. Movement rustled within the overgrown brush like an animal laid in wait. The holy words chased it out and branches broke with loud snaps. Memories of an expedition in India that ended with a spent tiger raced through Melissa's mind as her heart pounded.

"Do you know where Alex got the tools to bury the other?"

Unable to speak, Melissa led the way to the old carriage building behind the house. There they collected a lantern, shears, a shovel, and gloves. Claudio cut the twine that the rooster hung from, the motion of the tension being released flinging some of its blood onto her skirt.

"My apologies, *signorina.*"

"It's not your fault." She held the lantern with one hand and took the shears from him so he could scoop the fowl with the shovel. She led the way to the bush where Alex buried the other and watched as Claudio silently dug a hole.

"Claudio, whose grave did Alex dig?"

In the flickering light of the oil lamp, his olive complexion was darker, his eyes as black as his hair. "After the hurricane, when we were all at Seacliff Cottage, he volunteered to dig the grave of his half-sister. His father had an affair with the maid and left her destitute. She had come to seek monetary help with her newborn, but the storm trapped her with our unfortunate group. The baby was sickly, but I was able to baptize her before she passed. Part of Alexander's penance was helping with her burial."

As they returned the tools and gathered Claudio's supplies from the front porch, Melissa mulled over the new information. Maybe Freddy wasn't the most complex man she knew, but she preferred his straightforwardness to Alex's murky past.

Claudio went in for Naomi. A quick glance in the parlor window showcased the couple tangled in each other's arms. Melissa waited in the foyer and the priest returned with a worried look on his countenance.

"I offered to see Naomi to the streetcar, but she declined. The kitchen is done. Let us see to the dining room." He prayed and sprinkled salt in all the corners, flicking water about the space.

Melissa followed him until he got to the study. She hovered in the doorway, eyeing the chaise in the corner as Claudio continued.

He approached Melissa after he was done, fingering her cheek. "Anxiety does not match your sunny disposition." He sprinkled salt across the doorway and nodded to the parlor. "Let us see how well they behaved."

Melissa stayed a step behind, hoping Claudio would block any view of salacious happenings. Once they were through the door, the priest stepped aside. Though still fully clothed, Alex was on top of Lucy the length of the settee, scarred hands in her hair and her lace-covered ones all over his backside as they kissed.

"*Amico*, you may wish to halt in your pursuit while we bless the room."

Alex straightened, a devilish smile upon his handsome face. "Is the study clear?"

"*Sí.*" Claudio's mouth turned up.

Alex had Lucy in his arms a moment later.

"Allow me to lead the way, my angel." She walked backward, one hand clasped in Alex's.

"I love you, my queen."

The passion in his voice made Melissa's knees go weak. *Will anyone ever speak to me that way?*

"I love y—" Lucy's voice turned into a scream.

Nineteen

Melissa abruptly turned to Lucy shrieking in the study doorway. Lucy pushed past Alex, but shrunk from the kitchen as well.

Claudio looked to Alex, sorrow in his eyes. "She cannot cross the blessed doors. Hold her, she must be exorcised."

"Lucy, my queen, I'm here." Alex wrapped his arms around her from behind and rested his chin on her shoulder. "I know you're scared, but Claudio needs to make you whole."

"Don't let him touch us!" She thrashed in his arms, but miraculously Alex's hold remained. "He'll kill us!"

Claudio motioned for Alex to drop Lucy to the floor and he did it with a caressing flair, lowering on top of her as though preparing for a rapturous moment.

"My queen, if you want us to be together, Claudio must see to you first."

"That filthy priest and his bag of tricks?" She spoke with a guttural tone. "Get him out of our house!"

"I can't do that, Lucy." Alex kissed her and then brought her hands above her head, pinning her wrists to the floor with his weight. Lucy began bucking, her feet leveraging her body off the floor in an attempt to rid Alex from holding her down.

"Get her feet, *signorina!*"

Melissa stumbled toward Lucy's kicking legs. As she was barefoot, her strikes did nothing more than send her own skirt slipping to her thighs. Melissa watched the pattern of Lucy's movements a few seconds, then tackled her ankles.

Through gritted teeth, Lucy sputtered. "Mr. Noble sent an insufferable woman to pester us!"

Claudio pressed the heavy crucifix to Lucy's forehead, causing her to yell more. He said the Rites over her while Alex recited "Hail, Mary." Feeling she should help in some spiritual way, Melissa said The Lord's Prayer as she'd often heard Grandmother Stone do when life grew challenging. With each word, Lucy struggled less. Alex appeared to catch his breath when Melissa got to the end of the prayer. Only Claudio's Latin filled the space.

Melissa loosened her grip on Lucy's ankles. As though waiting to strike, she kicked and reared, pushing Melissa away with her legs and knocking Alex off her torso. Lucy flipped and clawed toward Claudio.

Alex sprang on top of his wife. "Claudio needs to rid the demon to end this!"

"You care nothing for this woman," Lucy's voice was gravely. "You only want her body. That's all this vessel ever was to you—a plaything. Take it here, take it now, and then leave her to rot in Hell!"

"Do not listen, *amico*. The demon is wearing you down so you give up the fight. Pray, both of you, pray! This has been with her longer than what Magdalene experienced. The struggle will be intense."

Having only heard secondhand stories about Seacliff Cottage, Melissa didn't know what to expect. She shifted her weight often to prevent fatigue, endured name calling—which made her wonder how much of it was demonic and how much was Lucy's true feelings—and did her best to keep reciting The Lord's Prayer because she wasn't comfortable enough with her own words to plead to Heaven. But worst of all was when Lucy bragged to Alex.

"You aren't man enough to fulfill her desires. We brought her to the other one." Lucy's body panted. "His strength nearly crushed us this afternoon. We had to tell him we couldn't breathe, though his hard body pressed against this one felt good. We wanted him inside as his big hands touched and his mouth kissed."

"Alex," Claudio snapped, "do not listen!"

The room appeared to fill with mist as Melissa's vision blurred.

"The insufferable one doesn't like to hear that," Lucy's spiteful voice said. "It pains her to hear about the man she has feelings for touching another. The man lusts after who will always possess his heart. He wants this woman, not you. No one wants you."

"*Silenzio!*" Claudio roared before more Italian words raced out, causing Lucy's body to tremor.

The priest scrambled alongside Lucy until he laid a hand on Melissa's shaking shoulder. "*Signorina*, you had no warning for this hardship. You need to take a moment to collect your thoughts and refocus on the task at hand. There is no shame is admitting weariness."

Melissa sat back, hands covering her face as she sobbed. Claudio pulled her to her feet and deposited her on the settee. She curled into a ball to protect herself, but the harsh words continued to inflict stabbing wounds.

***

The next thing Melissa knew, the grandfather clock in the corner struck ten. She stumbled to the hall where Alex lay upon his wife, head resting on Lucy's chest, though it looked nothing like the scene in the parlor earlier. Lucy's face stared blankly at the ceiling, Alex's face painted with exhaustion. As soon as Claudio was done speaking on the telephone, he did the sign of the cross over Melissa and blessed her before bringing her back into the parlor.

"I had to call the archdiocese for help. My experience is with infestation of a home, oppression, and short-term possession. This demon has a firm hold on Lucy and I do not wish to hurt her or not complete the process properly." He fingered Melissa's cheek, dark eyes searching hers. "The demon speaks what will wound the most to make us doubt ourselves. You must not allow what is said to affect you."

Melissa nodded, not knowing what to say.

"I shall need your help with Alex. Help him from slipping into despair. We must all support each other."

Claudio walked Melissa toward the bathroom. She kept her eyes averted from the prone bodies on the floor and shut the door to the little room. Her reflection in the mirror was ragged. After washing the residue of tears from her cheeks, she did her best to push aside the hurtful remarks, reminding herself it was the demon, not the woman. But she knew she'd have trouble forgiving Lucy, especially for saying the things in front of Claudio and Alex.

Somewhat composed, Melissa opened the door. Claudio sat cross-legged on the floor at Lucy's crown, balancing a crucifix on her forehead. Alex leaned against the wall, knees to his chest.

"Claudio," he moaned, "I cannot bear another moment of this."

"We have survived this before and will survive again."

"I'd rather it be me," Alex whispered.

"So your voice would say spiteful things to make your wife cry? You would rather Lucy sit in tears as she sees you wracked with spiritual pain and fear as you lose control of your body? Neither situation is ideal, but we must handle them as best we can. Take it as a blessing she is suspended at the moment after the exhausting display these last hours."

"I would do both to save her the pain." The rawness of Alex's voice testified of the depth of his agony. "I didn't think it possible, but my heart is breaking a thousand times more than it did over Magdalene in this position."

"Lucy is your wife, the keeper of your heart."

"My everything. Don't fail to return her to me."

Alex didn't see the fear on the priest's face as Melissa anxiously looked between the two men. Lucy's leg twitched, then an arm jumped. Her hands went to her face, then clawed down her chest, ripping the lace inset of her dress. Claudio grabbed her hands. As he shifted to her side, Alex sprung to her.

"Lucy, I'm here." His tender touch went unnoticed as he took her hands from Claudio and kissed her knuckles—Lucy's black gloves a stark contrast to Alex's scarred limbs.

"Get that filthy priest away from me!" she growled. "He'll try to have his way with me, like he did with the others."

Claudio crossed himself.

Melissa covered her mouth and stared as Lucy turned to Claudio. "Am I not good enough for you, priest? Are these eyes not as pretty as Eliza's? My manners not as comely as Magdalene's?"

Alex brought a finger to her cheek and turned her to him. "Don't concern yourself with Claudio. I'm here."

"Here to rule over me and have your way with me!" Her voice was venomous. "Drive this body you desire until I'm broken and bleeding once again. You only care for yourself!"

"That was a lifetime ago."

"Do you think this woman has forgotten your horrors?"

Alex fell upon her breast, unable to hold back his tears.

"*Amico*, do not engage in conversation. It is not Lucy. She has forgiven you a million times over."

"Says the sinner masquerading as a priest!" The demonic reply was broken by a loud knock on the front door.

Melissa retreated to answer it. A decorated priest flocked by two assistants stood on the porch. Assuming it was the help Claudio called for, she stepped to the side and motioned them in.

"They're around the corner," she said in a soft voice.

"Father De Fiore, this house reeks of evil. I expected better of you, but I assume you are too close to the situation to be of much use."

"Bishop, forgive me. Her situation is beyond my experience."

"Is there a blessed room she can be laid in?"

"*Sí*, over here." Claudio pointed to the study.

The bishop motioned to his helpers. "Bring her to a sofa."

Alex was still on his knees, holding Lucy's hands.

"Mr. Melling," the bishop said, "you need to remove yourself so I may begin."

The bishop's square face was firm, almost angry looking in his vigor. Claudio helped Alex to his feet, whispering something to him. One of the men lifted Lucy under the arms, the other took her legs. As soon as they reached the doorway, her body thrashed as she screamed. Her elbow struck the left doorframe, her head the other side.

Alex rushed to protect her from injury, but the bishop stopped him. "You are a hindrance to her healing, Mr. Melling. You need to stay out."

"When she comes around, she'll be scared and need a familiar face." His voice cracked. "Please, Bishop Allen, she's all I have in this life. She's the reason I'm alive."

"I am well aware of your life, Alexander Melling, as well as your family's history. I cannot have you in the room. It is for your wife's own good. Come, Father De Fiore."

The study door locked.

Remembering her promise to Claudio, Melissa guided Alex to the kitchen where he slumped into a chair and buried his face in his arms on top of the table. Melissa put water on the stove and readied two teacups to the sound of Alex's sorrow—which was sometimes eclipsed by Lucy's screams.

"God have mercy on her soul!" he cried. "If it's my folly that caused the possession, let her bitter cup pass to me."

"I hope it's not bitter," Melissa said as she set the tea before Alex, "but I have been known to make it too strong."

His hand went around the teacup as though seeking warmth. "I never thought I deserved her and often felt I'd ruined her after we parted ways. If this is my fault, I truly am a wretched man."

"Alex," Melissa worked to keep her voice calm, "from what I've heard, you've done an amazing job changing your life. And in all my travels, I've never seen a couple more in love than you and Lucy."

"It was our passion that got us into trouble." A smile flickered across his lips with the memory. "Her very being consumed my thoughts and desires, and in turn I consumed her innocence. We burned too hot. It took years to master the natural man so I was fit to even breathe the same air as my queen, but it will all be for naught if what torments her comes from my sins."

"I'm sure it will all turn out fine."

They sipped their tea in silence a few minutes. Another shrill scream followed by "Alexander!" split the quiet of the house.

He collided with the study door.

Claudio slipped out, but it immediately locked behind him. "*Calmati, amico.* Bishop Allen is making progress."

"Then why did she cry out like that?"

"Because she was herself a moment and wanted you." Claudio brought them to the settee, still keeping his arm around his friend. "But there is some concern."

Melissa lowered herself into the nearby chair.

"What more can it be?"

"When asked how long the demon had resided with her, it answered from her visit to Seacliff Cottage, though it was chased away when she was baptized for her marriage to Frederick."

"Then it *is* my fault. But how—"

"It said it has been tempting her for years and was able to take hold when the insufferable one arrived." Claudio and Alex both looked at Melissa.

"I may not be of your faith," Melissa sputtered, "but I live a decent life! Never have I experienced anything like the perils I've seen in conjunction with this trip. I've traveled the globe peacefully until arriving in Mobile."

"We are not saying you have done so on purpose, but if you unknowingly brought—"

"Father De Fiore," a voice called from the hall, "you are needed."

Alex rushed for the hall but wasn't brazen enough to push past the bishop.

"I will allow you entrance when it is safe for you to do so, Mr. Melling."

The study clicked shut and Alex stormed out the front door. He smoked and paced the porch for half an hour. When he returned to the parlor, Melissa sat in silence with him until after midnight. They listened to the sounds of struggle and cries that came from the study, afraid to speak lest they miss something important.

At two in the morning, the bishop and his assistants emerged.

"Mr. Melling, we are going to cleanse the house. Father De Fiore has instructions to see to your wife daily for at least a week, longer if she exhibits signs of trouble. But someone from the archdiocese will check with her before next weekend."

"Melissa, would you stay in the hall in case they need anything?"

"Of course, Alex. Go to Lucy."

Once he entered the study, the sound of sobbing filled the air once more. Melissa fingered her camera and purse, still in the foyer from when she returned with Alex nearly twelve hours before. Thinking of her outing with the Davenports later that day, exhaustion set in. Melissa closed her eyes as she listened to the heavy footsteps in the rooms above her.

"*Signorina*, you have done more than expected tonight. Thank you." Claudio cupped her cheek with a warm hand. "I will have to leave when Bishop Allen does, but I will be back tomorrow."

Gazing up at his exotic face, she was transported once again to Italy and the man she had a relationship with during her time there. "I'm not a sinful woman, Claudio. I've had deep feelings for men, but I have never taken a lover."

"Anyone looking upon you can see you have a true heart." He rested his hand on her shoulder. "Were the words spoken about your affections true?"

Melissa refused to answer.

"What the demon said in conjunction with it was to sting you. Lucy remembers nothing of what she said and did while possessed." He smiled with reassurance at her. "There is no shame in opening your heart to someone. I can think of no one more fitting for your affections than Frederick. Give him the option. You both deserve it, Melissa."

The way he said her name caused a sob to catch in her throat. She managed a nod, and then the other men were there. They blessed her and all those of the priesthood left the house. An empty stillness settled around her. After locking the front door, Melissa went to the study. Alex was on the chaise, Lucy curled in his lap like a slumbering child.

"Alex," she whispered, "they're gone."

He lifted his head, moisture beneath his eyes catching in the light. Then he kissed Lucy's tangled hair. "My queen, it's time for bed."

His lean strength allowed him to stand with her nestled in his arms. Lucy lay still as death, her lace camisole and gloves in tatters, scratches beneath the torn layers. A small bruise resided on her alabaster cheek, swollen eyes and tear stains smudged her countenance.

"Melissa, would you come with me? She's very weak."

She agreed and soon found herself in Alex and Lucy's bedroom—the last place she wanted to journey. He laid his wife on their silken bed and removed the ragged black gloves.

Lucy gasped as her eyes opened. "I'm sorry I ruined them. I didn't mean to!"

"You needn't fret, my queen. I'll get you a new pair." Her eyes fluttered closed and Alex motioned Melissa over. "I'll lean her forward, if you could undo the buttons on her dress."

With great care, the two removed the purple dress and bustier, replacing it with a simple chemise. It took both of them to see to her needs as she appeared to sleep through the whole ordeal.

Alex washed Lucy's face, hands, and arms with warm water, and then brushed her matted hair while Melissa held her upright like a doll. Then Alex lifted Lucy once more and Melissa turned down the bedding. He tucked his wife into the red sheets with care, not stepping away from the bed until he'd kissed her forehead.

He came to Melissa where she waited by the door and took her into his arms. Shocked, she started to pull away, then noticed his hold wasn't amorous but filled with relief. She allowed him a moment of surrender.

"Thank you, a million times, thank you. I wouldn't have made it through this night without your help."

She stepped out of his embrace. "You did well, Alex. Lucy could ask for no one better."

Twenty

Frederick sat at the kitchen table with Phoebe and Bethany as they finished their lunch. He'd survived Saturday morning Pancake Time and yard play with the girls, but it was overshadowed by concern over what happened at Lucy's house. He thought about calling to check, but didn't feel it was the best thing to do with the poem hanging over his mistake. Instead, he did his best to look carefree for his daughters, giving them the extra fun-loving attention he didn't always have time for during the week.

As he lifted Bethany out of her highchair, the telephone rang. Rather than standing in the hall to answer it, he carried his youngest with him and settled in the study at the desk Lucy used to write at.

"Hello?"

"Freddy, I hope it's okay I'm calling."

"Melissa," he breathed her name with relief. "I was wondering about everyone over there. Are you all right?"

"I'm fine and still look forward to this afternoon. I just wanted to let you know what happened without discussing it in front of the girls."

"We just finished dinner. I need to put them down for a nap so they have an hour's rest before we leave. Could I call you back in about ten minutes?"

"Or I could come to you if that would be easier. I'm not sure what way it would be better to hear the news, in person or over the wire."

"I'm happy to receive you, Melissa. I'm five blocks north from the stop at Dauphin and Joachim, but the blocks are small. Take a left on State Street. I'm two-fifty-four. We'd be able to let the girls sleep until they wake up on their own, which will make for a more pleasant afternoon."

He thought he could hear her smile. "I'll be there as soon as I can, Freddy. Number two-fifty-four?"

"Yes. I look forward to seeing you, even if you bring bad news."

"It has a happy ending, so far at least. Goodbye, Freddy."

He hung the earpiece on the cradle and hugged his daughter. "Time for a nap, Beth. Let's get Phoebe."

They cleared the kitchen table, and then he took the girls to their room and removed their play dresses for them to sleep in their underclothes. Doff settled at the foot of Phoebe's bed, but she tugged her cat up to her chest until it curled against her side and purred.

"Kiss, Daddy!"

Frederick covered Bethany before kissing Phoebe's cheek. "Rest well so you have energy for the park."

Downstairs he put water on the stove, opened the front door, and paced the length of the hall from porch to kitchen while he waited for the water to boil.

The kettle whistled.

When he came out of the kitchen after turning off the burner, Melissa stood in the open front door. She looked as lovely as the spring afternoon in a striped robin's egg blue and white walking dress. Her hair was piled under a jaunty straw hat and she carried her parasol, camera, and small handbag. He stared a moment too long.

"Sorry, Melissa, I was dazzled for a moment. Come in."

"You're too kind."

He held a hand out for her things and set them on the credenza. After she unpinned her hat, he took her hand in his, stroking the back of it before raising it to his lips. Her citrusy scent invigorated him.

"It's a pleasure to have you here, even if it's a bit unconventional."

Her brown eyes widened and her tanned cheeks pinked. "Should we sit on the porch?"

With his laughter he was set free. "My neighbors are unbearable gossips, and Darla's aunt next door is the worst. I'd rather take our chances indoors, if that's okay with you."

Melissa nodded, looking shy. "I'm sure it will be easier to hear the girls as well."

"That will be our excuse if anyone happens to ask." His grin was back, but it couldn't be helped. Nor could the fact that he hadn't even pulled on his suit jacket. At least Melissa was used to the informal air at Lucy's house. "I have water ready for coffee or tea."

"Coffee, please. It was a long night. I didn't get out of bed until half-past nine."

"Make yourself comfortable," he said as he motioned to the living room, "and I'll be back in a minute."

"Is it okay if I come with you? I'd like to see the house." She held her hands behind her back as though anxious to hear his response.

"You're welcome anywhere."

After he fixed their coffee, Frederick led the way back to the living room. They settled on the sofa a respectable distance apart, slightly turned toward the other. After a few sips, Melissa set her cup on the table and started in on the story, complete with dead roosters, an over-whelmed Claudio, and the bishop's takeover. Frederick listened to Melissa's carefully chosen words. They gave him an insight to her feelings—she'd been scared but pulled through because her promise to Claudio to help Alexander.

"But now that it's over, I feel like I might belong there. I know it's silly, but I have more respect for Alex, and Lucy was actually kind to me today. It's strange to think she might really have been ruled by a demon since I arrived, but that might explain her bitterness."

Frederick held Melissa's hand but didn't remember when he'd taken it. Maybe it was when she looked pained while talking about Lucy's screams. He also sat with their knees practically touching.

"You did well, Melissa. I'm glad you came."

"To Mobile or your house?" She leaned closer.

"Both." He looked from her lips to her eyes, trying to control the impulse to kiss her.

"Claudio advised me to let my heart be known." Melissa looked down, as though too timid to breach the subject.

He released her hand and raised his fingers to her chin, trailing across her jawline as he lifted her face. "Does your heart wish to speak?"

She nodded.

"May I go first?" When she nodded, he continued. "Melissa, you're the first woman that's turned my attention to wanting more. You're beautiful, smart, and savvy, plus you get along with my girls. I know you're leaving at some point in the near future, but I'd like to get to know you better if you'll allow me."

Her smile turned to a laugh. "That's close to what I was thinking about you."

Frederick's hand followed the curve of her neck until it rested at the base of her hairline. Instinctively they both leaned in, tilting their heads until their lips made contact. Not wanting to press on without restraint, he rested his cheek against hers. "That was delectable."

Melissa's breath was hot and he imagined her heart beat as fast as his did.

"Would it be too bold of me to ask for another?" she questioned.

He sat back. "First, I need to hear exactly what your heart has to say."

"You're an incredible man." Melissa rested a hand on his knee. "I admire your dedication to your family, job, and fitness. You're kind, intelligent, handsome, and enjoy my humor. I don't want to go back to New York without getting to know you."

"It seems our goals are similar." He gazed at her broad smile and placed his palm on her cheek, allowing his thumb to rest in her deep-set smile line. "I think we should move forward with what you want."

Frederick lowered his hand as they leaned together. The kiss started simple, but Melissa surprised him by trailing her hands up his arms and around his shoulders. He, in turn, wrapped his arms around her waist and tugged her closer, increasing the fervor. When his tongue began to part her lips, she pulled back, breathless.

Melissa's hands were on his biceps and her fingers moved over their firm lines through his shirt. "You feel as good as I've dreamt."

"We meet in your dreams?"

She leaned against his chest and his pulse quickened once again. "Nearly every night since I arrived."

"I'd hoped you considered me in the same way." He pressed his lips to her forehead and rested his head there while she nestled under his chin as though they'd had years to grow comfortable together. Warmth spread over Frederick's body from scalp to toes from the sensation of holding her. He always figured any woman but Lucy in his arms would feel wrong, but everything about Melissa was right.

Twenty-One

Just as Melissa thought she could sit in Freddy's arms all afternoon, he sighed.

"Is it bad that I want the girls to sleep another hour or two?"

"Only if you want to spend the time alone rather than with me."

When his laughter quieted, Freddy stood and pulled Melissa to her feet. Brown eyes intense, he rested his hands at her waist and she placed hers at his shoulders. "You'll be hard-pressed to be rid of me, Melissa."

Freddy covered her mouth with his. His left hand moved to the small of her back and tugged her against his firm torso. The sensation caused a scandalous wave of electricity to pulse through her body and she unwittingly opened her lips to him. His administrations were slow and matched the way his body moved against hers.

Lucy trained him well.

The thought jolted her and she leaned back until he loosened his hold.

His eyebrows pulled together in concern. "I'm not practiced in courting etiquette. Am I going too fast?"

Melissa hugged him a moment to reassure him. "You're perfect, Freddy. It's just—never mind."

"We won't get very far if we can't be honest with each other."

"Then kiss me once more and I'll tell you anything you want."

He kept it chaste, as though he wished to prove his staying power. Then they were back at a respectable distance on the sofa, coffee cup in her hand to keep from reaching out to him.

"I've never dated a man who's been married before, or a man with whom I'm acquainted with the woman who was his previous relationship."

"Lucy."

Melissa nodded. "I've been well-versed in the Mellings' passionate ways this week and every once in a while thoughts come to me about you and her."

"What was it this time?"

"It's probably insulting to even say it, but since you asked, it was that she trained you well."

His laugh was long and loud, and she expected the girls to come running. "Lucy was my first everything, my childhood infatuation turned bride. She came to me with more experience, but I like to think I brought my own level of romance."

"She was your first?" Her eyes narrow. "But you said she was your second wife."

"Few people know, but I'll tell you, Melissa. My marriage to Harriet was to give comfort to our fathers in their final days. Her father was dying and she herself had consumption. Her father wrote to mine asking him to care for her as he was her godfather. My own father had a failing heart but agreed. To ease his burden, I married Harriet."

Melissa covered her mouth in surprise, tenderness for him bubbling over.

"I bought this house and set the study as a bedroom for her so she wouldn't have to go up and down the stairs when weak. I lived in my room upstairs and worked as usual, taking over more of the management of the office from my father, and had nurses come in to care for her as her illness advanced. We became friends in our few months together, but never lovers. She knew where my heart lay. I was a widower before I turned twenty-one and put my life on hold eighteen months for mourning over an unconsummated marriage. During that time, my father passed away and my mother moved to Atlanta to live with my sister and her family."

"How unfortunate." She placed her cup back on the table and rested a hand on his knee.

"To survive, I spent my time at the gym. The Sunday before Christmas in 1904, I happened across Alex walking Lucy home from the cathedral and the rush of memories from having grown up with the Eastons flooded me. I was best friends with Eddie, Lucy's closest brother, and had spent countless hours playing and studying at their house. Before I turned fourteen, I knew I loved Lucy but needed to wait for her to grow up. Seeing her on the street that day brought it all back. My first love was on the arm of the worst cad in Mobile less than two weeks before I could respectfully return to society from mourning."

"How awful for you."

"That's the thing I regretted the longest—not having told her my feelings before she got wrapped around Alex, but he'd already found his way into her heart. It all worked out though. Our daughters are napping peacefully upstairs and you would never be in Mobile without Alexander distracting Lucy."

Melissa's laughter lightened the mood, bringing her back to their mutual affection. "That's one way to put it."

"While I'm more than pleased to bring you out today with the girls, would you take a supper date with me one evening this coming week, just you and me?"

"I'd like that."

"Good." Freddy leaned to her and quickly kissed her lips.

The sound of doors opening and shutting on the second floor, followed by the streak of a cat zooming down the stairs turned their attention. The tabby jumped onto the back of the sofa, meowing. Freddy ran his hand over the length of its back. "This is Doff, Phoebe's cat. And it seems the girls are awake now."

He stood and offered his arm, chivalrous enough to walk Melissa up the stairs. She took in the tidy space as he motioned to the first room. "That's mine, the guest room is at the end, and the girls are here."

As he reached for the knob, the adjacent door opened. Phoebe stepped out of the bathroom.

"Daddy, I rested good!"

"You sure did. Go get dressed and brush your hair." He winked at Melissa and tossed Phoebe into the air, bringing her to his chest after he caught her. "Is Beth awake?"

"Yes." Over her father's shoulder, she eyed Melissa. "You look different, Miss Melissa."

She looked down the length of herself. "Might be the dress. Vertical stripes make people look taller."

"That's not it." Phoebe frowned. "Why are you here?"

"Phoebe, that's not polite." Freddy put her down. "You know she's going to the park with us."

She crossed her arms. "But we're supposed to pick her up at Momma's. I want to see Momma and Mr. Alex!"

Freddy patted Phoebe's head and went for the girls' room. "You'll see them when we bring her home, Princess."

"Daddy," Bethany said as soon as he stepped in. Then she saw Melissa in the doorway and reached for her. "Sissa!"

Freddy's grin was huge as she lifted Bethany from her crib, but Phoebe's scowl deepened.

Looking about the pink room, much like the one at their mother's house, Melissa smiled. "Your room is pretty, girls."

Freddy pointed to the clothing hanging from a knob on the bureau. "Would you help Bethany dress?"

"Of course."

"The diapers are in the top drawer. I usually bring her to my bed to change her. The pail is in the bathroom." Freddy gave Phoebe a funny stare. "And I'll tackle the grumpy bug."

"I'm not grumpy!" Phoebe squeezed her arms tighter across her chest.

"You better not be. Grumpy girls don't get to ride the carousel or eat ice cream."

Phoebe dropped her arms and stalked across the room, giving Melissa an evil eye as she carried Bethany out.

Melissa had never entered a man's bedroom. She expected to be uncomfortable, but the room was decidedly Freddy and she didn't even blush as she sat at the end of the bed. All the furniture was rich mahogany with little embellishment. Functional, well-crafted, and handsome. She found her eyes roaming the space after she'd dressed Bethany.

"There's one piece of furniture I couldn't stand to see in here after she left. I moved it to the guest room." Freddy stood in the doorway, his expression somewhere between melancholy and resignation. "It wasn't part of the original set, but it did look nice."

Melissa stood Bethany on the bed. "What's that?"

Freddy crossed the room and set his daughter on the floor. "Get your shoes, Beth." They watched her toddle out of the room. "The dressing table. Even without Lucy's things scattered over the top, it was too feminine a piece for a single man to wish to look upon."

He left a whisper of a kiss at her right ear, a charming smile upon his gallant face when he stepped away. Then—lest he get the wrong idea about her keeping in his bedroom—Melissa went for the door, taking the soiled diaper with her. Bethany came in with her shoes and Freddy lifted her back onto the bed to put them on.

"I just need to get their hats," he told her when she returned from washing her hands.

"Sissa." Bethany leaned for her.

Freddy stopped before Melissa, longing in his eyes as he transferred his daughter to her arms. "It does me a world of good to know she likes you."

He leaned in as though he was going to kiss her, but fingered the corner of her lip instead. Then he disappeared into the girls' room, leaving Melissa wanting more. He returned with a floppy sunbonnet and a pink straw hat. He set the straw hat on his own head as he tied the white cloth one under Bethany's chin.

"Let me carry you downstairs." Bethany laughed and snatched Phoebe's hat off his head when he took her.

They found Phoebe on the sofa with Doff.

"You forgot to brush your hair, Princess," Freddy told her.

Phoebe gave Melissa another glare and trudged up the stairs.

"Sometimes," Freddy said as he set Bethany on the floor, "Phoebe does a scathing impersonation of her mother without realizing it."

Melissa's laughter filled the room. "I've received that very look from Lucy this week."

"Phoebe often wakes up in a mood. Don't make too much of it."

When they rode to the bay, Melissa sat in the backseat with Bethany, and Phoebe sat with her father. It was a large, splendid touring automobile with four doors and the canvas roof open to the sun. Mobilians flocked the waterfront park. The noise of the rollercoaster, the crack of a baseball at an early exhibition game, the cacophony of music from a brass band, and the food smells were an explosion on the senses.

"Can we get ice cream first, Daddy?" Phoebe tugged on his hand.

"We have a guest today, Princess." He turned to Melissa, one hand on Bethany's leg, who rode on his shoulders with her arms draped over his head. "What would you like to do first?"

"Ice cream sounds good to me." She smiled at Phoebe and received a frown in return.

Allowing Freddy to lead the way, Melissa paused a few times to take photographs of the rollercoaster and orange penny arcade building that were mentioned in Lucy's books. As they wove through the crowd, Freddy was often greeted by men and women alike. He had a smile for everyone and the girls were fussed over, but Melissa stayed a few steps behind and was overlooked. When they were in line for ice cream, she stood at his elbow opposite Phoebe and held Bethany so he could easier purchase the treats.

"Davenport!" a boisterous voice shouted. "Those were some smooth moves yesterday evening, but I'll take you down Monday."

A cocky young man with dark hair and long sideburns dropped a young woman's arm and approached Freddy in a fighting stance, working his mincing steps and giving short jabs while he guarded his chin.

Phoebe stomped her foot. "No one can hit my Daddy!"

"Chuck Brady sure can." He jabbed the air a few more times.

Melissa was aware of more stares their way and shifted slightly away from Freddy. The movement set the man's attention on her. He looked from her face to Bethany in her arms. Then his gaze went down the length of her striped walking suit before snapping back to Freddy.

"Davenport, you old dog. Where've you been hiding her?"

Freddy looked like he was chewing on the inside of his cheek, but grinned. "At Lucy's house. Melissa works with the same publishing company. Chuck, Melissa Stone. Melissa, Chuck Brady and Rachel Wiseman. Chuck is one of my sparring partners at the gym."

Melissa shifted Bethany to her left hip and her folded parasol to the other hand so she could greet them properly. "It's nice to meet you both."

"You're a writer like Lucy Melling?" Rachel asked. "Have I read any of your novels?"

"I write travel essays for magazines."

Freddy moved forward in the line, but paused to touch Melissa's shoulder. "She's traveled the world. What is it, five continents?"

"I only have Australia and Antarctica to go. I hope to visit both this winter."

Rachel gasped. "Down to the ice and snow in the winter?"

Phoebe stuck her hands on her hips. "Everybody knows the bottom of the globe is opposite from the top. Our winter is their summer!"

Rachel blushed.

Chuck laughed. "That's an impertinent firecracker you've got there, Davenport."

"That's my fault," Melissa said. "I've been teaching her a bit of geography this week."

"Getting on Davenport's good side with his girls is smart." Chuck winked at Melissa. "That might be the key, especially if you already put up with Lucy."

Freddy cleared his throat. "It's been nice talking with you, but you need to go. Now."

Chuck raised his hands in surrender before offering Rachel an arm. "We'll continue this Monday evening. Goodbye little Miss Davenports, and Ms. Stone. It was a pleasure."

It could have been her imagination, but from then on it seemed Melissa was no longer invisible. Once those that witnessed the conversation in the confined area of the line knew she was with Freddy, curious eyes began watching. She was grateful to move on with their cones to a shady bench across the path from the carousel.

Freddy held Bethany on his lap so there would be room for all of them on the bench. Phoebe sat between her father and Melissa, seemingly pleased to be a literal wedge between them. She licked the chocolate ice cream and kicked her legs like nothing would ever be wrong in her life. Bethany's ice cream ran down her cone, over her fist, and splattered drops on Freddy's pant leg. He used a handkerchief to wipe the worst of it off and smiled.

"I always throw a few extra hankies in my pockets when I go out with the girls. I have one for you if you get anything on your chin."

Melissa laughed. "I'll try not to use my allotted handkerchief just yet."

The carousel was next. Freddy stood beside Bethany to support her. Melissa laid her parasol on the floor and took a horse on the other side of Phoebe. The girl leaned over the horse and whispered in its ear.

"Do you name your horse when you ride?" Melissa asked.

"I've named them all," Phoebe replied. "When I turn five, Mr. Alex is going to teach me to ride real horses so I can be part of a cavalry. He's a fine horseman, did you know?"

"No, I never would have guessed."

The carousel began and the music increased, halting their conversation. Afterward, Freddy took Phoebe on the roller coaster. Then all four walked to the less crowded Yacht Club pier. Phoebe took Bethany's hand and Freddy offered his arm to Melissa as they strolled behind the girls.

"Thank you," Melissa told him. "I needed to get out today and you're wonderful company."

His smile tugged at her middle. "It's my pleasure. When I come with the girls Monday morning, I'll let you know about dinner. Is there a day that's better for you?"

"No, but don't interfere with your training the week of the tournament."

A hand wrapped around hers. "If you insist, but you'd be worth missing the gym for."

"I can't say that's the most romantic thing I've ever heard."

Freddy's laughter turned his daughters' heads. Bethany waved—nearly toppling over—but Phoebe held her up. They reached the Yacht Club building at the end of the pier and turned back, allowing the girls to continue leading.

"I love how you wear your joy on your face." His voice was deep, indulgent. "You aren't ashamed of being light-hearted and it's refreshing to see. I'd kiss you right now if it was proper."

"You may kiss me right now even if it isn't proper."

Her boldness seemed to startle him and he slowed his steps. "Do we need to rush things, Melissa?"

A nagging reminder that none of her romances on her journeys ended well—or the ones in New York for that matter—caused her to pause two seconds. "No certain speed necessary, Freddy. I say we blaze our own trail."

"In that case, I need to feel your lips once more." He leaned under the shade of her parasol and planted a firm kiss on her mouth. "That should hold me until I see you home."

Twenty-Two

Freddy's body rushed with giddiness he hadn't felt in years as he drove toward town. Phoebe sat against his side but every few minutes he chanced a look in the backseat to be sure he wasn't dreaming. Melissa was there, Bethany in her lap as they rolled by the business district on their way to shop for the girls' Easter dresses. He didn't care if Lucy got mad—she'd given him responsibility over their clothing and it was his choice to seek the opinion of another woman.

He bypassed the typical department stores he frequented for the girls because it was less of a hassle for a single man to shop in one of them than a specialty store. But with Melissa by his side, he felt comfortable walking into one of the boutiques.

"Mr. Davenport, it's a pleasure to have you in our shop today," the matron said. "I've seen you about town with your girls and have itched to outfit these cherubic figures."

Puzzled, he looked at the worker but didn't recognize her. "That's kind of you. We're here today for Easter dresses."

"Of all the blessings, we're to be the shop to dress these angels for the most important day of the season!" She waved an assistant over. "We'll need to take their measurements in the dressing rooms. Usually the mother attends, but as there is no one else in the shop and you're such a distinguished—"

"No need to bend the rules for me. Ms. Stone may attend them, correct?" He looked to Melissa.

"I'd be happy to." Melissa disappeared behind a curtain with the girls and two assistants.

Freddy noticed the way the matron appraised Melissa and was pleased the woman looked impressed.

"Now Mr. Davenport, do you have any colors in mind?" she asked.

"Anything but pink. They're positively swimming in it because that's what I usually fall to when I'm unsure."

"Never fear, Mr. Davenport. We'll take good care of your girls."

An hour later, they exited the shop with new everything from undergarments to hats and gloves for Easter Sunday.

"You really are admired in this town," Melissa remarked.

He shrugged. "It's difficult to predict what will captivate people."

"I'm sure a respectable businessman will always be sought after."

On their arrival at Lucy's house, Ruth Melling's chauffeur stood beside her automobile. Frederick groaned and was about to turn around when the front door of the house opened. Too late to retreat. He parked in the driveway, put a hand on Phoebe's knee, and turned to Melissa.

"Would you keep them here a moment?"

Melissa nodded but Phoebe protested. "I wanna see Momma and Mr. Alex!"

"You will, but wait until their company leaves."

He crossed the yard, getting to the bottom of the steps as Ruth and Alexander reached the top. It had been months since he'd seen her and Frederick was shocked at her frail appearance as Alexander held her elbow.

"Hello, Mrs. Melling."

"Don't tell me you've been around without a hat, Mr. Davenport. Your forehead and cheeks are quite red from the sun."

"It's no bother to you, I'm sure."

"Of course not, but you must take better care. Claudio was late arriving home, so I pressed him for details. I was most anxious about Lucy when I heard what happened and came to see my daughter-in-law. Are Lucy's girls in your automobile? Alex is so fond of them, I almost feel as though they are my family as well."

"They never will be, Mrs. Melling."

"Come now, you have been hiding them from me for over a year. I would have thought you would relax your attitude by now." She started down the steps, cane in one hand, Alex on the other. "I am not getting any younger, and if Alex does not give me a grandchild soon these girls will be the closest I have to—"

"You have no connection to my family."

"Alex, do talk some sense into this man."

"Phoebe and Bethany are his daughters, Mother. I have no claim over them."

Frederick's automobile door swung open and Phoebe dashed out. "Mr. Alex! Mr. Alex!" She leaped at him so he had to let go of his mother to catch her in his arms. "I got to ride Storm on the carousel again!"

Frederick couldn't deny the glow Phoebe and her stepfather had together—ultimate conspirators bound with love.

"No claim over them other than their hearts." Mrs. Melling's smile was laced with bitterness.

Frederick took pity on her, as well as Alexander's childless state, and waved Melissa over. She joined them with Bethany in her arms.

"Pass her to Alex," he whispered.

After Bethany kissed Alexander's cheek—and Phoebe kissed his other so she wouldn't be outdone—Frederick nodded to him and looked to Mrs. Melling. Alexander grinned like the Cheshire Cat in return.

"Knights of Kingdom Davenport, I'd like you to meet my mother, Mrs. Ruth Melling. Mother, Phoebe Camellia and Bethany Iris."

Frederick stepped back, taking Melissa by the elbow. "Let me help get your things inside."

When they reached the automobile, Melissa took his hand. "Have they not met her before?"

"I've never allowed it. She's caused more trouble to people I know than anyone else on this earth." He let go of her hand and gave her the wrist bag, keeping the camera and parasol to carry himself. "But I suppose allowing her to greet them won't hurt things."

"Alex looked proud to introduce them."

"He did." He glanced at where they all stood by the front steps and knew he did the right thing. "My own mother only met Phoebe once. She couldn't travel much the last years of her life, and by the time Bethany was born, Lucy and I were over, making traveling alone with them to Atlanta next to impossible at their young ages. I love that the girls have a close relationship with the Eastons because I hardly knew my own grandparents. Were you close to yours?"

Melissa took his arm. "Grandmother Constance Stone practically raised me. Mother was a factory worker and my father worked nights as a security guard. We had a three-generation apartment, but it was mostly my grandmother who saw to my care. She made sure I got a good education so I wouldn't be stuck in the filth of the city."

Phoebe was in the middle of explaining the differences of the carousel horses to Mrs. Melling when they approached. Alexander, still holding both girls, whispered in Phoebe's ear. She quieted and he nodded to his mother.

"Mother, this is Melissa Stone, from Noble Publishers, the one who's staying with us as Lucy's—"

"Assistant, of sorts," Melissa finished for him as she offered her hand. "Pleased to meet you, Mrs. Melling."

"The buzz around town has been about you this week, when people are not speaking about the boxing tournament." She gave Frederick a cutting glare. "I cannot abide violence in any form, even if masquerading as sport."

Frederick ignored the jab and clapped Alexander on the back. "Have them inside in a few minutes, please. They want to see Lucy before we go." Frederick led Melissa inside and set her things on the bench. "Goosy, are you up for another visitor?"

"I'm in the parlor, Freddy." Lucy was propped on the settee wearing her silk kimono, her legs covered with a small afghan. Her eyes were shadowed with smudges, her cheek marred, and she appeared paler than normal. Frederick took her hands into his and bent to kiss her forehead before sitting on the edge of the cushion.

"It appears Mrs. Melling's visit wore you out."

She gave a rueful smile. "It has nothing to do with a demon possessing me."

"I think there are safer ways to go about finding an adventure."

Her laughter, though weak, was still musical. "No one can make me laugh like you, Freddy. I'm sorry about what I asked you to do."

When her lower lip began to tremble, he smoothed a lock of hair behind her ear. "None of that, Goosy. I'm still here as your friend. It'll take more than a demon to keep me away."

"My protector." She kissed his knuckles, lowered their clasped hands to her lap, and closed her eyes. "Where are the girls?"

He stared at the slight smile on her lips and was pleased not to feel the need to kiss its teasing softness. "On the lawn, with Alex and his mother."

Lucy's eyes opened.

"I thought it was time," he stated.

"Are they still there?"

Frederick walked to the window. "Yes, just as I left them."

"Help me, Freddy. I want to see."

He scooped her into his arms and walked to the window. There he stood her on her bare feet and held her arm. Lucy covered her mouth with a trembling hand and leaned against him to keep herself upright.

"Do you see the smile on Alex's face? The light in his eyes?"

"Yes, Goosy." He passed her his final clean handkerchief.

She wiped her wet face. "Thank you, Freddy."

"It's not that great of a hanky."

Lucy laughed and rested her head on his chest. "You've brought us much joy today. Will you help me back so Alex doesn't get distressed at seeing me up?"

Frederick carried her to the settee and fixed the blanket over her legs.

"You don't need to hang about the hall, Melissa," Lucy called. "You're welcome to sit with us. The others should be in soon."

Melissa hesitantly entered the room. Not liking to see her unsure, Frederick led her to the loveseat. He sat beside her and gazed steadily at Lucy, wondering if she would say something.

A smile flickered on her lips but didn't stay. "Did you see all that you needed to at Monroe Park, Melissa?"

"Yes, Freddy and the girls are excellent guides. It's an exciting place." She looked to him and smiled. "And I got to meet one of his friends."

"Which one?"

"Chuck Brady and his date, Rachel."

Lucy snorted. "I'm sorry for you. Chuck is obnoxious and his dates tend to be dim-witted."

"He was nice enough, even if a bit like a puppy."

Frederick laughed. "Agreed."

"And Phoebe did school Rachel in simple geography," Melissa continued, "but she seemed sweet."

"I'm glad you two get along. Frederick needs variety in his life. I'm afraid he'll begin to grow moss if things don't change for him."

She's thinking more like "anything to save him from the clutches of Judith Smith." He cleared his throat. "We did find the girls' Easter dresses while we were out."

"Wonderful." Lucy's smile was back and when Phoebe ran into the room a moment later, it doubled.

"Momma, are you sick?" She quietly approached the settee and laid her hand on the afghan over Lucy's knee.

"Just a little, but it's nothing that can hurt you."

Phoebe climbed beside her and they kissed each other's cheeks before she settled against her. Alexander walked in with Bethany clutching his neck, but she reached for Lucy when she saw her mother. He gently sat her on Lucy's lap and then went to Frederick, pulling him into a hug like he often gave Claudio.

"Thank you, Freddy. You'll never know how much that meant to me, to my mother."

"Is she well, Alex?"

"She's too stubborn to admit anything, and if I asked after her health she'd take it as a slight to her looks. Claudio's told me he hears her coughing in the night and the pharmacy delivers many bottles to her each week."

Frederick rested a hand on his shoulder. "Let me know if there's anything I can do."

"You've already done it."

***

Monday morning, Frederick was eager to bring the girls to Lucy's, not to be rid of them but to see Melissa. Phoebe drug her feet to and from the breakfast table and refused to brush her hair. They were ten minutes later than usual getting into the car, but the memory of kissing Melissa Saturday kept him happy. The goodbye kiss he had left her with on the porch was mild compared to the minutes they shared in his living room, but together it added to the perfect day.

Alex was gone when they arrived, but Lucy sat on the porch swing looking more herself in a mauve tea gown.

"Who gave Daddy trouble this morning?" she asked as they climbed the front steps.

"Me!" Phoebe jumped onto the swing.

"It's nothing to be proud of, Phoebe Camellia. You need to apologize."

When Frederick brought Bethany to Lucy, his oldest stood on the swing to kiss him. "I'm sorry, Daddy."

"Just like her momma, she gives me a hard time and then looks so sweet when she apologizes I can't help but forgive her."

Lucy playfully backhanded his arm.

"My scrappy Easton."

She gave him a curling smile. "Would you bring us a storybook from the parlor?"

Frederick pinched her cheek affectionately. "Of course."

He found Melissa wrapped in a book, knees to her chest in the corner armchair. Creeping across the room, he fingered her loose hair. "Good morning, beautiful."

She startled and dropped the book. "Freddy! I didn't hear you arrive."

Frederick handed her the novel and went to his knee beside her. "Being lost in a book is a good excuse."

"I'm glad you think so." Her brown eyes were bright with joy, her smile radiant.

Testing her readiness, he trailed his hand from her hair to her cheek. She inclined her head and he moved in for a kiss without hesitation. Like the rising sun, her lips warmed him and brightened the morning.

"Oh, to begin each day like this," he whispered as he rested his forehead against hers.

"You know where to find me." Her hand went along his arm, squeezing its thickness.

"Yes, and I'll collect you tomorrow evening at seven. I've secured Darla to watch the girls and a seven-thirty reservation at the Trellis Room."

"That's where you took Phoebe last week, isn't it?"

"Yes, is that all right?"

"Of course, and I look forward to it." She wrapped her arms about his neck and took the initiative for another kiss.

His hands went around her blue walking suit as he leaned across her lap to get closer. He breathed in her sunny fragrance and deepened the kiss until she shifted back to end it. With a smile he kissed her once more, quick and firm. "I think I'll have a great day today, even though I'm running late."

Twenty-Three

Ever since Melissa went out with Freddy, the hours between seeing him stretched endlessly. Claudio's daily visits were enjoyable, but paled in comparison. Lucy acted so warm and inviting that Melissa felt as though she were in a different house, though Phoebe continued to snub her.

Tuesday morning, she returned from her walk at seven and found Alex looking over the newspaper in the parlor.

"Lucy's making breakfast," he said over the top of the paper.

"She's feeling better?"

"Her coloring is back to normal and she didn't toss about as much last night."

"That's wonderful. I have to admit that she's changed these past few days. She's kind to me now, someone I wouldn't mind calling a friend."

Alex folded the newspaper and looked at Melissa. "Her descent into darkness was so gradual I didn't notice. To me she's back to her regular self, but you see the drastic change because you only knew her when she was afflicted. You must have thought us all daft, but now do you see why we all speak highly of Lucy?"

"She's quite pleasant. Seeing all she's been through, I don't relish pushing her back to work, though. Mr. Noble expects me to report each Friday. After last week's good news, I fear this week's will be a washout."

"I'll encourage her before I leave but won't make today's goal too lofty. Let her ease back into it, and I can ease back into her." He sighed while Melissa felt her face heat. "Sorry, that sounded vulgar, but I didn't—"

Melissa looked away. "It was perfectly clear what you meant."

Alex chuckled. "So it was. Eliza would have appreciated that remark. My sister made me look tame."

It was Melissa's turn to laugh. "That's a scary thought."

He blushed and studied his scarred hands. "Claudio told me not to be intimate with Lucy this week, to make sure she's spiritually healed before we reunite."

"Feel free to ask me to take a long walk when the time comes. The warning might come in handy for my sanity as well."

Alex's dimples winked above his stubbly beard. "I'll keep that in mind."

"There's something I need mentioned to her."

Alex raised his eyebrows. "Yes?"

"I won't be here for supper. I don't know how to tell her but …"

"Going out with Freddy, are you? I saw how you two were when you came back Saturday. I knew the first hour you were here you'd get along with him, and seeing how Phoebe hasn't treated you the same since that outing, there must be something going on."

"She wasn't pleased when she woke up from her nap and I was at her house."

"And what did you and Freddy do while the children slept?" A challenge shone in his merry eyes.

Melissa stood and clasped her hands behind her back. "We talked."

"Breakfast is ready," Lucy said from the doorway. "I'm glad you're back in time, Melissa."

Alex rushed to Lucy's side, tugging her apron as he kissed her. "Melissa's going on a supper date with Freddy tonight so this will be our only meal together today."

Lucy's radiant smile turned to Melissa. "Do we get to keep the girls late or overnight?"

"Freddy has Darla coming to his house. I don't think he wanted to over burden you."

Her smiled faded. "He would think of that."

"He's thoughtful and correct." Alex kissed Lucy again. "Last night was the first time you slept well. You need a few more nights like that to be back to peak performance for writing—and other things."

Lucy giggled as he nuzzled into her neck. With an arm around her, Alex walked her to the kitchen, looking back to see that Melissa followed them.

"Do you think you can get two or three pages written today?" Alex asked Lucy after he blessed the food. He passed Melissa the platter of eggs and stuck a piece of bacon into his mouth.

"I think so, though I might want to sit with the girls the first hour. I enjoyed swinging on the porch with them yesterday."

"Try the gazebo and take in the sight of the last of the azalea blossoms," Alex suggested. "I've been thinking we should get a swing installed in it."

"That would be nice."

"I'll start making plans."

"Take it out of my account." Lucy stirred her coffee.

Intrigued, Melissa paused eating. "You keep a separate bank account?"

"I opened one when I started getting payments from Mr. Noble. When I married Freddy, he insisted I keep it. He ran the household comfortably with his own income and wanted me to save mine. I suppose he's seen too many widows with financial problems come through his door. Alex runs our home with his income as well. I used my money to buy the house from my father, but otherwise it's been mostly untouched."

"My mother originally didn't approve of Lucy because she thought she was after our family's money, but when I came back, it could have been said I was after hers."

"And I thought you were after my body."

"Body, mind, and soul. I want it all, my queen."

After breakfast, Melissa offered to clear the table so Lucy could wait for the girls. She was rinsing dishes when Freddy came up behind her. He left a gentle kiss on her neck that sent a pulse of longing through her body, and she leaned against him.

"Good morning, Melissa."

"Morning, Freddy." She dried her hands and turned to him, tilting her head up for a kiss.

"Is that what New Yorkers call 'talking' these days?" Alex stood in the kitchen doorway. "If so, Lucy and I really need to go back."

Melissa threw the dishtowel at him.

Freddy smiled and squeezed her hand. "I'll see you this evening."

"Come on, give her another one before you go. I won't tell."

Freddy shouldered past Alex. "I need to save something for tonight."

***

Melissa readied for her date as soon as Freddy picked up the girls, taking a quick shower and then brushing her hair. She sat in her underclothes at the dressing table in her bedroom when a knock sounded on the door.

Pulling on her Japanese shawl nearly as big as a robe, she called out. "Who is it?"

"Lucy. Do you need help?"

Melissa opened the door, holding her shawl closed with one arm.

Lucy smiled. "I have some time before supper if you'd like assistance."

Melissa stepped aside to allow her in.

"I don't think I ever told you, but your hair is lovely."

"Thank you, Lucy."

"How are you going to wear it tonight?"

"I'm not sure. I just finished brushing it."

"What about something like Lily Elsie?"

"The actress? I'm not as glamorous as that."

"You could be. People here don't know your style other than your smart everyday suits. You can be anyone you want to be. You do have lovely taste. What does your gown look like?"

She pulled the green silk and linen dress from the closet. "I hope it's okay."

"It's wonderful!" Lucy fingered the geometric trim at the bust and elbows. "It's very stylish, but more important, it's simple and elegant. Freddy will love it. A soft up-do will be perfect with it. I have a silver headband you could borrow if you'd like. May I fix it for you?"

"I have to admit," Melissa said, "it's odd to have you want to help me prepare for a date with your ex-husband."

"Freddy's my dearest friend. He deserves to have joy in his life, and spending time with you would give him that. He likes wit and intelligence and you have plenty of both. He has an appreciation for beauty and classic sensibilities, and you're blessed with those as well." Lucy took Melissa's hands. "I've been eaten up with jealousy, but that's behind me now. This week I've been reborn, and if there's anyone I'd want to share happiness with, it would be Frederick—to make up for all the pain I've caused him."

Lucy spent over half an hour arranging Melissa's hair. The result was a low chignon with her red waves expertly pulled loose enough to look like they were about to tumble around her shoulders. Only the exposed headband seemed to hold the tousled look in place.

"You're a miracle worker, Lucy. I never would have dreamed I could accomplish this style."

"Hopefully the rain will hold off. It's six-thirty now. I bet Freddy will be here by a quarter 'til. Do you want to make a grand entrance or wait in the parlor for him?"

"No theatrics, please."

"I think someone should take your picture together before you leave like you did for Freddy and Phoebe last week. May I bring it for you?" Lucy pointed to the camera on the dresser.

Melissa nodded. "I'll be down in a few minutes."

She pulled on her stockings and the silver slippers that—though unseen under the floor-length gown—highlighted the subtle diamond pattern on the silk fabric. After she hung her reticule on her wrist, she took a final look in the mirror, smiling at her reflection.

Downstairs, she walked in on the Mellings in the parlor standing before the hearth with Freddy. Lucy clutched Alex's arm with excitement as Freddy, wearing his tuxedo, appraised Melissa from head to train while holding a handkerchief to his nose. He lowered his hand, showcasing the remnants of a bloody nose.

"Freddy, what happened?"

"I caught the Jamaican around the corner when I came. I confronted him and he took a swing at me, just grazing my nose, but I got him in the mouth before he ran away. Alex called the police station and they're going to patrol the area tonight."

"Should we not go?" Melissa asked.

"Don't worry about us," Lucy told her. Then turning to Freddy, she pointed to the hall. "Go wash. You can't walk into the Trellis Room with blood on your nose and knuckles. What would people say about the noble Frederick Davenport if you did?"

"They'll say nothing because all eyes will be on Melissa Stone."

When Freddy was gone, Lucy turned to Alex. "I'm going to let Naomi know we're ready for supper and you need to take their photograph."

Alex escorted Lucy to the other room and met Melissa in the foyer. She had the camera open and showed him how to use it while Freddy joined them. The couple positioned themselves in front of the door and Alex took the final two photographs on the film.

"You both have fun," he told them with a wink.

"I hope that wasn't as awkward for you as it was for me," Freddy said as they walked to his automobile.

Melissa laughed. "They mean well."

With a hand on her door, he turned to her. "I plan to make tonight worth the discomfort. You're breathtaking. May I kiss you?"

She answered him with a smile, and after a light one on her lips, he worked his way to her throat. Reflexively, her arms went about his shoulders as his lips lowered to her collarbones. Invigoration left her ready to climb upon him with wanton passion. She settled for running her fingers through his thick hair and pressing her body against his. A sigh of longing escaped.

He stepped back a few inches and shook open her coat he had over his arm. "Let's go before we get ourselves in trouble."

Sitting in the automobile, Melissa kept near the door. When Freddy climbed in behind the wheel there was more than two feet of bench between them. He smiled as he started the engine and she realized that it was the first time she was alone in an automobile with a man. She'd traveled with men on public transportation and by foot, as well as by wagon both here and abroad, but never in the intimate space of a private automobile. Melissa almost wished for Bethany to hold to keep her from making a fool of herself.

Freddy parked near the hotel and hurried around to open her door. Gray clouds moved across the night sky and he grabbed his coat off the backseat. They checked their outerwear and paused under the domed ceiling of the lobby to pass the time before their reservation.

Melissa was about to remark on the decorative moldings when a man stopped before them.

"Davenport, it's good to see you."

"Spunner, allow me to introduce Ms. Stone. Melissa is in town on business, and Sean Spunner is one of the regulars at the gym."

The next ten minutes were a blur of introductions to a dozen people, several of which remarked on the upcoming boxing tournament. Melissa relaxed when they were shown to their table, grateful for the semi-privacy in their corner location.

"Would you care for an appetizer and wine?" Freddy asked.

"Yes, please." She wasn't one to drink much, but after her time in the Mellings' house it seemed like a treat.

Freddy ordered for them while Melissa studied the menu to decide on her main course. When they were alone again, he moved his setting next to hers at the round table.

"It will be easier to talk this way." He caressed her forearm.

Halfway through their crab-claw appetizer, Melissa sipped from her second glass of wine while telling a story of the time a hippopotamus charged her along the Omo River.

"The Karo tribesmen were doing some sort of battle cry as I climbed the nearest tree. The translator said they'd never seen a white woman run or climb so quickly. Fortunately I was wearing a split skirt that day so it wasn't too unseemly.

Freddy laughed and caught her hand in his as he reached for his glass with his other.

"Now this is a surprise." For the first time Melissa looked upon a person who had no admiration for Freddy—but rather disdain. The man's receding hairline and thin lips were punctuated with a crooked nose. "I didn't think you were one to go out on a work night, Davenport, especially cavorting with women and drinks."

"I see but one woman and one drink, but thank you for your concern." Freddy's harsh voice surprised Melissa.

"May I have an introduction?"

Seeing Freddy's jaw tighten, Melissa offered her hand. "Melissa Stone."

"Melissa Stone." The way he rolled her name off his tongue made her feel defiled. He leaned over her hand and kissed it, obviously coming closer to stare at her chest. She pulled her hand free. "I'm always pleased to meet a lovely woman. Rupert Lyons, at your service."

"Lyons from the Mellings' old law firm?"

"So you've heard of me?" He smiled.

Melissa shook her head. "I just know how to read."

Freddy covered a laugh with his napkin. The waiter arrived with their main course and Rupert excused himself.

"I feel the need to wash my hands after that encounter."

Freddy stood and took her elbow, kissing her lightly on the temple as she stood. "You don't know how correct that assumption is."

"I'd like to hear more when I get back."

While she dried her hands, a towering brunette came into the washroom looking at a timepiece she wore around her neck. Melissa stood to the side, trying to pass through the doorway. "Excuse me."

"In a hurry to get back to Mr. Davenport?" She snapped her watch closed. "He's well cared for at the moment."

"I'm sure I don't know what you mean, but please excuse me."

"If you think you can waltz into town and steal our most eligible man, you're in for an awakening." Her hand went to her sharp hip.

"I'm sorry if your feelings are hurt, but—"

She laughed and waved her left hand before Melissa's face. "Do you see this ring? No accountant would ever splurge on jewelry like this. I married for prestige, but I have a friend set on everyone's favorite numbers man. She married for money her first time. Now the young widow wishes to marry for stamina."

"This is none of my business."

"Precisely, which is why you need to quit seeing Frederick Davenport."

The counter attendant took pity on Melissa. "Mrs. Lyons, I'm sure our guest would like to exit now."

Melissa gave her brightest, forced smile to who she now knew was Rupert Lyons's wife, and pushed out of the room as though she nudged her way through a crowded subway station. Freddy was in the clutches of an equally demanding brunette, this one with voluptuous curves surrounding the tiniest waist Melissa had ever seen. Freddy stood behind his chair, a glazed look on his face until he saw her. He stepped around the woman, joining Melissa.

"Excuse us, Mrs. Smith, but we need to get to our supper now."

The woman studied each movement between Melissa and Freddy as he assisted her, eyes narrowing when he caressed her arm. When he moved back to his own chair, Mrs. Smith placed a hand on his biceps.

"Did you need my assistance Saturday during the tournament?"

"It's as I told you. Lucy and Alex are seeing to our girls." He took a step back and her hand fell away. "Goodnight, Mrs. Smith."

As soon as Melissa and Freddy were both situated at the table, the waiter came back, removing the silver covers from their plates.

"Let me guess," Melissa said as she cut her first piece of steak, "Mrs. Smith is the widow of an older, wealthy man."

Freddy sprinkled salt on his potatoes. "How did you know?"

"I ran into Mrs. Lyons and she told me how her dear friend had claim on you first."

"Judith Smith's been after me since I was still married to Lucy. She's persistent, but that's the only kind thing I can say about her."

"Well I can't fault her good taste."

"Not in the friendship department. Rupert and Kate are the worst predators in town."

"How so?"

"I don't wish to disturb a good meal with conversation about them, but the simple facts are Kate used to run a local gossip magazine, slandering the names of many young women, but she had a keen eye on Lucy."

"Lucy and Alex were easy pickings, I'm sure."

He nodded. "And Rupert's a devil. He used to be good friends with Alex, but he tried to have his way with Lucy at their Mardi Gras ball and then with Maggie during the Seacliff days."

"Maggie, otherwise known as Magdalene. I keep hearing her name in conversations."

"Her family is coming to town so Douglas can watch the tournament, and they'll be back next month for Darla and Henry's wedding." Freddy took her hand in his. "I see the pained look on your face. You were correct in your assumptions of Rupert, but let's change the topic and enjoy our meal."

"Agreed." She forced a smile that changed to a genuine one when he kissed her.

Twenty-Four

By the end of supper, Frederick's face was sore from grinning. They both declined dessert and spent another half hour chatting over coffee. Each time Melissa's smile lines creased her face, his heart beat faster. When he was down to the last inch of coffee in the cup, he got the nerve to reach under the table for her hand. Entwining their fingers, he rested them on his knee.

"Despite the rude interruptions, I had a great time," he told her.

"I'd face the Lyons and Mrs. Smith in order to see you again."

"The likelihood of running into them decreases as the prices decline. If you're a fan of diners, you're welcome to meet me on Mondays, Wednesdays, or Fridays after my training. I could bring you back when I pick up the girls. Chuck is often with me, sometimes Henry as well."

"That sounds fun. Tell me where to meet you tomorrow."

"I'll drive you by it on the way home."

Going through the lobby, they were stopped several times by people wishing Frederick luck at the tournament. After collecting their coats, they paused to button them closed against the steady rain.

"Where's your parasol when we need it?"

"A little rain never hurt. Come on, it isn't far." Melissa took his hand and dashed outside.

He let her set the pace, but overtook her as they neared the automobile so he could open the door. As soon as she was in, he went around the front and slipped behind the wheel. The rain on the canvas roof was muted, but it tinged off the hood, splattering on the windshield.

A few blocks later, he pointed out the gym and diner, telling her the nearest stop for the streetcar. They were still a mile from the house when the sky let loose with lightning and a blowing downpour. Frederick pulled to a side street, parking under a sprawling live oak to shield them from the rain. He turned to her, reaching across the bench in the dark for her hand.

In the next flash of lightning he saw her hands clasped in her lap, but yearning in her eyes. The darkness enveloped them and he slid toward the middle, right arm on the back of the seat until he touched her shoulder. Lightning struck again, revealing Melissa unbuttoning her coat. A heartbeat later, they surged together.

Their hands were on each other as a mood of playfulness permeated the storm. Frederick followed the wrapped trim of Melissa's gown to her back, pressing her closer as her hands trailed up his torso and around his shoulders. His lips made their way to her earlobe as he inhaled her exotic scent made heavy by the rain. Then he followed the trail of rain drops to the hollow of her collarbones, licking the wetness off her skin. She clung to him, and beneath her touch he sensed her struggle for control.

"Freddy, you're amazing, but the rain is letting up. We should go."

He lifted his head, waiting for another flash to lighten the sky, but it never came. His eyes adjusted to the darkness and he watched her watching him until his breathing calmed.

"You taste divine," he whispered before starting the engine.

Melissa shifted beside him. He placed an arm around her and kissed her cheek. They rode in silence to Lucy's house, surprised to see all the downstairs windows aglow behind closed drapes.

"That's unlike them," Frederick murmured as he shut off the engine.

Remembering the Jamaican, his body grew taut with the need to protect and he sprung out of the automobile. Outside Melissa's door, he raised his coat over his head, spreading the sides to make a roof for them. She paused before him, causing his breath to catch as she wrapped an arm about his middle. The other held her hem above the wet ground. She kissed him—firm and deep—and he let it be hers as he relaxed into the sensation of being held by a woman whose heart didn't cry for another.

"I had a great time tonight." Her lips brushed against his cheek. "I'll remember your attentions while I try to sleep."

"Melissa." He brought his mouth to her throat and down to her neckline. Frederick's arms still held his coat above them so he was helpless to cling to her when she tugged against him. He kissed his way back to her lips and they tasted and teased until they were both breathless.

"We should get out of the rain."

He tried not to stare at the way her chest moved with the words, but was unsuccessful.

"Keep an arm about me," he told her and they started for the front porch.

When the puddles threatened her dress shoes, Frederick let his coat drop onto his head and swooped her into his arms, reaching the cover of the porch a moment later. Under the glow of the gaslight, Melissa glistened with rain. Not caring that he dripped upon her, he kissed her once more.

"No one's ever swept me off my feet like that." She leaned her head on his shoulder. "You're amazing."

"You've said that twice tonight."

"That makes it doubly true."

They were sharing another kiss when the front door opened.

"It is an odd night for romance," Claudio said, "but come in and dry yourselves. Alex has a fire in the parlor and there are tea fixings in the kitchen."

The priest held the door open for them, but Frederick paused to set Melissa on the porch and take their coats. After shaking the excess water from them, Frederick hung the outerwear in the foyer.

"What are you doing here so late?" Frederick asked.

"They had an unwelcomed visitor shortly before I arrived. Lucy was distraught and Alex was busy with the police so—"

"What happened?" Frederick went to go for the parlor but Claudio stopped him.

He looked from Frederick to Melissa. "It was the stranger. He tried to come in the back door, but the blessing from the other night prevented him. He screamed out and was withering in pain when Alex saw him."

Frederick took both Melissa's hands. "We have to stop him from coming here. It isn't safe for you. It isn't safe for anyone. Do you have any idea what he's after?"

"I spoke with him once. He's after his power and said the name Hepzibah. I know of one woman with that name, but it's a common name in Jamaica. He could have me mistaken with someone else."

"I do not think so," Claudio said. "Not with what the demon said about your arrival."

Seeing Melissa shiver, Frederick hugged her to him. "We'll figure this out."

"Come in, sit down." Claudio motioned to the parlor.

"Just for a minute. Did you reseal the house?" he asked Claudio as he led Melissa down the hall, an arm still about her.

"*Sí*, everyone will be safe inside these walls."

Alexander was on the settee with Lucy curled against him, head resting on his chest and eyes closed. His eyebrows were pulled tight, his mouth set in a straight line.

"I'm sorry we missed the commotion," Frederick said. "I wouldn't have thought the man brazen enough to return after I caught him here this evening."

"I'm close to hiring a private guard. Do you have any friends at the gym who would want the position?"

"Not that I can think of, but it's those at the gym during the day you'd want to ask, not the guys who come in after work." Frederick nodded toward Lucy. "Careful there, Alex, she's liable to drool on you."

"Frederick Lionel Davenport, I'm not asleep."

"I do believe Goosy just admitted to drooling in her sleep."

She brought a hand up her husband's chest to his shoulder. "Only when dreaming about Alex."

A gleam brightened Alexander's eye. "That's because I like her w—"

Claudio saved the group from what Frederick knew was a lewd admission with a string of what could only be described as chastising Italian. Alexander looked remorseful, but Lucy looked ready to burst from holding in a laugh.

She caught Frederick's gaze and crossed the room, looking between him and Melissa. "How was your supper?"

"Wonderful," Frederick said.

"With one exception," Melissa added. "I was unfortunate enough to meet Mr. and Mrs. Lyons and Judith Smith."

Lucy frowned. "They would have to be there tonight."

"Cheer up, Goosy. It appears there's someone those women dislike more than you."

She hugged Melissa. "We're kindred spirits after all." Then Lucy turned on Frederick, embracing him next. "I'm glad you had a proper date. It's been long overdue."

"It was worth the wait." He smiled over Lucy's shoulder at Melissa.

"Yes, and I'm going to meet him at the diner tomorrow evening. You and Alex can have a family supper with the girls."

Lucy raised her eyebrows. "It must have gone very well! Don't hurry back. We're happy to keep the girls a bit longer, aren't we Alex?"

"Yes, and for that reason you should get to bed, my queen. You've had a long day." He came to her side, kissing her cheek as he wrapped an arm about her waist.

"I don't want to go upstairs alone."

"I'll come with you," Melissa said. "That will give Alex a chance to see the men out."

Alexander nuzzled against Lucy's neck. "I'll be up soon."

Lucy took Melissa's arm, then dropped it. "I suppose you want to say goodbye to Freddy."

Seeing the look of embarrassment flash across her face, Frederick quickly kissed Melissa's cheek. "I'll see you tomorrow."

When the ladies left the room, Alexander frowned. "Is that all you've got?"

Frederick crossed his arms. "We might have shared several minutes while we were caught in the thunderstorm on the way home."

"And he had her in his arms when I opened the front door," Claudio said.

Alexander's blue eyes sparked with amusement. "How does it feel to be back to romancing a woman?"

"It's great, but difficult this time around."

"She doesn't compare to my luscious Lucy? Does she need to be trained or has someone taught her wrong? In all her travels, she might have picked up some odd notions for ways to—"

"*Calmati*, Alexander. You are speaking of a daughter of God."

"She's amazing." Frederick couldn't help grinning. "It feels better, more real than anything before. There's no comparison other than I know how good the ultimate feels. It's taking every ounce of strength I have to control myself because it could only be more incredible with Melissa."

Alexander grabbed Frederick by the shoulders and tried to shake him. "Yes! She's the one for you! And the release you will feel after you—"

"After being married before God." Claudio crossed himself. "Lord bless these natural men."

Alexander raked his hands through his hair and groaned. "Then bless me Father De Fiore, for I have sinned. Your regulations for Lucy's healing this week are my downfall. If I cannot be doing it, allow me to speak of it! It's been four and a half days since I've had my sweet Lucy. We haven't gone without half this long since we've been married."

Days ago the information would have stung because Lucy could go weeks without being intimate with Frederick, but now it was just another rash statement from Alexander. What Frederick had with Lucy—beyond their daughters—didn't relate to him at present. He craved no touch or attention from a woman beyond Melissa Stone.

"You will survive, *amico*. Now let me bless each of you with strength and Frederick can bring me back to Mrs. Melling's house, no?"

"Yes, but bless Alex first. He looks as though he's about to faint for want of Lucy's touch."

Twenty-Five

At three-thirty Wednesday afternoon, Melissa found herself in a staring match with Phoebe—her blue-green eyes a startling mix of her mother and stepfather. The two were on the rug in the parlor, a small block tower Melissa helped Bethany build between them while the youngest was across the room with her doll.

"Would you like to build with me?" Melissa asked.

Nothing.

"You may use the blocks now. Bethany is done with them."

Silence.

"I had a lovely time at Monroe Park with you Saturday."

She snarled her pouty lips.

"Why are you mad at me this week, Phoebe?"

And there it was—a hint of her father in her clenched fists. She slammed them on the floor. "Daddy loves Momma!"

Melissa forced a smile. "Yes, he does. They're good friends and they both love you and Bethany."

"Daddy loves Momma, not you!"

"Your father and I are friends, but different friends than how he is with your mother." She picked up a block from the floor and added it to the top of the tower. "There are many types of friends and there's room for all of them in life."

"Not for you. You're no longer a knight in my kingdom!" Phoebe stood, hands on her hips, and kicked the tower over with a swift motion before running from the room. Bethany looked at the fallen creation and went back to hugging her doll.

Melissa, on the other hand, had to swallow a lump in her throat as Phoebe stomped around upstairs.

Lucy exited her study. "Are you about ready to leave?"

Melissa sighed and stood. "I suppose."

"What is it?" Lucy took the elbow of Melissa's gray walking suit.

"Phoebe." Melissa pointed at the ceiling to show that the girl was in her room. "Ever since Saturday, she acts like she hates me. I've tried everything I can think of, but she's not softening."

"Since you went out with them?"

Melissa nodded.

"Even when we were married, Phoebe preferred Freddy over me. Their bond is tight and she fears you're going to take his attention from her. She dotes on Papa more than Nana and some days I think she loves Alex more than me. I don't look forward to when she reaches courting age. She'll be flitting around men like a bee to flowers."

Melissa said her goodbyes then gathered her camera, parasol, and purse, making sure her used rolls of film were in her bag. On her way to the streetcar, she passed a policeman on Catherine Street.

"Good afternoon, Ms. Stone."

Stopping, she looked in his dark eyes. "Are we acquainted?"

"Mr. Melling has made the situation of your stalker known to the entire police force. We'll do our best to make sure there are no more instances with the Jamaican. Are you headed to the streetcar?"

"Yes, but Mrs. Melling is alone with her girls and the cook right now."

"It will just take a minute to see you aboard." He waited until she was securely on the trolley before walking back toward Lucy's house.

There was a sense of comfort in knowing a policeman was near the house, but it still wasn't the best situation for the Mellings and Davenports to be in. She'd never forgive herself if something were to happen to one of them. Determination to find the man and confront him once and for all took over.

After she saw to her film's developing and bought more rolls for her Kodak at the photography store, she wandered toward the cathedral to take photographs of the church. A policeman at the corner nodded to her as she passed.

At the newsstand, she bought the latest copy of *Noble Travels* magazine. Her article on springtime in Washington D.C. was in it. Usually, she supplied the photographs needed for the articles, but this one Mr. Noble purchased the visuals from a photographer in the capitol. The photographer had taken photos last spring and would cover the cherry trees being planted at the end of the month with First Lady Taft and the wife of the Japanese ambassador. Ms. Scidmore, one of Melissa's friends who paved the way for female travel writers, spearheaded the efforts of planting cherry trees. Melissa was invited to attend the ceremony on March twenty-seventh, but she knew she'd still be in Mobile at the end of the month. Only the image of Freddy helped soothe the wound of missing out on the historic event with her friend.

In her distracted state, she found herself before the jewelry shop she'd stopped in her first afternoon in town. The tinkling of the bell announced her entrance.

"Good afternoon, Ms. Stone," Mr. Hofstedder said. "I hope you're enjoying our city."

"Yes, very much. I'm just out on a stroll this afternoon. There's much to see here."

"Have you reconsidered about the brooch? I have a buyer interested."

Melissa tucked the parasol under her arm and fingered the folded camera hanging around her neck. "You've been seeking a buyer for it when it's not for sale?"

"Nothing like that. The gentleman came in the day after you and asked if I'd seen any Spanish gold and emerald pins lately. Said he was looking to replace something for his family. He was an islander and I assumed he must have come over on the ship with you and admired the jewel."

Melissa laid a hand on the counter. "Did he leave his name or contact information?"

Mr. Hofstedder rubbed his head. "No."

"I'm not looking to snub you a finder's fee because I'm not selling, but I think the man could help me with something else."

"He didn't leave his name, Ms. Stone, but he said he'd come in every Monday and Wednesday afternoon to check to see if I'd gotten it. You just missed him last hour."

Out of energy and tired of worrying, Melissa found herself sitting on a bench in front of the diner a quarter of an hour early. A few minutes later, Darla spotted her.

"I'm glad I don't have to wait alone." Her blue eyes were bright against her porcelain skin. "I was excited when Henry told me you'd be dining with us."

"And how was your day?"

She flopped onto the bench in a show of exhaustion. "I delivered a baby boy this morning whose lungs were so strong I thought he'd break every bit of glass in the house. Dr. Hughes was late, so I did it with the help of the mother-in-law and cook. Days like this make me want to run north to one of the medical schools that allow female students."

"Why don't you?"

"Henry." She smiled as she said his name. "Last year I was ready to leave—with his blessing mind you—but I couldn't get on the train. Even if I came back with my medical certificate and the title of Doctor, no one here would employ me."

"Then why not set up a new life somewhere else?"

Darla laughed. "You haven't had many beaus in your life, have you?"

"Nothing long-term," Melissa admitted with a blush.

"My heart is here. My friends are here. What's left of my extended family is here. Mobile Bay is home. Henry's arms my haven." She sighed. "And I figured I could do just as well helping women here with Dr. Hughes than I could as a fresh start-up elsewhere. Dr. Hughes is respected in these parts, and the fact that he believes in me and the option of home-birthing against the procedures the hospitals are doing does a world of good. Granted, some things are medical advancements, but many aren't. The risk outweighs the benefits in my opinion."

"Do you keep up with the research?"

"I read everything I can get my hands on, and Dr. Hughes has allowed me in on some of his surgeries. The few times he's had to rush a patient to the hospital for complications, I've been right beside them the whole time."

"Fascinating."

"Me? I'm just a girl from Dauphin Island." Darla tucked a strand of her dark hair behind her ear, an amused look on her face.

"You're smart, resourceful, and caring." Melissa took her hand in a show of friendship, surprised at the roughness of her young skin.

Reddened with embarrassment, she pulled away. "I forgot to moisturize after the scrubbing today."

"I'm almost out of facial cream. I was going to buy a jar while I was in town this afternoon." Melissa pointed across the way to a storefront. "I bet we have enough time to run in. I'll let you use some. It's a luxury on hands, but it works quickly."

Darla gushed her thanks on their way back to the diner as she rubbed the cream into her skin. "Henry will thank you too. He's never said anything, but I know he prefers a soft touch."

When they reached the diner, Freddy and Henry were waiting for them. Freddy slipped his hand around Melissa's.

"Hello, Beautiful." He kissed her temple and relieved her of the parasol, bag, and camera as they followed the younger couple to a booth in the back of the diner.

Henry and Darla used their menus as a privacy screen while they kissed.

"The wedding can't come soon enough," Freddy voiced above the clatter of the diner.

"Four weeks from today," Darla said from behind the menu. "You have to come, Melissa. That is, if you're still here. Or if you want to stay especially for the wedding, I could host you in my aunt's house. It's right next door to the Davenports."

"As I don't see an end date for Lucy's work, I think we'll be safe to assume I'll still be here."

"Good." Darla looked at Freddy and then Henry. "Where's Chuck tonight?"

"Having dinner with Rachel's family," Henry replied.

"I don't recall him taking a family dinner with any of his other ladies. Are things getting serious?"

"It would appear so." Henry brushed Darla's nose with his finger. "I think he wants what we have."

"I don't think he has the attention span for anything this deep."

The conversation over supper was carefree. After they said goodbye to Darla and Henry, the events of the afternoon returned to Melissa's mind—police guarding the house and the Jamaican coming to the jewelry store. Freddy would see the police presence soon enough, but she wasn't ready to share the information of the Jamaican frequenting Mr. Hofstedder's shop. Melissa wanted to decide how she could approach the man before telling anyone.

Freddy's automobile was on a side street behind the gym. Once Melissa was seated, Freddy handed in her things and hurried to his own door. Rather than starting the engine, he looked to Melissa.

"Why are you so far away?"

She slid across the leather seat. "Did you choose this parking spot because of the seclusion?"

The tilt of his head and sly smile answered for him as he cupped her cheek. "Do you mind?"

"Not in the least."

As she closed her eyes, she felt the heat from his breath feather across her face before his lips made contact. Freddy's kiss started soft, but he pressed on until she lost herself under his attentions. A blissful minute later, he kissed her once more and straightened.

"I fear I'm beginning to rely on moments like this to mark my days."

Though he didn't say it, she knew he was thinking about when she would leave, when she would no longer be there for a morning kiss when he brought the girls to the Mellings' house or stolen moments at the end of the day.

"Let's enjoy it while we can," she whispered.

He drove with her tucked under his arm. When they got to Catherine Street and his headlight shone across a man pacing the sidewalk, he slowed.

"Alex finally got the police to take him seriously," Melissa said. "One was here this afternoon and walked me to the streetcar."

Freddy pulled to a stop. "Evening, officer."

He tipped his hat. "Mr. Davenport. Ms. Stone. Your man showed up near sunset, but he got across Dauphin Street before the officer on duty could catch him. When it was telephoned into headquarters, Mr. Melling was assured someone will be on duty here the next forty-eight hours."

"I'm glad to hear that. My girls are here during the day."

"Yes, Mr. Davenport. Mr. Melling made us aware of all the precious souls within those walls, as well as when to expect everyone's comings and goings."

"Thank you." Freddy nodded and continued to the house.

Once he shut off the motor, they took another minute of privacy, which ended with Melissa breathless in Freddy's arms. Gazing up at him while she returned from the high his attentions gave her, she fingered along his arched brow and down his cheek. He closed his eyes and leaned into her touch. A simple act, but the rush of power and oneness it gave her surpassed everything she'd felt in her life until that point.

"Do you feel it, Freddy?" she whispered. "Do you feel the oath between our souls?"

"It's telling me I'll never feel this way with another."

And his kiss told her of his devotion like no words could express.

Twenty-Six

Melissa survived Thursday only because Darla arrived at noon. Frustrated from her morning with contrary Phoebe, Melissa took her sandwich to the gazebo for a few minutes of solitude while Darla and Lucy handled lunch.

Darla joined her not long after Melissa finished eating. "What happened to Lucy?"

"What do you mean?"

"She's happy. Pleasant and even downright witty, without the biting sarcasm."

When Darla was there for a few hours Monday, Lucy had rested the whole time. Today proved her first experience with Lucy post-exorcism. "Did you hear about what happened Friday night?"

Darla shook her head and settled on the bench opposite. She listened intently, her expressions changing from surprise to shock to understanding.

"It all makes sense now," Darla said when Melissa finished. "When I met Lucy, she was unstable, haunted by the memory of Alex. At times she would lash out at me, other days she would bare her heartache. When Alex appeared, she clung to him without a backward glance. I didn't believe any mother in her right mind would leave her children for a man—especially when she had such a fine husband as Mr. Davenport—but she was driven to the sin by the demons that came to her when she first gave herself to Alex."

"They do love each other." Melissa surprised herself with the conviction in her voice.

"Yes, sometimes I think too much for their own good." Darla smiled and blushed. "But my opinion might change when I'm married next month and see how it all works. I see the result of it every day, but the act—beyond basic anatomy—is still a mystery to me. Are you experienced?"

Melissa twisted the napkin in her lap.

"I'm sorry. It's none of my business. It's just I have no one to talk to, but I can ask Maggie when she's in town this weekend. She'll be back for the wedding, but there won't be time then. There's no way I'd ask Lucy. I'm sure her and Alex's relationship is beyond anything I could ever relate to."

Melissa giggled—something she hadn't done in years. "They're quite an eye-full at times. Alex walked out of the study in nothing but his pants the first day I was here. He didn't apologize or make excuses. He knew I was aware of what they were doing when Naomi interrupted him to take a telephone call. But I suppose it's romantic to them that they have no shame in their relationship."

Darla stood. "And then there are those of us who hide behind menus to kiss."

"You and Henry are sweet together. I'll tell you, Darla." She lowered her voice. "I've had several relationships, but nothing long-term as my work has me traveling so often. I've been kissed in more countries than I can count on my fingers, but only once did I come close to giving myself to a man."

Darla's eyes widened and she sunk to the bench beside Melissa. "Who? And what made you stop?"

"An Italian on his family's vineyard in Tuscany a few years back. I was there for several weeks to learn about wine-making and he wanted to share with me all the joys he had to offer."

"His name wasn't Valentino, was it?" Darla crossed her arms defensively.

Melissa looked on her with interest. "His name was Antonio. Who's Valentino?"

"Claudio's cousin. A violinist with a penchant for romance."

"Valentino De Fiore?"

Darla nodded.

"I saw him perform at Carnegie Hall the last time he was in New York. How small the world is!"

"He was here for a season with The Battle House Orchestra that crazy autumn Alex came to Lucy. My cousin, Alice, was one of his students and I chaperoned his lessons until Claudio came into town and abolished the use of Valentino's hotel room for instructions. Valentino tried to take me as a lover, and then my cousin when he couldn't convince me. I wouldn't be surprised if this romancer of yours was a relation."

Melissa laughed. "He very well could be. Claudio said his family has lived in Tuscany for hundreds of years and Antonio was as handsome as a De Fiore man, though his surname was Rossi."

"What gave you pause?"

"There was no depth. He was handsome, charming, and knew everything to do to weaken my knees. But in the end, it felt like a fling. A summer of love to be forgotten, but I didn't want to give myself to a man who would soon turn to the next tourist and never think of me again. I didn't want to be the lonely woman with nothing but memories and no one to hold when I got home."

"But what of Mr. Davenport? You've gone out with him several times and you two seem to get along wonderfully. Does it feel the same as with Antonio?"

"Can you keep a secret?"

Darla took Melissa's hands into her own. "I'm filled to the brim with secrets, but they never spill out."

"It feels like nothing before. Freddy reaches my very soul. Everything pales in comparison to my moments with him."

"I can tell he likes you, Melissa. I think you have what he needs."

"And what's that?"

"Complete adoration and devotion. You two are perfect for each other with your warmth, honesty, and humor. Those that haven't seen you together will see you with him at the tournament and there'll be no doubt where his affections lie."

****

Henry and Darla picked Melissa up after seven Saturday morning. Alex and Lucy were still dressing, so she let herself out and settled in the backseat of the little automobile. It was a starter vehicle, nothing like Freddy's big touring one, but Henry took a moment to shine the grill with his sleeve before jumping behind the wheel. Darla wore a pretty yellow dress and Melissa began to doubt her choice of a brown walking suit. At least she pinned her emerald brooch to the lapel to add a dash of sophistication, though she felt half-dressed being stocking-less beneath the skirt.

Henry was in the middleweight division and had to weigh in before those in the heavyweight, like Freddy. They arrived at Temperance Hall, a three-story building where the tournament was held—said to be the scene of Mardi Gras balls in decades past but had since been turned into a roller skating rink. A boxing ring sat in the middle of the wooden floor, surrounded by rows of folding seats and bleachers with narrow aisles at each of the four corners.

The audience was small for the featherweight division. Rather than trying for floor seats, the ladies took the first row of bleachers so no matter who sat in front of them they'd be able to see over their heads. Darla politely asked to keep the row when people stopped, explaining they were saving them for family of the contestants. Across the ring, Melissa spotted Mr. and Mrs. Lyons and Judith Smith in the front row, along with another young couple.

Melissa scooted closer to Darla. "Who's that with the Lyons?"

"That's Dr. John Woodslow and his wife, Grace Anne. She used to be best friends with Lucy until Alex ruined her reputation."

Melissa was sure the group consisted of Lucy's worst enemies and tried not to dwell on them. Gazing around the space, she was surprised at the number of women in attendance. Just before the top of the hour, two men approached Darla, one with almost as much gray in his hair as brown and a pleasant smile, the other heavyset and grouchy.

"Hello, Darla," the friendly one said, kissing her cheek. "Think we could sit here until the rest of the crew arrives?"

"There should be room even with the Mellings and Campbells. Hold that end for us so Melissa can sit by me." Darla motioned down the bench. "Have you met Melissa Stone? She's with Lucy's publishing company."

"I have yet to lay eyes on her." He walked down the row, hand extended. "I'm Maxwell Easton, Lucy's oldest brother. It's a pleasure to meet you. And this is our brother, Edmund."

While Maxwell offered a warm hand, Edmund silently appraised her as she joined Darla.

"Don't mind him," Darla whispered, "he's been sour for years."

Maxwell settled beside Melissa. "Have you been enjoying your time in Mobile?"

"Yes, very much. I find it charming."

"And at least one of our citizens has been charmed by you." He winked and leaned closer. "I took lunch with Freddy a week ago. He's quite smitten."

Melissa felt her face heat and looked at Maxwell long enough to smile. "I find him wonderful as well."

"A woman could do no better than Frederick Davenport."

When the first round of the welterweight began, the chatter stopped and the room was filled with shouts from the spectators calling for their favorite competitor. Toward the end of the hour, the Mellings arrived with the girls. Melissa watched them make their way down the aisle, Alex in a striking blue suit with Phoebe on his shoulders in pink and Lucy a beacon in one of her red tea gowns carrying Bethany in a sweet blue sailor dress. An outsider would have thought them royalty with all the attentions given them through looks and whispers.

Darla stood and waved them over. Edmund shoved his way off the opposite end from the approaching Mellings. Seeing the slight, Maxwell stood to welcome his sister and family.

"Uncle Max!"

He lifted Phoebe off Alex's shoulders, slapping him on the back in the process. He was smiling, but it looked rougher than necessary for a friendly greeting. Maxwell then kissed Lucy's and Bethany's cheeks.

"You all look well," he remarked. "How's the writing coming along?"

"It's going splendid." Lucy sat beside her brother. "Melissa's a big help. Darla too, as usual."

Maxwell resettled between Melissa and Lucy with Phoebe on his lap. Alex sat on the other side of Lucy, leaving more than enough room on the end for other arrivals.

"Sissa," Bethany's little voice said as she reached in front of her uncle to get at Melissa.

"What's this? Beth has a pet name for you like you're one of the family?" Maxwell joked as Melissa took Bethany.

She snuggled into Melissa's shoulder, still smelling more like Freddy than Lucy.

Phoebe crossed her arms and frowned. "She's not family. She's not even in the kingdom anymore!"

Maxwell took the girl by her upper arms and stood her before him. "You listen here, Phoebe Davenport. Ms. Stone is a guest in your mother's house and a friend to your family. She deserves your respect."

Her blonde head lowered. "Yes, Uncle Max."

"Apologize to her."

Phoebe's luminous eyes turned to Melissa. "I'm sorry I was rude, but you can't be a knight anymore!" Then she squeezed past her uncle's knees and dove for the security of Alex.

While the welterweight class finished, Freddy slipped through the crowd in a casual day suit. He mounted the bleachers on Alex's side and greeted him and Phoebe first.

"Why aren't you getting ready?" Lucy asked as he bent to kiss her.

"I wanted to say hello to everyone."

As Freddy made his way down the row, a man with a red beard came behind him with a young boy in tow.

"Looks like we barely made it in time," the man said as he took the end of the bench beside Alex.

"Kade!" Phoebe fell upon the gangly boy with a hug.

Darla crossed the row and threw her arms about the bearded man. "I'm so glad you and Kade are here, but where's Maggie and Tabitha?"

It was Maggie's husband, Melissa realized as she admired his handsome profile.

"Shopping. She didn't want to try to sit in the crowded heat in her condition, but she'll see you after it's over."

"And how are she and the baby doing?" Darla asked.

"Fine as anything." Melissa identified a Scottish brogue in his voice. "'Tis another strong and mighty Campbell."

Darla greeted the boy—who immediately returned his attentions to Phoebe—before returning to her seat. Freddy turned back to speak with Douglas.

"I don't blame Maggie for not coming," Darla said as she took her seat. "It's stuffy and will only grow worse in here."

"How far along is she?" Melissa ran her hand over Bethany's back, hoping to keep her calm amid the noise.

"Six months. At least she'll be over it before the worst of the summer heat arrives." Darla gripped Melissa's arm and pointed with her other hand. "There he is!"

Diagonally across from them, the middleweight contenders warmed up behind the spectators. Henry's tousled mop of dark-blond hair bounced as he moved up and down, stretching and doing squats. Melissa hadn't thought about seeing the men she knew in boxing shorts and bare-chested like the others athletes.

"I haven't seen him like this since the tournament last autumn." Darla sighed. "Less than a month until I can feel each and every one of those muscles for myself."

Melissa laughed and opened her purse with one hand while balancing Bethany. She pulled out the fan she'd purchased in Asia while on her tour with Ms. Scidmore three springs ago. Unfolding the jewel-toned paper, she handed it to Darla.

"Cool yourself off."

Darla laughed but accepted it. "Your time will come, Melissa."

Freddy had made his way along the row while the ladies spoke and crouched before Melissa. "And how are my girls over here?"

"Daddy. Stay Sissa."

"Yes, Beth, I won't take you away from Melissa." He leaned closer on the pretense of smoothing his daughter's hair, but stared Melissa in the eyes instead. "I wish I could stay in your arms too."

Her heart felt ready to burst. "Good luck, Freddy."

"Would you walk with me to the weigh-in room?"

"Yes."

"Come here, Bethany." Darla held out her arms.

"No, Sissa." She clutched the brooch on Melissa's brown suit with one hand.

"Will you let Daddy carry you?"

"No."

Melissa patted her back. "It's okay, Beth. I'll keep you."

She left her purse with Darla and followed Freddy down the aisle. In the entrance hall, the air lightened with the absence of the crowd's body heat.

Freddy took her free elbow. "It's up on the second floor, but I won't have you come with her in your arms. You'll have enough trouble getting back to your seat as it is. I shouldn't have asked you. It was selfish on my part."

Melissa smiled and brought her hand to his face. "I was happy to come along."

He closed his eyes and leaned into her touch. "I'm glad to hear that, Melissa. May I kiss you for luck before I go?"

"Five minutes left for heavyweight check-in," a man hollered from the second floor landing. "We still need Charles and Davenport!"

Melissa shifted Bethany onto her hip to free more space in front of her. "I'm here for you, Freddy."

He smiled and touched her arm supporting his daughter. "I'm glad you're in our lives."

Her hand lowered to his shoulder and his arm went about her middle. Melissa expected him to quickly kiss her cheek, but his eyes searched hers as he leaned closer.

"I feel like I can do anything with you by my side," he whispered.

Their lips met and separated, but then he was back for more. His cheeks and chin were rough as though he skipped his morning shave, but she accepted the sensation happily as they deepened the kiss. When Freddy pulled away with a slight nibbling tug on her lower lip, she sighed and opened her eyes.

"I'm falling hard for you, Freddy, more than you'll ever know."

Pulling her to his side with one arm, he brought his mouth to her ear. "Show me after I win." He kissed her and took the stairs three at a time.

Twenty-Seven

When Melissa returned to her seat, Darla was all smiles.

"Did he get a kiss?" Darla whispered.

Melissa nodded.

"You should have seen the fury across the way. Judith Smith practically spit when you walked out with Mr. Davenport. Mrs. Lyons and Mrs. Woodslow tried to calm her and it looked like Mr. Lyons passed her a flask."

Melissa adjusted Bethany to sit sideways in her lap in an attempt to stay cooler. The announcer quieted the crowd and broadcast the middleweight boxers and the brackets for the matches. Henry was in the third match with Sean Spunner as his opponent. Darla flicked the fan beside her face as she leaned forward, following Henry's every move. Thirty seconds in, he dealt a knock-out blow to Sean's jaw. The crowd roared and Darla dropped the fan as she rose to her feet, a look of something between nausea and elation on her face.

Henry jumped the ropes and ran up the aisle. He was still laced in his boxing gloves, but it didn't stop him from lifting Darla into an embrace and kissing her. Darla trailed her hands across his bare shoulders as the hollering heightened. A moment later, he set her down and returned ringside.

Darla sank to the bench as though her knees gave out.

Melissa patted her hand. "That was the most romantic thing I've ever seen at a sporting event."

"He's never kissed me like that in public." Darla retrieved the fan. "And his body—it was scandalous to touch him, but I don't want to erase it from memory."

Melissa smiled, remembering the feel of Antonio's bronze skin under her hands out in the vineyard one hot afternoon. It was replaced by thoughts of touching Freddy's muscles through his shirt. Soon she'd see what lay beneath, but the act of embracing him fully clothed was still more powerful than what she experienced in Italy.

As though summoned by her thoughts of his homeland, Claudio made his way through the crowd. "I arrived in time to see Henry strike down his opponent. That was magnificent!"

He kissed the cheeks of Melissa, Darla, Lucy, and the girls as he made his way down the row until he settled between Alex and Douglas. Claudio put an arm around each man and laughed over something Alex said. The three men were an unlikely trio: Alabama lawyer, Italian priest, and Scottish boat captain. Taken separately, it didn't appear they'd have anything in common, but together there was no denying the camaraderie they shared.

It was almost an hour before Henry was back in the ring. Since his first fight was so fast, he was still fresh, but his competitor had taken five minutes in the ring quarter of an hour before. Four minutes into the five-minute round, Henry dealt another knock-out, but he kept near his trainer. When the round with the other top contender began, he had a cocky bounce to his footwork.

"Oh no, Henry," Darla muttered. "Focus. He's just as good as you."

The crowd chanted "Knock-out! Knock-out! One-two!" as the men jabbed and ducked. Henry landed a good strike and turned, like he wanted to catch Darla's eye. His opponent recovered and caught him on the side of his head, bringing Henry to his knees. He tried to stand too quickly and fell. Darla cried out and rushed for the ring. She appeared to give instructions to his trainers, but it was too noisy in the cavernous room to hear her in the stands. Dr. Woodslow climbed in the ring, knelt beside Henry to check his vitals, and then waved the trainers over to carry him out.

They brought Henry through the back, where those warming up waited. Freddy was there in all his glory. Stopping the caravan, he looked Henry over and gave Darla a brotherly hug. When the others moved on, Melissa kept staring. Though he didn't have the full height of former world heavy-weight champion James Jeffries, Freddy was built like him. Even at the distance, his biceps looked like rocks and his abs were well defined above his high waistband. Melissa rested her chin lightly on Bethany's head in order to pick up the familiar cologne that brought images of Freddy's embraces to her mind.

"That's a shame about Henry," Maxwell remarked.

"It makes me not want to watch Frederick's match," Lucy said from the other side of her brother. "Melissa, you must be beside yourself with anxiety."

"He'll do well," she said in earnest.

"Here, Bethany Iris." Lucy held her arms across Maxwell. "Come to Momma so Miss Melissa can have some breathing room."

While Melissa enjoyed the reprise, she missed the comfort of holding Freddy's daughter. A short while later, the heavyweight rounds were announced. Freddy's match was fifth, but Chuck Brady fought during the third. Chuck was spry—like he was out of the ring—and wore down his opponent by his fancy footwork and jabs before going in for a winning strike.

When Freddy entered the ring, a silence passed through the room. Then the chatter and shouts began. Fans flickered as Frederick Davenport turned toward his family and friends, put a boxing glove to his lips, and raised it in salute. Men hollered, women swooned, and others seethed with jealousy.

"The clever man knows how to work the crowd," Maxwell muttered and Melissa smiled around the fullness in her chest.

The bell rang. The swaying motion of the fight and noise of the crowd took over. Freddy was a cross between an English nobleman and Greek god. The stretch of his taunt leg muscles—visible from above his ankle shoes to his bugling thighs—were beautiful. His high-waist trunks looked more gentlemanly than his competitor's low-waist ones. Freddy had two inches over the other man and put his longer reach to use with kidney punches when they were upon each other, which was often because the other man had no patience to wait for an attack. He ruthlessly plunged at Freddy but soon fought to get away from his plummeting strikes.

Melissa stayed silent, watching Freddy first, the crowd second. Maxwell leaned forward. Lucy hid her face behind Bethany. Phoebe bounced on Alex's lap. Claudio, Douglas, and even little Kade were on their feet, hollering like the majority of the men in attendance.

In the front row opposite them, Judith Smith stood—Mrs. Lyons holding one arm, Mrs. Woodslow the other. Behind them the faces of more society ladies loomed, all stretching on tiptoes to see around the men's shoulders in hopes of getting a better look at the specimen they called Frederick Davenport.

Melissa's body pulsed with nerves as Freddy took a blow to the face. After ricocheting off the ropes, he managed to stay upright. He dropped all decency after that, going at the other man with a relentless pounding. Freddy bloodied the man's nose and kept going until the referee called it over. Melissa knew it was Henry's youth and excitement that sent him running for a kiss, but in that moment she wished Freddy would do the same. She wanted to feel those glistening arms around her as they held her to his perfect chest. Instead, she opened her fan to cool herself.

Alex squeezed closer to Lucy, loosening his collar. "Having been at the receiving end of that strength, I feel for the other man."

"That was almost barbaric." Lucy trailed a hand up Alex's arm. "I'm glad you're on his good side now."

"Do you wish me to bulk up at the gym, my queen?" Melissa, watching the exchange from the other side of Maxwell, recognized the look in Alex's eyes and held her breath. *Surely they wouldn't go at it in the middle of a boxing tournament!*

But Lucy passed Bethany to Maxwell and pulled her husband into her arms. "You're perfect the way you are, Alex."

As the next round began, the Mellings were at each other's lips, but at least there wasn't room for them to lie down.

"I'm going to go check on Henry and Darla," Douglas called down the row.

Holding hands, Phoebe and Kade made their way to Bethany on Maxwell's lap.

"Our daddy is stronger and better than all of these men," Phoebe announced to her sister.

Lucy broke away from her embrace with Alex. "Yes, he is, Phoebe."

"My dad could beat those guys, too," Kade countered.

"Captain Campbell is an equally fine man. I'm sure if you lived in town he'd be out there competing with the others," Lucy assured the boy.

Bethany turned from her sister and reached for Melissa. Her uncle passed her over while Kade studied her.

"Who are you?"

She smiled. "I'm Melissa. I'm staying with Phoebe's mother for a few weeks."

"We're staying there tonight too."

Phoebe tugged his arm. "Come on, Kade. Let's go back to Uncle Claudio."

Lucy leaned over her brother to speak with Melissa. "When Freddy's last match is over, Alex and I will take the girls home and get things ready for the party."

Bethany snuggled onto Melissa's shoulder, clasping the brooch. Since she wasn't tugging on it, Melissa left it alone.

"You're ideal for them, you know." Maxwell patted her knee. "A perfect match for Freddy and a great match for the girls. They could use your level-headedness in their lives."

"I should be offended," Lucy told her brother, "but I know you never thought I was a good match for Freddy, though we were meant to have this family together."

Maxwell put his arm around Lucy and kissed her forehead. "I know it, Lucy. It all worked out for you in the end, I just want to see Freddy happy, too."

***

By the time Freddy made it to the final contenders, he'd won against three men and at least four women had to be carried out— whether from the heat or overwhelming feelings, Melissa didn't know. Judith Smith was practically heaving out of her dress ringside as she and her friends fanned themselves.

Melissa spotted Darla coming up the aisle, Douglas walking behind her with an arm around Henry. Everyone shifted down so they could settle on the end by Melissa.

"He's still a bit dizzy, but he insisted on seeing Freddy in the finals," Darla said. "I forgot how hot it is in here. Lucy taught me one thing I don't mind putting to use in situations like this. Why wear stockings when it's blazing hot and no one can see your legs?"

Melissa—thinking of her bare legs under her long skirt— smiled. "She advised me the same thing yesterday."

The final three in the heavyweight division were Freddy, Chuck, and Thomas Charles, who Henry said was another member of their gym. They each had to fight each other, and unless one of them lost both rounds to their opponents, they would match again for a two-out-of-three match up to determine the top two boxers.

Freddy barely beat Chuck, Chuck beat Thomas, and then Thomas—tired from only having five minutes to recover—put up a strong showing before being bested by Freddy. Freddy embraced Thomas and it looked like he apologized to him. Melissa's heart went out to all three for having to fight their friends.

It was Freddy's turn to only have five minutes rest before taking the ring against Chuck. All the contenders from their gym came ringside for a closer view, taking the space in front of the Lyons and their friends. Henry started laughing and pointed at Judith Smith trying to get the boxers to let them stand in front of them.

"They're holding rank because they know Freddy detests her. That's our boys!" Henry kissed Darla's cheek then looked beyond her to Melissa. "That's a show of respect for you as well. They've seen how happy Freddy's been the last few weeks."

In that moment, Freddy looked up from his stool in the corner of the ring closest their seats. His gaze began down the row at Claudio and he waved to Phoebe and Kade, who cheered for "Kingdom Davenport!" to the amusement of those around them. He nodded to Alex, Lucy, and Maxwell before settling on Melissa. She brought her fingers to her lips and blew a kiss his way. With a parting smile, the towel was removed from his shoulders and the stool lifted out of the ring.

"For the final match in the heavyweight division, we have Frederick Davenport verses Chuck Brady! No time limit. They'll fight until one no longer stands."

Across the way, Rachel Wiseman made her way through the crowd. When she tapped one of the boxers on the shoulder, he allowed her in front of him.

Darla nudged Melissa. "They'd let you in down there if you want to see each bead of sweat as it runs over his muscles."

Melissa elbowed her in return. "I'm pleased with the view and companionship here, thank you."

In the ring, Freddy and Chuck circled each other. They both gave jabs that were blocked and it appeared they were having a pleasant conversation while doing so.

"We came for a fight, not a tea party!"

"Give him the old one-two!"

Chuck surged on the energy in the room and came at Freddy harder. He kept throwing punches. Freddy blocked them but didn't take the offense when he had the openings. The crowd grew rowdy, yelling taunts and booing Freddy. Chuck did a dance around the ring, clearly giving Freddy any opening he wanted, but he stayed in his defensive stance.

"Come on, Davenport!" Chuck shouted. "Don't hold back. Give me all you've got in your old age!"

Freddy shrugged, closed the distance between them in two strides and caught him in the stomach with a left-right hook. The crowd yelled as Freddy landed a few kidney strikes as they rushed together. It took a minute for Freddy to reach his peek, and then it appeared he stopped seeing Chuck as a friend and accepted him as the competition. He became as brutal as he had during his first match. Absorbed with the fluidity and beauty of his movements, Melissa couldn't look away.

Seven minutes later, though he was getting a few good punches in himself, Chuck's eyebrow was bleeding as well as his nose. When Freddy got him on the head again, Chuck took a wobbly step and then threw his hands into the air.

"Davenport is king!" He sunk to his knee and bowed his head in surrender.

Phoebe's high-pitched squeal could be heard above the thunderous cheers. She squeezed past Claudio's knees and ran down the aisle, her blonde head like a moonbeam in the sea of spectators, shouting "Daddy is king!"

Thomas Charles picked her up and slipped her through the ropes. Freddy helped Chuck stand and walked him to his coach before going to his knees to hug Phoebe. The crowd's noise level climbed higher, the newspaper cameras rose above the ropes for photographs, and again as Freddy plopped his daughter on his shoulders.

"We present," the announcer called, "the winner of the Mobile Bay heavyweight division by submission, Frederick Lionel Davenport!"

Twenty-Eight

Frederick wanted nothing more than to climb out of the ring, get cleaned up, and find Melissa. But as winner of the heavyweight division of the tournament, he owed it to the crowd—who suffered almost as much as him in the heat—to appear gracious. When he saw Bethany atop Alex's shoulders making their way toward the ring, he set Phoebe down so he could hold his youngest. He lifted her from Alex and kissed her cheek before placing her on his shoulders and walking the ring. After shaking hands pressing in from all sides, he accepted his trophy and posed for a photograph with the tournament coordinators.

He returned to Alex and Lucy. Phoebe rode on Alex's shoulders and Lucy reached through the ropes for Bethany. Muscles burning, Frederick eased himself into a squat and passed Bethany to her mother.

"You were an animal, Freddy." Lucy gave him a teasing smile. "We'll see you at our house as soon as you can make it. Come hungry. Naomi and Sharon are cooking a feast."

He kissed the top of her head. "Thanks, Goosy."

Alex offered a hand through the ropes. "Well done, Freddy. It's much easier to watch you beat someone than be the one being thrashed."

He laughed, pulled himself up with the ropes, and reached out for more handshakes. Douglas led Henry and Darla toward the center of the room while Claudio kept track of Kade. Melissa held Maxwell's arm as they approached. Frederick slipped out of the ring and accepted a towel from one of his friends and congratulations from more. By the time the group arrived, he'd managed to wipe most of the sweat from his torso and many of the extra people were pulling back to the exits.

"Mr. Davenport, we need to clear the floor. Your friends can accompany you to the back."

Before he could say anything, they were urged toward the warm-up area. He took a moment to glance behind him to motion Maxwell and Claudio to follow.

Douglas kept beside him. "I don't see how you're still upright after that match. Not to mention the ones before it."

"I fear once I sit down I'll never stand again."

They gathered near the door.

"You were terrific, Mr. Freddy!" Kade shook his hand. "Phoebe sure looked swell sitting on your shoulders. I hope I'm strong enough to carry her one day."

"You're too young to worry over pretty girls, son," Douglas told him. "There's plenty of time for that as you get older."

"But Papa, I'm not worried over Phoebe. I'm worried over my strength."

Douglas laughed. "We need to catch up with Maggie and Tabitha. We'll see you at the house."

Maxwell excused himself as well. As the group shrunk, those remaining stepped closer.

Claudio cleared his throat and looked from Henry and Darla—still with an arm around each other—to Frederick and then Melissa, who he stood between. "And which of you couples needs a

chaperone more? Who do I get to accompany to the Mellings'
house?"

Darla grinned. "After that kiss I got from Henry, I fear it's
us."

"Yes, Father De Fiore. Could you help me back up to the
dressing room first and then drive us? I'm still a bit light-headed."

"Of course Henry, but only if you call me Claudio like
everyone else."

"I will when you remove your collar." Henry turned back to
Frederick. "We'll see you soon."

Frederick gave them a head start as he stared at Melissa. Her
suit was a bit rumpled from holding Bethany in the heat, but she still
glowed with happiness.

"You were wonderful, Freddy."

"I couldn't let the opportunity pass me by for you to show
me how you feel."

Her smile renewed his energy. Frederick stepped into the
empty back hall and led her out. He dropped the towel from around
his shoulders and placed his trophy on the floor next to it. Then he
looked into Melissa's brown eyes with what he hoped was more love
than yearning.

"Do you mind us embracing when you're dressed like this?"
She looked expectant.

"Not if you don't. It will help you get your curiosity out of
the way, at least. Do you still think I'm built like James Jeffries?"

Her smiled widened. "Even finer."

Frederick opened his arms to her and she stepped within his
sphere of reach. He gently held her waist. Trailing her fingers down
his chest and across his abdominal muscles, Melissa created a shiver

of pleasure deep within his frame. He closed his eyes, savoring her touch as her hands played over his biceps and around his shoulders.

"You're marvelous, Freddy, inside and out."

They kissed and he pressed Melissa against him as tightly as he could without fear of hurting her. Her hands kneading across his sore back muscles melted him further as his lips parted and his tongue baited. Lost in the moment, he didn't hear the approaching footsteps.

"Leave it to a Yankee to teach our men to expect liberties when they win a tournament."

The voice grated, but the moment wasn't spoiled—only put on hold. When Melissa pulled back an inch, Freddy kissed her again and smiled. Then he brought his mouth to her ear. "We'll continue this later."

He stepped back, picked his things from the floor, and offered Melissa his arm as though the fact he was in nothing but his boxing shorts was typical. The bold way she made eye contact with Judith invigorated him.

"Really Mr. Davenport," Judith's sharp voice stung, or would have if he cared. "I'm beginning to question your choice in women."

"As long as you realize it doesn't include you, I have no problem with what you think." At the base of the front stairs, he looked to Melissa. "Would you hold the trophy while I change?"

She nodded and carefully took the heavy statue from him, one hand roaming up his arm. "Do you have to get dressed?"

Frederick laughed, and then kissed her as he pulled her against him once more. "I love the feel of us together, Melissa. You rejuvenate me, body, heart, and soul."

"Davenport, how about an interview?"

They turned to the question and a photographer snapped their picture.

Frederick took a slow step back from Melissa, their hands linked together a moment. "Allow me to change. I'll give you a few minutes when I return."

He found Darla in the upstairs hall.

"There's a reporter in the lobby," he told her. "I'm afraid he might heckle Melissa. Would you mind waiting with her? Claudio is more than capable of getting Henry down the stairs."

She grinned up at him. "I hope you at least kissed her before leaving."

"You may be certain of that."

***

By the time Frederick led Melissa to his automobile, the afternoon was nearly gone. After the newspaper interview, what little strength he'd clung to poured out of him as though through a sieve. When he climbed behind the steering wheel, he rested his arms upon it and dropped his head.

"You must be exhausted."

"Not too tired for you." He took her hand in his right one and brought it to his lips. "The wash basin in the changing room didn't do much for me. I need a hot shower if I'm to be fit company at Lucy's party and I should change into nicer clothes. I'll drive you home first."

"There's no need to drive me across town."

"I don't want you riding the streetcar like I've abandoned you."

"I'll accompany you to your house."

In his present state, he didn't think the implications through, but started up the Owen Touring and drove home. He carried his bag of soiled clothes and Melissa carried the trophy.

"You can find a place for it and make yourself comfortable," he told her in the front hall. "I won't take too long."

Only when his muscles relaxed under the rain of hot water did he realize he brought Melissa to his house. Alone. No children. No chaperone. And he was disrobed. Yes, it was her idea, but he should have insisted otherwise. He could have grabbed a change of clothes and showered at Lucy's. Frederick hastily dried and pulled on his underdrawers and gray suit pants. His body was still too heated to put a shirt on, but he was parched.

He clamored down the stairs and looked in the living room for Melissa. The trophy was artfully placed on the left corner of the mantel and her beige suit jacket hung in the foyer. With a smile and a spring in his step, he went for the kitchen. Melissa stood at the counter looking fresh in her white blouse as she rubbed an orange against the juicer lid of the glass pitcher. Beside the container were the rinds of several other oranges as well as a grapefruit.

"I thought you'd be thirsty." She looked up and her eyes widened. Biting her lip, she looked back to the task and finished the orange. "You still look hot."

"That's why I didn't put a shirt on. It's not too immodest for you, is it?"

Melissa's laughter brought more energy to him. "I'll never complain if you wish to go around without a shirt."

"I'll keep that in mind." He came to her side and she placed the glass in his hand.

"Drink first," she told him. "I don't want you going weak in the knees if we start kissing."

"*If*? How little you expect from me." He raised his eyebrows, took his first gulp, and then kissed her forehead. "It's good, thank you. I'd like to relax for a moment while I finish it. Join me?"

"That's why I'm here." She slipped her hand into his and they settled on the sofa.

"You're an excellent juicer, Melissa. Mine never tastes this good."

"Everything tastes better when someone else prepares it." She shifted closer.

"I'm beginning to think I won't be able to live without you." He ran his hand down her sleeve, gently urging her toward him.

Melissa leaned against him. "If only I could tuck you in my trunk and bring you back with me."

Frederick swallowed the rest and set the glass on the table. Seeing his moment, he seized it like a champion. "Let's enjoy what we have right now."

She was quick to kiss him and wasn't tentative about touching his displayed strength. They moved together to a sensual rhythm— their kisses thoughtfully executed as her hands caressed his torso and his trailed her back. Wanting to feel more, Frederick shifted sideways and slowly leaned back the length of the sofa, bringing Melissa on top of him. Seeing she didn't resist, he stretched his legs so her lower body nestled between them. He softened his kisses and reached around her head to undo her hair.

"You're beautiful, Melissa." His fingers brushed the copper strands behind her ears. "I'm honored your choices have led you to me."

She rested upon him, cheek on his chest, a finger trailing his side. "I've never felt this way before," she whispered. "It's glorious but frightening."

"Don't be scared." He tightened his arms about her, loving the feel of her body against his. "I'll protect you with my life if you accept my heart."

Melissa raised her head and fingered through the patch of hair across his chest. "I don't want to hurt you, Freddy."

"Promise me you won't and my world is yours."

"I can't promise that because I'll have to leave at some point."

"Promise me you'll be true to your heart. You owe yourself that much."

Melissa planted a kiss on his neck. "You've been wonderful to me."

His hands progressed across her back until they converged on her hips. With a grasping tug, he held her to him, watching her smile turn to hunger as her breath grew faster. He rose, urging her up and then laying her back on the sofa. Kneeling over her, he brought his lips to hers with fervent need. Her reciprocation was immediate, hands skimming along his waistband as they tasted each other. Frederick lowered upon her, trailing kisses down her jaw as he opened the top button of her shirt to get at her neck.

"Freddy," she breathed, "it all feels wonderful."

He shifted against her as he brought his kisses back to her salty neck. "I'm trying to be a gentleman."

He let their passion flare a minute more, and then he stood and helped her up. "We need to leave."

"Is this you protecting me?" She kissed the base of his throat as they held each other.

"Yes." He trailed a finger down her cheek. "How experienced are you, Melissa?"

"As much as we've shared together," she whispered.

"That makes my decision easier. I want to safeguard your purity, not overcome you."

Twenty-Nine

Melissa sat beside Freddy on their cross-town drive, her hand resting on his knee. His suit jacket was in the backseat, but she wore hers because she didn't want to return less dressed from when the others last saw her. Thinking about the sensations being with Freddy evoked warmed her cheeks, and his insistence in protecting her increased his appeal.

When they pulled in at the Mellings' house, sounds of children playing squealed across the yard. Alex paced the front porch smoking a cigarette, appraising them both as they approached.

"Everything okay?" he asked when they reached the steps.

"I had to do an interview before we left and then needed a shower to feel human. We stopped at my house for a few minutes."

Alex smirked and exhaled a ring of smoke.

Freddy held to Melissa's arm as though afraid she would run. "We're both mature adults."

"Don't I know it." He took another drag. "The honorable Frederick Davenport is always above suspicion, but a cad like Alexander Melling is guilty until proven innocent."

Freddy laughed. "You and Eddie that winter. Well, I suppose there's nothing to laugh about, but at least it's in the past."

"So it is." Alex snuffed his cigarette in the ashtray.

"Why do you smoke out here?" Melissa asked in hopes of changing the subject.

Alex smiled. "Unlike New Yorkers, we southern gentlemen still abide by the etiquette that it's rude to smoke in front of women. I have no den in the house and Lucy doesn't like the smell, so I keep my habit to the porch." Alex nodded to Freddy as he held the screen open. "I suppose you still don't indulge."

"Those that smoke are out of breath first in the ring. And living with Lucy four years prevented me from picking it up. She doesn't like the taste of it." Freddy's voice was more cutting than teasing.

In the foyer, Alex grabbed a few mints out of the bowl on the credenza and tossed them in his mouth with a smirk. "But she does like peppermint."

Melissa stepped between the men. "I'm going to freshen up."

Freddy kept hold of her elbow. "Why don't you say hello to everyone first?"

"The women are in the parlor and the men are with the kids out back," Alexander informed them.

As soon as they were in the parlor doorway, Lucy embraced Freddy in a way that left no room for Melissa to stay by his side. Lucy's blonde veil curled at the sash of an exquisite lavender evening gown that accentuated her figure. The cream colored lace camisole gave the illusion that she was bare beneath the open areas of the top and beckoned one to look closer.

"You were wonderful Freddy, though I don't think I'll be able to look at you the same ever again." Her hands were on his chest in a way that showed she claimed him as a pet.

He took her hands in his and kissed her cheek as he stepped away. "You won't have to, Goosy. Let me greet Maggie and introduce her to Melissa."

Freddy went for the armchair where a pretty brunette rested in a classic blue gown. He helped her stand and kissed her cheek. "You look glorious, Maggie."

"You're too kind, Frederick." She hugged him in return, causing Melissa's stomach to churn. "I'm sorry I missed your tournament, but after hearing the reports of the heat, I know I chose well."

"You did all right with Tabitha by yourself?"

"Yes, and we left the packages at the stores until Douglas could collect them. I was able to purchase Easter clothes for the children and this new dress for myself."

"Wonderful." He tucked her arm under his and stepped toward Melissa with shining eyes. "I'd like you to meet Melissa Stone. Melissa, this is Magdalene Campbell."

"Welcome to the fold, Melissa. Please call me Maggie. I feel as though we've already met with all I've heard about you." She hugged Melissa and took her hands. "I'm not afraid to say it, so forgive me if this is too bold, but as much as he claims not to need us, we're all protective of Frederick. Tread lightly."

Freddy crossed his arms and looked at Maggie with exaggerated disdain. "Then I suppose I'll leave you ladies to swap stories with her."

"Don't give Lucy any ideas, Mr. Davenport." Darla's voice was too hard to pass as teasing.

He looked at the younger woman with disappointment but kept quiet as he crossed to Melissa, leaving a kiss at the corner of her mouth that stirred a smile to the surface of her unease. Freddy turned to Lucy on his way out. "Thank you for hosting us, Goosy. That gown is perfect on you." He leaned in and whispered something that caused her to smile and her cheeks to pink.

"And what was that about, Lucy?" Maggie reclaimed her seat and motioned Melissa to the settee with Darla.

"He always knows how to cheer me up." Lucy flounced to the armchair opposite Maggie and poured more lemonade into her glass.

"And?" Darla leaned forward, staring at Lucy. "Don't you think Melissa deserves to hear?"

"There's nothing to be concerned about. If Freddy had wanted everyone to know, he would have spoken out loud." Lucy crossed her ankles, smoothed her skirt, and sipped her lemonade.

Darla offered a noise of disgust.

Maggie started laughing, and then Lucy joined in.

"Really, Darla," Maggie said. "You treat Lucy as if she's the most uptight woman in the world. She's teasing you."

"I've yet to understand her humor." Darla huffed and leaned back.

"If you'd all excuse me, I'd like to freshen and change," Melissa said, hoping to escape the tension in the room.

"Feel free to shove our things out of the way," Maggie said. "I try to keep the bathroom tidy, but it's not always easy with the children running about."

Melissa stood. "I won't be long."

Lucy followed, stopping her at the base of the stairs. "Darla fusses over how Freddy and I are. She doesn't understand our relationship and she doesn't need to hear what's between us, but I want to tell you, Melissa."

She set her hand on the banister. "Don't feel you have to explain."

"I'm glad you didn't hold anything against him after my episode last week."

"Lucy, you're a beautiful woman, his first love, and the mother of his children. Only a fool would expect him to not have a connection to you. Or worse, try to sever it."

"Thank you, Melissa." Tears welled in her green eyes. "I've feared the day when I'd have to share Frederick with another woman. He's my dearest friend and I won't be able to live without him."

"I'd never ask that of either of you."

Lucy gave a hiccup-sob-laugh. "He always knows how to cheer me up. He saw how biting Darla was—she gets that way when she's defensive of Freddy—and wanted to lift my mood. He told me I look as good as I smell and Alex won't be able to keep his hands off me."

Melissa smiled and took Lucy's hand. "Your dress is gorgeous."

Half an hour later, Melissa returned to the parlor showered, changed into the sage green afternoon dress Freddy only had a peek of the week before, and hair braided and wrapped into a bun.

"Where'd Lucy go?" Melissa asked as she settled beside Darla.

"Stepped out a minute ago to check on the food preparations," she explained.

"Now," Maggie said, "what was it you wanted to ask me, Darla?"

Her cherubic face blushed. "About my wedding night. I didn't want to ask in front of Lucy, but if she comes in while we're talking, don't stop. I'm not sure how much longer the men will be outside."

Melissa straightened in her seat, trying not to look too interested.

"You've delivered enough babies to—"

"I know the body parts, both male and female. I know he"—Darla dropped her voice—"will enter me, but what do I do, lay there?"

Maggie laughed. "If you have enough restraint to lie there, I'd be surprised. Douglas could hardly keep me off of him our first week. Of course, that could have been something to do with Seacliff Cottage, but I like to think it had more to do with my passion for him than possession."

Darla's blue eyes widened. "*Off of him?*"

Maggie leaned closer. "Have you ever been able to kiss, I mean really kiss and touch without an audience?"

"You know how my aunt is, but we've managed a few times. Most recently was on the visit at his family's house. We were on horseback and stopped for a break by a creek. We laid in the grass together." Darla's hands covered her rosy cheeks. "I could tell he was very much in the moment. We were facing each other, kissing, and then he jumped up claiming a bee was buzzing him."

"Let me guess," Maggie teased, "there was no bee."

"Not at all. Just my sweet Henry, whose muscles look and feel much better without a shirt covering them."

Maggie laughed. "Have you felt stirrings in your body when close to him. Impulses? Cravings?"

"What started as a flutter in my stomach has grown into tingling and blood rushing and all manner of electricity." Darla clasped her hands. "Is that normal?"

"Yes," Melissa and Maggie said at the same time.

They all laughed, and then Maggie continued. "Those feelings will help guide you to do what's pleasurable."

Lucy slipped into the room in her lavender glory, silently taking her previous chair.

Maggie took Darla's hand. "When there are no barriers for you and Henry, just let those feelings run free. You'll find what you both enjoy. Start with kissing and hugging as you're used to, and it will all go naturally from there."

"After your wedding. Everything will be more enjoyable when it isn't a sin."

The three women turned to Lucy.

Maggie heaved to her feet and crossed to her with open arms. Lucy stood and embraced her. "Your thoughts and experiences are just as important, Lucy."

Maggie brought her to the settee and the four squeezed together. Their dresses overlapped in a giant green-purple-yellow-blue stripe.

"What should I expect, Lucy?" Darla whispered.

"It's like the heavens are created and everything is right in the world. There can be slight discomfort when he goes in the first few times, but it won't last and you'll feel so much of everything else you won't care. But more importantly, you'll fall more in love with him than you thought possible after sharing the experience."

Maggie reached across Darla to take Lucy's hand. "You're so right."

"I wrote a poem for Alex after our first time. Would you like to read it?"

"Yes!" Maggie practically jumped off the seat.

Darla nodded in agreement.

"Melissa?" Lucy raised her eyebrows.

All she could think of was Lucy's poem confessing her sin with Freddy. "If it's not too personal."

Lucy dashed to her study and returned with a red leather journal. "I had a special compartment built into the chaise to hold my poems for Alex."

"I'm sorry about my first day," Melissa said. "I had no idea it was such an important piece of furniture."

Lucy waved her hand. "It's forgotten, Melissa. All the poems I wrote Alex when we courted I thought were lost as he had the only copies. He had them all memorized and kept originals at the Government Street house when he traveled. After the Seacliff Cottage fire, Claudio went to say goodbye to Mrs. Melling before he left for Louisiana. He went into Alex's room and retrieved a few of his personal things he asked for, including my poems. I've since recorded them all in here and add new ones to it."

Maggie stroked the cover. "The secret love poems of the great Olive Kent."

Lucy's radiant smile reflected on all their faces. "I'll read aloud."

Forever

We became man and wife by our actions

Before anyone could turn us away

You recited poetry

My words on your lips seduced me

As they had seduced you on paper

The sweat and sounds we created together

Salty and sweet awash in my mouth

Your hands over my skin

Mine on yours

Your scent all around me

In me

Your impassioned words as I cried out

You showed me much

But there is more to learn

Know that I'm forever yours

And I'll need this again soon

Melissa stared at the open book trying to process the inner workings of Lucy's emotions. "That's not the same author who wrote *Azalea Blossom*."

"No," Lucy said as she shut the book, "I was a changed woman from the time these poems begin. I'd never been kissed when I wrote my first four books. Excuse me a moment while I return this. Alex will expect a new entry if he sees me with it."

When Lucy returned to the parlor, Alex followed. His hands went about her middle from behind.

"Watch," Maggie whispered to Darla, "Alex is a master in the art of love making. See where his hands and mouth touch. Those are areas that give the most response. Kissing her ear and neck, hands on her ribs and hips. And he keeps it all light, not having to use force to entice her."

Darla's face reddened. "I usually look away when they go at it."

Alex turned Lucy to face him, lips lowering to her collarbones.

Maggie's exhale was sharp, her hand on her throat. "He was the first to kiss me there."

As though he knew they were talking about him, Alex raised his head and looked over Lucy's shoulder at them with a sultry smile. "And what do you think, my darlings?"

"I remember how good you felt against my skin," Maggie boldly stated.

A fire lit within his clear blue eyes. Alex waltzed Lucy to the settee and she dropped into her place between Melissa and Darla.

"My rainbow of beauties." Alex smiled at each in turn before offering a hand to Maggie. "Come, Magdalene."

His hand was low on her back, the other caressed her arm as he danced her around the room in a sinuous flow.

"He is good," Darla whispered.

Melissa looked to Lucy, witnessing her face as her smile fell into terror. Alex's eyes clouded with a sinister gaze of longing as his face lowered to Maggie's neck.

"Darla, get Claudio!" Melissa ordered as she took hold of Lucy's hands. "He must be overcome, Lucy. He loves you, you know he does."

Lucy's scream rang in Melissa's ears, but Alex and Maggie continued their sensual dance.

Thirty

Upon hearing Lucy's scream, Frederick rushed in the house. Darla collided with him in the hall. He gripped her arm to steady her.

"I'm getting Claudio!" She hurried out the back.

Frederick assessed the situation in one glance—Lucy crying on the settee and Alexander locked in an erotic dance with Maggie. He went for the couple.

"Release her."

"Magdalene is ours." Alexander's lips brushed against her cheek as Lucy's sobs increased.

"Maggie, please step away." Frederick took a fist full of Alexander's hair from behind, stopping his movements.

Maggie tried to oblige by lowering her arms, but Alexander still had an arm around her middle and her hand in his.

"The dance is over, Alex. Release her."

"She belongs to us!"

"Look at me, Maggie." Frederick held her gaze over Alexander's shoulder. "Can you get free without hurting yourself?"

Maggie struggled a moment before raising her free hand to slap Alexander's cheek as Douglas and Claudio ran in.

Douglas caught his wife by the elbow, narrowing his eyes at Alexander. "What the devil has come over you? I thought you were beyond this, Alex."

Alexander dropped to his knees. Seeing his penitent stance, Frederick stepped to the side.

"Forgive me!" Alexander looked to the Campbells, agony etched on his face. Then he rent his shirt, buttons flinging across the room. "It's in me once more!"

His scars burned red across his chest and up his arms as he tore the shirt from his limbs. Alexander lunged at Claudio. "Kill me! Kill me before I do more harm!"

Frederick went for Lucy, wrapping both her and Melissa in his embrace. Speaking directly into Melissa's ear, he gave directions. "You need to go to the yard and be sure that under no circumstances any of the children come inside the house. Do you understand?"

She nodded, releasing Lucy to his care.

"I trust you to safeguard my girls."

Melissa squeezed his hand before stumbling from the room.

It was difficult to tell who had hold of whom between Claudio and Alexander. There seemed to be a grapple for hold on Alexander's slim body between priest, demon, and man. Claudio brandishing his crucifix and the Melling scratching his own skin.

Lucy cleaved to Frederick as she watched her husband's plight. "Help him, please!"

He smoothed her loose hair from her face. "You know I would if I could, but I don't know how, Goosy."

Alexander began thrashing and slipped to Claudio's feet. Douglas motioned Maggie to the settee and dropped to the floor to help.

"It's in me! Cut it from me before I wound Lucy!" His body broke into a sweat.

"Alex!" Lucy sprung from her seat, Frederick catching her around the waist.

In a surge of emotions, Lucy tore free and fell beside Alexander in a heap of tears. Frederick went for Lucy, but Claudio raised a hand to stop him before he could pull her away.

"My queen, I've failed you once more."

"You haven't, Alex. I love you." She kissed his lips. "Please don't hurt yourself."

"I feel it battling to take control." He arched away from her, teeth gritted. "Claudio, you must ask about the power. I'll not continue to fight. Find out how the evil came into the house when I lose myself. We need to end this infestation. Take her, Freddy! Take Lucy out of the room!"

Frederick lifted Lucy with one arm and swung her over his shoulder. After placing her on the chaise in the study, he took her hand, kissing her knuckles. "Claudio won't forsake him. I know you're scared, Goosy, but try to pray."

Maggie came in and laid a hand on Frederick's shoulder. "They need your help. I'll stay with her." She sat beside Lucy. "I'm sorry, Lucy. He swept me away like no time had passed. I forgot myself a moment."

Frederick left Alexander's lovers to come to their own understanding. He closed the parlor's pocket doors behind him, dropping to the floor beside Claudio, who held Alexander's shoulders while Douglas pressed his ankles to the ground. Frederick couldn't help but think they were lucky it wasn't him in need of controlling.

"Frederick, take his wrists and hold his arms straight over his head so he can no longer wound himself."

As soon as Frederick took over subduing Alexander, Claudio had a crucifix on his friend's forehead and prayed. Alexander's strength seemed to grow, taking more effort to hold him. He grew talkative, speaking what appeared to be fluent Italian. Claudio asked questions, and based on his tone, Alexander gave biting replies.

After several minutes, Claudio seemed to lose his patience. "Where is the source of your power?"

"Pirate treasure, brought by the outsider. But now we're home with the ones from the house on the cliff." Alexander broke a leg free from Douglas and tried to leverage himself away. "We want our loves. We need to take one once more. This body was created for pleasure. This vessel isn't complete without it and you, filthy priest, have made this mortal wait. He's weak from his needs. He craves whatever flesh he can get."

Douglas yanked Alexander back into submission. "Insufferable wretch."

Frederick caught his eye and nodded his agreement.

"It is not him," Claudio reminded. Then he was back to speaking in such a way that Frederick knew he was casting out the demon.

He watched the minutes tick by on the mantel clock.

Five minutes of constant struggling against Alexander's fit.

Ten minutes later, he seemed to calm.

Quarter of an hour.

"We're almost there," Claudio whispered.

Frederick caught movement outside the front window. Melissa in her lovely dress holding a lifeless Bethany to her chest. He bolted to the front door and snatched his daughter, feeling like he touched a hot stove.

"Was there an accident?" he asked, checking Bethany's body for harm.

"No, she grew increasingly lethargic, whimpering a little. She's burning up. Darla thought you should know. I don't think it's good for her to be out in the breeze. At least pass me a blanket for the time being."

"No." He held her to his chest, swaying on his feet. "She needs a bath to help regulate her temperature. Will you go draw a cool one?"

"Of course."

He grabbed her hand. "And the others?"

"Phoebe is fine and the Campbell children as well. Henry and Darla are watching over them." She tenderly touched Bethany's cheek before running up the stairs.

"Claudio!" Frederick called. "Is it done?"

"*Sí*, what is going on?"

He carried Bethany toward the stairs. Claudio came to him in the hall, reaching with his hand holding the cross. Bethany shrieked in pain.

"Frederick—"

"I know! Cleanse the house and find the evil, then come to us."

"Was that Bethany?" Lucy exited the study, Maggie at her side.

"Stay back." Frederick held his daughter tighter. "See to Alex, I've got her."

"But what—"

"Fever. I've handled it before." He took the steps as quickly as he could without jostling his precious load.

In the bathroom, the tub was half full. Melissa went to turn it off.

"No, take her first."

Melissa cradled Bethany to her shoulder and Frederick started pulling off his clothes. "Freddy, I think someone else—"

He looked at Melissa's tight face as he dropped his pants. "There's no time." He hopped into the claw foot tub in his underdrawers, muscles tightening at the coolness of the water. "Take off her clothes and hand her to me. Let the rest of the space fill with warm water. Shut it off once it's as high as her neck."

Frederick leaned against the porcelain back, taking Bethany to his chest as the bathtub continued to fill. She fussed but didn't cry. She hadn't strength for tears. He wrapped his arms around her, hugging her to his bare chest.

"God, please don't take her." Her forehead was unearthly hot beneath his lips. "Daddy's here, Beth. Stay with me, Little Princess."

"Tell me what to do," Melissa whispered.

"Pray." He closed his eyes against the pain.

Thirty-One

Freddy asked the one thing Melissa felt inept doing. She couldn't come close to the beautiful prayers Claudio offered or the prayers Alex gave over their food. She tried to remember the words to "Hail, Mary", but then remembered Freddy wasn't Catholic. Was Bethany? She assumed the girls attended church with their father on Sundays, but Freddy had allowed Claudio to bless them. Melissa settled on whispering The Lord's Prayer while she hung Freddy's clothes on the hook behind the door. She leaned against the far wall, trying not to look upon him because seeing him raw with pain took a toll on her heart. The sound of someone running up the stairs brought her unrealistic hope.

Douglas came to a halt on the tile floor, looking first at Melissa and then into the bathtub. "Claudio wanted me to check on Bethany."

"She's holding on," Frederick replied. "Could you light the fire in the girls' room?"

"Yes." He stroked his red beard, an eyebrow arched over a blue eye as he looked to Melissa. "Claudio needs to speak with you."

She looked to Freddy. "Do you—"

"Go. I'll stay a few minutes more. Please get the fire going, Douglas."

Melissa went in search of Claudio and found him blessing Lucy in the parlor. She was on the end of the settee, Alex lying across her lap, a bandage wrapped about his shirtless chest. The priest looked up when he was done, catching Melissa's eye.

"Come." Claudio took her by the elbow, stopping to tell Maggie to keep an eye on Alex. "But not too good of an eye, *Posseduta.*"

Maggie's punch struck his upper arm, generating a sharp laugh before Claudio turned serious. He came to a stop with Melissa in the hall.

"Alex willingly gave himself to possession so we could learn where the Voodoo power is and destroy it."

"What?"

"*Sí*, he stopped fighting the demon so I could question it. It said you brought the power here with a pirate treasure. Do you know what that means?"

In startling clarity the brooch loomed in her mind. Hepzibah. The jeweler. She was blind not to have put it together before now. *Has the evil addled my head?*

Claudio followed her up the stairs. When they reached her room, he began praying as though he sensed the presence of the talisman. Unable to touch it now that she knew what it was, Melissa used a handkerchief to lift the gold and emerald brooch from the drawer and dropped it wrapped into Claudio's outstretched hand.

"I wore it today." Her eyes filled with tears. "I wore it to the tournament and Bethany touched it the whole time she was in my lap."

"It is not your fault, *signorina.*"

"Freddy will despise me."

"No, *sig*—"

"If something happens to Beth—"

Claudio dropped the cursed item onto the bed and took hold of Melissa, speaking soothingly in Italian until her breathing calmed. "Go, see if help is needed."

She felt her guilt displayed on her face as she entered the bathroom. Freddy was still there with Bethany on his chest.

"Take her. We need to get her warmed."

"But Freddy—"

"There's no time, Melissa. You saw me in my boxing shorts today. This isn't much different."

Melissa needed to explain that it was her fault—that her "treasure", as Phoebe called it, caused his daughter's illness. She took a lavender scented towel from the shelf in the corner and spread it wide to accept Bethany. As she wrapped her in the white softness, Bethany began to convulse.

Freddy stumbled out of the tub, reaching for her as he slipped on the tiles in his dripping state. Steadying himself, he tucked Bethany to his chest and charged for her bedroom. Melissa paused to look into her own room. Claudio continued to pray over the brooch.

"Claudio, help us!"

Freddy knelt on the rug before the hearth, trying to keep the towel about his daughter as her body twitched. Claudio came in, still reciting over the brooch.

Melissa took his arm. "Go to Bethany instead."

"The object must be cleansed. She should heal when it is done."

"She might not make it that long!"

The priest stood over Freddy and his daughter, the pin on the handkerchief in his hand.

"God, don't take her from me," Freddy pleaded.

Hesitating over them, Claudio continued to recite his prayers in Latin. Unable to stand idle a moment longer, Melissa caught the corner of the handkerchief and flung the brooch into the fireplace. With a hiss and flare of green flames, the fire consumed the jewel.

Bethany's seizure abruptly stopped.

No chest movement.

No twitch of a finger.

Freddy looked with horror from his daughter to Melissa's raised hand. "What did you—"

Then Bethany's body heaved with breath and she cried. Freddy scooped her into his arms, hugging her to his damp chest.

Unable to face the fright in Freddy's eyes with which he'd looked upon her, Melissa locked herself in her bedroom. None of them would wish to speak to her when they discovered she was the means by which the evil had infested their lives. The man stalking their house, leaving dead roosters and hexes. Because of her, Lucy tried to seduce Freddy, and Alex Maggie. Alex, who had overcome so much only for her to bring it all back. And worse still was Bethany, near death with fever and convulsions.

Eyes blurry with unshed tears, Melissa pulled her trunk to the middle of the room and began folding her clothing into it. It was halfway full when a knock sounded on her door.

"I'll telephone for a taxi within the hour," she called.

The knob rattled. "Melissa, what do you mean?"

Freddy. "I won't be here much longer. You needn't worry."

"Open the door!"

She wanted to, but his pain was too fresh in her mind.

The door swung inward and Freddy—still in his wet underdrawers—stood on the threshold, Bethany in a cotton nightdress clinging to his neck. He looked from her surprised face to her open trunk. "What do you think you're doing?"

"Packing. Everyone will be upset with me for—"

His right hand went to her shoulder. "You saved her, Melissa. Claudio was stuck in his procedures, but you did what had to be done. Thank you."

She closed her eyes, reflexively leaning into his touch. "But it's my fault. I brought the evil here."

"You saved us." Freddy nudged the door shut with his foot and set Bethany beside him. His hands came to either side of Melissa's face as he lowered his mouth to hers, thumbs stroking her neck. Without meaning to, her arms went about him—his skin cool from the tepid bath. "We still have weeks together, Melissa. Don't leave me."

She brought a hand to his jaw, shadowed with stubble. "Everyone will be upset with me."

"It wasn't you." His lips touched her throat, weakening her resolve to blame herself.

"But Alex—"

"He has purposely caused more harm to people than you think you've done accidentally."

There was a tug on her dress.

"Sissa."

Melissa and Freddy looked down. Bethany clung to the green skirt, one arm reaching up.

"Even Beth wants more time with you." Freddy handed her to Melissa, kissing them both. "Don't disappoint us."

"You've made your point." Melissa rested her head against Bethany's. "Now do you think you could get dressed before someone finds you in my room like this?"

Freddy blushed but pulled her to him once more. "You'll watch Beth for me?"

"Of course, but how did you get in here when I'd locked the door?"

"I know all the tricks in the old Easton house."

***

When they returned to the parlor, Freddy was fully dressed. Even Alex wore a fresh shirt as he lounged beside Lucy. Maggie and Douglas were in armchairs they'd pulled together, leaning against each other's shoulders. The priest gazed into the darkening front yard.

Lucy stood, arms open. "She's all right now?"

"Yes, thanks to Melissa and Claudio." Freddy brought Bethany to her, and then placed a hand on Alex's shoulder. "Thank you for your part. Your sacrifice was great."

Alex's eyes were the color of the sky on a crisp spring morning as he smiled. "It's Melissa who solved it."

"Only because the information that came through you." Melissa stood beside Freddy, facing the Mellings. "I'm sorry. I had no idea that the brooch harbored such evil. I never would have—"

Alex kissed the back of her hand. "We never thought that of you."

"It is time to bring the others inside," Claudio announced. "One at a time, so I may bless them."

Maggie stood. "Please allow me get Tabitha first."

Freddy brought Melissa to a chair and stood beside her. They watched in silence as Tabitha, Kade, and Phoebe were blessed, followed by Darla and Henry.

Soon after, the large dining table was full—Bethany's high chair the thirteenth seat. Lucy wasn't pretentious enough for name cards, but Melissa was pleased when Freddy kept her at his side when they chose seats. If anyone could claim the head and foot of the table it would have been Phoebe and Claudio, which was a perfect example of who ran things around the place. Throughout supper, Melissa was alert to those across the table—Alex, flanked by Lucy and Maggie. While Lucy was the focus of most of his attentions, he played charming with the other woman. After witnessing the dance the two shared, Melissa wondered more about the happenings in the infamous Seacliff Cottage. Surely there was something between them because Lucy hadn't minded the other woman dancing with Alex until his gaze darkened with lust.

When Henry finished eating his slice of lemon cake, Darla sent him to his automobile to collect a surprise, which they set up in the parlor. All the furniture was pushed to the edges of the room and the gramophone sat ready in the corner. They started a ragtime recording, which sounded strange in the space so often filled with Tchaikovsky. The couple began with a flourishing cake walk, to which the children clapped along.

"And this is the dance causing scandals in social halls across the country," Darla said as Henry set the next recording. "The Turkey Trot."

Only in the Mellings' house would the cheek-to-cheek dancing not be scandalous. Coupled with the press of their bodies together, Henry's and Darla's fast footwork and flapping elbows were remarkable.

"They move well together," Melissa said.

Freddy leaned toward her. "I bet we do as well, but I'm not one to dance like that."

"Wouldn't you even try?"

"And make a fool of myself?"

"I doubt that. Even Alex said you're a fine dancer."

Noticing Melissa trying to sway him, Henry joined the urging. "Come on, Davenport. Take Melissa for a spin."

"After the day I had in the ring?"

"Dance, Daddy!" Phoebe bounced in front of him. "Dance with Miss Melissa!"

As though he found the change in Phoebe's attitude toward Melissa as heartening as she did, Freddy wasted no time getting to his feet. He held Melissa's hands as they stood beside Darla and Henry, watching their instructions a minute. Then Alex restarted the recording and the young couple took off around the room full speed.

Melissa and Freddy stumbled through the first song, laughing and enjoying themselves. By the second tune they had the rhythm, even if their moves were slightly different from the others.

"You'll have to go dancing with us one night," Darla said as the record ended. "You're better than most people we see out."

Freddy hung his arm around Melissa's shoulders. "Would you like that?" he whispered.

She nodded.

"Just tell me the night and I'll keep the girls," Lucy assured them. "Alex, I'd like to take a turn. That is, if you aren't too tired from your ordeal this afternoon."

"You know better than to question my stamina, my queen." He pulled her into his arms and flashed a roguish grin.

Maggie laughed and snuggled against Douglas on the settee as Freddy switched recording for the familiar strains of "Swan Lake."

"Keep dancing," Lucy told the others. "Alex and I don't need the floor to ourselves."

"*Sí*, privacy or not, they will do as they please." Everyone laughed. Claudio approached Maggie, hand open. "*Posseduta*, will you share a dance with me?"

Claudio and Maggie, Henry and Darla, Alex and Lucy, and Freddy and Melissa twirled about the room. Kade and Phoebe joined in, trying to emulate the adults. Everyone smiled over the four-year-olds except Freddy.

"What's wrong?" Melissa asked.

He rested his head against hers. "I'm not ready for that."

"Children play at being adults, that's what they do."

"But is this unconventional group the right one to show them how to behave?" He sighed. "I fear I'll lead the girls wrong."

"You're a gentleman and a fine example."

"I'm a twice married, divorced man who wants nothing more than to take his dancing partner back to her bedroom where he was with her earlier in only his under shorts. What type of example is that?"

Melissa laughed. "A human one, but you don't act on all the thoughts you have, which proves you're honorable and brave, qualities your girls will cherish."

Freddy dropped the pretense of the dance as he pulled her against him, one arm low about her waist, the other around her shoulders as he walked her backward into the hall. "I need you. I need your insight and wit. There's too much doubt in my head these days, but you chase it all away. Everything is clear when I'm with you."

He took her hand and brought her to the stairs. Fearing for a brief moment that he was going to bring her to her bedroom, Melissa sighed in relief when he sat several steps up. He guided her to sit between his legs, lightly rubbing her back with one hand.

"I enjoy being with you, Freddy. As much as you claim I'm good for you, you're equally great for me."

His hand rested on her shoulder. "Am I moving too fast for you? I don't want to chase you away by being too forward."

"Not at all."

"At my age, I know what I want and I've learned not to put off expressing it."

"At *our* age, Freddy. And I respect that about you. I can't get a straight answer from people in the city about anything. Your honesty is refreshing."

The music ended and Phoebe peeked around the parlor doorway. "It's okay. They aren't kissing!"

Melissa savored the rumble of Freddy's laugh. "I'm pleased Phoebe appears to like you now. I'm beginning to think it was the brooch that turned her against you."

"That would be a convenient explanation."

New music started in the parlor, followed by Phoebe squealing in delight.

"And easier for you to meld into my family."

The taste of his kisses loomed in Melissa's mind as the sadness of what was to come overshadowed her. "Freddy, I'll have to leave when Lucy finishes the manuscript. I have to turn in her book and I have my project I need to pitch to Mr. Noble. I can't walk away from my responsibilities and the career goal I've been working towards for a decade."

"The essay collection?"

Pleased he'd remembered from their previous conversations, she smiled. "Yes."

"I'm sure you'll do well, Melissa. Though I can't say the same for me once you're gone."

"Daddy, come see! Momma and Mr. Alex taught me and Kade how to tango!"

Freddy's forehead dropped to Melissa's shoulder. "Now do you see why I worry about the example this group sets?"

Thirty-Two

Sunday afternoon, the Campbells left after dinner. Claudio stayed to bless the house and inhabitants, and then Lucy settled in the study to write. The parlor window was open. Melissa, curled in an armchair in the front room with her journal, couldn't help but witness Alex and Claudio on the porch.

The odor of their cigarettes wafted through the window along with Alex's words. "Are we safe now?"

"*Sí*, Lucy has been clear since the exorcism last weekend. And you seem as good as ever after the incident yesterday. I even checked the remains of the brooch and there is no lingering curse on it. I do not know what Melissa plans on doing with it, but it is now a harmless lump of gold and gemstones."

Alex exhaled a smoke ring. "So Lucy and I are—"

"Why do I think that this week you have been as concerned about your own needs as much as the safety of Lucy?"

"Because it's true." He stuck the cigarette in his mouth and thrust his hips in an obscene manner. "I crave Lucy, the rhythm we share."

Claudio threw his hands in the air. "I can do nothing for you when you are like this."

"It's been a long ten days, Claudio. It's no wonder the demon was able to take me. I'm weak for lack of sharing flesh with my wife."

"You are shameless." He clapped Alex's shoulder and tightened. "You may go to her, but wait until night when you can take your time. I will see you tomorrow."

Alex paced the porch a minute after Claudio left and then hurried inside.

When he got within view of the parlor door, Melissa called out. "Don't you dare interrupt! She got nothing done yesterday."

He laughed. "Claudio told me to wait as well."

"So I heard. Everything. And saw your outlandish moves."

"I'm sure you didn't find it as thrilling as Turkey Trotting with Freddy."

Melissa laughed. "You're surprisingly humble after your impetuous display."

"I know when I'm bested by Frederick Davenport." Alex's cocky smile was contagious.

"And don't you forget it."

Alex settled with the newspaper on the settee. It sported a photograph of Frederick with Bethany on his shoulders on the front page under the headline CROWD FAVORITE AT TOURNAMENT.

After supper, Melissa took a shower and washed her hair. When she stepped into the hall in her pajamas and robe, the sounds of Alex and Lucy in their bedroom filled the space. Knowing that they had waited an eternity according to Alex's standards, she couldn't complain, but she did clamp her pillow around her ears until she fell asleep.

When Melissa returned from her Monday morning walk, Alex stood in the kitchen staring out the back window.

"Is everything okay?" She went for the kettle.

"Wonderful." His eyes gleamed.

"I think the whole neighborhood might know how wonderful things are for you and Lucy after last night."

Alex took his toast and coffee to the back porch table, gyrating his hips on the way. "All is great with the Mellings." As though thinking better of his display, he turned back. "You will join me, won't you?"

"Only if you behave yourself."

His charming smile nearly broke her resolve to keep a safe distance from him. After witnessing Maggie with him all weekend, she promised herself she wouldn't to turn into another swooning female around him. But Alex drew Melissa into his fantastical world more so than anyone else. His life of demons and romance, death and life, lust and bravery. A knight for the modern world, shadowed by his past.

Phoebe found them laughing in the breakfast nook ten minutes later.

"Miss Melissa!" Phoebe offered her a bouquet of bridal wreath—clusters of tiny white flowers that usually grew beside azalea bushes about town. "For you!"

To Melissa's astonishment, the girl threw her arms about her for a hug before clinging to Alex for attention.

"Thank you, Phoebe. They're beautiful." She gathered her dishes and brought the flowers to the kitchen to locate a vase for them.

She carried the filled glass through the swinging door and found Bethany toddling around the front hall holding her doll. "Good morning, Beth."

"Sissa!" She reached for Melissa.

She picked up the girl. "I need to bring these flowers to my room."

The first thing she noticed when she walked in was a box of chocolates in the middle of her bedspread. Melissa set the flowers on her dresser and then placed the sampler beside it. Bethany wiggled to be set down and then went for her bedroom across the hall.

Melissa followed and came face-to-face with Freddy.

"Good morning, Melissa." He hugged her. "Yesterday was incredibly long without you."

"Thank you for the chocolates." She wrapped her arms about his neck and kissed him. "And Phoebe was a surprise with her flowers."

His shy smile warmed her more than the coffee. "That was her idea."

She leaned against him, inhaling his aftershave in an attempt to memorize the scent.

"I'll find out from Henry which night we'll go dancing." He started into the steps of the Turkey Trot.

Melissa laughed. "I'm glad you enjoyed the new style. It's fun, and we do move well together."

"Yes, we do." Then his mouth was upon hers, playful and soft. "But I need to get to the office. May I see you and Bethany downstairs?"

"Daddy." His daughter reached for him, her doll and a stuffed puppy wedged under her arms.

"Could I ask a favor?" Melissa took his arm as they went for the stairs.

"I'd be forlorn if you didn't think you could ask me."

"I need to go downtown this afternoon to pick up my photographs and see to a few things. If I can make it to your office by five, would you mind giving me a ride back?"

"I'd love to."

Melissa released his arm downstairs. "But it's your gym day. Never mind."

"Do you think you could get to my office by four-thirty? If so, the bookshop isn't far from the gym and it's open until six. You could browse while I workout and then we could grab dinner before coming back."

Melissa thought of her plan to be at the jewelers before three o'clock to confront the Jamaican. "Yes, that should be plenty of time."

***

Lucy didn't come out of her bedroom until close to nine and drank her coffee with a wistful expression. Every so often, one of the girls would lay a hand on her knee or climb beside her on the settee to show her a toy or a picture in a book. She would focus on them when prompted, but then was back to daydreaming. When Darla arrived at ten, Phoebe begged to play outside.

"Keep them in the back please, Darla." Lucy looked to Melissa. "Could you come with me a moment?"

Following Lucy into the study, Melissa noticed her hair was braided recklessly. "Are you all right today?"

"I had a late night with Alex, but everything's great." Her curling smile unwound. "It was magical, like the first time after we were married, but even better."

"Did you call me in here to discuss your bedroom practices?"

Lucy laughed. "No, but I thought I might find a sympathetic ear." She turned serious and placed her hands low on her abdomen. "I feel different. Full, like Alex is still within me."

Melissa shifted the weight from one foot to another. "Lucy, this is more Darla's specialty than mine. I don't see how—"

"It's probably my imagination, but still it's there and I have hope."

Melissa's smile was one near pity. "I'm glad for you. Now what can I do to help you with your deadline?"

"I should have the draft done by the end of the month, but then I'll need to go back through it with my notes and insert the details to help lay the groundwork for the mystery. I was thinking once I mark the pages with what needs to be added, you might help me retype them. The chapters from wherever the additions are will need to be retyped."

"The whole manuscript might need to be retyped?"

Lucy nodded. "We could fit another desk and typewriter in here, if you're willing."

"Of course, that's why Mr. Noble sent me. I'll do whatever it takes to see that you meet your deadline."

Lucy hugged her. "I'll work hard, Melissa. I remember what you told Alex when you came. I'll see that it happens so you can enjoy your special day with your friends in New York."

Melissa went out the back door, a dazed look on her face.

"What is it?" Darla led her to a bench in the gazebo.

"Lucy's going to apply herself and finish the draft by the end of the month."

"But you have to be here for my wedding!"

"What day?"

"April tenth."

"I'll be here for it, Darla." She patted her hand. "We're going to have to retype the whole manuscript after she marks it for edits. She just wants to make sure she's done well before the deadline so—why did I even say that?"

"What?"

"The first day I was here, I told Alex and Freddy I wanted to be back in New York by the deadline because it happens to be my birthday and I wanted to spend it with friends."

"But aren't we—"

"Of course you all are now, but that was weeks ago. A lifetime it seems."

"Sissa, flower." Bethany came into the gazebo with a daylily picked from the back flowerbed.

"Thank you, Beth." She accepted the yellow flower and looked at Darla. "I need to leave at two this afternoon to get downtown on errands. I'm meeting Freddy at the end of his day and we're going to take supper together. Are you meeting Henry tonight?"

"I just might have to now. Let me run in to telephone him."

By dinner time, the girls were tired and hungry from playing in the yard, Lucy added another seven pages to her story, and Melissa was already half gone in her mind. She reminded Lucy she was going on errands and would ride back with Freddy after supper.

Phoebe and Bethany were still napping when Melissa gathered everything she needed in her purse. At the last minute she put her camera around her neck, vowing to immortalize more of her personal time in Mobile. Before going downstairs, she went into the girls' room. Phoebe was a little angel with her blonde halo on her pillow and Bethany a silent beauty with her dark features. Melissa opened her camera and took a photograph of each girl.

She was downtown by two-thirty and walked into Mr. Hofstedder's shop with her parasol under her arm.

"Good afternoon, Ms. Stone."

"Hello, Mr. Hofstedder. I was hoping you could help me out."

"If you're looking for the islander interested in your brooch you haven't missed him today." He looked to the clock on the wall. "He should be here soon."

"Good. I'd like to speak with him before he comes in. Could you keep an eye out for me?"

"Of course, Ms. Stone."

"Thank you."

Melissa settled at a corner bench in Bienville Square under the shade of her green parasol, watching the shop as she waited for the Jamaican. But another evil found her first.

"Ms. Stone, how good to see you." Rupert Lyons offered a cigarette from his gold case, but Melissa shook her head. "I saw you at the tournament but never got a chance to say hello."

"I'm not sure I'll be able to get over that loss."

"Has mild Davenport decided he likes his women feisty?"

"I'm sure that's none of your business, Mr. Lyons."

"Should you find yourself bored with the accountant, come to me. I'll be sure the remainder of your time in our fair city is pleasurable."

Melissa tilted her head. "I'm afraid I don't correlate you and pleasure in the same sentence, Mr. Lyons. Have a good afternoon."

She found walking away from vile man after having the last word worth losing her prime location. Melissa walked to Royal Street and turned back toward the jeweler's. In mid-stride she caught the movement of a dark man in a derby hat, smoking against a brick wall. She turned her attention to him and her heart began to race. Before she could talk herself out of it, she approached him.

"Excuse me. Seeing as though you've made a point of following me about town the last few weeks, may I ask your name?"

His smile was surprisingly friendly under his thin mustache. "Tolman Bailey, Ms. Stone. Have you decided to part with my power?"

"Yes, I have." She stepped in the direction of Mr. Hofstedder's store, keeping close to the store fronts rather than the street in case she needed to bang on a window for help.

Tolman stayed right behind her. "That's smart of you."

"I'm afraid to say it's caused much folly."

"Obeah has been known to do that."

She paused in front of Mr. Hofstedder's window. "It was one thing when it caused issues with the adults, but when one of the girls took ill, something had to be done."

Tolman's smile turned to a frown, his brown eyes narrowed. "What did you do?"

"What did *you* do to imbed the power within the object?" she countered.

"Nothing you need to concern yourself with. It is the way of my people."

"Then why did Hepzibah give it to me?"

"She was a meddler. That jewel had been in her family for generations and she claimed it was a gift from Captain Calico Jack to his lover, the pirate Anne Bonny, famed for her red hair. Her son lost it to me in a bet, but the crazy woman said it was better to go with another red-haired woman than be in the possession of a black magic man like me, but I had already made it my charm. Now return it to me." He held out his hand.

Melissa reached into her purse and pulled out the handkerchief wrapped item. "I'm afraid it will be no use to you now, Mr. Bailey." She opened it in her palm, exposing the mangled gold and gems. "It was blessed by a Catholic priest and found its way into a fire."

He reached out for it and yanked his hand back as though stung, cursing under his breath. Melissa tucked it back into her bag. She removed the lens cap from her camera. "It appears there are some powers stronger than yours. Now leave me and my friends alone."

"You've given a death sentence to Hepzibah for taking what I'd rightfully won."

"And you'll find yourself on wanted posters in Alabama and Jamaica if you continue your revenge." In a swift movement she opened her telescoping camera and took a picture of him.

"This isn't over," he hissed.

Mr. Hofstedder reached the door and Tolman ran toward the river.

"Are you all right, Ms. Stone?" Mr. Hofstedder asked.

"Yes, thank you. I don't think you'll see him again." Melissa closed her camera and reset the lens cap before bringing out the destroyed brooch. "But if you are interested, I have gold and emeralds for sale, but I'm sorry to inform you it is no longer a functional brooch."

Thirty-Three

After four o'clock, Frederick couldn't concentrate on the simplest tasks. His final appointment ended half an hour before—one of many blessings that day, beginning with the minutes he shared with Melissa. He loved greeting her in the mornings and after work. It made him yearn for days when he'd once again wake with and come home to the one he loved. Down the hall at Henry's office, his hand was poised to knock before he heard the tell-tale sounds of a business conversation. Frederick paced the length of the waiting area, and then poured himself half a cup of stale coffee just for something to do.

"Go on if you need to, Mr. Davenport," Ms. Neves said from her desk. "There's no need to wait around when you can be off to the gym for the day."

"I'm waiting for Ms. Stone before I leave. Would you send her to my office when she arrives?"

"Certainly, Mr. Davenport."

Frederick shut his office door and hung his suit jacket on the rack. He smiled as he thought of the day Lucy had waited in the corner chair before going to the lawyer to discuss their divorce. She was glorious, growing Bethany and out-witting Judith Smith.

"Goosy," he muttered to the ghost in his memory, "it was worth all the pain to make it to this point in my life."

He smoothed a hand over his hair and forced himself to sit at his desk, relaxing his muscles. A moment later, the knock came.

"Come in."

Melissa, managing to look both unsure and bold at the same time, closed the door behind her. Frederick went to her side to relieve her of the package and parasol.

"Thank you, Freddy." She placed her purse and camera beside the slim box he'd set on the chair. "You looked so official sitting there when I came in, I felt like I was about to be interviewed."

"I'd never hire you."

Shock registered on her heart-shaped face. "Why not? Am I over qualified?"

"Most likely, but it's because I'd never be able to do this." Frederick took her in his arms and initiated a kiss that encouraged her hands to explore his body.

"Mr. Davenport," she whispered, "I'd have to agree that I don't wish to work in your establishment. The perks of not being an employee are too good to pass up."

He laughed and hugged her to his chest. "I love moments like this."

"I have something else I think you'll enjoy." Melissa led him to the box she'd brought. "Prints from my last few rolls of film."

The top photograph was of him and Phoebe on their way out for supper, when he'd been smiling over Melissa and Phoebe gazed up at him.

"It's perfect." He flipped to the next one in the pile—the forward facing one—and sighed. "She looks just like Lucy did at that age. Perfection."

"You can have them both. They're a good framing size for table top, but I can have larger prints made if you want to make a wall hanging out of one."

"I'd like that, of this one we're looking at each other. Thank you." He went through the pile. "You captured some amazing pictures around town."

He laughed when he got to one of him and the girls eating ice cream at Monroe Park. Phoebe and Bethany looked to have ice cream everywhere but in their mouths.

"That's one of my favorites," Melissa remarked. "And the last ones in the pile."

The final photographs were the ones Alex and had taken before their supper date. Melissa captured well on camera, her jovial smile, the curve of her body in her evening gown. "We make a striking coupe, if I'm allowed to say that about ourselves. May I claim one of these as well?"

"Yes, but let's sort them when we get back to the house. You need to go to the gym." She closed the box.

"Would you like me as well if I stopped working out?"

"The better question is if you'd like yourself. I think you need it, at least at this point in your life."

Freddy set the box on the desk and his hands cupped her face. "You know me well."

He brought his mouth to hers, nibbling her satin lips until she returned the attentions. Deepening the kiss, he tasted of her as his hands went to her hips.

Melissa pulled away. "This all feels too good to keep doing safely."

"Am I dangerous?" he teased.

"Extremely dangerous, from your sincere eyes to your strong hands."

"In that case, anything to keep you safe." He pulled on his jacket and carried her box and camera.

Frederick stopped to introduce her to a few people in the office. Then they were at his automobile to drive to the gym. Melissa kept her purse and parasol when he walked her to the book shop, though the sun was past needing shading from. She used it as a walking stick but never put her weight on it—a handy weapon for a single woman. The emerald hue of the fabric reminded him of her pin.

They stopped outside the store. "What did you end up doing with the brooch?"

"Claudio picked it out of the fireplace for me yesterday. I kept it until this afternoon so I could secure my safety."

His hand tightened on her elbow. "How's that?"

"Don't be mad, but—"

"I already don't like where this is going." Frederick crossed his arms.

"You want us to be honest, so I'm telling you." She let out a deep breath. "Mr. Hofstedder runs a jewelry shop. I met him my first afternoon here."

"I know him well. I bought both wed—never mind."

"Both your wives' wedding rings from him? Honesty, Freddy. It goes both ways." She smiled.

He looked at his shoes. "I don't want you to be uncomfortable if I talk about Harriet or Lucy."

"Your past makes you who you are. Harriet is an example of your chivalry and I've been around Lucy enough to know her shortcomings and not be jealous."

Frederick laughed and hugged her, ignoring the stares from passersby. "You're perfect for me, Melissa. You even understand my ex-wife."

"I suppose it does take a special person to accomplish that feat." She tapped her parasol on the ground and looked up at him. "Last Wednesday, Mr. Hofstedder told me a Jamaican was coming in a few days a week enquiring about a brooch like mine. He expected him today at three, so I watched for him on the street. When I saw him, I asked his name. Tolman Bailey it is, if he told me the truth."

He touched her cheek. "He could have hurt you."

"I kept in front of the stores and stopped outside Mr. Hofstedder's. I told him I was going to speak with the man, and he was watching for me."

"I wish you would have told me so I could have been there with you."

"I figured he wouldn't talk unless I was alone. I wanted to know what he'd done to it." She explained the history of the supposed pirate treasure. "Hepzibah sold fresh flowers to guests at the hotel. I'd seen her about several times on my walks about the grounds. When she finally spoke to me and presented the brooch, she said it had been in their family for generations and wanted it to be returned to a red-haired woman. He had to come after it—Obeah, he called it—because he'd already endowed it with power, which he wouldn't explain to me."

"But surely that's enough to satisfy you."

"Yes." She smiled up at him as though she was grateful for him understanding her need to unravel the mystery. "And he was upset when I showed him the piece, more so when he couldn't touch it. I took his picture and warned him he'd be wanted in Alabama and Jamaica if he continued to seek retribution."

"You threatened him armed with only a parasol?" She nodded and Frederick crossed his arms. "So where is the brooch now?"

"I sold it to Mr. Hofstedder. His jewelry designing friends can salvage the emeralds and reshape the gold into something new."

"You weren't interested in keeping it? Emeralds are your birthstone."

"Not after all the trouble it caused. There were too many bad memories."

"Well I'm glad you're safe and it's refreshing to know how brave you are." He kissed her forehead. "You should get the film developed and give a copy to the police in case he comes back."

Melissa hesitated. "I think he meant to leave. As for the photograph, I've only taken a few pictures on the roll. I'd rather use it first."

"Then let's fill it." He took her hand. "How about pictures of the guys at the gym? I'm sure they'd be more than pleased to pose, especially coming off the excitement of the tournament. The owner has wanted to do a display board. It would be perfect, unless you'd rather go to the book shop."

"Take me to the gym, Freddy."

After retrieving her camera from the automobile, Frederick escorted Melissa to the gym. She waited in the lobby while he changed to his workout clothes and received permission for her visit. He proudly led her between rowing machines and punching bags, making introductions before he started his workout. Attention divided between her and his sparring partner, Frederick took a beating in the ring. All the men were respectful to Melissa, and none more than Chuck, who left blatant hints about Frederick's good mood since she arrived in town.

***

Back at the old Easton house, Melissa told Alexander and Lucy about the Jamaican and Alexander contacted the police so she could give her statement. Within thirty minutes, the daytime watch was pulled from the house, though a police officer would stay nearby the next two nights. If Tolman Baily didn't reappear, that would be the end of it—though Frederick would have preferred the police to wait a full week before writing off the danger.

After the situation was settled, Frederick sat on the rug in front of the fireplace with Melissa and the girls as she sorted the pictures: a pile for each the Davenports, Mellings, herself, and business purposes. She made a list of which pictures she wanted in larger sizes as Phoebe squealed over her portraits.

Running them to Lucy and Alexander on the settee, Phoebe beamed. "See how pretty my dress looks, Mr. Alex?"

"It's lovely, Phoebe Camellia."

"And Daddy is the best king in his fancy suit."

Lucy's fingers entwined in Alexander's. "He does look handsome."

When Phoebe turned back to the photograph pile, Lucy leaned to Alexander's ear, whispering. Frederick watched, surprised at the glow Lucy possessed. He hadn't realized how troubled she'd been lately until he saw her with pure happiness.

"Here, Freddy." Melissa handed him the pictures from before their date. "Show Alex what he captured."

"Those turned out good." Alexander looked them over with Lucy resting on his shoulder. "Proof that Frederick Davenport still knows how to enjoy himself."

"You two make a handsome couple." Lucy hopped off her seat and fell to her knees before Frederick, pinching his cheeks. "Just look at that face! Does it ever bother you that he's so charmingly handsome?"

Melissa laughed. "I'd never complain over that."

"Leave him alone, my queen. He has a woman to fawn over him now."

Her green eyes glistened as her smile increased. Frederick had never seen her so vibrant, and it was just Lucy at home with Alexander and their broken family. She threw her arms around him. "I'm happy for you, Freddy."

It came to him like a jolt. The first time he'd gone to the duplex when Alexander and Lucy were engaged. She glowed with joy, threw her arms about him, and insisted Alexander show him around. And as it was seven years before, he awkwardly put a hand around her and patted her back with the others looking on. The memory of him thinking he'd never hold her mixing with the thought that he'd never have her as he once did. He leaned out of Lucy's reach and looked to Melissa, smiling because knowing he and Lucy were over no longer smarted.

"Listen to your husband, Goosy. I don't need you to fawn over me."

She pouted, but Frederick only tweaked her nose. Lucy's laugh flittered through the room. "You're still my best friend, Freddy."

"So long as Alex is fine with it, I'm happy to claim that title."

"Just leave me all the others, my queen." Alexander winked. "Husband, lover, tango partner—"

"Momma." Bethany climbed into her lap with a copy of the ice cream picture.

Lucy snorted, which made Frederick chuckle.

"I must have one of these, Melissa. Look at those faces! And Freddy with an 'at least it'll wipe off' look of defeat behind his smile." She laughed and handed it to Alexander.

His smile lacked the proper emotion behind it to make it credible, but only Frederick seemed to notice the hollowness. "Father and daughters. Sweet." He handed it to Lucy and leaned back, closing his eyes.

Frederick stood. "I need to get the girls home and to bed. You may have that honor Thursday, Alex."

"Your dance night?" Lucy asked as Frederick helped her stand while she held Bethany.

"Yes, Henry's going to pick up Darla and Melissa here at five and I'll meet them for supper downtown." He looked to Melissa. "If you want, I can drop off your film in the morning."

"Thank you." She handed him his copies. "And the negatives for these, with numbers and sizes of what size prints I want to order, if you don't mind."

"Not at all." He helped her straighten her piles and then stand.

"The film is in my purse in the foyer."

"I'll meet you by the door, girls. See you tomorrow, Goosy. Alex."

Frederick focused on Melissa as she held his arm on their way to the front door.

"I had a great evening, Freddy."

He set his photographs on the credenza and ran his hands across her back, tugging her closer. The feel of her resting against his chest brought as much tenderness as kissing. "I look forward to dancing with you again."

Her hands trailed up his torso and around his neck. "In the meantime, I'll delight in our moments together between now and then."

He breathed in the exotic scent behind her ear, leaving a kiss on her neck.

When their lips met, they shared a provocative moment until Phoebe squealed with delight. "They're kissing!"

Thirty-Four

Thursday afternoon while Melissa was in the front yard with Darla and the girls, a black limousine drove up the lane.

"Get the girls and take them inside," Darla told Melissa.

Recognizing the automobile, Melissa stood her ground. "But Freddy said it was fine for them to see Alex's mother with supervision."

"You're sure?"

"I was here when she last came."

"Then I'll run and get Lucy. I'd rather not speak to that woman."

The chauffer helped Mrs. Melling exit as Melissa took Bethany by a hand and approached the vehicle.

"Good afternoon, Mrs. Melling."

"Ms. Stone, the woman of the hour. How are you and Mr. Davenport getting along?"

"Just fine, thank you."

"And those precious girls. Hello, Bethany. Do you remember me?"

She hid behind Melissa's skirt.

"She's the shiest of the two," Melissa said.

As though proving her point, Phoebe ran over and dropped to a curtsy. "Hello, Mrs. Melling! Mr. Alex is at work right now."

"I know, dear girl." She steadied herself with her cane and then reached out to Phoebe. She accepted the woman's hand and rubbed the back of it against her cheek, which caused Mrs. Melling to smile. "I am here to speak with your mother."

Lucy came onto the porch, her scarlet dress billowing around her legs and her loose hair waving in the breeze.

Mrs. Melling appraised her as she approached. "Alex always had an eye for beauty and Lucille is exquisite."

"Hello, Mrs. Melling." Lucy offered her an awkward handshake. "Would you like to come inside? I could have tea or coffee ready in a few minutes and we have cookies."

"Cookies!" Phoebe bounced on her toes.

"You can take Bethany inside and Darla will help you, Phoebe."

The three watched the girls to the porch in silence.

"I saw the Beauchamp girl when we pulled up. Will she be with you much longer?"

"She wants to stay on as long as she's able. Dr. Hughes keeps her busy, and marriage will change things, but she's only here two days a week as it is. Do you wish to come in?"

"No, thank you." Mrs. Melling shifted her weight and took a heaving breath. "I cannot stay long. I only stopped by to give you an invitation."

Lucy looked to Melissa when she tried to step away, her eyes pleading not to be left alone. Melissa stopped and waited for Mrs. Melling to continue.

"Alex is taking Claudio on the ferry Saturday to see to the Seacliff property. I would like to host you for tea that afternoon. We see so little of each other and I do want to make amends before I die."

Lucy's hand went to her heart. "I don't know what to say to that."

"There is no point in pretending I will live forever or in hoping Alex and you will be heartbroken when I am gone. We have grated each other from the beginning of your relationship, and it is entirely selfish on my part to wish to amend the wrongs so you might become at least a little fond of me before my time comes."

"How morbid can you be, Mrs. Melling?" Lucy's voice tremored.

"Very, but you shall humor an old woman and we can keep each other company while the men are across the bay."

Lucy clasped her hands behind her back. "May I bring Melissa? That is, if she isn't busy."

"Yes. I shall send my driver for you both."

"All right, Mrs. Melling. I'll come."

Her smile was one of a woman who'd gotten her way. "Splendid, Lucille. I shall send my driver at a quarter to three Saturday."

Melissa and Lucy stood silent while Mrs. Melling got into her limousine. When it was around the corner, Lucy fell against Melissa's shoulder.

"What have I done?"

"Agreed to tea at your mother-in-law's house."

"The last time I set foot in there, Mr. Melling found me in Alex's suite after we'd lain together. That instance set off most of what ruined things. The demons were only in my head until that point. After that, they were tempting Alex through his father, alcohol, and Consuela."

"Consuela?"

"His regular whore he forsook when we started courting. His father found out that day and sent her to him several times before our wedding. We may have sinned for the first time at Seacliff, but we ruined ourselves in his parents' house."

***

The day after Darla was over always seemed longer, and the Friday after the dance outing was the longest yet. Between dreading Mrs. Melling's tea party—which Freddy encouraged her to attend—and replaying the wondrous moments dancing, Melissa was more than ready for the girls to take their naps. She tried staying in her room after they were in bed, but she was too restless.

Lucy found her in the kitchen waiting for water to boil. "You can finally tell me about your date last night!"

Melissa turned to Lucy with a look of incredulousness.

Lucy poked her in the ribs. "Come on, how was it? And is there enough water for me to make a cup of coffee?"

"There's enough water, but I'd rather not—"

"Please, Melissa. I've never been to one of the dance halls. Henry and Darla are fabulous dancers, and you and Freddy did well last Saturday."

"Darla and Henry were terrific, but Freddy was amazing. There were a few double rushes and he was taken from me each time. Darla and Henry dance so fast, no one dared cut in." Melissa poured the boiling water through the tea bag holder. "I'm sure it's silly for me to enjoy dancing, but I've always found pleasure in it."

Lucy accepted the kettle from Melissa. "I could never get into the fast ones, but Freddy was always a fine dancer. He taught me to waltz, and then again when I was with Alex and needed to learn how to hold a train."

She followed Melissa to the parlor, her spoon tinkling against the China teacup as she stirred her sugar into the coffee. "I'm not sure if it annoys you to hear about Frederick from me, but he's part of my life—past, present, and future. I wasn't right for him, though I loved him. Those weeks leading up to Alex returning I knew I hadn't been fair to Freddy. I hadn't given him the love and attention he deserved."

Melissa took the chair near the window, hoping the woman had spoken enough to be satisfied with silence. On the settee, Lucy tucked her legs under herself and kept talking.

"He was tired of me—of my moods and obsession over Alex. We fought, well as close to fighting as he'd ever get with a woman. Harsh words and we barely touched for weeks. I think it was a bit of a relief for him when Alex came. He had a target on which to release his frustration. He nearly killed Alex that first night." Lucy took a sip of coffee. "He was strangling him when Douglas and the others burst in, then he went after Claudio because he'd helped Alex in his lie all those years. But he punched through the wall rather than hit me. Does that shock you?"

Melissa's laugh was hollow. "No, I've seen some of his responses to Alex in my time here. Are you trying to shock me?"

"I'm trying to help you understand how Freddy and I are woven together. Looking back, I see the flaws in our relationship, but the strength that we had is still with us as parents and friends." Lucy gazed from her cup to Melissa. "I've seen the way he looks at you. He never looked on me that way. To him I was his fair maiden he wanted to rescue and protect. But he sees you as you are—a woman with real needs and desires. Where I was the childhood role-playing companion, you're a lady who stands beside him as an equal. Part of me wants to envy you, but the larger part of me is thrilled for Freddy."

Melissa held her breath as a tear slipped down Lucy's alabaster cheek.

Lucy swallowed hard and refocused. "If you're going to walk away from him when your work here is done, please warn me so I can help him through it."

"I'm under instructions to deliver your manuscript to Mr. Noble in person. Besides that, I have a book proposal of my own to pitch to him."

"A book proposal?" Lucy's gaze narrowed.

"I've been planning a collection of travel essays for years. Freddy knows that's why I took this job, so I'd more likely get a personal audience with Mr. Noble to pitch my idea."

"He knows you're leaving?"

"Yes."

"What have you promised him?"

"I've promised to be true to my heart. He's never asked for more."

Lucy frowned as she went for the door. She locked herself in her study and Melissa was left to be restless with her thoughts. Before she could begin pacing, Phoebe tiptoed into the parlor, still wearing only her underdress.

"Miss Melissa, I can't sleep. May I sit with you?"

She set her teacup on the side table and opened her arms. Phoebe's grin lightened her heart. Snuggling against her, Phoebe rested her head on Melissa's chest. She in turn wrapped her arms around the girl to provide some warmth.

"I'm glad you've been happier around me this week. I like being your friend."

"May I call you Sissa like Beth does?"

"Of course." She kissed the top of her head.

Phoebe fingered the green tie on Melissa's sailor dress. "Does Daddy love you?"

"I think he does."

"Then he does." Phoebe reached up and touched her cheek. "Can I love you too, Sissa?"

A lump formed in the back of her throat. "If you'd like to, Phoebe."

The girl closed her eyes, a curling smile like her mother's on her lips. In that moment, Melissa understood Lucy's mood. How could she gain the love and devotion of a family that had already been ripped apart only to leave in a few weeks?

Thirty-Five

Frederick left the office early so he'd have time to pick up the prints and new photographs for Melissa before going to the gym. He purchased frames for his portraits, and while the photographs were placed in them he flipped through the new prints. The one of the Jamaican reminded him of what could have happened to Melissa when she approached the man.

I can't lose her.

"I'll need another of this one, please." He put in the order so there would be one for the police.

Next, he came across the pictures of Phoebe and Bethany sleeping, bliss washing over him at the sight of his daughters. "And these, please. Two of each in the next larger size." He wanted to give a set to Lucy and have one for himself.

"We can rush them all, Mr. Davenport, if you want to get them in the morning."

"Yes, thank you."

He filed the photographs into the envelope, placed it in the box with his frames, and headed for the gym. He was in and out in an hour, not taking time in the ring because he was anxious to see

Melissa. He went to the kitchen at the house, lightly knocking at the back door.

"Mr. Frederick, you gave me a fright." Naomi frowned. "With that Voodoo man running around, I've kept the door locked."

"Sorry, Naomi. He hasn't been about, has he?" He set his box on the table.

"Haven't seen him all week, but it's not something I'll soon forget."

He nodded toward the dining room. "How far along are they?"

"Still the main course." She looked him over. "You need something, Mr. Frederick? I've got more soup and sandwich fixings."

He smiled. "Yes, please. I forgot to eat before I came."

"Too much of a certain lady on your mind. You want me to bring a tray in there for you?"

"No, thank you. I don't want to disturb them. I'll eat here."

"Get yourself a drink and I'll fix your food."

He'd finished off a sandwich and soup when Alexander came in. "Naomi told me you were here. No need for you to hide. Join us for dessert."

"I didn't want to impose." He wiped his mouth with the linen napkin.

"If you think either of those women will complain about your company, you're daft."

Frederick laughed. "All right. Are you really going to Seacliff tomorrow?"

Alexander nodded. "Claudio is taking the ferry with me to Montrose. Leroy Watts, the caretaker of the property, is going to meet the boat and bring us to Ecor Rouge. He has the automobile Father bought for Douglas to chauffer Mother and Magdalene around that year. Six long years, but sometimes it feels like yesterday, especially with the events of last week fresh on my mind." He ran a hand through his hair. "Thank you for talking Melissa into going with Lucy tomorrow. It will bring her comfort to have a friend with her at Mother's house."

"Are they friends?" Frederick carried his dishes to the sink.

"Close enough. There's an understanding, like Lucy and Darla have, but they have more in common, being closer in age and both writers." Alexander lifted the pedestal platter holding a carrot cake.

Frederick collected the pile of plates and forks Naomi had ready and followed him to the dining room.

"Look what I found in the kitchen," Alexander announced when he entered.

"Cake!" Phoebe caught sight of her father. "And Daddy!"

"You know how to please us, Alex." Lucy kissed Frederick's cheek. "You look well this evening."

"I feel good, thank you." Frederick kissed Bethany's forehead to keep away from her messy face. "Hello, Little Princess."

Then he was to the far side of the table with a hug for Phoebe.

"Sit between me and Sissa, Daddy." She jumped off the chair and moved down a seat.

"Sissa now, is it?" He took in the details of Melissa's sad eyes and turned down mouth. Reaching a hand to her face, he fingered her chin. "What's wrong?"

She forced smile and shook her head. "Nothing."

Frederick dropped to the seat, hand skimming around to the back of her neck, and kissed her on the lips. "Honesty," he whispered in her ear. "But we can talk later."

Melissa studied her hands in her lap. He glanced across the table at Lucy. Despite the fact that Alexander set a large piece of her favorite dessert before her, she scowled.

"Did you have a good day, Phoebe?" he asked in search of pleasant conversation.

"Yes! We played outside this morning and had story time. After dinner I couldn't sleep, so Sissa held me. I've decided to love her, Daddy, because you do."

Melissa nearly took out the bottle of milk when she stood.

"Excuse me. I don't feel quite right." She rushed from the room.

Frederick stood, laying a hand on Phoebe's shoulder. "I'm glad to hear that, Princess. Would you save me a piece of cake while I go see Melissa?"

"And one for Sissa?"

"That would be good."

He stopped at Lucy's chair. "What happened today, Goosy?"

"Nothing beyond letting her know I don't take kindly to people hurting those I love."

"She's hurt no one."

Frederick went for the door but heard Lucy whisper, "Yet."

Melissa wasn't in the parlor, so Frederick climbed the stairs.

He knocked on her bedroom door. "Melissa, please let me in. You know I can open it without permission, though I'd rather it be your choice."

He heard her sniffle and the floorboard creak. A handkerchief was extended in his hand when she opened the door. She gave a choked laugh and dabbed it under her eyes.

"Thank you."

He folded her into his arms, relief flooding his heart when her arms went about him in return. "Whatever it was Lucy said to you, remember that it's her opinion, not fact. She can be both fanciful and pessimistic. You needn't be upset over anything she says, especially about something that hasn't happened."

"But she's right. When I go back to New York, you'll be left with nothing. And the girls! It's not fair to them for me to get close and then leave. They're too young to understand I have responsibilities."

"Is that all?" He lifted her chin and gazed at her tear-stained face. "Melissa, I've known since the day we met you were here temporarily. My heart saw fit to open to you despite that. Whatever happens next month, I'll not let go of what we have today."

Frederick pressed his lips to hers. Restraining himself, he kept the kiss chaste. But when Melissa's hands went to his hair he found himself nudging her toward the bed. At the last second, he turned so she fell on top of him.

He fingered around her wide eyes, grinning. "I'm living in the moment and want to collect as many of them with you as possible."

"But the girls—"

"They have big hearts and are resilient." He lifted his head to kiss her, and then fell back with the satisfaction that she now smiled. "I'd like it if you'd come over in the morning. I do a pancake breakfast Saturdays at eight o'clock. Come to the kitchen door. The girls and I are in there about an hour, baking and being silly."

Melissa stood, gazing down at him. He must look a bold fool, stretched across her bed, but she laughed in her unrestrained way with her ear-to-ear smile. "That sounds fun."

"Good, and afterward we can pick up the extra prints I ordered this afternoon."

"You got my order?" She extended her hand to help him up.

Sitting on the edge of the bed, he pulled her to him, resting his head on her middle. "Yes. And we can bring the gym photographs by there, too. Saturday mornings usually have a crowd of regulars."

"I was going to shop for something suitable to wear to Mrs. Melling's tea, but with Lucy upset with me she might not want my company."

"Upset or not, she won't go there alone. And I know just where to take you, if you'd like me to see to shopping with you."

"I'd enjoy that."

"Then it's a date. Now let's claim our dessert before Lucy and the girls eat it all."

***

Frederick was in the middle of a two-step to the beat of Phoebe and Bethany banging pots with wooden spoons when Melissa opened the backdoor.

"Sissa." Bethany reached to be picked up from the floor but Phoebe kept playing, so Frederick kept dancing.

When the song came to an end, he held out the edges of the apron to curtsy. Melissa and the girls clapped. He needed to turn the sausage before greeting their guest, but she came to him first.

Nestled against his side, she kissed above his morning stubble. "When you said you acted silly, I didn't quite believe you. Now I know better than to doubt your word."

He chuckled as he turned the last link in the cast iron skillet. "Pancake Time is serious business around here. More so than ever since Beth is big enough to cause a ruckus of her own." Hands free, Frederick embraced Melissa fully. "I'm glad you've joined us."

"I should have known it was a wild time. Alex gave me a look of pity when he heard where I was going."

"He took Saturday breakfast with us once when Goosy was still living here. Some things are too drastic from the way he was raised for him to appreciate." He kissed her hard. "You don't mind our rowdiness, do you?"

"Not at all."

"Phoebe, get a pot and spoon for Melissa." He trailed his hands across Melissa's back. "I need a good rhythm to whisk the pancake batter."

"Here, Sissa!" Phoebe handed her a stockpot and ladle.

Melissa held them up. "Really?"

"I expect much from you." He slung an arm low about her waist, tugging her back to him. "Don't disappoint me."

He tilted his head, going for her cheek, but she met him first with a deep kiss he didn't want to end. It did, with a thunderous clash from the girls.

"We want pancakes!" Phoebe led the chant. "We want pancakes! We want pancakes!"

Melissa pulled away. "You heard the girls. We want pancakes! We want pancakes!"

She clamored the ladle against her pot on her way to sit with them. Hiking up her slim navy skirt, she sat on the tiles between Bethany and Phoebe in their nightgowns.

If every Saturday was like this, I'd be a happy man the remainder of my days.

Standing at the counter before his pre-measured ingredients, Frederick cracked the eggs into the mixing bowl. He carried it around with him, dancing as he beat the eggs. Then he was back at the stove, removing the sausage from the heat before adding the milk to the batter. He was so distracted by Melissa's playfulness he nearly spilt the mixture three times before he poured the first scoops into the buttered skillet.

"Time to clean up the pots and wash hands." He instructed the girls.

Phoebe gathered the noise makers into a pile and ran for the bathroom. Without being asked, Melissa picked up Bethany and brought her to the kitchen sink, helping her wash as Frederick flipped the first batch.

"Could you watch the pan while I get the highchair from the dining room?"

"Of course, Freddy."

Chairs set, Frederick put plates on the counter and cut half a sausage on Bethany's dish while Melissa settled her in the highchair. He put a pancake on each of the girls' plates before adding more batter to the pan. By the time he turned back to the plates, Melissa was cutting Bethany's pancakes.

"I didn't mean to put you to work when I invited you."

"It's no trouble. I'm enjoying myself."

"You are?" He wrapped an arm around her.

"It's the most interesting breakfast I've ever experienced. I never would have thought to bang pots to demand pancakes. Is that what you had to do as a boy?"

"Hardly. My father did make pancakes on Sunday mornings, though."

"We want pancakes!" Phoebe resumed her chanting when she got to the table.

"You get the plates," he said, "and I'll get the syrup."

Melissa saw to the girls and Frederick flipped the next batch, making a show of tossing them into the air. By the time the girls were done eating, he had the last batch in the skillet and Melissa had started on her own plate. He took a sip of coffee from the cup she'd poured for him and leaned against the counter, smiling over her wiping syrup off Bethany's face.

This is it, what I've been waiting for my whole life. She's leaving, but I need to make sure she wants to come back to me.

To us.

Frederick went to the table with the last two batches of pancakes and several sausage links just as Phoebe left in search of Doff.

"You're an amazing father," Melissa said. "Thank you for sharing this bit of your life with me."

"To serve as a warning?" He took his first bite and stood to look for his coffee cup, but Melissa was already reaching for it off the counter.

She kissed his cheek as she handed it to him. "To show me how magical daily life can be. I thought Kingdom Davenport versus Melling Militia was something, but Pancake Time wins overall."

"You're welcome every week. I think you have just what our rhythm section needs."

And with the dip of her head and her blush, he knew she understood the deeper meaning.

Phoebe carried Doff in and Melissa poured milk into a saucer for the cat, allowing Frederick to keep eating.

"You're spoiling me," he said as she returned to the table. "This is the hottest breakfast I've had in I don't know how long."

"You deserve a break."

"In that case, would you like to dress the girls for me?"

"But the dishes, Daddy!" Phoebe took his arm.

"Not this time, Princess. We're going shopping with Miss Melissa so we'll do the dishes later."

"I'll pick my clothes!" Phoebe dashed for the stairs.

"We usually wash the dishes together after eating on Saturday mornings. It gives Miss Sharon a break and teaches the girls how to maintain a house. I try not to rely on the help for everything or let the girls take advantage either. I learned that from the Eastons."

"You're doing great with them, Freddy." Melissa left him with a kiss and carried Bethany upstairs.

When he was done eating, Frederick peered around the doorframe into the girls' room. Phoebe bounced on her bed while brushing her hair. Melissa sat on the rug singing children's rhymes to Bethany as she buttoned up the back of her dress. The glimpse of his possible future gave him hope like nothing before.

In his room, he tried to contain his joy so he wouldn't scare Melissa.

"Freddy," her soft voice came from the doorway, "the girls are ready."

"I was going to shave before we go."

"Do you always shave after breakfast on Saturdays?" She stepped toward him.

"I let it go half the time."

"Then leave it. It's a nice change, like you had it at the tournament." She ran her hand over the stubble. "Do you ever grow out facial hair?"

He wanted to disappear into her touch. "I've done a mustache or goatee a few times."

Melissa traced his features with her fingertips, stirring his passion with a new force. "You have a face that would work well with anything."

He brought his hands to her shoulders. "Do you have any idea what you do to me?"

"If it's like what you do to me, we're in trouble."

"It's the type of shake-up I'd take any day." He kissed her and she melted against him for a blissful moment. "Now let's bring our band of trouble around town."

Thirty-Six

By the time Melissa returned to the Mellings' it was almost one o'clock. She expected Lucy to be pacing the hall, but her study was shut and the sound of typing could be heard. Leaving her packages in the foyer, Melissa returned to Freddy's automobile.

"Sorry girls, she's writing."

"But—" Phoebe started.

"No, Princess." Freddy's voice was stern. "I told you we wouldn't disturb her if she's working. You'll see Momma another time. I know you're cranky, but that's okay because we're going home and you're getting a nap."

Melissa climbed on the running board and hugged the girl. "I had fun today, Phoebe."

She smoothed Bethany's hair, who was half asleep between her sister and father. Then she was around to the driver side, stepping up to kiss Freddy.

"It was a perfect morning. Thank you for everything, from Pancake Time to bringing me to Mademoiselle Bisset for my dress."

His shy smile sat playful on his handsome face. She kissed him once more and made herself return to the house.

As Melissa gathered her packages to bring to her room, Lucy emerged from the study still wearing her kimono.

"Do you need help?" she asked.

"If you don't mind, thank you. I just arrived."

Lucy fingered the pink and white striped box. "Mademoiselle Bisset's shop?"

"Freddy took me. I wanted to get a new dress for the tea and he said that was the best place to go for anything substantial. Mademoiselle Bisset said to give you her greetings and she expects to see you next month for new summer frocks."

"Did she dote on Freddy and the girls?"

Melissa laughed as she walked into her room. "Most enormously. Peppermints for the girls and praises for Freddy. There is something for you from Freddy in one of these. Give me a moment."

She restacked the boxes on her bed until she found the one from the photography store. She handed it to Lucy with a smile.

Lucy opened the gift and then the clamshell frame, displaying the sleeping portraits of Phoebe and Bethany. "Thank you, Melissa."

"It's from Freddy."

"But I know it was you who took the photographs." She gazed at the pictures before closing the frame and hugging it. "I'll put it on my dresser. How was breakfast this morning?"

Melissa took in Lucy's straight-faced stare, trying to judge her opinion on rowdy Pancake Time. "It was delightful, even if a bit loud. Freddy's a wonderful father."

She pursed her lips. "I was scared being alone all morning, but I locked myself in the study and wrote a full chapter."

"Excellent."

Lucy frowned. "I'll meet my deadline with room to spare."

"I'm sure you will."

She motioned to the striped box. "Did Freddy help you pick it out?"

"He guided Mademoiselle Bisset on what to choose."

Lucy nodded with a spark in her eye like she remembered times when Freddy helped her at the dress shop. "I'm sure it will be perfect for you. Be downstairs by two-thirty if you can."

Melissa washed and dressed, pulling on the new cream chemise for the foundation of the lace tea gown. The buttery gold of the lace overdress was decorated with peach and pink embroidered flowers on trailing green ivy that offset her hair and sun-kissed skin perfectly. She unwrapped her new gold shoes and set them at the foot of her bed before going to work on her hair. With the replicated style that Lucy had done for her date night with Freddy, Melissa felt ready to face the superior-minded Mrs. Melling and descended the stairs.

"Melissa, you look divine!" Lucy fingered the sheer, elbow length sleeves and eyed the scalloped neckline. "Freddy always had fine taste."

While Melissa was subtle in Earth-tones, Lucy was striking in a royal blue silk and chiffon dress trimmed with fringe on the overlays.

"You're gorgeous as always. Even Mrs. Melling remarked on your looks the other day."

"It was never my looks she or her wretched husband had a problem with."

"What was the trouble between you two when you were first engaged to Alex?"

"Society and money." Lucy pulled on a pair of white fingerless gloves. "She thought my family too beneath hers to be a proper match for her darling Alexander, though she invited my mother to plenty of social events throughout the years. She didn't like my fashion choices either. I'm sure she'll find this blue too last season for her taste but I love it and I'm going as a service to Alex, not to please the woman."

The ride only took a few minutes, but when the chauffer opened the door for them in the driveway of the mansion, Lucy sat rigid.

Melissa gave her hand a reassuring squeeze. "I'm right here. Think of Alex, how much he loves you."

Lucy lifted her chin and led the way to the veranda.

A uniformed maid answered the doorbell. "Please come in, Mrs. Alexander Melling and Ms. Stone. Mrs. Melling will receive you in the front room."

Ruth Melling sat in a gilded Bergère chair in a black lace gown.

"Lucille, my dear." Mrs. Melling rose with the help of her cane and crossed the carpet to plant a kiss on her cheek. "Come sit with me. Ms. Stone may take the couch."

Since Lucy stayed silent, Melissa spoke. "Thank you for having us, Mrs. Melling."

Mrs. Melling took Lucy's hand. "I would do anything for Lucille. She is the crowning jewel in the Melling family and the talk of the city with her literary talents. You always had a style all your own. Alexander appreciated it and I have grown fond of it myself. I am pleased you came today. There is not much time left for me to make things up to you. When does your next book release?"

Slipping her hand out from her mother-in-law's, Lucy crossed her ankles. "In the fall. I'm not sure of a date yet, but the manuscript goes to Mr. Noble in April."

"Then Ms. Stone will be returning to New York?"

Lucy nodded.

"I am sure the women about town will be pleased to hear that." She gave a cutting look to Melissa, as though she blamed her for stealing Freddy from the local ladies.

The maid brought in a rolling tea cart. Mrs. Melling tried involving Lucy in topics of interest as they ate and drank, but she kept her responses closed. The front door opened and Melissa turned toward the foyer. A second later, Tolman Bailey shadowed the marble space. Melissa reflexively stood, reaching for her parasol that wasn't there.

"What do you think you are doing here?" Mrs. Melling demanded.

"I have come for revenge." He stepped onto the plush carpet and advanced toward Melissa. "I must have something from you to replace what was lost."

Mrs. Melling reached for her bell, but Tolman lunged forward and knocked it from her hand, causing the woman to whimper in fright.

"What is it you want?" Melissa moved to stand in front of Lucy, who'd grown pale. "Allow me to step outside with you so we don't bother the others."

As though sensing her willingness to protect them, Tolman lashed out to wound. "Obeah tells me there's evil within these walls, in this family."

Lucy moved to stand but clutched the arm of the chair instead—eyes closing, head lolling to the side. Melissa caught her and leaned her back against the chair while Mrs. Melling looked on with an open mouth.

"Obeah tells me she is with child this week," Tolman's voice was raspy, his gaze absent. "The Melling name will continue for another generation, though it was almost by another her child would be known."

Melissa's horror was eclipsed by Mrs. Melling's joy. "A child for Alexander!"

From her discussions with Claudio, Melissa understood those claiming to be in touch with the other side might be conversing with demons, and while truth could be learned, it was at a high price. As Lucy was susceptible to possession, Melissa knew she needed to remove her friend from Tolman Bailey's presence.

"You must leave!" Melissa snatched the cane resting between the two Mellings. "There's a Catholic priest staying here and evil is not allowed!"

"He is gone for the day, and the priest's opinion," Tolman said in an ominous tone, "should not matter since he wronged the Mellings."

Mrs. Melling fingered the cross at her neck. "He's been my dearest advisor and confidant since Eliza passed away."

"It was by his choices that she died."

"No!" Mrs. Melling gripped the cross.

"Obeah does not lie!" Tolman shouted. "The priest is a sinner! They were lovers. Your daughter died the night she ran to him."

Melissa turned her head to look at their hostess. "He's speaking through demons and you know what pain those have caused your family. Claudio is a good man."

But even as she said the words, Melissa knew what Tolman said was true. She'd seen the heartache on Claudio's countenance whenever Eliza was mentioned.

"I must speak to Eliza." Mrs. Melling looked at the man pleadingly. "I need to know—"

"Eliza is through the veil." Melissa rested the cane on her shoulder as Tolman took a step back. "Whatever this man claims to speak as, you can be sure it would never be Eliza. Think of your daughter now with you—Alex's wife. It's possible she's with child. Don't tempt fate by allowing demons near her. You'll expose her and the child to great danger."

Mrs. Melling nodded, and then looked to the Jamaican. "Take all that you brought or conjured and leave my house."

"The truth often hurts and your family's past is riddled with sinful stories, from your wicked children to your adulterous husband."

"But it is my family, and I love them. Please go."

"Fool!"

As he extended his arm to slap Mrs. Melling, Melissa swung the cane, striking him on the side of the head. He went down, but Melissa didn't trust him to stay there long. She rushed for the fallen bell and rung it furiously, afraid to leave Lucy and her mother-in-law alone.

The maid entered, eyes wide at seeing the man on the floor.

"We have an intruder," Melissa spoke firmly. "Call the police immediately and tell them to hurry!"

When the maid ran out, Melissa yanked the cord holding back the velvet draperies. Dropping beside Tolman Baily, she turned him to his stomach and pulled his hands together behind his back. Just as he was beginning to stir, she tightened the binding around his wrists.

The maid returned with the cook and chauffer. Seeing the Jamaican moving, the driver sat upon his back to still his means of escape, allowing Melissa to see to Lucy.

Thirty-Seven

Phoebe and Bethany played on the living room floor with Doff and their dolls when the phone rang at four-thirty. Frederick answered it in the study, leaving the door open so he could listen for his daughters.

"Davenport."

"I'm calling to vent, as you suggested."

He would have smiled but he heard the concern in her strained voice. "What happened, Melissa?"

"Tolman Bailey burst in while we had tea."

The knuckles of his left hand strained white around the arm of his chair. "Are you home safe now?"

"We're still at the mansion. Lucy and Mrs. Melling are both resting."

"Is he finally captured?"

"I struck him down with Mrs. Melling's cane and bound him with drapery cords before the police took him away."

"Must you always rush toward danger?"

"I had to protect Lucy and Mrs. Melling. She was overcome and Mrs. Melling was stirred with the words he spoke. Tolman said some truths, even if speaking by demons. After the police left, she collapsed."

Frederick drummed his fingers on the desk. "What was said?"

"That Lucy is with child and the Melling name would continue, though it was almost by another name her child should be known."

Frederick felt the color drain from his face and rested his elbow on the table while he held his head. "I swear to you I haven't—"

"I know, Freddy," her voice whispered through the line. "Claudio told me demons speak truths to wound, but I don't think Mrs. Melling heard the last part. Whatever prevented Lucy from becoming pregnant must have changed. Maybe her possession being cleared or the fact that she and Alex abstained so long had something to do with it. But Tolman said it was Alex's."

"But if she's pregnant so soon after what she attempted, will anyone believe it?" He twisted the receiver's cord around his hand.

"Only a few of us know what Lucy did and no one doubts you stopped it."

"What else was said? What upset Mrs. Melling?"

"It's about Claudio and her daughter. He told her they were lovers and Eliza died the night she ran away to him."

"When Claudio met with me after what I did with Lucy, I told him he couldn't understand and he admitted to his sin with Eliza to prove that he knew of my pain."

Melissa sighed. "Then Lucy must truly be pregnant with Alex's child."

"Do I need to bring you two back home?"

"I think we should wait until Claudio and Alex return, but thank you. I'm going back to Lucy now. She's been placed in Alex's old suite. The chauffer carried her upstairs."

"Melissa, I don't like the thought of you there after all that happened this afternoon." He hoped she didn't think him melodramatic.

"I don't like it either, but Claudio should see to Lucy here rather than possibly bringing some lingering evil back to the house with us."

"Would you like me to telephone Naomi and tell her you'll be late?"

"Yes, thank you, Freddy."

"Call me later and let me know you made it back, all right?"

"Of course."

"And call if you need anything, Melissa." He cleared his throat. "I'm here, and I love you."

"I ..." He heard the hesitation in her voice. "I appreciate everything. I'm very fond of you as well."

The line went dead between them. Unease settled in Frederick's gut, but whether it was for the predicament the two women he cared most about were in or the fact that Melissa hadn't said she loved him, he didn't know. He pressed down the lever on the receiver and then rang the operator to be connected with the other house.

"Mellings' residence," Naomi answered.

"And I was looking for the Eastons."

"That it will always be, Mr. Frederick, but the Mellings reside here now, though none at the moment."

"That's why I'm calling. There was a bit of trouble at the tea Lucy and Melissa went to. They're going to stay at Mrs. Melling's until Alex and Claudio return, but Tolman Bailey has been arrested."

"That does my soul good, but I've already got supper going. I'll set it in the warming oven."

"That would be best. And don't wait for them, it could be late."

"Don't you worry about me, Mr. Frederick. You watch those girls of yours. I've got things covered here."

"Thank you, Naomi."

He sat for a moment, sorting his thoughts, then went for the kitchen.

"Miss Sharon, do you have a few minutes to watch the girls so I could run next door?"

"Sure thing, Mr. Davenport." She wiped her hands on her apron and set about turning off the burners on the stove.

Frederick perched on the edge of a chair in the front room.

"Daddy." Bethany came for a hug.

"Beth, my little princess." He pulled her to his knee and kissed her chubby cheek.

She squirmed to return to her play, but Phoebe soon replaced her. Frederick smoothed her hair and kissed her as well.

"I'm going next door for a minute, but Miss Sharon is going to watch you."

She took his cheeks in her little hands. "You okay, Daddy?"

Frederick stuck his tongue out and crossed his eyes. "Just worried a bit, Princess."

"Do all big people worry?"

He smiled. "At some time or another."

"Then I never want to get big. I like being happy."

Hugging her to his chest, he kissed her forehead. "Worry isn't constant, Phoebe. And Daddy only worries over important things long enough to see that they are taken care of. You see me happy, don't you?"

"At Pancake Time, when we go to the park, with Sissa, and right now, hugging me."

"That's right, Princess. I'll be back in a few minutes."

At the Beauchamps' house, he learned Darla was out on a call with Dr. Hughes. He left the message for her to come over when she returned and gave his thanks.

Not long after Frederick dished up the girls' food, a knock came at the front door. Darla stood on the porch wearing an old work dress. "I came right over when Aunt Ida said you'd asked after me. Is everything all right?"

"Here, yes, but not with Lucy and Melissa." He quietly told her what happened at Mrs. Melling's tea. "I want to meet Alex and Claudio at the dock to warn them what they're coming home to."

"I already cancelled my plans for tonight when Dr. Hughes called. Let me clean up right quick, and I'll be over."

Frederick finished supper with the girls and ushered them into the living room to play while they waited for Darla. They were in a pile on the floor, Bethany bouncing on her father's back and Phoebe trying to tickle behind his knees when she arrived.

"All right, Knights of Kingdom Davenport, your king must see to business in a neighboring land for a while. Hugs and kisses for the princesses, and I'll be back after Miss Darla has you in bed."

At the waterfront, he parked next to Alexander's automobile. When the lights of the ferry approached, he joined the other people meeting the returning day trippers.

Alexander joked with Claudio as they disembarked, but as soon as his gaze passed over Frederick's, he quieted. "What's happened?"

Frederick nodded to their automobiles and they grouped between the parked cars. He kept his voice low when telling the tale, but Alexander spewed profanities.

"The Jamaican was able to make a few pronouncements before Melissa took him down."

"It is of the devil," Claudio was quick to say.

"But haven't you said demons speak the truth?" Frederick asked.

"*Sí*, but often to wound."

"I'll leave it for Melissa to inform you."

Alexander took him by the shoulders. "You must tell me!"

"I'm afraid of how it will affect your driving."

"I can drive," Claudio offered.

"But there's news of you as well."

Alexander tried to shake him but couldn't move Frederick. "Out with it!"

"Supposedly, Lucy is pregnant this week with your child."

Alexander fell to his knees and grabbed Frederick's legs, clutching them in a hug that nearly toppled him backward.

"Get off me, Melling." He tried to nudge Alexander with a gentle kick, but he held fast. Frederick turned to Claudio.

"Do not set your hopes too high. It might have been spoken to wound you if the child is soon to be lost. We cannot count on the word of a demon. But what of me?" Claudio asked.

"Yours and Eliza's love affair was announced, and how she was running away with you the night she died. Mrs. Melling collapsed after the police left."

"I meant to spare her the stress and disappointment."

Alexander turned to the priest and clapped his friend on the back. "You may move in with us if needed."

"I'm closer to the parish," Frederick offered.

Claudio shook his head. "Allow me see to Lucy and *signora* before plans are made."

Thirty-Eight

Melissa watched the doorway from her chair by the fireplace. Alex entered and crossed himself, eyes focused on the still form of Lucy in her blue gown upon the bed. He quickly slipped beside her, a quivering hand lowering to her abdomen.

"My queen, is it finally to happen for us?"

"Alex," Melissa whispered, "she was already overcome when it was spoken."

Alex was swift to pull Melissa to her feet and embrace her as Freddy entered the room.

"Thank you for watching out for her." Alex kissed her cheek before stepping away.

"Lucy doesn't know what was proclaimed, but she did tell me something Monday morning."

"Monday after we—"

"After that fine display of vocalizations your first night back together." Across the room Frederick and Claudio hid their smiles. "She said she could still feel you inside her and she hoped it meant that things were happening."

Alex's dimples were on full display, his eyes the most jubilant blue she'd ever witnessed. She turned to Freddy rather than be swept away with Alex's dreams of fatherhood. Melissa opened her arms to the one she loved and he held her.

"Are you all right?" Freddy whispered in her ear. "You survived tea with Mrs. Melling and then a kiss from her son."

She laughed. "Don't tell me you're jealous."

"So long as his lips never touch yours." He kissed her. "I had to meet them at the dock to warn them what they were coming to. And I wanted to see you in this dress again. You're gorgeous, you know."

"Not compared to her." She motioned to Lucy, still sleeping while Claudio prayed over her and Alex held her hand.

"But you are. You're gloriously you." His hands trailed the pink sash around her middle.

She closed her eyes and leaned against Freddy, absorbing the warmth of his arms and the soft murmur of Claudio's prayers. Complete satisfaction—that's what she felt in his embrace with their friends surrounding them.

"She is good, *amico*." Claudio left the bedside. "We need to see to *signora* now."

Lucy bent a leg, then moved an arm.

"My queen, my life, my everything." Alex trailed a finger down her neck. "How do you feel?"

"Rested." She opened her eyes and blinked at the ceiling, clutching Alex's hand. "We're in your—"

"Yes." With a flash of his impish smile he knelt over her body. "You haven't been here since the weekend before our broken wedding. You healed me and then my father came and ripped it all apart."

"I'll heal you now." She reached for his buttons and he lowered onto her with a control Melissa didn't think him capable of.

"Calmati, amico."

Lucy screamed and Alex laughed as she backhanded his arm. "Why didn't you say we weren't alone? Better yet, why are you climbing upon me when Claudio—" She gasped when she sat up. "And Freddy and Melissa are here!"

"I can't help myself when it comes to you, my queen. You're enchanting in this dress." His hand went to her waist as he leaned in for a kiss. "We need to see to Mother, but you rest until I return. Would you like tea or something to eat?"

"A little bite would be good."

"Naomi has your supper ready at home," Freddy said.

"I'll get you something to tide you over." Alex looked to Melissa. "You'll stay with her or will Freddy whisk you away?"

"I'll stay."

"As will I," Freddy said. "At least until everything is settled."

Once Alex and Claudio were gone, Lucy waved Melissa over, patting the space beside her. "Sit with me so Freddy may have the chair."

Lucy took Melissa's hand and leaned back on the pillow. "It was a nightmare when the man came in like that."

"He can't bother us anymore, but he did share a few prophecies before he fell. Lucy, one thing he said was about you." Melissa held her gaze a moment before continuing. "He said you began carrying Alex's child this week."

Her hand went low on her stomach. "Didn't I tell you I felt something?"

Melissa nodded. "But Claudio warns of getting too attached to the news. It's too early to know for sure—"

"But I've known it since the next morning." A tear escaped the corner of her eye. "I know a part of Alex grows within."

"Excuse me." A maid stopped in the doorway. "Mr. Melling asked me to bring this up."

"Thank you." Freddy accepted the tray and carried it to the bed. "It seems Alex allows you to have dessert before supper."

"He lets me partake anytime I wish." She giggled, laughing more heartily when she saw Freddy's red face.

"I suppose I asked for that with my teasing."

"You did." She sat up and he handed her the first cup. "But I accept your apology, so long as I get the largest piece of cake."

"You drive a hard bargain, Goosy. Just never ask for a pony."

They laughed over their shared joke while Freddy readied a cup for Melissa. When everyone was served, Freddy retreated to the chair. They ate and drank in silence.

"I want to leave this place and never return." Lucy set her cup on the side table next to her empty cake plate. She stood and slowly made her way around the room. "These walls, the color of Alexander's eyes when he's determined, have the power to subdue me. The memories in here are passion and fear. The only pleasant times in this house were when Alex was beside me."

"Even though he treated you harshly?" Freddy's tone was cold.

"You only remember the bad, but I remember the good. God knows he loved me—that he still does—and I him, imperfections and all." Lucy paused before Freddy, a hand going to his scruffy cheek, causing an ache in Melissa's chest. "Not everyone is as noble as you in staying their desires."

"I'm glad you have each other now." He moved his head to kiss her palm. "I know how happy you are with him. And he's straightened himself out like I never thought possible, even if he's willing to climb upon you in front of your friends."

Alex strode into the room with Freddy's words, arms extended, slim hips gyrating. "My queen is my one desire."

Lucy turned at the sound of his voice, hunger in her eyes at seeing her husband's actions. She raised her lithe arms and danced to him. Alex caught her around the waist and nuzzled into her neck. After a moment of indulgence, he turned to the others.

"I need to stay a little longer. Mother's doctor is on the way and I want to speak with him and find out what's going on with her, beyond today's upset. Claudio is packing. He's afraid she'll become upset when she sees him." Alex looked to Freddy. "Will you see the ladies and Claudio to the house?"

Claudio walked in. "It would not be proper to stay at your house, *amico*. Not with an unmarried woman in residence. Frederick, does your offer still stand?"

Lucy flung herself at the priest. "You must come to us!"

"If word gets out about my sin with Eliza, it would be best not to be in a house with two beautiful women."

"Go ahead and say it," Freddy said. "You don't wish to subject to the Mellings' lovemaking."

"That may be true as well."

Lucy backhanded Claudio's stomach.

"And this, also." He patted his middle. "I am growing to the size of a comfortable, old priest with the *signora's* chauffer at my disposal. Frederick's house is a fine distance from St. Joseph's. Two weeks of walking will condition me back to my regular self so I may return to my parish without a priestly bulge."

Lucy hugged him. "You must continue to take supper with us when you can."

"I will. Miss Naomi is a fine cook and I enjoy the company of you all."

At Lucy's house, Freddy saw the ladies inside and walked the rooms to make sure all was well. Lucy kissed his cheek and went to finalize supper, leaving him alone with Melissa.

"I'm sorry your day was ruined with the tea." He pulled her to him.

Her arms went about his shoulders, fingers teasing his neck. "The morning with you and the girls outshine any darkness."

"Will you join us next Saturday? Claudio might need a support system to make it through Pancake Time."

Melissa's head went back in a laugh and Freddy tugged her against him. As soon as she straightened, his mouth was on hers. After several moments of smooth kisses, his lips trailed to the base of her throat, artfully displayed with the scalloped neckline of the lace dress. There he teased and tasted while Melissa did her best to stay upright under his attentions.

"Freddy," she whispered as he worked his way toward her lips, "I think you better go."

"Are your knees weakened?"

She laughed. "It might be good to set me on the bench before you leave."

He did, with a final kiss on the lips and a whispered "I love you."

***

Sunday, the Mellings slept late and stayed home from church, wrapped in each other's arms in the parlor. Darla called, changing her day to come from Monday to Tuesday due to the patient load she had with Dr. Hughes. Melissa took the afternoon to go for a long walk and contemplate her feelings for Freddy. She loved him, but did she love him enough to come back after leaving? Should she tell him how she felt or would it make it harder for him if she decided to stay in New York?

Monday morning, Melissa didn't return from her walk until she was sure Freddy would have already come and gone. Lucy was in the parlor with the girls, still in her kimono.

"There you are. Freddy had to rouse me because Alex had already left."

"I'm sorry, Lucy. Time got away from me." Melissa sat cross legged on the rug.

"Good morning, Sissa!" Phoebe hugged her and then kissed her cheek. "Daddy said to give you one from him."

"Thank you."

Then Bethany climbed down from Lucy's lap and hugged her too, flooding Melissa's nose with Freddy's scent.

"You two are the sweetest girls I've ever known. What are we going to play today?"

"It's time to plan another attack on Melling Militia." Phoebe took her best fighting stance, arm extended with an invisible sword. "I need to gather our weapons!"

She ran from the room and Lucy opened her arms to her youngest. Lucy kissed Bethany's shiny brunette hair. "Can you imagine this one as a big sister?"

"It's early yet. Remember what Claud—"

"I know." Lucy bit her lip. "But I can still hope. And Alex, God bless him, he'll drive me crazy in the coming months. He was a wreck when I was in labor with Bethany. Darla will probably throw him out of the birthing room."

Melissa couldn't help laughing. "She would at his first obscene remark."

When Phoebe returned with an armload of swords, Lucy excused herself. Melissa spent the morning in the backyard with the girls. When they came in for dinner, Lucy was aproned and cooking omelets and grits.

"I forgot to eat breakfast," she explained, "and eggs sounded easy."

After they were done eating, Lucy insisted on putting the girls down for their naps. Melissa used the time to list in her journal all the good points in returning to New York. Half a page, including multiple career goals, as well as friends and favorite places. She flopped onto her bed, more confused than ever.

By the time Phoebe roamed the hall, Lucy was back to work. In the few hours before Alex was expected, Melissa and the girls created a fort on the front porch with dining chairs and blankets, stocking it with newspaper balls. Melissa held position in the fort to help Bethany, and Lucy watched from the parlor window.

Alex came around the porch and whistled. "And what do we have here? A new castle erected on my turf?"

"Halt!" Phoebe shouted. "Kingdom Davenport secured the island for our purposes and you're trespassing. Come any closer and suffer the consequences!"

Alex made a show of stomping up the stairs like a giant. The girls giggled and Phoebe reached for a paper ball. Melissa handed one to Bethany as Alex faced the door to the hideout.

Phoebe jumped at him, a basket of ammo hanging from an arm and one ball in her hand ready to strike. "For the king!"

The pelting began.

Alex used his briefcase as a shield while Phoebe bombarded his torso. Bethany managed a few ankle strikes before he collapsed on the floorboards, groaning in false agony. "The knights of Kingdom Davenport are too strong! I fear I've lost this battle."

The girls were on him, bouncing on his stomach and sitting on his knees as they poked at him with play swords.

Phoebe peeled off one of his gloves and struck his cheek with a *thwack*. "We win!"

"Phoebe Camellia!" Lucy pushed through the screen. "That isn't ladylike."

Alex laughed and hugged Phoebe to his chest before letting her go. "She won the battle and all's fair in war." He brought his ungloved hand to Lucy's ankle with a mischievous grin. "Do you still love me, my queen, even though my palace is overrun by ruffians?"

"They can't be any worse than a rascal like you." Lucy bent to Bethany who sat on his knees.

"Don't strain yourself." Alex sat up with Bethany.

Lucy sighed. "I'm fine, Alex. You can't coddle me for nine months."

"But I can and I will." He lifted the hem of her red gown as he massaged her calf. "Pampering, honoring, and loving you, but never spoiling, Lucille Amelia Melling."

Thirty-Nine

Frederick planned for an extra half-hour at the gym to help relieve his stress from the weekend. Besides the ordeal at Mrs. Melling's, there was the fact that he'd professed his love for Melissa and she hadn't returned the favor. He was glad the first time was over the phone, so she couldn't see the disappointment on his face. The second time he turned away quickly to guard his feelings. But maybe he walked away too fast after their parting kiss.

Chuck circled him in the boxing ring. "Come on, Davenport. You need to focus. I saw you on the punching bag and your form was sloppy. Don't waste my time."

Henry watched from the ropes, waiting to take on the winner. "Forget your lady and let him have it so I don't have to."

"Lady troubles is it?" Chuck increased his footwork. "Did you and the redhead have your first fight as a couple?"

"We aren't a couple." Frederick's jab went too wide and he was back to defense.

"Then what are you? I sure don't want to go dress shopping with a woman unless there are clear expectations for our relationship."

"I don't know what we are, but I'd give anything for her." Frederick's light jabs turned to punches with all his weight behind them.

"What the hell, Davenport?" Thomas Charles called from the ropes opposite Henry. When Chuck went down with a bloodied nose, Thomas was there with a towel.

"You're out for the day, Davenport!" the gym manager hollered.

Henry held the ropes apart for Frederick and followed him to one of the full-size punching bags, holding it steady against the brute strength of his strikes. For fifteen minutes Frederick punched and Henry absorbed the force. When he finally stepped away, gloved fists hanging limply at his sides, Henry loosened the laces for him.

"Thanks, Henry. I'll see you at the office tomorrow."

Chuck was in the shower room holding ice to his nose.

"I am sorry, Chuck."

"It's been a while for you, but you've got it bad. Might want to keep it in perspective because word is she's going back to New York in a few weeks. Remind me not to get in the ring with you when she leaves."

After a hot shower, Frederick redressed in his office clothes and stopped at the diner for a quick supper. On the drive to get his daughters, he thought of Melissa's absence that morning. He knew she loved her walks, but she hadn't missed him dropping the girls off since her first week there, making him think it was deliberate. Had he gone too far Saturday night, either in going to Mrs. Melling's or his attentions to Melissa as they said good night?

He trudged up the front steps, eyeing the blanket fort on the porch. It transported him to his childhood sword battles with Edmund to rescue Lucy from imprisonment. A smile found his face at the memories and he entered the house without the guise of sadness.

"Daddy! Did you see our fort?" Phoebe ran to him in the parlor, hugging his knees.

"I sure did. Looks like a solid structure."

"Sissa helped us. We beat Melling Militia!"

Frederick's gaze settled on Alexander and Lucy, snug together on the settee with Bethany on his lap.

"You look no worse for the defeat."

Alexander smiled. "I've recovered, but Phoebe was a fighter, just like her dad. She even slapped me with my own glove when it was all said and done."

Frederick couldn't help the laugh that blurted out. "I can't say I've ever done that."

"Has Claudio settled in at your house?" Alexander asked.

"All is fine."

"He's coming for supper Wednesday," Lucy said, "if you'd like to join us."

He thought of his open invitation to Melissa to join him in town on his nights at the gym, but wasn't sure if that would ever happen again. "I'll let you know tomorrow."

"Daddy, I left Rummy upstairs. Will you come with me to get him?"

"Lead the way, Princess."

He waited in the hall when Phoebe ran to her bedroom, checking in Edmund's old space but it was empty. Phoebe rushed by, tossing her stuffed rabbit at him.

"I gotta go! Sissa's in the bathroom, so I'm going to Momma's!"

As soon as Phoebe was in the next room, the hall bathroom opened. Melissa, in a long, white cotton nightgown covered partially by a fringed Asian shawl of blues and reds, stared in disbelief as she clutched her wrap closed.

"Good evening, Melissa." He awkwardly held the rabbit under his arm. "Phoebe asked me to come up while she got Rummy and then she ran to Lucy's bathroom, leaving me to look a fool when you emerged."

"You're hardly a fool, Freddy."

"Then why are you avoiding me?" It came out harsher than he expected.

Melissa looked to the floor. "You have been good to me, but I don't trust myself to do the right thing when it comes to my feelings. I don't want to hurt—"

"Haven't we been through this before?" He gripped the rabbit around its neck.

"Yes, though I don't think it's Rummy's fault."

Frederick smiled and moved the rabbit to his other hand.

"Every day things between us advance." She spoke to his shoes as though afraid to meet his eyes. "I don't see the proper path that would be fair to both of us."

"I'm sorry if I went too far Saturday night with my attentions. I warned you I'm not accustomed to courting practices. If my touch or kiss makes you uncomfortable, I'll withhold them."

She raised her head, a rare, controlled smile on her face. "They feel wonderful, but I'm afraid they make me doubt my own intentions."

He stepped before her, a hand going to hers with a gentle caress. "I've told you I'll take what we have one day at a time. Don't worry about when it will end."

"Okay, Daddy!" Phoebe snatched the rabbit and wrapped her arms around Melissa's legs. "Good night, Sissa! See you in the morning!"

Frederick released her hand and moved to follow Phoebe. "I hope to see you in the morning as well."

"Freddy, I didn't mean to slight you."

He shrugged. "It's one of those things."

Then her hands were on his chest and she leaned against him as she angled for his mouth. "I don't mean to hurt you," she whispered before she pressed her lips to his.

He kissed her back but refrained from touching. When she pulled away, he was quick to reply. "Then don't ignore me. I'd rather be friends than nothing."

Melissa's smile was pained. "Agreed. I'll see you in the morning, Freddy."

***

Tuesday was back to normal with greetings from Melissa when Frederick left the girls and returned after work. They set plans to meet Darla and Henry for supper the next day, and he returned home with the girls to supper prepared by Miss Sharon and the added benefit of Claudio's company.

"It is good to be here," Claudio said as the girls ran off to play. "*Signora's* house was suffocating me. I have felt better these past few days than any other time on my stay. Thank you, Frederick."

They carried the dishes into the kitchen. "I love my girls, but there's something about adult conversation that brings meaning to the day. Do you play chess?"

"*Sí*, but I am out of practice. I have not played since Alex left Monroe."

They settled in the living room, Claudio on the sofa, the board on the coffee table, and Frederick sitting on the floor across from him. The girls and Doff played around them as Claudio blundered through a game.

"Maybe you should play against yourself while I get the girls ready for bed."

After Phoebe and Bethany were down for the night, Frederick carried a tea tray into the living room. Memories of the time Alexander roomed with him when he tried to stay sober and make amends with Lucy filtered through Frederick's mind as he and Claudio played the next game.

"After the fire, was Alex immediately changed or was it a slow process?"

Claudio shook his head. "Much had changed to him that last day at Seacliff Cottage, but it took him a while to completely give up his old ways. He was impulsive—like inviting Consuela to go with us to Louisiana."

"What?" Frederick's knuckles whitened with strain. "After claiming to still love Lucy and his display of longing with Maggie?"

"Alexander was scared and desired a familiar face. He wanted to take her away from a life of sin and help her start new like he was doing. He paid for her separate room and meals and only asked that she tend his burns twice a day. But do not be upset with him—he told Lucy all this when he returned. He even told her he planned to marry Consuela when he healed and took a job."

In his anger, Frederick missed taking Claudio's bishop. When he saw his mistake, it was too late.

Claudio moved in for a check. "Finding Consuela with a client in the hotel room he was paying for helped him understand his own mistakes. He could not force her to change, just as loving Lucy was not enough for him to defeat his demons. Alex washed his hands of her. His health improved without the alcohol, but his heart still ached for Lucy, though he was happy you were there for her."

"I find that hard to believe."

"He was joyous for her when he saw your wedding announcement. He said out of all the people in her life, you were the best one to care for and love her. But he did gloat in having her first—in being the one to teach her what it meant to love and be loved."

"Alex will always be Alex."

"But we love him in spite of his flaws because none of us are perfect, though he is perfect for Lucy." Claudio smiled. "And I think I have finally made it to checkmate."

***

On his lunch hour Wednesday, Frederick walked to Mr. Hofstedder's jewelry store. When the bell on the door announced his entry, the owner smiled.

"Mr. Davenport, it's good to see you. What can I help you with today?"

"It's not time for another ring, if that is what you are thinking."

Mr. Hofstedder laughed and rubbed his balding head. "It's always fun to wait on a pleasant customer. I will cut a discount if you keep me entertained."

"And you know the way to loyalty from an accountant." Frederick smiled. "I'm here for a gift for a special friend."

"*Special* indeed, Mr. Davenport." He winked. "What type of piece for this lady?"

"A brooch, nothing flashy. Something classic that could be worn with a walking suit or gown."

"You can never go wrong with a cameo."

Frederick followed him to a display case in the corner. It took him mere seconds to spot the perfect piece. Trimmed in gold, the oval background was a flesh color much like Melissa's tanned complexion. The ivory woman depicted in profile had her arms crossed on top of a globe, a roll of parchment at its base.

"This one, please. Second row, third from the left."

"Shall I bring out another to compare?" the owner asked.

"No, thank you. That is the one."

"I insist you hold it first, Mr. Davenport."

Looking down on it in his hand, he knew it was meant for Melissa. He handed it across the counter. "Please box it, Mr. Hofstedder."

"We haven't discussed price."

"I will pay whatever you ask for it." He pulled his checkbook out of his suit pocket and readied his pen.

"You have always been a man who knows what he wants and it is a lovely piece, Mr. Davenport."

Frederick returned to his office with a bagged sandwich, the gift in his pocket, and a spring in his step. He might have danced to the coffee pot.

Henry let out a laugh. "Easy there, Davenport, or people will get the wrong idea on how you spent your lunch."

He set the coffee down and punched Henry's shoulder. "Careful how you talk to the boss, Adams, or he might get the idea you don't value your job."

"I'll save my banter for the boxing ring."

After eating, Frederick took two appointments. At four o'clock, he organized the files from his last client when someone knocked on the door.

"It's open!"

He expected it to be the intern or secretary and finished sorting the last few pages. When he finally looked up, he met Melissa's steady gaze. She wore her brown walking suit, parasol under her arm and a wristlet hanging at her side.

"I hope I'm not a bother."

"Never, Melissa." He crossed to her and set her things on the corner chair before pulling her in for a hug that turned to kissing.

"You caught me more relaxed than typical." He reached for his jacket off the coatrack.

"I'd never think badly of you being comfortable." She ran her hands down his white shirtsleeves.

"I'll leave it off then, but there's something I need to get from the pocket." She caught her breath when he removed the gold box. "I wanted to replace your brooch so you leave with what you came with, though hopefully with more fond memories than when you arrived."

"Freddy," her voice softened, "you didn't need to."

"I wanted to. It's not as fancy as the other, but I hope you like it." He opened her palm and placed the box in her hand. "Please accept this token of my admiration for you."

"You're sweeter than Naomi's iced tea." She kissed his cheek, hand trembling as she lifted the lid and gasped.

"I hope it meets your approval."

"It's perfect, Freddy. Grandmother Stone always wore her cameo on special occasions. I was to have it after she died, but my father sold it to help pay her burial expenses. I always meant to buy one when I started earning a decent living, but I never could bring myself to do so. Thank you."

"May I pin it on you, my globe-trotting writer?"

"Only if you place it over my heart."

Forty

On Friday, Melissa helped Phoebe and Bethany ready for their naps. She waited a few minutes in her room until their noises quieted, and then she went to the parlor with her journal to curl in the armchair by the window.

Half an hour later, Lucy emerged from the study with a pile of papers in her arms and a smile on her face. "I finished and already called Alex. Do you wish to call Mr. Noble or shall I?"

Melissa hugged her. "Congratulations, but I don't think we need to tell Mr. Noble until you're done with the edits."

"He needs to know so you can set your travel plans." She stared at the cameo on the ribbon choker about Melissa's neck as she spoke. "April thirteenth will be good. I'll go through with add-ins and the edits the next few days, then we'll take a week with typing. You'll be here for Darla and Henry's wedding, plus two days to pack and say your goodbyes."

Hearing a date two weeks away sent Melissa's heart crashing. She managed a nod. "You call him with your news. The secretary is more likely to put you through than me."

Melissa paced by the study door as Lucy settled at her desk. From the drawer she pulled a small notebook and hunched over the phone. When the operator picked up, she informed her of the long distance call to New York and held for the transfer before reading off the number. As she waited, Lucy's posture straightened.

"Good afternoon. This is Mrs. Melling, otherwise known as Olive Kent."

Melissa blinked at the pronounced southern accent Lucy placed in her voice.

"I have important news to relay to Mr. Noble if you would be so good as to put me through to his secretary." She smirked as she listened to the reply. "Why of course, and thank you."

Shock to know Lucy played the office staff froze Melissa.

Lucy caught her stare and covered the mouthpiece. "It helps that they think little ol' me can't lift a finger without dear Mr. Noble." Her eyes widened and she lowered her hand. "Yes, Ms. Lamont, it's me. It's so good to hear your friendly voice. We've seen our azaleas and have moved on to the magnolia blossoms. Has spring finally reached your fine city?"

Bile rose in Melissa's throat, but she finally understood why Mr. Noble never pressed Lucy's previous contracts. She knew he was charmed by Lucy, but didn't know the extent of her cunning portrayal to the whole office staff. No wonder Mr. Noble thought she needed a babysitter to finish her manuscript—she was all gushing Southern Belle! Melissa could not stomach listening to the details, but Lucy waved her over a minute later.

"She's pulling him out of a meeting to take my call."

Lucy sitting in her home a thousand miles away could get Mr. Noble pulled out of a meeting because she'd written a few fluffy novels, while Melissa in the same city had to wait weeks for a minute of his time when she'd penned the man hundreds of articles and traveled the globe on his business for almost a decade. It wasn't fair, and it wasn't right. She couldn't hide the anger that began to boil.

Lucy's smile turned to a frown and she picked at the corner of her typewriter rather than look at Melissa.

"Why, good afternoon, Mr. Noble! I have news sure to give you joy." Lucy listened and then laughed that sickening enchanted bell sound.

Melissa wanted to grab the letter opener off the desk and—

No!

She took the job helping Lucy because she knew how Mr. Noble felt about her. Olive Kent was her ticket into Mr. Noble's office. She couldn't resent that when the end was in sight.

The end.

Leaving Freddy.

Leaving Phoebe and Bethany.

That's what she was upset about—Lucy pushing her away, trying to protect her family like Melissa was an ailment they needed to keep away from because she lived in New York rather than Alabama.

"Ms. Stone has been such a blessing."

Melissa snapped back to attention.

"She did just what you said she would, lending a hand so I could focus on writing, and she'll help with typing after I work edits."

Lucy bit her lip as she listened to Mr. Noble.

"No, sir. We'll be done within two weeks. Ms. Stone will be ready to leave on April thirteenth. Feel free to book her train ticket for then so she'll be in the office the following Monday. That should keep your lawyers happy."

A frown, a smile. "Yes, I'm quite certain. And it's no rush, but a pleasure."

She twirled the cord around her finger. "Thank you, Mr. Noble. Yes, she's right here. And I expect a phone call from you after you read it."

Lucy stood and motioned to her seat. Melissa reluctantly took her place behind the desk. "Hello, Mr. Noble."

"Ms. Stone, I must offer my thanks for all you've done this month. Many people told me it would never work, but I had faith in you. And the article and photographs about Mobile were perfect. The magazine department was thrilled. We expect a great response when it goes to press."

"I'm glad to hear that. I'll be sure to bring the new manuscript directly to you when I return. I also have—"

"I look forward to it, Ms. Stone, but I must get back to my meeting. My secretary will handle your travel plans."

A pause.

"Ms. Stone?"

"Yes, Ms. Lamont."

"What day will your departure be from Mobile?"

Melissa glanced up at Lucy's stabbing smile. "April thirteenth."

***

Melissa and Freddy dined alone after his gym time that evening.

"Two weeks?" His soft gaze held her captivated across the table at Klosky's New Italian Garden and Buffet.

"Yes. Lucy insists she'll be done by Darla and Henry's wedding. She wants me to turn in her manuscript the following week."

Freddy's mouth turned down. "I'm sure she does."

"The publishing company will call Monday with my travel itinerary." Her hand reached out and they held each other across the table. "We knew the day was coming."

The string quartette playing across the room made the moment lighter than it was, but Melissa felt the warmth of Freddy's smile. "Then we'll enjoy each moment, starting with dancing after supper."

She looked around the airy space, eyeing the tables between the bricked archways. "Is there dancing here?"

He squeezed her hand. "There will be this evening, though no Turkey Trotting."

Melissa felt like a princess on Freddy's arm. His navy suit was complementary to her sage ensemble and they turned many heads as he led her toward the music. It felt as though the whole restaurant watched as they danced a flowing Viennese Waltz amid the greenery. A few other couples joined in, but Melissa only gazed upon her partner. She tried to memorize the feel of his hand snug on her waist, the scent of his cologne, and his delightful smile.

Freddy twirled her to a stop at the end of the Vivaldi score, curling her to his side. "Would you like another one?"

"Yes, but then you need to return for the girls, don't you?"

He nodded and started them in with the next tune. It was quicker, but he kept her close so they could talk. "I like how you're wearing the brooch today. It's almost as if your tasty neck is a package to be unwrapped."

"Not tonight, Freddy." She smiled. "But you may taste of my lips if we have privacy later."

After the ride home, Freddy parked in the Mellings' driveway. He came to the shadowed side of the automobile and opened the door for Melissa. She stood and wrapped her arms about his broad shoulders as he fingered the brooch on her choker.

"May I kiss you, my beloved?"

Her heart swelled with his words. "Yes."

His hands went to her waist then skimmed to her back. Freddy's mouth tasted of the wine they'd had with dinner and his caressing hands on her back a savory dessert. He turned their positions so his back was to the automobile and took her by the hips, pressing her against him. Electricity tingled from her core outward, wanting nothing more than to touch him and have him explore her in return.

"Melissa." His breath was hot on her ear. "I hope you enjoy this as much as I do."

He kissed her earlobe with a flick of his tongue and worked his way along her jaw to the other ear. She was near breathless and all she could think of was the conversation about sex Maggie and Lucy had with Darla the other week. She had never felt like this and knew she would give herself to Freddy if he asked it of her. But she also knew he never would—unless a ring and ceremony were a part of the deal.

Her hands ran down his chest, feeling the definition of his muscles under his shirt. "I think we better go inside, Freddy. You've weakened my knees and eroded my inhibitions."

"Then my job here is done."

They held each other in a tight hug, neither speaking before stepping apart.

"Two more weeks of this and I'll be a spoiled man."

She clasped hands with him and they started for the porch. "There will never be another time like this for me."

Before opening the front door, he paused for a quick kiss. Then they joined the hoopla in the parlor—Alex giving pony rides to the girls.

Lucy looked between them with her cold, green stare. "You two appear to have enjoyed yourselves this evening."

"We did." Freddy saw Melissa to an armchair and turned his full attention to Lucy as his daughters rode by on Alex's back. "For one claiming to be concerned about my happiness, you don't seem pleased to see me smiling."

"When I know it to be from something temporary, I can't delight in it."

Freddy dropped beside Lucy on the settee and took her chin in his hand. "Do you see any hint of sadness or regret on my face, in my eyes?"

She was silent for what seemed like minutes. "No."

"Do you see joy or fulfillment?"

A longer pause. "Yes, but that's the prob—"

"No, that's *your* problem. We know what is coming. It's not going to be a surprise heartache." He released her stubborn chin. "If you cannot be happy for us, please feign indifference."

He stood, looking nobler than ever as his eyes went to his daughters squealing in delight as they tumbled off Alex's back.

"It looks like your horse needs to be set out to pasture, princesses."

Alex took a swipe at Freddy's ankles, and he allowed himself to fall. He easily wrestled Alex into a headlock with his massive arms, his legs catching the smaller man in a scissor hold.

Lucy jumped to her feet. "Frederick Lionel Davenport, that's my husband!"

"Yes, and he tripped me."

"Another win for Kingdom Davenport!" Phoebe raised a hand in triumph.

Bethany clapped and Melissa laughed.

Lucy huffed. "These battles are getting too realistic for me."

Freddy released Alex, who collapsed on his back gasping theatrically for the girls benefit. "Melling Militia is officially done for the week. I shall report for battle Monday."

Phoebe cheered and climbed onto her father's lap.

Alex raised his arms. "I need my queen to put me to bed."

"How about I ready a hot bath for you first?" Lucy went for the door.

"That's good for a start. Say goodnight to your momma, girls."

While they said their goodbyes to Lucy and then Alex, Freddy gave Melissa a firm kiss.

"Eight o'clock tomorrow morning?" he asked.

"I wouldn't miss it."

The girls each hugged her and then the Davenports were gone. Alex still lay on the rug and Melissa nudged him with a foot.

"Show's over, Alex. You can get up now."

He groaned and rolled to his stomach before getting to his knees. "Parts of me are sore I didn't know existed. Either Phoebe is getting too big or I'm getting too old."

"Both, I think." Melissa laughed.

Alex held to the edge of the coffee table to stand. "Are you off to Pancake Time tomorrow?"

"Yes, around seven-thirty I imagine."

"When you return there will probably be strange men here, and Lucy and I might be out. I plan on taking her to breakfast and then shopping for another desk and typewriter for you. I've arranged for carpenters to install a swing in the gazebo, as well as another surprise." He put a finger over his mirthful mouth.

Melissa made the motion of buttoning her lips.

"And next week, an architect will be drawing plans for a new cottage on Seacliff, though Lucy doesn't know it yet."

"Are you trying to spoil her?"

His grin was pure, eyes bright. "She's not one to spoil. I, on the other hand, am rotten to my soul."

She joined him near the hall, laying a hand on his arm. "You no longer play a convincing bad guy, if you ever did."

"If you'd like to make inquiries, I'm sure you'd find witnesses to dispute that claim." He shifted toward her in a playful manner.

"Anyone that's seen you with Phoebe and Bethany couldn't think poorly of you." To change the light-hearted mood and release the hold his charm had on her, Melissa switched the subject. "How has your mother been the last few days?"

His eyes darkened. "Not good. I've been going to her on my lunch hour. She's still in bed from the episode Saturday. The nurses sitting with her say she babbles about Eliza. Her breathing is weak and she isn't eating much. It doesn't look good."

"I'm sorry to hear that, Alex." She put a hand on his shoulder. "Has Claudio visited?"

He shook his head. "But I think he should. They need to make amends."

Could Mrs. Melling forgive someone she had held in high regard for being human and sinning with her cherished daughter?

"Let me know if there's anything I can do."

He gave a solemn nod and kissed the back of the hand she'd placed on his shoulder. "Thank you, Melissa."

"Alex," Lucy's voice called from the top of the stairs, "it's ready."

He released Melissa's hand with smile. "My queen awaits."

Forty-One

The following Friday, Alex stayed home. Freddy sent the girls' Easter dresses with them and midday Alex, Lucy, Phoebe, and Bethany walked to St. Mary's for Holy Friday Mass. Phoebe was exquisite in baby blue and Bethany striking in the daffodil yellow gown Melissa picked out. From their frilly bonnets to their gleaming white shoes, the Davenport girls were sure to stop traffic on their way to church, especially with Lucy in pink from head to toe and Alex in a blue suit with a pink bowtie and handkerchief. Melissa almost wished to attend Mass with them to gage the reaction of the congregation, but she settled at her temporary desk in the study. It was smaller than Lucy's, but large enough to hold the new Underwood, the manuscript sitting under the lamp beside it, and a fresh stack of paper on the other side. They were only halfway through retyping, and she felt her time best served working than following the Mellings to church.

A few typed pages later, the telephone rang.

Melissa went to Lucy's desk. "Mellings' residence."

"How did the girls look?" Freddy asked.

Melissa smiled. "Gorgeous. Lucy and Alex couldn't get over how fine everything is. It's sweet of you to allow them to wear the clothes first with Lucy. I took a family portrait before they left, which they also appreciated."

"Our patchwork family. You still don't think we're too crazy for you, do you?"

"Not at all, Freddy."

"Good because Claudio informed me this morning he has to be at St. Joseph's early tomorrow. He'll miss Pancake Time."

Melissa laughed. "It was your idea not to warn him last week. How would you have felt being woken up to all that banging, and then running into a kitchen full of people staring at you in your nightshirt?"

It was Freddy's turn to chuckle. "I think that Italian he spoke had more than enough choice words, though he was a good sport about it." He was silent a moment. "The girls and I are going to their grandparents' for Easter dinner. You are invited and can ride with Alex and Lucy or I will pick you up. But you're coming, I insist. Lucy wanted me to invite you. She thought you would be more willing to accept this way."

"You really want me there?"

"The Eastons are as close to parents as I have now and Lucy's siblings are like cousins. I would like you to meet them."

"Then I will come, but I'd rather ride with you if it isn't too much trouble."

"Never, Melissa. I'll let you get back to work. I had to call because I was an inch away from running over there to kiss you once more. You tasted divine this morning."

Melissa felt her cheeks warm with the memory of his lips upon her. "Tonight you may have more. Where are we taking supper this evening so I know how to dress?"

"At the diner with Henry and Darla. Then we will have all day together tomorrow. Phoebe is looking forward to Monroe Park."

"She let me know many times this morning. I'll see you at the gym at six, Freddy."

"I will count the minutes, Beloved."

Replacing the telephone, Melissa relished the surge of energy Freddy's words created. She gazed out the window to the double glider swing under the magnolia—Alex's surprise from the previous weekend—and thought to the evening before when Freddy joined her and the girls on it. He had sat with Phoebe and Melissa with Bethany, each pair looking at the other as the twin benches swung.

To focus her mind, she boiled water for tea and made herself a sandwich before settling back at the desk.

When the family returned from church, Alex looked in on her. His jacket, tie, and shoes were removed, shirt half-unbuttoned to showcase his scars. "Would you like to join us for dinner?"

"I already fixed myself a sandwich, but thank you."

"When we're done eating, I'm sending Lucy in here while I watch the girls. What time do you need to leave to meet Freddy?"

"I'm not going early, so about five-thirty."

"I'll watch the clock for you. Would stopping by five give you enough time to prepare?"

Melissa smiled. "Yes, plenty. You're very thoughtful."

"The more work you get done today, the less Lucy will need to do tomorrow. And with the house to ourselves all day, I'd rather see her reclined somewhere than stuck behind her typewriter." Alex winked.

"Always an ulterior motive when it comes to you."

"I'm incorrigible when it comes to Lucy." He absentmindedly stroked his chest. "I did decide to save the Seacliff plans until after the manuscript is finished. I don't want any distractions for her until these pages are retyped."

"Then what will tomorrow be if not a distraction?"

"A deposit in the bank of love."

Melissa laughed and tried to refocus her thoughts on the mundane task of typing when Alex had firmly planted seeds of sensuality in her brain. Her mind wanted to wander over Freddy—his loving attentions and firm muscles. The way his strong hands felt on her hips and his mouth at her throat. She groaned and leaned her head against the bookcase behind her.

"One more week," she whispered. "Will it be enough to satisfy us?"

Lucy, changed from her church finery into her kimono, came in. "Is the story so bad you want to bang your head against the wall?"

"Not at all. I got distracted and needed a moment to clear my thoughts. Freddy called while you were out. He insists I come with him to the family dinner Sunday."

"You cannot be alone on Easter." Lucy sat regally behind her desk.

"So you don't mind?"

"I told him to invite you, didn't I?" She twisted her hair into a bun and shoved two pens through it.

"It sounds important to him. He said your parents are as close to parents as he has and your brothers and sisters are like cousins."

Lucy's eyes narrowed. "My family has always loved him. Except Edmund, who now despises him, but that's because of me and Alex. I doubt he'll be there, but Susan is coming from Grand Bay, so you'll be able to meet one of my sisters."

"That will be nice."

"Susan adores Frederick. She is always trying to set him up with eligible ladies from south Mobile County. She loves to play big sister to him. Don't be upset if she questions your motives or gives you a colder shoulder than I do."

Melissa wanted to ask if that was possible, but held her tongue.

"Pass me the next chapter, please." Lucy offered a hand and they worked to the sound of dueling Underwoods for several hours.

***

After attending Easter sunrise Mass with Lucy and Alex, Melissa went back to the study while the Mellings disappeared into their bedroom. Six chapters remained and she was determined to complete another before Freddy picked her up at twelve-thirty. She kicked off her shoes and loosened the sash on the gown she'd purchased for Mrs. Melling's tea before settling at her desk.

At ten, Alex strode in with a cup of coffee and scone, leaving them at the corner of the desk.

"Don't let Lucy see you being nice to me."

He laughed. "She's sleeping right now, but she does like you, Melissa. She feels guilty for breaking Freddy's heart and as she's the reason you're in town, anything that might happen between the two of you—good or bad—she feels responsible for."

Melissa crossed her arms. "Her logic is flawed."

"Of course it is. She left a comfortable life with a respected husband for a scarred, drunken attorney who'd treated her horrendously the last time she was with him."

"Because she loves you."

"And love does not always make sense, like you and Freddy falling for each other when you live so far apart." Alex held her gaze with his piercing blue eyes. "But like for me and Lucy, if you and Freddy are serious, it can work out."

"It's that easy?"

"You're smarter than that, Melissa." He smirked. "You've heard what we both went through, but in the end, all the sacrifice was worth it. You have to know your limits. For Lucy it was not leaving the town where her children live. I had to come to her though I wished never to return to this place, the family I forsook, the old friends who witnessed my many sins. Lucy has undergone more gossip and scrutiny for her divorce than anything before. You and Freddy need to discover what you're willing to live with or without to make it work."

She stood and hugged him. "Thank you, Alex. I've come to respect you and enjoy our friendship. And yes, even your bawdy sense of humor."

He flashed a naughty smile as he lifted her hand to his lips. "I'll miss you, too."

Melissa tried to understand all that Alex had told her as she sipped the coffee and ate the pastry. A minute later, Alex crossed the backyard. He settled on the double glider, placing an ashtray beside him and lighting a cigarette. In all her time with the Mellings, she never heard them mention friends beyond Freddy, Darla, Claudio, Maggie, and Douglas. They never went out to supper parties or had visitors except those few—three of which lived out of town. Their choice to reunite appeared to have left them isolated.

She finished eating and returned to work. When she typed the last period at the end of the chapter and laid the page face down on the pile of completed ones, she sighed in relief to see it wasn't quite noon. Melissa paused in the parlor doorway. Alex rested his head on Lucy's lap as she read poetry aloud.

Lucy looked up when she finished the poem by Lord Byron.

"We are down to five chapters. I'll try to complete another before going to bed tonight."

"It's a holiday, Melissa." Lucy closed the book over her finger marking the page. "You don't need to push so hard."

"I want to be sure it's completed before Wednesday like you wished. We'll all be at the wedding that day and then Thursday and Friday I'll need to see to packing. You won't expect anything from me those days, will you?"

"Of course not. You're here to help me fulfill my contract. As soon as one of us types *the end*, you're a guest."

"Would you like that honor, typing the last page?" Melissa asked.

"However it falls is fine. You've typed more of this draft than I have. If you have the final chapter, don't wait on me."

A short time later, Alex helped Lucy into their automobile while Melissa waited on the porch for the Davenports to arrive. Phoebe was out the door as soon as Freddy rolled the automobile to a stop, a blue streak running for her mother.

"Momma! Mr. Alex! May I ride with you?"

Freddy lifted a hand in agreement as he went to the passenger side to keep Bethany from tumbling out the open door. Melissa crossed the yard and kissed his cheek before accepting his hand to climb inside.

"Sissa." Bethany reached for her.

Melissa pulled her into her lap. Freddy closed the door and shouted over to Alex. "We'll see you there!"

Forty-Two

Frederick always felt a pang of guilt when he went to the Eastons'. He knew they didn't need a huge home, but the single-story row house seemed cruel though it was the right size for them. Maxwell and Lottie were already there with their five children, as well as Susan and David and their seven. Maxwell took Melissa to introduce her to his wife and their brood running around the little yard. Then Frederick brought her inside because he wanted to be the one to make the introductions to his old in-laws.

Mrs. Easton rearranged the centerpiece on the dining room table—always having to fuss over something, and he loved her for it.

"Thank you for having us, Mrs. E," he said when they stopped in the doorway.

"Freddy, you need to visit more often." She turned around, seeing first Bethany in her yellow dress. "There's my sweet girl. I heard about Lucy parading them to St. Mary's on Friday. If it's not—"

Her eyes went to Melissa. She gave a not-so-subtle appraisal before smiling. "Here I am babbling away when you want to introduce me."

"Mrs. E, this is Melissa Stone. Melissa, Evelyn Easton."

Melissa offered a hand but Mrs. Easton pulled her into a hug, whispered something, and then stepped to Frederick for a hug as well.

"She's pretty as a picture." She spoke into his ear before taking Bethany from him. "James will be out in a minute. Wait for him in the parlor, Freddy."

He led Melissa back to the front room, leaving Bethany with her grandmother.

"What did she tell you?" Frederick asked once they were on the settee.

Melissa laughed. "That if I hurt you, she'll wring my New York neck. Now I know where Lucy gets her pluck."

"The Easton women are something else, that's for sure."

Mr. Easton entered from the hall, leaning heavily on his cane. Frederick stood and helped Melissa up. "Good afternoon, Mr. E."

"Freddy, my son." He hugged him with a strength Frederick didn't realize he still possessed. "I hear you've brought along a special friend."

The screen door slammed shut, everyone turning to stare a moment at Lucy.

"Yes, Mr. E. This is Melissa Stone. Melissa, James Easton."

"Thank you for having me today," Melissa said as she shook hands.

"Anyone with Freddy is welcome here. Our family is yours, dear."

Lucy stomped through the room, the sound of her shoes on the hardwood a novelty for the usually barefooted woman. Frederick watched her go for the kitchen and knew he needed to approach the topic he'd avoided all week. He saw Melissa seated, excused himself, and found his ex-wife in the kitchen with a pilfered sweet roll.

"I know exactly what you're doing, Frederick Davenport, and I won't stand for it!"

Both her mother holding Bethany and the cook turned to stare.

Without speaking, he took Lucy by the elbow and marched her out the rear door. He didn't stop until they reached the back fence.

Frederick released her arm and stood facing her. "To let you know, next Friday night I am going out of town with the girls. We will return the following Thursday morning."

"You're not chasing that woman with my daughters in tow!"

"I figured it would be a good time for a change of pace, to help us all with the transition. We are going to see Angela. I haven't been since before Bethany was born and the girls are old enough for me to handle them on the train by myself."

Lucy scowled and crossed her arms. "I know Melissa is going through Atlanta. I suppose you're going to tell me you happened to get tickets on the same train as hers."

"As a matter of fact I did, though Melissa doesn't know it."

She took a bite of the roll and glared.

"You gave up your right to interfere in my life when you divorced me."

"You're introducing her to your surrogate parents and then you'll introduce her to your sister at the train station. You want your family's approval before declaring yourself to her, I know you do!"

"I am a grown man and need no one's approval, though family support is welcomed."

"You have no right to put our daughters through such games!" Lucy shoved against his solid chest. "Leave them with me and go chase her all the way to New York for all I care!"

Alexander ran from the house, taking Lucy around the waist from behind. "My queen, you need to calm down. The whole street can hear you."

"Then let them!" She shoved Alexander away. "Let this whole town know that Frederick Lionel Davenport is a romantic fool who deserves every ounce of heartache he has coming to him!"

Lucy ripped the pink hat from her head and slapped Frederick across the chest with it twice before flinging it on the ground. She ran a few steps, removed her shoes, and threw them at him as well before running for the front yard.

"Sorry, Freddy!" Alexander called before chasing Lucy down the sidewalk.

Frederick collected her shoes and hat, laying them on the back porch before returning to the kitchen.

"I don't know what gets into her," Mrs. Easton said. "She's most unreasonable when it comes to you, Freddy. I think it's because she loves you so much. Don't take it personally."

"Maybe I should go home and let Alex bring me the girls later."

Mrs. Easton put her arm around him and walked to the front of the house. "If Lucille wants to act like a spoiled child, that's her problem. And Alex's for indulging her too much. I'd much rather keep your company than hers if she insists on behaving in such a manner."

They reached the parlor just as Maxwell ushered all the children inside. "Now that was a fine display! Your neighbors will have enough gossip to keep them busy all week, Mother."

"How did she end her tirade?"

"Running barefoot down the sidewalk with Alex in pursuit."

Phoebe bounced in her scuffed leather shoes. "We have Melling Militia on the run!"

Frederick smiled. "That we do, Phoebe."

At dinner, Frederick was pleased to see Melissa getting along with Susan. They let the cousins play after eating, and then Frederick sought Maxwell in the backyard.

"Leave it to Alex to create more of a spectacle on the way back than Lucy did on her way out." Maxwell referred to Alexander carrying Lucy inside when he brought her back after her tantrum. He'd taken her to the bathroom and washed her feet before they came to the dining table. "You put up with a lot from those two."

"They mean well." He clapped Maxwell on the back. "Call me at the office sometime. We'll meet for lunch."

Then he gathered his girls and Melissa. "Would you like to come over for a little while?" Frederick asked once they were all in the automobile. "I think these two will be asleep before long."

"That's tempting, Freddy, but I'd like to get another chapter typed today."

"Would you like to spend the day together Thursday or come home with us after the wedding Wednesday?"

"We'll see what happens in the next few days, but I'll meet you for supper tomorrow, if you'd like."

"I'd enjoy that."

Frederick glanced at her before turning onto Government Street. Her smile set his cravings on edge. With Bethany sleeping in Melissa's lap and Phoebe drowsy between them, he knew it was good they weren't going home because he couldn't trust himself when his yearnings were so strong. He was persuasive enough when he walked her to the front porch. Roaming hands, active lips—he let his passions loose and Melissa returned the affection.

A sigh of contentment escaped her as they hugged. "I'll see you tomorrow, Freddy."

***

When Frederick parked in front of Lucy's house Tuesday afternoon, Alexander's automobile was gone. He always got home before Frederick arrived. With an inkling of worry, he mounted the porch steps. Only the sounds of Naomi in the kitchen reached his ears once he stepped inside. Frederick checked in the parlor and study before going upstairs. All the rooms were empty except one.

Melissa lay on top of her bedspread, sleeping curled on her side. Her pale blue day dress was slightly rumpled, but she was prettier than ever in her relaxed state. The bed squeaked under his weight and her body naturally curved toward his when he lay behind her, following the bend of her knees with his own. He felt her awaken as his arm went about her middle and he nestled his face against her hair.

"Good evening, Melissa. I take it your work here is done."

"Yes." Her body tensed. "But what time is it?"

"Ten after five. Everyone's gone."

"Alex came home at two and took Lucy and the girls out to celebrate the manuscript's completion. I would have thought they'd be back by now." She turned to face him, a smile replacing the look of worry that first creased her face. "It's lovely to wake up to your voice and touch."

His fingertips traced her lips before he left a soft kiss there.

Tears welled in her brown eyes, and she buried her face in his chest as though trying to hide her emotions. "I don't know how to be true to myself and you at the same time."

"Melissa, I want you to know that I'd never hold you back from your goals. I'd follow you to New York if I didn't have the girls to think about, but I do, and they need to be near their mother."

"I'd never ask you to break your family apart, Freddy."

He grasped her hips, pulling her against him for a probing kiss.

"Every piece of me wants you—to talk with you, kiss you, hold you, make love to you, and be with you every day for the rest of my life. I love you, Melissa. I love you and you're free to accept my love eternally or enjoy it as a brief moment of your life. But should you come back, I'll be waiting with a wedding ring."

"But it wouldn't be fair. I don't know how long I'd be gone, how—"

Frederick stopped her with a kiss. "The only thing unfair would be for us to have never met. Do you deny your feelings for me?"

"I think you know how I feel though I've been reluctant to say the words in fear of hurting you when I leave." Her hands went to his cheeks as her tender gaze pierced his soul.

"Will you tell me now?"

"You've charmed me since day one. Your honorable character, fine dancing, and loving ways have captivated my heart. I love you, Freddy. I love you like I never thought possible and can't see my future without you in it. I'll come back to you, I promise."

"That's all I need."

They lay in each other's arms several minutes, but sat respectfully in the parlor when Alexander, Lucy, and the girls returned at six o'clock.

"Sorry to keep you waiting, Freddy." Alexander brought Bethany to him. "We went out for ice cream and came across the Campbells and Walkers. They'd just arrived from the island and we let the kids play in the square. Time got away from us."

Frederick smiled. "It's no trouble. We've enjoyed the quiet."

Alexander smirked and started to swivel his hips, but Melissa threw a needlework pillow at him.

"Attack on Melling Militia!" Phoebe sounded the battle cry.

"It is too late to start that up." Lucy said from the doorway, arms crossed in front of her purple dress.

Alexander caught Phoebe around the middle and swung her over his shoulder. Her rambunctious giggles chased Lucy away before he set Phoebe back on her feet.

"Go find Momma and tell her we're sorry. Then kiss her cheeks until she smiles." Phoebe ran from the room and Alexander turned back to Frederick with a grin. "I'm off the whole day tomorrow and we are hosting the captains and all their children in the morning while Maggie and Claire help Darla before the ceremony. The kids will eat doughnuts and play, and then we'll get them dressed and bring them to the cathedral. You're welcome to stick around. I'll call Claudio tonight and invite him too. It will give him more of a chance to see the others before he heads back to Louisiana. And don't forget supper here tomorrow night as well, if you would like to eat with us."

"I might stay for a little while in the morning, but I do have a ten o'clock appointment I cannot miss. And supper …" He looked to Melissa, who nodded. "That sounds nice, thank you."

Forty-Three

Melissa allowed herself to sleep in, though when she woke at eight and realized she'd missed time with Freddy, she felt guilty. Then she remembered he was staying later to see the visitors and hurriedly dressed. Wearing a basic blouse and skirt, she laid out her sage dress for the wedding.

She found Freddy filling a carafe with coffee at the kitchen counter.

"Morning, Handsome."

He set the containers down and embraced her. "Good morning. Did you sleep in?"

"Yes." She kissed him. "Thinking of you kept me up late."

"All good things?"

"The best." She kissed him again, slower. "I love you."

The kitchen door swayed on its hinges. Melissa looked to Freddy.

"Lucy," he said in response to her unasked question

"Did she hear?"

"Yes."

"Good. Let her know how I feel about you. Maybe she'll begin to understand."

He smiled, cupping her cheek. "I love you, Melissa. The girls are with Alex and Claudio out front, waiting for their friends. I came in to collect the coffee. If you could help with a tray of cups we can join them."

"Should we bring milk for the children?"

"Will there be enough for eight of them?"

Melissa opened the ice box. "It looks like they requested extra today."

Alex waltzed in. "I was responsible—it happens from time to time. I pulled myself out of bed last night at eleven to post a note by the back door asking for three extra milk bottles. It was quite the hardship, mind you. Lucy was soft and warm in my arms and I could not quite get as comfortable when I came back to bed."

"However do you look so rested this morning?" Freddy teased.

Melissa saw the gleam in Alex's eyes and covered his mouth before he could speak. "It was a rhetorical question."

Freddy, understanding how his question could have been twisted, frowned. "Should I be concerned you read his thoughts so well?"

"I think that shows you've found a keeper," Alex said. "Every good woman needs a bit of mischievousness in her. Have you discovered her playful side?"

Freddy's knuckles whitened. "I've had enough of your banter."

As the three emerged from the house with the coffee and milk, two hired automobiles pulled to a stop in front of the house. The newcomers surged in the middle of the yard with Phoebe and Bethany, complete with squeals and giggles from the children.

Freddy set his load on the porch table and took Melissa's hand. "I haven't seen the yard this full since I was a child. It brings back good memories."

Lucy turned to him from her wicker chair. "We had such fun here."

"We did, Goosy. And I'll always love my fair maiden, even when you scream at me."

"I was awful Sunday, but I've decided I cannot be indifferent like you asked. I am trying to change my opinion." She glanced at Melissa. "It's not working."

Douglas Campbell came to the porch with an armful of clothing. Once Lucy helped him bring it inside, there were handshakes for the men and hugs for the women. "I am glad you're still here, Melissa. It means a lot to Darla for you to come to the wedding."

"I've become great friends with her."

"And you and Frederick are good?" Douglas asked.

Melissa nodded, her smile huge. "Very good."

The other man with chin-length light brown hair and a crooked smile carried two boxes up the front steps, all eight children following him as though he was an enchanted piper.

"Everyone in to wash up," Lucy called out. "Biggest help the littlest in the washroom."

Alex held the screen door for the clamoring herd, his face shining with joy.

Freddy took the boxes and nodded to Melissa. "Joe, I'd like you to meet Melissa Stone. Melissa, Captain Joe Walker."

"It's always a pleasure to meet a pretty redhead, though I can't say I've met one as tanned as you."

"She's probably logged as many hours on the water as you have," Freddy said. "She's sailed to Europe, Asia, Africa, South America, and everywhere in between."

Melissa laughed. "But all in the comforts of a cabin, not at the helm."

"I've heard about you through Darla's letters to Claire. It's good to connect a face to the name. Here, let me introduce my ruffians." A boy and girl came out from the house, along with Tabitha Campbell. "This is my oldest, Emmett, and my youngest girl, Mary. Those are two names you get when you marry an Irish-Catholic."

Phoebe, Bethany, and Kade Campbell returned next, all holding hands. Then another boy and girl emerged.

"And my oldest girl, Clara Jane, and youngest, Abraham." The freckled, redheaded boy looked to be the age of Phoebe and Kade, and the three soon flocked together.

Alex and Claudio spread a blanket on the lawn and Freddy set one of the doughnut boxes on it. Then Alex poured milk for the children and Lucy saw to distributing it. The adults enjoyed a few minutes of quiet on the porch while the children ate. Then it was like no battle Melling Militia and Kingdom Davenport had ever seen, such was the running and screaming.

An hour later, Freddy was more than happy to excuse himself for work. "Would you like me to leave my automobile, Alex? I think you could fit everyone between yours and mine. Douglas or Joe can drive it and you won't have to hire an automobile or put anyone on the streetcar."

"That'd be swell, Freddy."

"Allow me to come with you." Claudio stood. "I should like to pray in the cathedral before the ceremony. I shall miss the beauty of that place."

Freddy leaned over Melissa's chair and tilted her chin up with a finger. "I'll see you in a few hours. Save a seat for me if you get there first."

"I will."

What she expected to be a quick kiss grew longer.

"Davenport's going deep!" Joe called, and all the men laughed.

Melissa broke the connection, her face warm.

"I love you, Melissa." Freddy pranced down the steps like a school boy with Claudio following him.

Alex still laughed as Freddy stopped to tell the girls goodbye. "Leave it to the wharf rats to be crasser than me."

Joe opened his arms in a show of humility. "I call it as it is."

Lucy huffed and crossed her arms.

"What is it my queen? Are you feeling left out?" Alex pulled her into his arms and spun her around, nearly upsetting the coffee tray. He went at her neck until she giggled.

"No wonder the priest wanted out." Joe smirked. "Y'all are worse than the kids."

***

When the group reached the cathedral's portico, Melissa adjusted her white hat. She took Phoebe's hand back into her own and looked behind them at Alex, Lucy, and Bethany, who were at the base of the stairs. Lucy appeared to be trembling.

"Melissa and Phoebe, you two are prettier than ever."

"Maggie"—Melissa turned to her as she spoke—"could you please watch Phoebe a minute?"

"Of course."

She turned the girl's care over to their friend and hurried down the steps in time to pull Bethany from Alex's arms as he caught Lucy.

Then Freddy was there. "Alex, get her to the side garden."

Alex brought Lucy into his lap on a bench.

Freddy knelt before them, taking Lucy's hand. "It's okay to be nervous, Goosy. The last few times you were here were choked with emotions. You are happy with your life and Alex is holding you, not running away. There is nothing to stop you from walking in there with your chin high except your own fears."

She shook with sobs and her black mantilla slipped off. Alex lovingly replaced it.

Freddy gave her a handkerchief, squeezing her fingers around it. "I saw you into the cathedral the last two times you entered, and I would do so again today. Alex on one side and me on the other. I will even help you out when the ceremony is over. Would you like that?"

She nodded and sucked in her breath to slow her tears.

"I will be right here. Take a moment longer." Freddy came to Melissa's side, kissing her and Bethany. "I'll be in as soon as I can."

"Don't worry, they need you. We will save you a seat."

Melissa settled midway up the nave with the girls snug against her in their Easter dresses. She left enough room for Alex and Lucy as well, but only Freddy came several minutes later.

He whispered, "They are sitting in the back."

Then he lifted Phoebe into his lap and took Melissa's hand. An itch in her throat started, like she wanted to cry. This would be her family—Freddy and his girls. For the first time, her promise to return to him felt real and it was magnificent to know their love would continue beyond the end of the week.

Darla was gorgeous in white lace as she came down the aisle on her uncle's arm. Henry practically bounced like he was warming up in the ring at the front of the transept. Melissa half expected him to run to Darla for a kiss like he did after his win at the tournament.

"Steady, boy," Freddy murmured. "She's almost there."

Melissa smiled, knowing Freddy thought the same thing.

The ceremony was beautiful to Melissa with Freddy's hand in hers. Afterward, she waited with the girls while Freddy saw to Lucy. When he returned, he offered a smile.

"She made it through but is skipping the reception. She needs to relax before playing hostess tonight." He took Bethany into his arms. "Come on, girls, let's say hello to Miss Darla and Mr. Henry."

When they reached the couple on the portico, Darla squeezed her in a tight hug. "You're glowing, Melissa, or is it me?"

"I'm coming back," she whispered. "I'm coming back to Freddy and the girls."

Darla embraced her again. "We all look forward to it."

Once they got to the Beauchamps' house, Melissa helped keep an eye on the Davenport, Campbell, and Walker children in the backyard. As the children played tag, she was finally introduced to Claire Walker. While Joe was all weathered and rough looking, Claire had soft lines and fair, freckled skin. Her hard determination was only seen on second glance.

"Darla stays so busy with her work, I was pleased to start hearing about you in her weekly letters. She needs more women she can turn to. Maggie comes to the city monthly, but this will probably be her last trip until after the baby is born and I only make it quarterly. For some reason Darla doesn't like going to Lucy with troubles."

Melissa smiled and stretched her legs out for a moment from her perch on the back steps. "They have an interesting relationship, but I've seen her accept Lucy's guidance."

"The infamous talk on Maggie's last visit? I fell out laughing when she told me. Those Mellings are something else, as is Maggie. The poor woman is tainted by her time in their house. The way she is with Alex is shameless at times. And Claudio." Claire motioned to the bench in the shade where Maggie sat leaning against the priest, his arm about her. "I don't know how Douglas stands it."

"There is a strong bond between them all, that's for sure."

Behind them, Douglas came out the door. They stood to clear the stairs.

"I'm supposed to make sure you ladies come in for refreshments." He scratched his red beard and shook his head before hollering, "Claudio, you look a wee bit too comfortable!"

Claire laughed. "I thought the same thing, but it wasn't my place to say it."

"If you ever see the Seacliff friends being overly chummy with Maggie, please say something." Tabitha ran by and Douglas scooped his youngest into his arms upside-down. "Is Kade looking out for you, Tabby?"

"Yes, Papa."

"Good." He kissed her and set her back down. "Now you ladies go in before I am accused of neglect."

Melissa was in the crowded house five minutes without seeing Freddy. She saw Darla—changed into a lavender traveling suit—and Henry while she ate a tea sandwich, and heard Joe's laugh from another room. Just when she was about to go back outside with the children, Freddy's familiar touch caught her elbow.

"You are a difficult woman to keep track of."

"That comes with the travel writer skillset."

Freddy laughed. "Alice Beauchamp is doing a violin performance in a few minutes. I would like to listen before getting the girls down for their naps. Do you need me to bring you home first or would you be comfortable coming next door when you're tired of the party?"

She slipped her hand into his. "I'll stay with you."

"I was hoping you would say that." Freddy led her into the parlor, squeezing into a space beside Joe and Claire Walker.

Alice was a solemn-faced beauty. When she started in on Mozart, the whole house quieted. Melissa recognized the flowing movements the young woman made as reminiscent of Valentino De Fiore's style and smiled at the smallness of the world. If an Italian violinist crossed paths with the same family in Mobile that she from New York had stumbled into, that showed fate was at play. Freddy stood behind her, holding her loose about the waist and subtly swaying to the music. It could have been the company, but Melissa found it the most moving performance she had ever witnessed.

Forty-Four

At three o'clock, Frederick and Melissa walked next door and readied the girls for naptime.

"Miss Darla looked like a fairy princess," Phoebe said as her father covered her and Doff with a blanket. "I want to look like a princess when I get married."

"You will, Phoebe."

She held her father's cheeks when he leaned over to kiss her, blue-green eyes sharp. "How can you be sure?"

"Because your mother looked like a princess when we married, and you look just like her."

Satisfied, Phoebe accepted his kiss and snuggled down with a yawn. Frederick stopped to leave a kiss with Bethany in her crib, closed the door, and joined Melissa in the hall. Her eyes shined, smile wistful.

He leaned close. "What is it, Beloved?"

"Are you really offering me your life and family when I return?"

With tenderness, he kissed her lips and placed her hand on his chest. "And my whole heart, but I give it to you now. You needn't wait until you return to know I lay it all at your feet."

Her arms went about his neck as she kissed him. He lifted her into his arms and went for his bed before stopping himself. Placing her feet on the floor, he stepped back and studied her.

"What is it?" She linked her hands before her self-consciously.

"You belong here, but not today. One day, when you return and we're joined together, I'll carry you up the stairs, lay you upon this bed, and take you on a trip like you've never experienced."

Melissa's smile was the reply he sought and her touch on his arm an added bonus. "Will you give me a taste of it now?"

"I don't trust myself in here with you."

He carried her downstairs and placed her on the sofa. His jacket and tie were already removed, as well as her hat, but he kicked off his shoes and removed Melissa's as well. Then he pulled her upright and clutched her to his chest, dropping onto the sofa with her atop him. His movements were slow, as not to arouse his body with her weight above him as he shifted until she nestled between his legs. With hunger in her eyes, her lips parted seductively. His muscles constricted as he sucked in his breath. Seeing his response, she paused.

"It's all up to you, Melissa. If you give me attention, I can't promise I'll stay a gentleman."

Through the open windows, sounds of the party next door drifted in. Doors slamming, laughter, a few piano cords. But in that moment it was just him and Melissa—closer than ever.

Her gaze softened. "I love you too much to purposely tempt you, though I'm sure I'll enjoy that at some point in the future."

"I hope so."

She sighed and nestled against him, turning her head sideways so her cheek rested over his heart. The weight of her warmed him from his loin to neck, but he tried to rest while his body told him he needed to urge things along. He drew languid circles with his finger on her back as she relaxed further against him.

"It's heaven on earth with you, Freddy."

At some point, Frederick noticed her breathing was even, her hand limp rather than firm against his side.

The next thing he heard was the front door. His hand pressed against Melissa's back to keep her stationary as he opened his eyes.

"I am sorry to interrupt, but maybe it is good I am here so I may chaperone."

"Claudio, come in."

Melissa pushed up from Frederick, touching her face. "I'm sorry. I fell asleep."

Frederick chuckled. "So did I."

"It is not the worst thing I have walked in on. Darla and Henry are off to the hotel for the night. We are taking the same train to Louisiana in the morning, though I continue to Monroe and they go to New Orleans. I told them I will leave them alone, but Darla insists we share a cabin. What will I talk to newlyweds about for so many hours?"

"Whatever you do," Melissa said as she straightened her skirt, "don't ask Alex's opinion."

Frederick and Claudio laughed.

"You've been to New Orleans?" Frederick asked.

"*Sí*, many times." Claudio's smile was dark, bittersweet.

"Then give them suggestions on where to eat, what to see."

"I know just the restaurant. The proprietress is a special friend of mine."

"I'd like to go there when I return," Melissa said. "And Dauphin Island."

"When you return?" Claudio looked at her.

"I leave Friday night, but once I settle things in New York, I'm coming back." She locked her fingers through Frederick's. "I finally expressed my heart like you suggested."

Claudio took their joined hands into his own, kissing their knuckles, and prayed over them in Italian. "It is good. Very good." He rested a hand on Melissa head. "You will travel safe and return to this happy family."

***

Frederick, his daughters, Melissa, and Claudio arrived for the Mellings' supper party just before six o'clock. Claudio immediately went for Maggie, who sat on the porch swing with Tabitha. Claudio kissed them both on each cheek, then patted Maggie's rounded middle.

"I've never met a Catholic priest before," Melissa said as she lifted Bethany out of the automobile. "Are they all like Claudio?"

Frederick watched Phoebe run around the back of the house, following the sound of Kade's shouting. "He's a bit of a rogue priest, but he loves the Lord and means well."

"I enjoy his company, as well as everyone else's I've meet at this house. But yours most especially." She put her arm around his, Bethany tugging at her other hand.

"Momma." Bethany pointed to the house.

"I'll help you find her, Beth." Melissa waved to Maggie and continued into the house, followed by Claudio.

Maggie called Frederick over.

"Good to see you again, Maggie." He kissed her and she clung to his hand.

"Claudio told me, and I'm delighted for you. A piece of my heart has ached for you since the day we met and Lucy's fractured devotion was revealed. Melissa is just the type of woman I would have picked for you. She's wonderful and you deserve happiness."

"Thank you Maggie, that means a lot. And I look forward to meeting your new one."

"Me too." She placed her hands on her belly and smiled. "Would you mind taking Tabitha to Douglas? He's supposed to be supervising the children in the backyard with Joe."

"I'd be happy to." He held his arms open and Tabitha jumped into them. He placed her on his shoulders and went around the back of the house.

Douglas ran after Emmett, the oldest Walker.

"Papa!" Tabitha called.

Frederick transferred her to her father's shoulders, who continued his pursuit of aiding the young children against the twelve-year-old. Then Frederick went for the double glider where Joe and Alexander swung.

"Time to put out the cigarettes, Joe. Freddy can't abide them." Alexander leaned his head back and exhaled a perfect smoke circle.

Frederick stepped onto the swaying platform, arms on the cross bars of the benches. "I thought this glider was a gift for Lucy, but I see you out here on it smoking more than I see Lucy enjoying it."

"You can be sure she enjoys it, Davenport. Look at the floor you're standing on and imagine a few blankets and pillows for cushioning, and luscious Lu—"

Frederick took Alexander by the throat, not roughly, but enough to stop his speech. "Do you really want other men imagining your wife draped across here?"

He released him and nodded hello to Joe.

"Always her protector, even when you have your own woman you could be ima—" Alexander laughed as he ducked.

"If you ever talk about Melissa the way you do Lucy, you'll not be able to work for months, if ever again."

Joe put out his smoke and jumped off the glider. "Take my spot, Freddy. Alex is in high form today."

Alexander smirked and took another drag. "Weddings make me feisty. I suppose that comes from waiting so long for my own."

Frederick sat across from him and cracked his knuckles. "That was your own fault."

The back door opened and they both turned to the sound. Alexander immediately put out his cigarette.

"Magdalene, my beauty. Come swing with me!"

"Only if Frederick stays with us."

Alexander hopped off the glider and brought it to a stop, holding Maggie's elbow as she stepped up. "I've always loved watching you swing, especially on the one Douglas built for you when it involved blue silk."

Frederick couldn't see Alexander's face, but the blush on Maggie's spoke volumes as she looked up at him.

"Sit," Frederick commanded, "so I can keep a better eye on you."

Alexander turned to him. "Don't fault me because I make her remember our shared past. I can't control the effect I have on women."

"He's harmless, Frederick." Maggie took Alexander's hand and tugged him toward the bench as the glider picked up speed from his movements.

"See, she wants me."

"Douglas," Frederick called over the din of the children, "you might wish to protect your wife!"

He was there in an instant, stroking his red beard, eyebrow cocked at Alexander cozy beside Maggie. "It's your turn to run with the children, Alex."

And so the evening went. Happy children, bantering adults. Good food and company. The islanders were still going strong when Claudio sought to return to Frederick's house to complete his packing.

"I wanna play with my friends, Daddy!" Phoebe protested when told to find her shoes while Bethany snored in Melissa's arms.

Lucy caught his eye. "She could sleep over, Bethany too, if you want to lay her down in the crib. Tomorrow's laundry day, so her sheets will be changed and I can bathe her in the morning."

Phoebe's arms were around Kade, blocking Abraham Walker as she turned their trio into a duo. "Please, Daddy! I won't see him for a long time and he's my bestest friend."

"All right, Princess, but be mindful of Abraham."

She squealed with excitement and pulled Kade out of the parlor, remembering after the fact to wait for the freckled boy. "Let's find Rummy!"

Frederick went to take Bethany from Melissa.

"Let me carry her so we don't switch her around too much," she told him.

Frederick helped Melissa stand and walked with a hand on her back.

"Need a chaperone up there, Freddy?" Joe teased.

"If you've seen them Turkey Trotting, you wouldn't have to ask," Alexander replied.

Frederick ignored the jokes and saw Melissa and Bethany to the girls' room. Phoebe was there with the boys, each grabbing an armful of animals before running for the stairs. Melissa transferred Bethany to the crib, removed her clothes, and covered her without disturbing his little princess.

"You'll be a fine mother figure to them, Melissa. And they already love you." Frederick held her to his chest.

"And I love them. Since you don't have to bring the girls in the morning, would you like me to meet you downtown?"

"Breakfast at the diner at seven o'clock? Then all day together, just the two of us." He pulled her tighter for a kiss, memorizing the way their lips fit together.

Claudio and Frederick said their goodbyes to the group, the priest clinging to everyone longer than necessary. He whispered to Lucy, then Alex, and finally promised Maggie he'd send word about how Darla handled her first day as a married woman.

As Frederick drove, Claudio was silent on the passenger side, his head leaning against the seat as he stared at the stars. Not until they were inside the house did Claudio speak.

"Do you think me a bad priest? Too sinful to do my job properly?"

"You're filled with love for God's people and that's the most important part of being a shepherd."

"I have always missed my friends, but now I am worried about Alexander. Today he was in tune with his old ways. The stress of *signora's* health and Lucy's pregnancy could become too much for him. He might revert to his previous ways of relief."

Remembering the way Alexander was with Maggie made the picture all too clear. "I noticed a change, coupled with a nervous energy."

"*Sí*, and because of that, I am going to submit a request for transfer to this archdiocese. He will need me in the months ahead. Will you keep me posted?"

"Of course. Anything to help Lucy and Alex."

Forty-Five

The next day was a blur for Melissa. Breakfast with Freddy, then a drive to new parts of town and the Bayfront, where they enjoyed a picnic while watching the ships. They stayed within touching distance whether eating, driving, or walking. The afternoon returned them to the city and they strolled downtown arm-in-arm.

Five o'clock came before they wanted it to, and Freddy returned her to Lucy's house. Phoebe and Bethany were ecstatic to see their father, but Lucy wasn't pleased.

"How could you take a day off when you'll be gone next week?"

"Goosy, there are competent people like Mr. Peabody to field questions and handle any difficulties that might arise."

"But Henry's gone right now."

"He'll be back on Monday, so next week isn't a hardship to the office."

Lucy stomped out of the parlor and slammed the door to the study. Alex, lounging on the settee, counted to ten before going for his wife, and Freddy sent the girls to make sure their room was tidy.

Melissa took his hand. "What was that about with Lucy?"

"The girls and I are leaving this weekend to visit my sister. She thinks I'm running away because I'm distraught."

"Are you?" she couldn't help but ask.

He smiled, his eyes soft. "I'll be sad to see you go, but I have faith you'll return. It's not the end, but the beginning of the next stage of us."

She hugged him. "I plan to spend as much time with the girls as possible tomorrow and then kiss you as long as I can when you pick them up."

When the girls came back to the parlor with their special dolls and Rummy, they left without waiting for Lucy or Alex to emerge.

Lucy was silent during supper. Over dessert, she made eye contact with Melissa for the first time. "People are saying you're coming back. Is it true?"

"I promised Freddy I would after I settle things in New York."

"That's not what I asked." Lucy looked from her half-eaten cobbler to her house guest.

"I said I promised. Isn't the answer obvious?"

"Promises can be broken. Promises to never hurt someone, promises to never sin, promises to love and honor all your days. All breakable. All broken."

"My queen." Alex touched her hand but she pushed him away and stood.

"I know you're driven in pursuing your career goals, and you should be. A woman in the professional world has to work twice as hard as the men she's up against. Mr. Noble told me had you not agreed to come here, he was going to send you to England to report on the Titanic. You would be sailing right now on the maiden voyage of the finest ship in the world. Instead, you had to babysit a wayward novelist while the other travel writer—a man with three published books—is sailing in style. Can you sit there and tell me you're going to let those opportunities pass because you feel something for a man you've known six weeks?"

The news of the Titanic smarted, reminding her of missing the cherry tree planting in Washington last month with Ms. Scidmore. But in the scheme of her life as she now saw it, both meant little compared to Freddy.

Melissa stood, but with Lucy's society trick, she still appeared to look down at her. "I won't tell you because I don't answer to you. I appreciate your concern over Freddy, but keep your place and remember you're the *ex*-wife and neither of us owes you explanations."

"But my daughters—"

"Your girls are amazing. I'll not take your place in their lives, but be to them similar to what Alex is—another adult who loves them and is there to help."

"Help with the shenanigans," he said with his impish grin.

"I'll leave that part to you, Alex."

"You'll leave it all to us because you won't return when the call of your next job assignment stirs you to new adventures!"

"If you believe that of me, you haven't gotten to know me in my time here, and I'm sorry for that. I was sent here to make sure you worked, and in doing so it kept a barrier between us. I love Freddy, the girls, and even you and Alex to a different degree. I can't picture my future without Freddy, and if you don't understand that, you shouldn't have the right to call yourself a romance novelist."

Melissa stalked to her room and spent the remainder of the evening packing. She sorted the clothes for the next day and what she would need on the train, packing the rest into the trunk and large suitcase. When she was about to climb into bed for the night, there was a knock. Throwing her shawl around her shoulders, she opened the door.

Alex in his striped pajamas bottoms and no shirt smirked. "I believe you'll come back."

"Thank you, Alex." She tried not to look at his scarring.

He leaned against the doorframe. "You said you love me and I know you won't want to live without gazing upon all I have to offer at least a few times a week."

"It's not like that and you know it." She shoved him and he laughed.

Alex used his new position a few feet away to appraise her as he ran a hand across the puckered skin on his chest. His eyes wandered her covered form as though he expected to see beyond the nightgown. "Your wrap is reminiscent of Lucy's kimono, but it makes me think more of Magdalene's shawl she used to wear about Seacliff Cottage. All you women create a rainbow of succulent fruit to feast upon."

Suppressing a shiver, she took hold of the doorknob. "Goodnight, Alex."

She locked the door and hoped he didn't know the secrets of the house as Freddy did.

***

When Freddy brought the girls over Friday morning, Melissa—recently returned from her walk to avoid being downstairs alone with Alex—walked with him to the automobile after he brought Phoebe and Bethany to Lucy.

"Would you do me a favor?" she asked.

"Of course."

"I need a hotel room this evening. I decided it would be easier to have a hired car collect me downtown to get me to the train station at midnight. Would you make a reservation and bring me there when you get the girls tonight?"

"Gladly." Freddy fingered the puffiness around her eyes. "But tell me what happened."

She kissed his hand. "Alex is acting strange, for lack of a better word. Yes, he makes lewd comments, but last night he behaved like a predator. He knocked on my door half-dressed and leered at me, comparing me to Maggie and Lucy."

Freddy's hands balled into fists. "Did he touch you?"

"No, but it gave me a bad feeling."

"He hasn't been himself this week. Or rather, he's like his *old* self. Claudio and I both noticed it. I'm glad you're moving on from this household." He left her with a determined kiss.

Melissa, not wanting to directly challenge Lucy for time with the girls, hovered nearby all morning. Often Phoebe would ask for help with folding newspaper swords or Bethany would climb into her lap for a few minutes. At noon, they held court beside their mother, affording Melissa the chance to study their sweet faces across the table.

When the telephone rang, Lucy left the dining room to answer it in the hallway. A few moments later she returned.

"It's for you."

Melissa hurried to the telephone. "Hello?"

"Are your cases packed, Beloved?"

"Everything except what I need for the train."

"My intern and I are going to get the trunk and extra luggage now. The hotel will hold them in the coat check so they don't need to be brought to and from your room."

"Thank you for seeing to it for me."

"It's a husband's privilege to see to things like this. I'll be there within the half-hour."

Heart racing, she spoke the words which now came to her easily. "I love you, Freddy."

After hanging up the telephone, Melissa leaned against the banister, soaking in the feeling of Freddy referring to himself as her husband. They'd discussed the options during their day together and decided when she returned they'd go to the courthouse to be married. Freddy had already been through a house wedding with Harriet, and then a wedding in Trinity Church with Lucy. As Melissa had no family to attend and her friends there were Freddy's, she was happy to keep things simple.

"Freddy is on his way to get my trunk and large suitcase," she said as she entered the dining room. "He'll bring them to the hotel, where I'm staying this evening. It will be easier for me to get to the train station from there."

"We're riding a train too, Sissa!"

Lucy frowned at her oldest.

"I heard you get to visit your aunt."

"A Kingdom Davenport Adventure!" Phoebe tugged on her mother's red sleeve. "May I wait for Daddy on the porch?"

"Yes, Phoebe Camellia. Bethany, too, if she wishes. Stay on the swing with her."

The girls hurried outside, and Lucy stood by the front window watching them. Melissa gathered dishes off the table.

"Have you told the girls you're returning?" Lucy asked.

"No, the promise is between Freddy and me."

"And breaking a promise to a grown man is easier than to an innocent child."

"I'll break no promises, but what the girls are told is up to Freddy."

Melissa came back for another load of dishes, ignoring the blonde at the window. When the girls called out to their father, Lucy turned to Melissa.

"Why are you moving to a hotel?"

Melissa looked away.

"I've opened my home to you for weeks. Are you shunning your last supper here with us without notice as well?"

"I'm happy to take supper with your family tonight. Freddy will come for me afterward when he gets the girls."

They both watched Freddy out the window as he greeted Phoebe and Bethany.

"You owe me an explanation for why you're moving out."

"Goosy, tell me the girls haven't been out there without supervision more than a moment," Freddy called when he stepped inside.

She crossed her arms and held her spot. "I've been watching them out the window."

He wrapped his arms about Melissa, causing her muscles to release some of their tension

"What is it?" he whispered.

"Lucy wants to know why I'm moving to a hotel."

"Tell her." His voice was hard. "What are we taking from your room?"

"The trunk and large suitcase by the door."

When Freddy and the intern went up the stairs, Melissa approached Lucy's ridged figure. "I'm leaving because of Alex. I respect you both, but he made me uncomfortable for the first time last night. I don't wish to feel that way again. It's best for me to remove myself before an issue might arise."

Her green eyes widened in fear. "What did he do?"

"He came to my door at eleven, half dressed."

One hand went to her stomach, the other clutched the credenza to steady her trembling.

"He told me I was coming back because I love him and wish to look upon him, teasing like he often does, but then his manor changed and he rubbed his scars and told me I reminded him of you and Maggie. That we were all succulent fruits to feast upon."

Lucy's hand went to her mouth and she rushed for the hall, nearly colliding with Freddy and the intern carrying the trunk.

Sounds of retching came from the half-bathroom.

Freddy looked to the intern. "Let's set this down. If you could get the suitcase and wait outside a minute, we'll see to this afterward."

The young man nodded and went for the stairs.

Freddy took Melissa's hand. "If you could entertain the girls, I'll see to her."

"It's naptime. Could you kiss them when I bring them through?"

"Only if I get to kiss you as well."

She gave an exaggerated sigh. "If you must."

"That will cost you one now."

Melissa tucked the girls in bed, hoping Bethany would remember her and Phoebe would still love her when she returned. Her relationship with Freddy she didn't worry about, it was the girls—and Lucy and Alex—that concerned her the most.

Forty-Six

Frederick knocked on the bathroom door. "Goosy, do you need help?"

Sobs were the reply.

He let himself in and found Lucy on the floor before the toilet. The memory of her retching in that same room over the news of Mr. Melling sending a whore to Alexander's duplex filled his mind. Frederick did as he had that winter morning—he brought a damp washcloth to her face and helped her rinse the taste from her mouth at the sink.

"We've been happy, Freddy. And then Melissa came with the evil and everything changed."

"That's been gone weeks. Don't blame Alex's recent behavior on Melissa." Frederick led her to the settee in the parlor, an arm about her shoulders. "Claudio and I noticed his change. He was a scoundrel with Maggie after the wedding."

"He flirted with her horribly, but Douglas put a stop to it." Lucy accepted a handkerchief and blew her nose.

"You keep that one, Goosy. I insist."

Her laughter lasted a few seconds before it turned to tears.

"I'll speak with Alex this evening. Make note of any changes to his behavior and tell me everything when I come back."

Lucy hugged him. "Do you have to go, Freddy?"

He kissed her forehead as Melissa walked into the room. "The visit is long overdue and it's the right time. If something happens while I'm gone, call Maxwell. He is strong enough to control Alex if needed."

"Control him?" Lucy wiped her nose. "He's refused to do more than hug and kiss me for weeks."

"When I come tonight, give me time with him. I'll make sure he understands what appropriate behavior is."

Lucy sniffled. "All right."

"I need to get Melissa's luggage to the hotel." He pressed his lips to her forehead again. "I'll still be here for you, Goosy."

"I know how much you mean to each other," Melissa said. "I won't stand between your friendship and what you share as parents. I got the girls down for a nap so you can rest."

"Thank you."

Frederick stood. "Do you need help upstairs?"

"No, thank you." Lucy stopped to give Melissa a hug. "I'm sorry for my husband's behavior. Please forgive him."

"I love and respect you both. I hope you'll come to accept me as a friend."

Lucy nodded and went up to her room.

"Allow me to leave you something to remember me by because we might not have privacy tonight." Frederick pulled Melissa into a hug and kissed her. "I'll see you this evening."

Her hands roamed his biceps. "I'll count the minutes."

When the trunk was in his backseat, Frederick drove to The Battle House after a quick stop at the candy shop along the way. A small sampler of chocolates was left at the front desk to be waiting on Melissa's bed, along with the retrieval tickets for her luggage.

At the office, he met with Mr. Peabody to go over responsibilities for the next week, followed by two appointments before he left for home. He skipped the gym for the second time that week so he could pack suitcases for him and the girls without rushing them at bedtime. He made himself a simple dinner before going back to Lucy's to pick up his girls—all three of them.

He jogged up the front steps, giddiness bubbling inside until he remembered Alexander's transgression. He paused on the porch to look in the parlor window. Alexander had his arm around Lucy on the settee, but his smile and eyes were focused on Melissa in the armchair. Phoebe held a book in her lap, and Bethany played on the floor near her feet.

He shook the tension from his limbs and entered. "Good evening."

"Daddy!"

"You stay there a minute with Sissa," he told Phoebe. "I need to talk to Alex about what I need him to do when we're out of town."

"Don't tell me I'll be expected to water your flowers, Freddy."

"Miss Sharon is seeing to the house and Doff." He lifted Bethany for a kiss and set her beside Lucy, taking Alexander by the shoulder. "Let's step into the study."

He shoved him into the room and locked the door.

"What the hell, Freddy?"

Frederick took a fistful of his button-down shirt. "I should be asking you that! What gives you the right to knock on Melissa's door half-dressed, making innuendos and leering at her—which I also witnessed for myself through the parlor window?"

Alexander smirked like the Melling scum he was. "I've always fancied having a redhead."

Frederick punched without thinking. He realized as Alexander went down that he should have slapped. But it was too late. Blood poured from Alexander's nose and he collapsed on the chaise.

He pulled him up quickly. "Don't drip on your stupid sofa. Lucy would never forgive me."

Frederick held Alexander upright with one hand as he went for his spare handkerchief with the other. Seeing that the hanky could hold but for a few more seconds, he ripped the shirt off Alexander's back, which tumbled the man to his knees. Frederick shoved Alexander's shirt at his face.

"Let that slow a bit and I'll check your nose for you. In the meantime, think long and hard about where your choices are leading you this week."

"I've done nothing."

"First it was your shameless displays with Maggie, and now you're hunting Melissa. I'll not stand for it, especially with the damage you're doing to Lucy."

"This isn't about Lucy," he said through the shirt.

Frederick yanked Alexander to his feet. "It's everything to do with Lucy! Your choices have the potential to destroy her. In the past few days, her faith in you has weakened. She fears she'll lose you once again to sin just as you're closer than ever to seeing your dream of creating a family to fruition. You need to pull yourself together."

"It's nothing but flirting."

"And I suppose next you'll be saying 'I couldn't help it if she found me irresistible' or 'just once' and 'what my wife doesn't know won't hurt her.' Is that how your *father* rationalized his behavior?"

"Don't speak to me of my father!" Alexander slung the bloodied shirt, catching Lucy's green shaded desk lamp. It brought the light to the floor with a thud of the brass base and a shattering of the bulb.

Frantic hands pounded the door. "Alex!" Lucy yelled. "Freddy, don't hurt him!"

"You're slipping, Alex, and you're going fast. If you don't stop you'll become the man you hated your father for being, complete with a displaced wife and children who despise you."

"You know nothing!"

"I know what you look like on your descent into sin. I know what Lucy looks like when you drag her with you. And I know how horrible the aftermath is because I've dealt with it!" Frederick shoved Alexander, not caring that he still dripped blood.

"You with your steady patience and iron will can't understand what a weakling like me goes through!"

"What can you possibly lack right now? You have the woman you claim to love as your wife, a job, a nice house, two step-daughters who adore you, and news of a child of your own. How is any of that validity for pursuing other women?"

Alexander racked his hands through his hair. "I thought I knew what I wanted, but I'm scared."

"Of what?" Frederick's lip curled in a sneer.

"I'm falling apart after two weeks. How am I to abstain for more than nine months?"

"Nine months? Alex, are you daft? Don't tell me you think you can't—"

"When I came back from Louisiana, you said Lucy was under doctor's orders for no intercourse because of her pregnancy."

Frederick's laughter rumbled out and wouldn't stop.

The pounding on the door started back. "Freddy, I don't like the sound of that!"

Frederick put Alexander in a headlock and rubbed is knuckles into his scalp like he used to do with Eddie. When he pushed him away, his own white shirt was smudged with blood.

"You're an absolute simpleton! That was the just for the final weeks, not the whole time. It's fine to enjoy your wife." He grabbed his shoulders, a rush of words spewing from him. "You'll want to marvel over her changing body. The way the curve of her belly grows as it holds your seed, the swell of her enlarging breasts. Some days it might feel a sin to be with her because she's so changed from the body you clung to on your wedding night. The feel of her beside you in the dark can be titillating because except for her familiar scent, it's as though you're exploring a new woman."

Alexander's eyes rivaled Eliza's in luminosity as they widened in understanding. "You mean I don't have to wait to be with Lucy?"

Frederick playfully slapped his cheek. "No, you cad."

"I can pleasure her and get my sweet release?"

"Yes!" He shook him by the shoulders, which started his nose back to dripping. "Just care for her comfort more than ever."

"And her body ..." Alexander cupped his hands in front of his chest.

He laughed, grabbed Alexander's shirt from the floor, and threw it at him. "Yes, her curves increased each time. Marvel over and treasure Lucy, because if I *ever* see or learn of your attentions roaming elsewhere, I'll rip your head off."

"Please do, Freddy. I'd deserve it."

When Frederick opened the door, Lucy looked at his bloodied clothes and then to Alexander holding his shirt to his nose and shrieked. Frederick caught her elbow in case she went weak, but she backhanded him.

"What did you do?"

"I knocked some sense into him, but everything is fine."

Alexander opened his arms to Lucy. "I've been a fool, my queen. Please forgive me."

They converged. Ignoring the blood on his face, her lips went to his and her hands trailed over his scars. "Always, Alex. But please tell me if I fail to satisfy you."

"My thinking was muddled, but Freddy set me to rights. You are all I need." Unabashed, Alexander's hands roamed her red gown. "May I pleasure you tonight, my queen?"

Her answer was given by backing him toward the chaise as her hands went to his waistband.

"Can you at least wait until you say goodbye? The girls will be gone from here five days, and Melissa an unknown amount of time. Then you will have all the privacy you need to do whatever it is you two enjoy."

Lucy paused, but Alexander rubbed himself against her, a frisky gleam in his eye.

"You should take a moment to wash your face," she told him. "And soak your shirt."

"Might be better off tossing it," Frederick said. "Most of the buttons popped off. I will buy him a new one."

Lucy's eyes narrowed. "You mistreated him terribly, Frederick."

"No more than I deserved, my queen. I was a naughty flirt, but now I know better." He put his arm around her waist, hand gripping her hip. "Let us say goodbye to the darlings, then we can ready for bed."

In the parlor, Phoebe ran for her stepfather. "Mr. Alex has an ouchie! Are you okay?"

"I am great, Knight Phoebe. King Davenport wanted to play boxing with me but I am not as good as he is."

"Another loss for Melling Militia!"

Alexander knelt before Phoebe. "I will have to regroup while you are on your adventure. You be good for your daddy."

"I will, but I'll miss you and Momma." She hugged him before loving on her mother.

Melissa stood, Bethany in her arms, and looked to Frederick. He collected his youngest and brought her to Alexander. Without prompting, she snuggled against him.

"I'll miss you, Bethany Iris. Momma and I will be here for more hugs when you come home." He stood and handed her to Lucy, then looked to Melissa. He pointed to his swollen, blood-stained nose. "That was for you, and I deserved it. Forgive me for being a scoundrel. I wish you safe travels, and I look forward to your return—for Freddy's sake."

"It's fitting to say goodbye to you when you are half-dressed." She smiled. "You were a shock to me the day I arrived. Little did I know what all was in store for me during my time here."

He took her hand with a light touch and raised it to his lips. "It's been a pleasure, Melissa. We'll all be blessed when you return."

"Even bloody and disrobed, you could charm the stripes off a tiger." She gave Alex a hug. "Take care of Mr. Noble's best-selling author while I'm gone. She'll need to be in top form for edits."

Lucy surprised Frederick by taking Melissa into an embrace.

"Thank you. Thank you for everything. You've put up with us and saw me through this deadline. I've not always been kind, but know I respect you. I have never seen Freddy happier. I hope you do come back for him."

"I will."

Lucy took Frederick into her arms next, hugging him like she hadn't in months. "I owe you much, as always. Take care of our girls, and I hope tomorrow goes well for you. You deserve all the happiness in the world."

"No more than the next person, Goosy." He kissed her cheek and leaned to her ear. "Be kind to Alex this weekend. The poor sop thought he couldn't make love to you during your pregnancy."

"What?" Turning to Alexander, Lucy looked at him with a mixture of mirth and sadness. "My angel, you should have said something! Did you think the times I approached you I didn't know better?"

He shrugged, his boyish smile hinting at the corner of his lips. "I know how you are when you have your mind set on something."

Frederick saw the fire burning between Alex and Lucy and nudged Melissa toward the door. "I'll see you both Thursday morning. I'll lock the front door on our way out."

Forty-Seven

Thanks to her ample travel experience, Melissa forced herself to sleep at eight o'clock. The New York Limited left Mobile at the ungodly time of 12:23 am. After her scheduled wake-up at eleven, she asked for an automobile to be called and set to readjusting her hair and clothing.

Once her trunk and extra luggage were checked at the train station, Melissa took her handbag and small suitcase onto the first class train car before searching for the dining car to collect a cup of hot chocolate and a snack to help ease her back to sleep.

On her way through the dimly lit middle-class seating car, Melissa scanned the faces of the passengers. Most sat with their heads back, a few looking out the window. But in the last row a man watched her. She caught her breath.

"Freddy," she whispered, "are you really here?"

His authentic smile shone in the dark space. As she stepped closer, she saw the girls sleeping beside him.

"Didn't I tell you my sister lives in Atlanta? It's the first stop in the morning."

Melissa leaned close, resting her hand on his shoulder. "This is the most romantic thing a man's ever done for me, but you must move to my cabin and allow the girls a proper bed. Mr. Noble always puts me in first class the final leg of a journey. Let me find help."

She explained running into a friend and his children to a porter, offering to pay for their upgrade to first class.

"It's your room, Miss. You can invite other passengers to visit, but I don't think the conductor will take kindly to an unmarried woman hosting a man in her private cabin."

"I'll keep the drapes open. The important thing is allowing the girls to sleep easier."

She tipped the porter and brought him back with her to carry Freddy's bag to the cabin. She carried Bethany and Freddy cradled Phoebe in his arms, his hat haphazardly perched on his head. The porter folded down the low bunk on one side of the cabin before leaving them. Freddy slipped off the girls' dresses and hung them on a coat hook before tucking them into the sleeper side-by-side without them knowing they'd been resituated.

Then Freddy brought a hand to Melissa's cheek. "Call me sentimental, but I want you to meet my sister if she's at the station when I disembark. Angela is seven years older than me and we were never close, but she's all I have left."

"You've brought your girls on a midnight train to Georgia to introduce me to your lone family member?"

"That's how important you are to me. To us." His thumb trailed along her lips. "Now where were you headed? May I fetch something for you?"

"It doesn't seem important now, but I was going for hot chocolate and a pastry."

He kissed her. "I'll be back soon."

Melissa paced the narrow floor, smiling at the sleeping girls while she waited for the love of her life to return. They settled on the bench seat opposite his daughters and spent an hour whispering over hot chocolate and muffins. Sometime near two, she snuggled against Freddy's side and his strong arm went about her.

"Goodnight, Beloved."

"Thank you for surprising me. I love you."

Melissa awoke with the sun through the opened window. She carefully leaned free of Freddy's arm to pull the curtain closed on the side closest to Phoebe and Bethany, hoping to afford them more sleep.

"You're gorgeous by morning light." He took her hand when she turned back. "Did you ever think we'd wake together before marriage?"

"It's wonderful." She took her travel case off the rack above the bench, ignoring her warm cheeks. "I'm going to freshen up."

Freddy went after Melissa but returned much the same. "I left my shaving kit at home. I'll be a bearded man by the time I get back to Mobile."

"You could go on a shaving strike until I return."

"Why not? It might be good to see if you recognize me with a whiskered face."

The girls woke to their father's laughter. Melissa accompanied Phoebe to the washroom while Freddy changed Bethany. After allowing the girls to watch out the window at the novelty of the landscape rushing by, they trouped to the dining car. Even with the rattling train, it was the quietest pancake breakfast the Davenports ever ate.

When the call for the Atlanta station came, they regrouped in the cabin to ready their things. Freddy jumped off the nearest exit without using the stairs and rushed into the waiting crowd to find his sister while Melissa and the girls watched from the window. He emerged from the crowd with a trim, middle-aged woman. Leaving her on the platform, he met the others in the cabin, taking Bethany in one arm and their overnight bag in the other.

His sister watched them approach, her stare cool as she appraised Melissa. As soon as they were before Angela, Frederick introduced Phoebe, who left Melissa's side to curtsey and hug her aunt.

"You look every bit your mother's beautiful daughter." Her smile was kind, her voice soothing, like Freddy's.

"I'm strong like Daddy, Aunt Angela!" She held her arms up for approval.

"And the newest, though a big seventeen months now, Bethany Iris. Beth, this is Aunt Angela. She's Daddy's big sister, like Aunt Susan is Momma's and Phoebe is yours."

She smiled and lunged for her aunt.

"And finally, though she has only minutes to spare before needing to return to the train, Melissa Stone, who will soon be part of our family. Melissa, Angela Garrett."

"It's good to meet you."

The women hugged and Bethany transferred to Melissa's arms in the process.

"Frederick," Angela said. "Collect your other luggage while we wait."

Phoebe clung to Melissa's skirt and Bethany to her neck amid the bustle of the station. "Daddy will be right back, girls."

Angela smoothed the touches of silver in her brunette hair. "I'll get right to the point, Ms. Stone. When Frederick telephoned me last week, I worried when he said there was a woman traveling on the train he wished me to meet. But seeing you with him and the girls, all my fears are washed away." She turned to look at Freddy making his way back with two suitcases and a huge smile. "He's practically glowing like a bride."

Melissa laughed. "I feel about ready to burst myself."

The conductor called out the fifteen minute departure warning as Freddy returned. He moved the group a safer distance from the platform and set the luggage at Angela's feet.

"All right girls, it's time to say goodbye to Sissa, but she'll return to Mobile sometime."

"Are you working with Momma again?"

"Not to work with your mother, Phoebe, but I'll return in a month or two."

"She's coming back," Freddy said, "to be the queen of Kingdom Davenport."

Phoebe's squeal rivaled the train's whistle as she bounced. "We could use an evil queen's plotting against Melling Militia! Sissa will do well!"

"I'm not sure if I should be proud or take offense."

"It's the greatest compliment, Beloved."

The littlest smooshed a kiss on Melissa's cheek and Freddy set Bethany beside Angela, who took her hand. Then Phoebe was in for a hug.

"We'll need to strike Melling Militia before the heat of summer so hurry back, Sissa!"

Tears built in Melissa's eyes, but she worked to keep them at bay as she said farewell to Angela. Freddy instructed Phoebe to hold Bethany's other hand while he walked Melissa to the train. At the steps to her car, the tears spilled out as Freddy embraced her.

"Thank you for a glorious morning. The gift of time with you is all I'll ever need."

"I want to give you much more," Freddy said as they hugged. "Return to me, and we can continue where we left off. You have my heart, now here's a kiss to keep you."

Their kiss was long and deep, drawing the attention of the conductor. "That's enough, folks. The railroad frowns upon displays such as that. Move along."

Freddy plucked the hat from his head and used it to shield another kiss.

Melissa laughed. "Keep being amazing, Freddy. I'll return as soon as I can."

The ghost of his touch lingered as she settled in her cabin. From the window, she waved to the Davenports until the engine took her out of sight.

***

The train pulled into Penn Station in the pre-dawn hours Monday. A hired driver waited for Melissa, collected her luggage, and brought her to her apartment in a women's boarding house on the Upper East Side. She had to ring the landlady to gain entrance to the building at that hour, and then she escorted her and the driver to Melissa's apartment to see that the man didn't stay longer than necessary.

Once she was locked in, Melissa roamed her space, hand trailing over the shabby sofa, adjusting the dusty trinkets on the mantel she'd picked up during her travels. Shells from the African coast, a Buddha from Tibet, a pewter Viking ship from Norway. Then Melissa took a hot shower, wound her silver alarm clock, and set it for seven o'clock.

After a few hours' sleep, she stumbled out of bed feeling like a stranger in her own room. It was well over two months since she'd left for Jamaica. Where she was once comfortable now felt like a fishbowl. A jumbled, colorful, cramped space with the noise of the city held back only by the third floor windows that illuminated her space by a narrow alley.

Melissa dressed in a cornflower blue suit with a men's style tie and straw hat and pinned the cameo over her heart. After finding Lucy's manuscript, she transferred the box into her leather messenger bag she used in place of a briefcase, along with her own manuscript proposal and sample essays. As a bonus, she added a file of photographs from Mobile she thought Mr. Noble would be interested in seeing.

The regulars in the corner diner she often ate breakfast at were pleased to see her, but the relationships felt hollow compared to the camaraderie she had with those in Alabama. By the time she took the subway and walked into the magazine department at Noble Publishing, she ached for those in the south. Melissa spent the first hour making small talk with her office mates, and then a secretary sent word Mr. Noble had to postpone Melissa's eleven o'clock meeting until three in the afternoon.

Not long after that, buzz about the Titanic reached the department. The ship had stuck an iceberg in the middle of the night and the unsinkable ship went down. The survivors were on their way to New York via the Carpathia, which Melissa had traveled aboard several times. She spent her lunch hour with her head on her desk, trying not to think that it could have been her stuck in the middle of the disaster.

When she reached Mr. Noble's outer office five minutes before three, she was numb from worry. *Am I really willing to risk everything on this emotionally charged day?* One arm clutched the bag and the other hand fingered her cameo while she waited.

"Mr. Noble will see you now," the secretary announced at three-fifteen.

Melissa walked into the paneled room lined with bookshelves displaying hundreds of books the company had published since the previous Mr. Noble started the business. The space, dark and masculine, reminded Melissa of Lucy's study so much she expected to see a blue chaise in the corner. Mr. Noble's gray head raised, a stiff smile on his face as he gestured to the leather armchair across the desk from him.

"Ms. Stone, it's good to have you back. I'm sure the news of the disaster has reached the magazine department by now. There's still no word on whether or not our star travel writer made it onto the Carpathia, but I hope the ship can handle the extra passengers without trouble."

"She's a fine ship, Mr. Noble. The crew is gracious and the captain generous."

"What will the public think of luxury travel after this? You have an important job right now, Ms. Stone. Travel could become feared if a great ship like Titanic can be brought to its grave on her maiden voyage. More people will take to the roads in their automobiles rather than risk crossing oceans. We need to focus on continental travel. America—sea to shining sea. Pieces like your view of Mobile, a pleasant, friendly city."

"I did bring some photographs I thought you might be interested in seeing. Pictures of Mrs. Melling and her family."

"That's just the thing to cheer me up, Ms. Stone." He motioned to her bag as she opened it. "If her manuscript is in there, I'm happy to receive it."

Melissa slid the manuscript box across the chestnut desk to him. Mr. Noble looked like a boy opening a Christmas present as he lifted the lid. *"Under the Gardenia Bush: A Mystery Romance* by Olive Kent. Just what I need to take my mind off the terrors of the day. I'll start it tonight. How about those photographs?"

She handed him the Mellings' Holy Friday Easter portrait taken on the front porch.

"She's still a beauty and those girls are adorable. Does the littlest take after her father?"

"Yes, that's Bethany. Freddy Davenport, Lucy's first husband, is father to both. Here's a picture of him with Phoebe."

"He's a sharp one. Not as flashy as Mr. Melling, but solid." He poured over the photos. Melissa handed him the final one—of her and Freddy dressed for their supper at the Trellis Room. He looked from it to Melissa and back again several times. "You look happy."

"I had some wonderful moments. I love the city, the pace of life, and people."

He raised his eyebrows. "And the man? Don't tell me you went and fell in love with Olive Kent's ex-husband."

Melissa couldn't tell if his tone was teasing or annoyed, but she wasn't going to lie. "I did, Mr. Noble. And he loves me. I'd like to give my notice of resignation so I may plan my return to Mobile."

"Out of all my girls on staff, you're the last one I would have picked to walk away from her position because her heartstrings were tugged by a handsome face." He held his hand up to stop her from protesting. "That being said, I know how sensible you are. These emotions must be the real thing to move you to do such a thing when you're on the cusp of something great with your career."

"Mr. Noble, I appreciate—"

"I'm not done, Ms. Stone." His tone was kind, but firm. "You're one of my best writers on staff. Even if you have your heart set on returning south, I'd like to keep you on. Your article on Mobile, coupled with your passion for the area and the new slant toward regional travel has given me an idea. How would you like your own monthly column about the Southeast? Provide me with the flavor of the area in cities like New Orleans and Atlanta to give our readers a reason to explore their country. I'll assign a travel writer to each region, but yours would be 'Southern Charm'! How about it? Would that man of yours support you in a monthly assignment of your choosing?"

It took all her control not to spring out of her seat and hug him. "He would, Mr. Noble. And he has a fine touring automobile and train travel is no problem either."

"To finish out this month, I'd like you on the Titanic. Start gathering information on the disaster. When the survivors arrive, I want you on the docks interviewing whoever you can, focusing on how the passengers' experiences will affect their future travel plans. We'll hold your Mobile piece to use for the following issue and start it as your first 'Southern Charm' piece."

"That sounds wonderful, Mr. Noble. Thank you."

He smiled and folded his hands on his desk. "I'll have my lawyers draw up a contract. Would committing to six months' worth of articles be a good choice for you?"

"Yes, thank you."

"Excellent. Now share this book proposal Mrs. Melling told me you have. It sounds most interesting."

Forty-Eight

On the afternoon of April fifteenth,

Frederick received a telegram at his sister's house stating that Melissa was safe in New York. A few days after he returned to Mobile, a five page, hand-written letter arrived. Melissa told of her job to report on the Titanic disaster from the angle of traveler safety and that she would be free to leave after it was turned in, and her apartment was rented so she wouldn't be penalized for breaking her lease. She wrote of Mr. Noble's offer for her own column about the south, but if the travel was too much stress on the family, she would pass if a renewal contract was offered. But Frederick didn't see it as a burden. He wanted to experience the world with Melissa by his side—beginning with Dauphin Island, as she requested.

Phoebe asked daily if Melissa would return. Though he loved that his daughter was excited to have Melissa in their lives, it stung not to be able to tell her when it would happen.

As of that afternoon, he had last kissed Melissa two and a half weeks before on the train platform in Atlanta. There were five long minutes left on the clock, but he was the boss and decided to leave for the gym. After rowing, he moved to the punching bag. That's where Chuck found him.

"Has your woman made it back yet?"

"No." Frederick gave the bag a series of jabs. "The inquiry on the Titanic is still happening. She might have to wait for that to finish."

"That could be weeks."

"I know." Sweat dripped into his eyes as he exerted every muscle in his body.

"Easy, Davenport. That bag hasn't done anything to you." Chuck threw a towel at him. "Meet me in the ring and take out that frustration on something that can hit back."

By the time he was in the ring with Chuck, Henry arrived. "I get the winner."

"Get in line, Adams," Thomas called. "I've got next. If a match is so important to you, you shouldn't have stopped to see the missus before getting here."

"Naïve Adams is going to be weak if he just took a turn with his wife," Chuck teased. "I think he should get the loser."

Henry climbed through the ropes and went straight for Chuck. Frederick stepped back and let him go.

"I have more understanding than you, Brady." Henry swung and missed. "That is, unless you pay for your experiences."

The men in the gym egged on the two. Frederick ducked out of the ring and returned to the punching bag, listening for the result of Chuck verses Henry.

Henry's righteous anger won and then took on Thomas Charles. When Frederick emerged from the showers, Henry was still going strong against another opponent, proving that exertion with his wife wasn't going to interfere with his performance in the ring.

Before getting his girls, Frederick took a seat at the diner counter and ordered the special.

"There's nothing as sad as a handsome man dining alone."

He clutched his coffee cup and turned to the voice long enough to acknowledge her. "Evening, Mrs. Smith."

"You and your formalities, Frederick Davenport."

She leaned against the counter in a pose attempting to capture his attention, but he focused on his roast beef and greens. When she didn't leave, he swallowed and glanced at her.

"If you need help choosing something off the menu, I'm sure a waitress will assist you."

"I've been doing you a favor for a year and a half by offering myself as a respectable option, but you were ruined by your ex-wife and you don't even know it! And then that New Yorker breezed through town, leaving you so wretched you can't even shave." She took his water glass and tossed the contents on his bearded face. "Frederick Davenport, you're utterly hopeless!"

Judith stalked out of the diner while Frederick calmly removed a handkerchief from his suit pocket. *If a cup of water was all I needed to be rid of her, I would have dowsed myself last year.*

***

Friday morning, Frederick woke to his alarm at six o'clock. He took the small box he'd carried around for weeks off the side table and kissed it.

"Happy Birthday, Melissa. I'll be able to give this to you one day."

Gazing in the bathroom mirror, he found himself ragged looking and decided to tidy his beard and mustache with a trim before breakfast. Once he and the girls were fed and dressed, they set off for Lucy's house.

Alexander was on the front porch swing smoking. He hugged the girls and sent them inside, asking Frederick to stay behind. "The doctor telephoned about my mother. She's not expected to make it through the weekend. I'll be with her for the day, possibly until she passes. Would you check on Lucy for me?"

"Of course." Frederick gripped his shoulder. "I'm sorry you have to go through this."

"I wish Lucy wasn't alone."

"The girls will keep her grounded."

"She's been tired lately."

"Tiredness at this phase of pregnancy is normal."

Alexander smiled and took a drag. "That's what Darla said, followed by her admonishing me not to tire Lucy with my own needs." He looked to Frederick, turning serious. "And I'm not. I'm gaging her energy levels and comfort. I'm being good."

Frederick laughed, lightly punching Alexander. "I believe you."

"I followed Darla's lecture by offering to explain a few techniques to Henry, but she scolded me."

Frederick laughed and went inside. His fair maiden was snug in the middle of the settee, a daughter on each side and a book on her lap. Frederick waited until she reached the end of the page of the story about two bad mice before speaking.

"Alex told me what's going on. Call me if you need anything and I'll be over in a jiffy."

"Thank you. You look polished today, Freddy."

"Thanks." He looked to his oldest. "You be a big helper to Momma, Phoebe."

"I will Daddy!"

"Daddy love."

"I love you, too, Beth." He kissed all three, the girls giggling over his tickling whiskers.

"I'll talk to you later, Goosy."

As he approached the front door, a familiar figure crossed the yard. The shine of her copper hair was unmistakable, the shape of her figure in her green dress that of his dreams. Screen slamming behind him, Frederick leapt off the porch, spinning her around when he caught her.

"Happy birthday, Melissa," he said as he nuzzled into the citrusy-tang of her neck.

"Thank you, Freddy, but let me see your face." She ran her fingers over the beard. "You're positively striking."

Then he was on his knee before her, a hand pulling the box free from his jacket pocket. "Beloved, I promise to love and honor you all the days of my life if you would accept me as your husband."

"Yes, Freddy. But you didn't have to—"

He'd forgotten to open the box until that moment. She sank to her knees in front of him, staring at the ring.

"I'm blinded from over here, Freddy!" Alexander hollered from the porch.

Lucy and the girls came out the door.

"Sissa!" Phoebe ran until she fell upon Melissa, knocking her to her backside on the lawn.

Frederick laughed and settled himself on the grass as well.

Phoebe's attention turned to her father when she was done hugging Melissa. "Daddy got you a treasure, but this one doesn't bite."

"I wanted you to have a replacement birthstone for the brooch you came with." He removed the ring, a cushion-cut emerald over a carat in size flanked on the diagonal by two European-cut diamonds half as large and framed with a row of smaller diamonds bound in gold. It slipped perfectly onto Melissa's left ring finger. "Mr. Hofstedder is an excellent judge of ring size by looking at a woman. All I had to do was tell him who it was for and he sized it."

Bethany interrupted their kissing by settling on Melissa's lap.

Alexander and Lucy came over with congratulations, he whistling over the ring as he held it up next to Lucy's solitaire. "Impressive, Davenport. That's the flashiest thing I've ever known an accountant to purchase."

"I decided I have had enough of practical marriages. It's time for me to live more." He put his arm about Melissa and kissed her. "Melissa is going to help me explore the world and be adventurous beyond the confines of Kingdom Davenport."

Lucy took Melissa into a hug. "Thank you for proving me wrong."

"My pleasure, Lucy, but I must thank you for telling Mr. Noble about my book proposal." She turned to Frederick. "I didn't send word about it in my letters because I wanted to share the news in person. Mr. Noble accepted my travel essay collection. It's going to press this fall. He wants me to continue to build my readership in the magazine the next few months before releasing it. I was so excited about the column offer I would have walked out of his office without mentioning it, but he brought it up because of you."

"After helping see my book to fruition, the least I could do was help give yours a chance."

***

Ruth Melling died on May fifth while Frederick and Claudio stood with Alexander at her bedside. She slipped away with a genuine smile on her lips—not unlike when she was introduced to the Davenport girls two months before.

Alexander stormed about his old bedroom, throwing pillows and cursing his parents' choices while the nursing staff and priest saw to his mother's body.

"Eliza and I were ruined by the time we moved here, but this house has the potential to be a real home for a family rather than a showcase. I want Claudio to cleanse it and for you to help me talk Lucy into moving here."

Frederick stared at Alexander from his seat beside the fireplace. "She would never abandon the Easton house."

"No, but she'd turn it over to you in a heartbeat. That was the original plan before she bought it. It was supposed to be the home the Davenport girls were raised in. There's hardly room at your house to grow your family, and with Melissa you might want a few more children. If we're both on this side of town, it'll be easier to see each other. Only a mile separates the houses, a pleasant walk even for little legs. Leinkauf is close should the girls be placed in public school, but I'm sure Lucy will insist on private. And dropping the girls here would be on the way to work. Think of it, Freddy. The yard sizes alone compared to your little space make it worth it." He gestured to the back wall. "Imagine Phoebe fortifying the camellia maze from an attack. The possibilities would be endless if the girls had this as part of their childhood coupled with the Easton property."

"Do you really think Lucy would want to live on Government Street, with all the staring eyes? And with the traffic in front, it wouldn't be safe for the girls to play."

"It's a double lot to Church Street in the back, Freddy. There's plenty of space to play and it's completely enclosed. As for Lucy, she's starting to accept her role as Olive Kent. We attended two balls this year and the house is far enough from the road for traffic noise not to be an issue."

"I'd need to discuss it with Melissa."

That evening after supper with Lucy and Alexander, Frederick brought Melissa to the gazebo and told her Alexander's plan. "Would you consider this home an option or is it too tied with Lucy and Alex for you to be comfortable with calling it your own?"

"Wherever you are is home, Freddy. The girls love it here, and as you've said, you know all the secrets. But if we do move, what do you think of us being married here? Could Claudio officiate while he's in town rather than a courthouse ceremony with a stranger to join us?"

"Whatever you wish, Beloved. It's your day to shine as the queen of Kingdom Davenport."

The week continued with planning, Melissa spending her nights at the hotel and her days with Frederick or Lucy. Frederick helped Alexander see his mother buried on Thursday by staying beside Lucy in the back of the cathedral service. Melissa sat on Lucy's other side with the girls and their grandparents. Lucy wore Mrs. Easton's old Christmas dress she'd had refitted for her wedding gown when she was first engaged to Alexander, along with the gold and garnet cross from Mrs. Melling—a spot of red amid the black-clad mourners like a stain of sin to haunt the Melling name.

The following Wednesday was Frederick's and Melissa's appointed day. What they originally thought would be a few people at the courthouse turned into a family affair at the Eastons' old property. Alexander, Lucy, and the girls were there, as well as Henry and Darla, Mr. and Mrs. Easton, Maxwell and Lottie, plus Susan and David and half the Easton cousins. Angela took the train in from Atlanta for the day, and at the last minute, Edmund appeared. Naomi and Sharon, who oversaw the meal, came out to witness the ceremony.

At precisely two o'clock, Melissa emerged from the back door in a white lace, short-sleeved gown with a wreath of flowers encircling her head. Frederick's pulse quickened and he thought he'd never make it through the afternoon.

Phoebe, carrying a tall bouquet of yellow gladiolas, walked beside Melissa, coaxing her to move faster. "Come on, Sissa."

Melissa only smiled, trying to keep her laughter contained, but when she caught Frederick's gaze, a bubble of joy burst out. Frederick held her hand and didn't let go until they needed to exchange their rings. Claudio oversaw the happenings with a bittersweet smile.

When it was time to kiss the bride, Frederick held nothing back, only breaking for air when Bethany tugged on his trouser leg. He assumed Lucy set her loose to bring their display to an end and Alexander's smirk confirmed his theory.

After the family dinner, Frederick and Melissa made their goodbye rounds. They planned on staying in his house until Saturday morning, when Lucy and Alexander would bring the girls for Pancake Time. Three nights of togetherness and packing to ready for the move.

When they got to Edmund, he mustered a smile.

"I was wondering if I could join you at the gym a few times a week." Edmund patted his bulging suit jacket. "It's time I gave up old grudges and get back into shape."

Frederick clapped him on the back as he shook his hand. "I go Mondays, Wednesdays, and Fridays at five. I'd be happy to see you there, Eddie."

Then Alexander walked the couple to the front porch and pulled them into a group hug. "Looks like third time's the charm for you, Freddy. Treat her right or I'll come for you—legally. We'll see you Saturday morning. Lucy and I will even stay for your blasted pancake chaos if you'd like."

"It's an open invitation." Melissa hugged Alex in return. "Come whenever you want."

Frederick lifted her into his arms and crossed the yard to his automobile where he placed her in the front seat. At his house, he carried Melissa inside. Doff ran out the front and he locked the door behind the cat.

"Welcome home, Beloved." He paused to kiss her before climbing the stairs. Gently setting her on their bed, Frederick tugged the fluttery sleeve over her left shoulder and brought his mouth to her skin. His kisses followed the deep cut of her lacy neckline and up to the other shoulder, which he exposed as well. "Are you ready to explore each other as we set out on this grand adventure of life together?"

Melissa lay back, tugging Frederick with her. "It feels like I've waited my whole life for this moment, Freddy."

He trailed a hand along her side to pull up the hem of her gown. "You've blessed my life Melissa. We'll be one, forever."

THE END

Bonus

"Revelry's Requiem"

A Chateau Rouge/Possession Chronicles Short Story
By
Jolie St. Amant
And
Carrie Dalby

New Orleans
1911

Carnival season was in full swing in the lounge area of the Chateau Rouge. Every night was a party at the hotel, but the revelry of Mardi Gras added a whole new level of lewd debauchery. Women danced with wild abandon wearing dresses that exposed creamy shoulders and raised the hems of their gowns to show way more skin than was socially acceptable as they kicked up their heels. In the center of the melee was Ivy, shimmying to the rhythm and smiling at her new lover, Valentino. Shivering when he raised one dark eyebrow and smiled, it was a silent promise of tantalizing things to come later in the evening.

As the most talked about bordello in the French Quarter, Chateau Rouge had the best girls. Members were among society's elite—the movers and shakers of New Orleans. Many deals had been made in the hotel's card room, with a pretty girl on either side of each gentleman.

Every evening started with the women coming down the hotel's staircase, decked out in the latest fashion. The men watched as they glided into the lounge, hoping to get some time with one of their favorite "girls". Ivy had been preferred by many until she had met the handsome musician, Valentino De Fiore. She had taken one look at him and had decided instantly that he would be hers. His passion matched her own, their affair had been a whirlwind.

When the song ended, Valentino set his violin down and rushed to join Ivy on the dance floor. He enveloped her in an embrace that left her breathless, his lips devouring hers as his hands slid over her small waist.

"Drinks?" Ivy asked when they finally came up for air.

"Yes, *amore mio*."

"I will be right back," she ran a finger across his collarbone within his unbuttoned shirt and smiled when he trembled.

While she left to retrieve the refreshments, he took a seat in a lounge chair plenty big enough for two. When she returned, she sat on his lap. He took a sip from his drink, set it on the side table, and trailed a hand up her thigh.

She turned in his lap to straddle him. Taking his face in her hands, she traced kisses along his soft neck. Her hunger for him almost taking over, she scraped her long teeth over the spot where his pulse thrummed just below the surface. The fast rhythm only encouraging her for more.

"Ivy…" the stern voice of Alcide coming from off to the side, effectively ruined the moment. "You know the rules."

She rolled her eyes, "Never in the lounge."

"Perhaps," Valentino said, "we should play some more music. Ivy, would you please do me the honor of accompanying us for a song?"

"I would love to."

"That is a grand idea," Alcide said before leaving to attend to his security duties.

Valentino held Ivy's hand as they walked to the piano area. To get Winston's attention, who currently had his head buried in the ample bosom of one of the girls, he picked up his instrument and played a few notes.

Hearing the music, Winston slowly raised his head and grinned at the woman, "Later, my beauty."

He took a seat at the piano, while Ivy and Valentino sat on top of it. They began a lively tune, kicking their feet to the rhythm while they sang.

***

Father Claudio De Fiore hopped on the streetcar with a group of passengers, a suitcase in one hand and his black bag of Holy relics in the other. The trolley was crowded compared to the train he rode that evening from Monroe. He smiled and motioned an elderly lady onto a bench as he leaned against a pole.

After the short ride, he stepped onto the banquette in the French Quarter. A charged atmosphere greeted him with shouts and loud music from a nearby bar. Claudio had learned about the wickedness that occurred during Mardi Gras in Mobile and Carnival season in New Orleans was not something the priest wished to experience. But his cousin had begged him to visit so he could brag about his success in the Southern city firsthand before returning to Italy.

Chateau Rouge wore a crisp gray façade, decorative wrought iron balconies servicing the three floors above the entry. Claudio received a few choice looks from passersby before a doorman stepped aside for him.

The pale blue, cream, and gold Grecian style could not disguise what Claudio had learned to recognize as dark spirits within a beautiful setting. Whispering a prayer, he passed his bag to the hand with the suitcase so he could do the sign of the cross. The women sitting on the couches in the lobby stared at him—the men with them nervously adjusted their collars.

Touching the cross he wore about his neck, he approached the desk.

"*Bienvenue*. Welcome to Chateau Rouge ... Father."

He met the azure gaze of the brunette behind the desk and pushed aside his thoughts of Eliza Melling. "*Grazie, signorina*. I am here to meet Valentino De Fiore."

An amused laugh escaped, her words cutting it short. "Excuse my candor, but I don't think a confession will save our young guest."

Claudio met her red-lipped smile with one of his own. "That does sound like my cousin. I am here on a social visit not business, though I am always happy to assist in that regard. I am well versed in blessing buildings."

Her laugh shifted the loose hair bun on the back of her head. "That will not be necessary, but thank you, Fath—"

He offered his hand. "Claudio De Fiore. Do not feel you need to use my title if you are not of my faith."

She accepted his handshake with her small, cold grip. "Josephine Jacobson, owner of Chateau Rouge. Valentino did set a reservation for a Claudio De Fiore, but do not feel pressured to stay if my establishment is not to your liking."

A door across the lobby swung open. Ragtime tunes being pounded out on a piano filled the elegant space, accompanied by the high keen of a violin. A couple danced through the lobby to the beat that quieted when the door swung shut. As they came to a halt by the elevator, the man's hands roamed down her hips.

The proprietress cleared her throat. "The merrymaking in the lounge, if you couldn't tell, is supplemented by your cousin this evening. He has made himself very much at home during his stay in New Orleans."

One of the men on a couch stood and kissed his companion's hand. He gave a curt nod to Claudio and a mumbled farewell to the owner as the sounds from the bar surged into the room once more. A middle-aged man gave chase to a feisty redhead. They bypassed the elevator cage and went directly for the stairs. The second man in the lobby took one more look at Claudio before rushing out the front door.

Claudio watched the retreat with an amused smile. "It appears my staying in your establishment has the potential for being bad for your business. If you would like to ask me to leave, I will understand."

Smiling, she shook her head. "Do not worry about me, Mr. De—"

"Claudio, please."

"Claudio. Business will be the least of my concerns this Carnival. Besides, it would be next to impossible for you to secure a room anywhere else in town this week." She took a key from the rack behind her desk and held it out before him. "You are most welcome. Your room is on the fourth floor, number 408. Valentino's room is across the hall."

Claudio squeezed her hand in thanks as he accepted the skeleton key. "*Grazie, signorina.* I assume I can find my cousin through those doors after I place my bags in my room."

"Yes, but I can have someone bring them up for you if you would like to go straight in."

"No, but thank you."

The quaint room overlooking the courtyard showcased more classic lines and colors like those found along the Mediterranean Sea. After setting his luggage on the bench, Claudio removed the St. Benedict's crucifix from his smaller bag. He kissed it and fell to his knees in supplication—to protect himself and his cousin for what evils lurked within the walls of what he now knew to be a bordello. He retrieved the Holy water and salt to bless his room. Then he slipped the wood and metal crucifix that had saved him and his friends within cursed Seacliff Cottage into the pocket of his cassock.

When he passed through the lobby, he looked to the front desk. A man clad in all black stood beside the proprietress like a demon in men's clothing. They both watched the priest so he smiled before stepping into the gaiety of the bar.

The dark paneled room was alight with swaying bodies, chatter, the clink of glass, and music. The upright piano was played by a man with garters over his white sleeves and a jaunty straw hat set crooked on his head. Valentino perched on top of the tall piano, legs kicking to the ragtime song as he fiddled along. Beside him, a buxom brunette in a skirt much too short for the frigid temperatures outside sang in a clear voice.

Claudio made his way across the room, creating a trail of silence before he stopped beside the piano.

"Claudio!" Valentino jumped to the ground and embraced him with one arm as he kissed his cheeks. "Why did you not leave off the coat and collar before joining me?"

His eyes swept the bar's occupancy before answering. It was lessened by half a dozen men from when he entered. "Why did you not inform me where you were residing?"

Valentino ran a hand through his chin-length, black hair and grinned. "I can assure you this hotel is better than the one the orchestra put me in when I first arrived. I found Chateau Rouge my second week here and moved in immediately." He set his violin and bow on the now silent piano and helped the singer to the ground. "*Cogino*, meet Ivy. She has the voice of a songbird."

Her gray eyes were as arresting as her figure, but Claudio felt the danger she presented before touching her cold hand. She leaned in for kisses—the hallmark of Valentino's seductions always included making his women accept and give Italian greetings.

"I have never been so close to a priest before. You smell delicious."

"It is lovely to meet you, Ivy." Claudio's hand went into his pocket to rub the crucifix. "It appears my vestments in a brothel are more inspiring than a Sunday sermon."

"Such weaklings! They need to be content with their actions to enjoy them fully. No regrets, no guilt." Valentino waved a dismissive hand before banging it on the piano. "Begin, Winston, I want music while I drink with *mio cogino*. Did you not bring vacation clothes, Claudio?"

He narrowed his eyes at the twenty-year-old. Ivy placed a hand on Claudio's shoulder and ran it down his sleeve—bringing back memories of his lost love, Eliza.

"You're about the same size as Alcide." She smiled and turned to Valentino. "Surely the head of security would loan a few things for the cause of protecting the guests from their own beliefs."

Valentino's bravado faded with the mention of the man in charge of security. "You better handle that, Ivy."

"Happily." She nipped his neck before sashaying out of the bar.

"Is she not glorious?" Valentino nudged Claudio toward the now empty section of stools along the far counter. "I can no longer remember the names or faces of those girls in Mobile. Mere children compared to Ivy. She is perfect. I hope to join her for eternity."

***

When Ivy didn't see Alcide at his normal post where he could see both the lobby and the lounge, she assumed he would be in the office area with Josey.

She could hear their voices murmuring behind the closed door.

"We must keep an eye on the priest. His presence here can put us in great jeopardy," Alcide said.

"Should I call on Selena?" Josey responded. Selena was the oldest vampire in town, and thus the person who attended to all problems pertaining to mortals.

"I do not think that is necessary. Yet. I will keep my eyes on him. And his cousin." The last word said almost like a curse.

Ivy's eyes widened when Alcide mentioned Valentino. To be put on Alcide's watch list was never good. She was tempted to listen more, but she knew it wasn't appropriate. Besides, being caught listening to a conversation with Josey and Alcide would get her into serious hot water with the two, and she was not willing to risk that.

"Come in," Josey responded after Ivy knocked. She entered the room and stood in front of Josey's elegant antique desk.

"Miss Josey," she said in greeting, then nodded to Alcide who stood across the room. He carved a red apple with a small knife. It was an interesting action for a man who typically did not concern himself with human actions such as eating.

"Valentino's cousin is visiting."

"Yes," he nodded, then waited for her to continue.

"Well, see, he's a priest, and he didn't bring anything else to wear besides his robes. We were wondering if you might have some things he can borrow. He sticks out here like a sore thumb."

Alcide raised a black eyebrow, "You don't say?"

"It may be a good idea," Josey said. "His presence has already caused quite the stir here. If he blended in, it might work out for the best."

"Very well," Alcide said, then crooked a finger at Ivy. "Come with me."

Ivy followed him to his suite on the fourth floor where the important people stayed. She hoped to have her own room there one day, but hadn't acquired that status yet. She was lucky now because she stayed with Valentino. As they walked, there was no conversation because Alcide did not make small talk, nor did he have patience for anyone who made the attempt to engage him in thus.

He unlocked the room with his special skeleton key—adorned with a black heart—and pushed the door open to allow her to enter first. She had never been in his lair, and the decor was just as intimidating as he was. The room was black. The walls, the window dressings, the furniture. He waved a hand and the candles in the votives mounted in crystal fixtures flared to life. Their flames cast eerie shadows all through the room. The room smelled of sandalwood and something darker.

"Wow!'" Ivy breathed as goosebumps raised on her arms.

"This way," he gestured for her to follow him down a dark hallway. Anyone with sense would be apprehensive, but not Ivy. She was far too fascinated. She was sure he could hear her heartbeat reverberate around the room as she walked down the hall.

If his living room was intimidating, his bedroom would make one's knees weak. A giant four-poster bed took up most of the room, the black canopy creating a gothic room-within-a-room. And not somewhere even Ivy would want to venture into.

He opened the door to his closet and began pulling out clothes. He gathered several suits that would be acceptable for daily wear.

He nodded, "These should be sufficient. Advise him to send the clothes to housekeeping when he is finished. Be sure he informs them that they are mine."

"I will. But, Alcide, what about the ball?"

"Ivy ... Selena will not like this. He is an outsider."

"He's family Alcide. Valentino's family."

He raised a dark eyebrow, "He is potential trouble. But, for now, I will send something appropriate. Ivy, if he causes any ... disruptions ... he will be dealt with. And there will not be anything I, or his God, can do to save him."

Ivy scoffed, "It's just a Mardi Gras ball, Alcide. What could possibly go wrong?"

He shook his head morosely, "There is much for you to learn, yet. This world is new to you. Please do not let your innocence be your undoing. Or someone else's."

Ivy gathered the garments close to her, "Thank you Alcide, I'll be careful. I promise." She turned to leave the room. She halted for a moment when his raspy voice said softly, "It is not you that I am concerned about."

***

Claudio stared at the suits laid across his bed. How could he decide which to wear when they all reeked of death? Turning away from the collection of black articles, he stalked to the dresser to retrieve the aspergillum. Flicking Holy water over the clothing, the priest allowed his irritation to display on his face with a scowl as he recited the words to cleanse the man's tainted fabric. Claudio would never have traveled to New Orleans for his cousin were it not for the fact he was lonely in Monroe since his best friend returned to Alabama two months before. Gone was his chess opponent, as well as the conversations and confessions the men enjoyed several times a week during their four years in Louisiana. Losing Alexander Melling's companionship hurt Claudio as much as when he lost Eliza five winters ago. There was no doubt the Melling siblings were well-versed in causing pain.

Claudio winced as he tugged on the black suit. His cousin was just as gifted in that regard. The weeping women he left across the globe were testaments to his cruel game of seduction. Though this time Valentino appeared to have been caught in a siren's spell.

"May we teach him a lesson between the two of us," he whispered as he stepped into the hall.

After a few minutes of waiting, Valentino exited his room wearing a look of dazed satiation along with a crisp tuxedo.

"Have you no self-control?" Claudio snapped. "Thirty minutes was afforded to change, yet you—"

A stupid grin filled his face. "I cannot help what she does to me, *Cogino.*"

"Which is what exactly?"

Valentino laughed and fell against him as though drunk. "I do not know, and that is part of the beauty of it! I rejoice in it—this splendor of love! I want it always and will have it."

Claudio gave a dry laugh. "You never want something longer than your contract lasts."

***

Ivy surveyed the handiwork of the young girl the hotel used to assist with hairdressing. She fluffed the dark curls that were left long and flowed down her shoulder. A golden barrette held the hair in place.

"You did well, Marie." She reached into the small purse on the vanity and handed the girl a few silver coins.

"Thank you, Miss Ivy," she said beaming.

"You're very welcome."

The girl nodded, still smiling and left Ivy alone in the room.

Ivy poured a glass of champagne and walked out onto the balcony. With her right hand, she brushed the train of her gown away then rested her arms on the railing. She looked up into the night sky, seeing the fat, full moon. Valentino would be there soon, along with his cousin. They were all going to Claire de Lune, one of the best restaurants in town. Ivy hoped Valentino would behave. He had already drawn enough attention at Chateau Rouge. Selena's attention could be deadly. As she was the owner of the Claire de Lune, it would be hard to avoid her.

When the men came to her door, she took Valentino's arm as she tasted his lips. "We'll grab one of my friends on the way out for Claudio to escort to supper."

"No, please." Claudio followed them to the elevator. "I am used to dining alone. Being with the two of you will be pleasant enough for me."

"I told you, Ivy." Valentino smirked. "Even without the robes, my cousin has no natural male urges left inside his priestly body."

They stepped into the lobby and Ivy ran a finger across Claudio's lapel. "We'll see about that. We're dining at Claire de Lune, a place where even your archbishop enjoys dining."

A cab drove them to the few blocks so they arrived at the restaurant fresh. The roadster pulled to a stop in front of the Claire de Lune. Valentino exited first, then extended a hand to Ivy. More than a few heads turned their way as they walked into the restaurant, Claudio following at a respectable distance.

The host greeted them with a smile, "Your table is ready, Miss Ivy."

"Thank you, Maxwell."

The trio followed the tuxedo-clad man through the white topped tables lit by candlelight that sparkled off of the fine china and silverware. Soft music played from a quartet situated on a small dais in the middle of the room. They stopped in the back of the restaurant in a VIP room. It was secluded and intimate, a favorite for the patrons and employees of the Chateau Rouge.

Valentino stopped in the entryway, "We need a table in the main room, please."

Ivy touched his arm, "*Cher*, this is the best table in the house."

"But, it is so…quiet. I require a table in the main room where everyone may see me."

"Well, sir," the host said. "We have no tables available at this time. However, if you would like to wait, I can seat you at the first available."

"Good. We shall wait at the bar."

"That sounds like a grand idea," Ivy said.

The three took the remaining seats and placed their drink orders.

While they waited, Valentino looked around. "This place needs more passion. I wish I had brought my violin so I could play a few songs. Clare de Lune would love me!"

"As we all do," Ivy said, reaching out to play with a wayward strand of his hair.

He reached out to pull her close for a kiss and Ivy leaned out of his reach. She slapped his hand playfully. "This is not the Chateau Rouge, Valentino. We must have a modicum of decorum here."

"Decorum," he scoffed. "That's not for people like us, *amore mio*. We are special. Chosen. All three of us—even my *cogino* here, chosen by God."

He grabbed his goblet of wine and raised it into the air, clearing his throat. "Ladies and gentlemen of the Clare de Lune, I am the violinist Valentino De Fiore! I have played in concert halls in cities all over the world, and there is no place as grand as New Orleans! I would be pleased if you would come and see me perform. I can even be found accompanying the fine pianist at the Chateau Rouge."

The restaurant went silent. Ivy, who was always pale, turned a shade of gray when he mentioned the hotel. Although the Chateau Rouge was a popular location in the French Quarter, it was unwise to draw undue attention, it could even prove to be dangerous.

"Valentino," she whispered, shaking her head.

"What is it, *amore mio*?"

"You don't understand."

"Understand what?"

"I cannot explain here. Could we leave? We can have a fine dinner at the hotel." She tugged on his jacket.

"We are just getting started. Aren't we, *Cogino*?" He looked over to Claudio. "We need to show my cousin a night on the town!"

The flames on the candles danced as a cold wind blew through the room. Ivy exhaled a breath, her hand falling away from Valentino's jacket.

A regal blonde approached them with such a sense of elegance, one would swear she was royalty. She stopped in front of Valentino, who for once, was silent.

"Good evening," she said, nodding to Valentino and Claudio. "My name is Selena Prosperie, I am the owner of the Clare de Lune."

Valentino reached out a hand in greeting. Selena glanced at his hand and ignoring it, looked him in the eye. "I provide a setting of elegance that my customers have come to expect. It is my job to see that atmosphere is maintained. If it is revelry you are looking for, I can suggest other places more to your liking."

Ivy tugged on his jacket again, "I am sure we will find a place."

Valentino looked at Selena again, and opened his mouth to speak.

Claudio took Valentino's elbow and stood between his cousin and Selena. "We apologize, *Signorina* Prosperie. I fear my cousin is too eager to show me the highlights of your fine city that he forgot where he was for a moment. We mean no offense."

Ivy looked between the two, noticing the priest fingering something in his hand. A crucifix!

Selena looked to it as well, a smile softening her hard stare. "Thank you for understanding." She nodded and took a step back to signal their expected departure.

As the three turned to leave, Selena stopped Ivy with a touch on her arm. "I expect to see you in my office tomorrow night, directly after sundown. Bring Josephine with you."

Ivy blanched and lowered her head, "Yes, Selena."

"Now, go along. This boyfriend of yours has done enough damage for the evening. See that he and his cousin return to the Chateau Rouge at once."

Ivy hurried to catch up with Valentino and Claudio.

"Why did she not appreciate having a world-renowned musician in her establishment?"

She pasted a smile on her face, "It's nothing against you, Valentino. Let's return to the Chateau Rouge, shall we? There will be a party going on there."

He kissed both her cheeks. "That sounds like a grand plan! Back to the Chateau Rouge we go!"

***

When Claudio followed the lovers out of the hired automobile in front of Chateau Rouge, Ivy's grey eyes flashed intriguingly at him before she attached herself to Valentino. The red evening gown played off her lips that looked as though they would drip blood with their lush color. She smiled at him sweetly and mouthed the words "thank you." Claudio nodded to her acknowledgement of his help in defusing the situation with Selena Prosperie—who he was certain was as dangerous as she was beautiful. Were all gorgeous women in New Orleans harboring unholy secrets?

Inside the lobby, Claudio met the dead glare from the head of security. This time, he could not muster a smile.

Valentino swept Ivy into his arms and deposited her at the center table of the lounge with a flourish. "Stay. My cousin will guard you until I return with my violin."

Ivy grabbed his hand before he could turn away. "Wait, please. Claudio must be starved. Let's eat before you turn to music. You cannot forget your cousin's needs."

Claudio took the chair diagonally across from the woman and smiled. "*Grazie, signorina.* I have to admit that without food, I will soon be forced to retire."

"Then food, music, and love making it shall be!" Valentino declared. "We need—"

Ivy interrupted his shouting command with a kiss. "Allow me to order at the bar. I'll be back in a moment."

If he wasn't so concerned over the state of Valentino's soul, Claudio would have admired the way Ivy was able to handle his cousin. Smiling, he watched the young man follow the hypnotizing movements of his current lover. "Will you play '*Boccherini*' for me tonight, Valentino?"

He took the seat opposite and shook his head, long hair brushing his cheeks with the movement. "I do not play Vivaldi unless paid handsomely. You, *Father* De Fiore, cannot afford me to play your antiquated baroque tunes. I had enough Vivaldi in Mobile to last me years! If it was not for the Tchaikovsky and Paganini, I would have gone crazy in that town."

"And in New Orleans?"

"Here I have the French influences of Chopin and Debussy, coupled with the locals' lively tunes. And Ivy. The songbird and I create beautiful music together. We shall be celebrated for our music and attractiveness forever."

Forever. Eternity. Valentino had never before looked beyond his current contract in whatever city he found himself in. What hold did Ivy have over him with these eternal plans?

The platters of blackened fish with seasoned rice and vegetables were excellent—Ivy's choice of wine an exquisite match. It was the broken conversation concerning a masquerade in two nights that concerned Claudio. He could tell it was of great importance to Ivy though she appeared reluctant to speak of it before the priest. Valentino's questions involving some sort of ritual seemed to aggravate her the most.

"This all sounds most interesting," Claudio said to ease an awkward silence at the table though the bar sounds continued around them. "I shall be most curious to learn more. It appears the carnival festivities here are different than what I learned of in Alabama."

Ivy fingered the corner of her napkin. "Alcide promised to provide a tuxedo for you. Someone will come tomorrow for a fitting, but if you don't think it proper for a man such as yourself to parade about masked, we can surely find you entertainment elsewhere."

Valentino took her hand. "Do not lose your nerve, Ivy. You know I sent for Claudio to be here this week especially for my moment of glory."

She bit her lip and nodded.

Valentino clicked his tongue and fished his key out of his suit pocket. "Fetch my violin, Ivy. It will bring you to a better mood to hear me play and then I shall remove the remainder of your cares within my chambers."

Surprisingly, she did as he asked. As soon as they were alone, Claudio pressed Valentino for answers.

"What is this plan you have in conjunction with the masquerade?"

His head tipped back with laughter. After drinking the rest of his wine, he held his cousin's gaze and grinned. "I shall be known from now until forevermore as the greatest violinist of all time! Sarasate and even Paganini himself will be forgotten as the years roll by. My name—my very face—will be immortalized as I take my place as the true master, an undying flame in the music world."

The new heights of his cousin's inflated confidence nauseated him. Possibly it was the undercurrent of dark power that he could feel but not name that soured him the most, but Claudio suffered through only thirty minutes of music and drinks before he excused himself for the night.

Locked in his room, he immediately stripped the borrowed clothes from his body and sealed the door with blessed salt and prayers. Clutching St. Benedict's Cross, he curled in the bed and willed himself to sleep.

A short time later, noises in the hallway roused him. Claudio lay in the darkness repeating the sign of the cross as he gripped his relic. In an attempt to block out the fevered procreation that pounded against the wall while moans split the night air, he prayed aloud for Valentino—and himself. He must not succumb to the memories of his violet-eyed beauty. Her scent and taste must be repressed though the sounds brought him back to the hours he had spent in her arms. He should not feel the softness of her curves nor crave the forbidden pleasure of ultimate release after five years.

"God help me," he whispered. "Take the agony of losing Eliza Melling from me. I cannot keep enduring the pain. If I am truly forgiven, please take the ache once and for all."

Cries of ecstasy shouted and moaned from across the hall, but it didn't sting.

A slamming door—a distant groan of submission.

The sharpness in his loins transformed into a dull ache in his chest.

Emptiness filling with hope, charity, and complete surrender.

"I am yours, Lord. Eliza's life was given to see it so."

The granted sleep was restorative. Claudio woke with the sun, dressed in the second borrowed suit, and left Chateau Rouge. The morning stroll to clear his lungs of the dank spirits that surrounded him within those deceptively pretty walls fed his soul. The *café au lait* and *beignets* boosted him as well.

***

The chimes signaling a customer roused Madame Vivian from her back room. A tall man dressed in a sharp black suit walked through the store, casually looking in the display cases filled with various treasures curated from all over the world.

"*Bienvenue,*" she said softly in greeting so as to not startle him.

He looked up, his brown eyes connecting with hers. She felt his intense faith. But, also a pain that haunted him though his friendly greeting was capped with dimples of a deep smile.

"Good morning. You have some interesting items in your store."

Vivian smiled in return. "Yes, we do. It is called *Enchanteé* for a reason."

She stepped closer to clasp the hand he offered. He smelled of sandalwood and spice. Intriguing. She knew that scent well.

"Are you staying at the Chateau Rouge?"

"*Sí*. How do you know?"

"Your suit. It belongs to Alcide Santiago."

He looked at his outfit with a slight frown. "*Sí*, do you happen to sell clothing? I would love to return his things."

Vivian grinned. "Nothing in your size, I am afraid."

"I am here to visit my cousin who is staying at Chateau Rouge. As a priest, my presence in the vestments made the other guests uncomfortable."

"I can see how that could happen. You must be a special guest if they afforded you the luxury of Alcide's closet."

"My cousin, Valentino De Fiore, has taken quite a liking to a woman there named Ivy."

"Ah, so *you* are Valentino's cousin!"

"You know him?"

"I know everything about the Chateau Rouge."

It was his turn to look surprised. His eyes filled with questions that Vivian could not and would not answer. "So, Father, what brings you to *Enchanteé* today?"

"I was merely taking a morning walk through the Vieux Carré. I happened upon your shop and felt compelled to come in."

"We are always glad to entertain our visitors. I take it you would not enjoy a card reading today."

He smiled. "No, but thank you. I am intrigued by these rosary beads." He gestured to a long set of small dark beads attached to a carved cross by a fine metal chain.

"Ah, the bone beads. Those are quite special. They belonged to a casquette girl, Angelique. Are you familiar with the history of the casquette girls, Father?"

"No, I am afraid not."

"In 1728, a group of girls of marriageable age were put on a ship and sent to New Orleans from France. They were escorted by a member of the Prosperie family and taken in by the Ursuline nuns upon their arrival until a suitable partner could be found. Angelique was one of those girls. She formed quite the friendship with the woman who escorted her. Madam Prosperie also encouraged the girl to work on her art, as she was very talented."

Vivian stopped for a moment and retrieved the rosary from the case, holding it out to the Priest. "When a husband was found for Angelique, they were wed and resided in a house not far from here. Unbeknownst to the nuns, the man was an alcoholic and abusive.

One night, in a fit of rage, he shoved her and she tumbled down the stairs. She died, so young.

"Madam Prosperie was enraged. She appeared at his home the next night. What happened after that was only whispered about from servants' gossip. But the man was never seen again. Some of the belongings she had ended up here, including that rosary. It's been here since but I only placed it on display today. If you ever meet Selena Prosperie, she is a descendant of the family. Some of Angelique's artwork can be found in her restaurant."

The priest rolled the beads in his fingers. "I met *Signorina* Prosperie last evening, though I am afraid that it did not go very well. My cousin can be uninhibited at times. I would, however, love to see this art. Perhaps I will go again tonight."

"If you should go, tell her Madam Vivian sent you."

"Excuse me, but is *Signorina* Prosperie well? She seemed more than upset over Valentino's minor disturbance. Surely she is used to boisterous guests, especially during Carnival."

"You are very perceptive, Father." Vivian patted his arm. "Selena's main concern is her friends. They are her family now. Anything that causes undo attention to Chateau Rouge and its special inhabitants causes her alarm."

His caressing touch on the carved beads turned into a grip. "There has been trouble at Chateau Rouge before?"

Madame Vivian shrugged. "What do you think?"

His brown eyes narrowed. "The staff seems well equipped to deal with any issues. Then the trouble has been with *Signorina* Prosperie?"

"It is not my story to explain further, Father." They held each other's gaze for several seconds. "However, I am happy to help you however I can."

"I would like to buy this rosary."

"Very well," Vivian completed the transaction and handed him a small bag.

"It was nice to meet you, Father …"

"Claudio. Claudio De Fiore." His dimples creased his face once more.

"Please come and visit me again. I so enjoyed your company."

"And I as well."

Vivian watched the priest exit the store. If anyone needed divine intervention, it was Selena. And the handsome priest was just the one to offer it.

***

That evening, Claudio looked down on Valentino from his stance atop a footstool while a tailor reinforced the bottom hem of the borrowed tuxedo pants. "I tell you I will be there, Valentino."

"Do you need a guide? One of the girls downstairs could—"

"Just because I have lived several years in Monroe, does not mean I cannot handle navigating a city, especially one as compact as New Orleans." Claudio smiled over his cousin's pouting frown. "All will be well. You do not perform until after intermission, so even if I go astray, I will not miss your grand entrance."

A knock sounded on Claudio's door.

"*Entrare!*" Valentino shouted from where he lounged on the floor, paying no mind that it was not his place to invite others in.

Ivy's beautiful form appeared in the opening door.

Was that a wince as she stepped inside? Did she feel the barrier of protection though the invitation brought her safely through it?

As soon as she was close enough, Valentino snaked a hand around her ankle and tugged her to the floor. Hands roaming her little black dress, the two bodies surged together.

The tailor cleared his throat and glanced at Claudio. "I am almost complete, sir."

"Thank you."

Claudio ignored the passionate kissing until the tailor was out the door. Crossing the room to the tangle of limbs, he nudged Valentino's backside with his foot. "Come, or you yourself will be late."

"My public awaits!" Valentino jumped to his feet and ran his fingers through his black hair, no concern for the woman he left behind with her dress askew.

Offering Ivy his hand, Claudio helped her stand, turning away from the expanses of skin exposed in several sensitive areas while she straightened her gown.

Valentino slipped on his own tuxedo jacket that was slung over a chair and came back to embrace Ivy once more. "*Amore mio,* please escort Claudio to the theater. Two tickets are waiting at will call."

Claudio used his most authoritative voice. "I require no escort, Valentino. I will attend the show and meet you afterward as planned."

"Having a woman on your arm is no sin, *Cogino*." With that, Valentino and Ivy left the room.

Alone, Claudio studied the fit of the altered tuxedo in the full-length mirror. It would be pleasant to escort a lady to the orchestra performance that night, but none that were within those walls would be right. Not even Josephine, with her coloring similar to Eliza's. No, he could never attempt to play-act with someone in residency of this cursed hotel. Bordello. *Alexander would laugh at me if he knew Valentino tricked me into staying here.*

He took his latest acquisition from the dresser, pocketing the carved rosary from *Enchanteé*. Claudio knew Selena Prosperie had something to do with what was going on at Chateau Rouge—as well as the connection with Madame Vivian at the shop—and he was going to find out how it related to Valentino before it was too late.

After he descended to the lobby, Claudio stopped at the sofa where Ivy perched on the arm. "I pray you do not take offense to my refusal of your company, *signorina*."

She shook her head. "I understand it's about your commitment to your faith, nothing against me."

He kissed the back of her hand. "*Sí*. A man would be foolish to reject your company. A fool or a priest—perhaps I am both."

"You're neither, Claudio. But let me know if you change your mind." She glanced at some of the others about the room. "There are many who would—"

He laughed and kissed her cheeks in parting. "You are too kind."

"Do you need a cab?"

"I am used to walking, but thank you."

"Be sure to watch for puddles and grime. Alcide won't share a second tuxedo. I'm afraid that one will have to service you tonight and for the masquerade tomorrow, but it can be sent for cleaning in the morning if needed."

"I will mind myself on the walk, *signorina. Arrivederci.*"

Claudio skirted Bourbon Street as he made his way to Claire de Lune. Several times he turned around because it felt as though he was being followed, but no familiar faces met his sweeping glances.

At the restaurant, he informed the host he was there to see Selena on behalf of Madame Vivian. Claudio was immediately ushered to a private office and asked to wait. He took in the space rich with Victorian furniture and red hues under the electric light before settling on a straight-backed armchair. Displayed above the fireplace was a painting of the French countryside.

Selena Prosperie arrived a few minutes later. Lean body draped in a gold silk gown and white gloves that reached over her elbows, she presented a cold shell with her unearthly beauty.

Claudio greeted her with a bow.

"I am sorry to keep you waiting, Mr. De Fiore. I was on my way out when I was told you have word from Madame Vivian."

"I am sorry to disappoint you, *signorina*. I am not here on Madame Vivian's errand but my own." He noted the way her body went rigid, as well as the distance she carefully put between them with a few mincing steps toward the door. Claudio fingered the scrolling designs carved on the beads and the delicate metal chain connecting them within his pocket. "I can only describe that I was led to her shop this morning for a purpose I do not yet fully understand."

Her lips curved into a sneer of skepticism. "I have heard things like that before, but I doubt there is anything within the store that would interest a man like you."

"And what type of man am I, *signorina*, who earns such contempt from you?"

"You are Valentino's cousin, are you not?"

"*Sì*, and I suppose that is enough for you to judge me by. You are not the first to do so, but I assure you I possess neither the arrogance nor the seductive wiles of my young cousin."

Her laugh was cruel. "I'm afraid this is something you cannot blame on Valentino."

Confused at her hostility, Claudio studied the way she tugged at her gloves. "I do not understand. Perhaps if I called at a better time we could—"

"I am not in the habit of accepting personal visits from priests." She crossed her arms as her venomous words continued. "Yes, if the archbishop comes to dine, I will pay a call at his table if asked, but I do not seek the company of those who claim to protect God's children and then do the opposite."

"I must apologize for whoever wore the vestments of my faith that wounded you—"

"If only it was me!" Her gloved hand trembled as she clutched a fist to her heart, eyes flashing red. "Pain to me I can live with—even if the one inflicting it could not."

Seeking to comfort her tempestuous spirit, Claudio ignored the possible danger of her viciousness and moved forward with a hand outstretched. "*Signorina*, I know what it is to have heartache, but there is nothing the Lo—"

Selena knocked his hand away with a motion powerful enough to send him stumbling back several steps. "I was in the process of losing my faith before I left my homeland. The betrayal here solidified my decision. I have gone nearly two centuries without the aid of God so do not expect me to fall on my knees before you tonight!"

Claudio hastily crossed himself and stared at the hand on her stilled chest as she sucked in a breath with the admission. Selena immediately advanced, her former blue eyes shining crimson with fury.

"Go, Priest!" Fangs could be seen within her snarling lips. "Forget this meeting ever happened before it is too late for you."

"I must know something first, *signorina*." Arms open in a show of peace, he held the vampire's deadly gaze. "I do not fear for myself."

"Then you're an imbecile! No man has failed to shrink before my wrath since—"

"What is to become of Valentino?"

Her laugh raised goose flesh on his skin. "He has chosen to become his own god, forsaking the one you pathetically cling to."

"How much time do I have to stop him?"

She shook her head, blonde chignon as stiff as her will. "It's too late. He's made his choice and the rituals are prepared. Now leave, Father De Fiore. My office is no place for you, especially tonight."

Catching the hint of softness in her last phrase, he gambled on the perceived weakness that she wasn't as vile as she wanted him to believe.

Claudio gave a chivalrous bow, hoping to capture his vision of escorting a woman to the orchestra and help Valentino at the same time. "*Signorina* Prosperie, I fear you do not know what you welcome with your diabolical plans. I beg of you to accompany me tonight. Attend the concert with me that I might show you Valentino's true self."

"It would be foolish for you to be in my company."

"As I said before, I do not fear for myself. In that regard, lovely Selena, I believe we are the same." His genuine smile brought a look of surprise to her face. "I know you are capable of caring for yourself, but your friends might not be as skilled. Valentino would be dangerous to them."

He saw the battle raging in her mind as she simultaneously licked her lips and leaned away. "I am overdue to feed. You are in danger every minute you stay in my presence."

Pulling the rosary from his pocket, he fingered the cross.

"Where did you get that?" Her voice snapped.

"Madame Vivian sold it to me." Claudio nonchalantly crossed the room and motioned to the painting over the hearth. "That is Angelique's too, is it not?"

Selena nodded, a faraway look in her eyes—once more their natural blue.

"My sister was taken from this life prematurely. I was sixteen when she died from fever. That was when I decided to give my life to others through service."

"A death from fever would have been a Godsend compared to the hell Angelique lived in!"

Selena snatched at the rosary, but Claudio quickly pocketed it.

"I too loved an artist who was taken from this world through the greed and sins of others. I understand the anguish and loneliness, the guilt and suffering because I did not do enough to protect her."

Inches from his face, her lips curled once more. "You can never understand."

The intoxicating sweetness of her scent, the womanly curve of her chest angled defiantly before him washed a wave of cold sweat over his body. Fingering the rosary in his pocket for strength, Claudio held her stare. "I am no man set above another, Selena."

"Prove it." Her lips brushed his cheek and her gloves encircled his neck as though she prepared to feast. "Prove your humility before I end your life."

"The artist was my lover." He kissed her cheek and leaned away to watch her startled reaction. "Our hidden love affair spanned several months and I planned to run away with her. Yes, even I once found something I loved more than God."

Her bittersweet smile brought him a semblance of peace. "Oh how the righteous fall with sins of the flesh, Father De Fiore."

"I was a deacon then, but even with my new title, I still stumble through life. We are all imperfect. Anyone claiming perfection is deceived by the devil and deserves not the vestments of the priesthood." He offered his arm. "Will you attend the orchestra with me, *Signorina* Prosperie?"

"Be careful what you ask for, Priest." She took a fur wrap from the coat tree by the door.

He helped her into the cloak and smiled when she took his arm. "Call me Claudio, a man blessed to bring the most beautiful woman in New Orleans to the orchestra."

***

Claudio and Selena were shown to a private box during the final movement of the first half of the performance. The dreamy strains of Bach vibrated to a low hum before the crowd burst into applause. Immediately after the houselights came up, a gentleman entered their alcove.

"Selena, my dear!" The gray haired man took her gloved hand without pause and pressed his lips to the back. "How good it is to see you outside of your restaurant."

"Good evening, Mr. Charbonnet." Her manner was cool and clipped. "It is kind of you to stop by. Allow me to introduce you to Claudio De Fiore."

Her hand went to Claudio's knee with an intimate squeeze while she flashed a seductive smile at him, accompanied by a wink.

Mr. Charbonnet stepped forward to shake Claudio's offered hand when he stood. "A pleasure, Mr. De Fiore. Any relation to—"

"They are cousins," Selena said before the conversation could be expanded upon.

"Splendid. I shall see you next week when I dine at your restaurant."

"Of course, Mr. Charbonnet. Goodnight."

When they were alone, Claudio shifted his armchair closer to Selena's before sitting. Her eyes darkened and her nostrils flared.

"I figured after your actions with me, word will spread about us." Claudio touched her gloved forearm and nodded to the curve of box seats stretching away from theirs. "There are many eyes on you."

Selena smiled. "I grow weary of turning away suitors. I hope you don't mind being brought into my scheme for peace."

"I am here to help you." Fingers trailed her cheek and he leaned close to whisper. "Your beauty shines, though you appear to be struggling. Do you need fresh air?"

"No, but thank you for being a considerate escort. It is past time, but I will wait until after the performance before slaking my thirst."

The orchestra returned to their seats, followed by the conductor to the center. The theater hushed until the buzz of the electric chandeliers were heard, making the thunderous praise when Valentino took the stage deafening.

"He loves being the center of attention," Claudio spoke into her ear. "He will not hide in the shadows if he is turned. You saw how he was in your restaurant last night—that was minor compared to most instances. He has no filter in his speech. He will brag to all who will listen"

Selena twisted her fingers in her lap as the crowd settled into silence. Bach's *Violin Partita #3* began, Valentino mastering the simple beauty with warmth and charm.

Claudio put his arm about Selena so he could whisper easily. "He will not be content to hide within Chateau Rouge, or even the whole city of New Orleans. His personality is one that feeds off others in a different way—he is a parasite of adoration. Ivy might hold him captive for the moment, but it will not last. He collects women in every city, leaving them with no thought when his contract is complete. Valentino is a gypsy, roaming from the highest paying client to another and sets himself as a prince wherever he is."

She gripped his hand with strength that almost caused Claudio to blackout from pain.

"Please," her voice tremored, "give me space."

With the release of her grip, she leaned against the far corner of the velvet wingchair—eyes closed. Even at rest, there was tightness in her features showcasing pain.

Your dependency on the blood of others makes you vulnerable, lovely Selena. You cannot rely on yourself all the time. You need more and I will help you find it.

Valentino's solos received a standing ovation, for which Claudio helped Selena from her chair. He shouted *"Bravo!"* but kept an arm about her as she weakly clapped.

By the time *Orchestra Suite #2* began, Selena was ashen. Claudio eased her to her feet and allowed her to gently fall into him between the back curtain and the side wall of their box. The space warm and private, Selena's lean frame cold against his length.

"Partake of me, Selena. You need strength to deal with Valentino after the performance."

"No." She tried to push away, but Claudio locked his wrists around her slim waist. Her ebbing powers were no match. "You do not understand what you're saying."

"Will it kill me?" he whispered.

"No," she replied in kind.

"Will it be painful?"

She shook her head. "I can take the pain and replace it with pleasure, but you will crave more of it."

"That is no concern for me." He caressed her bare neck and tried to ignore the press of their hips in their precarious position. "You must get relief. Take what you need to see you through the next few hours."

After a moment's hesitation, Selena pushed up his left tuxedo sleeve. She fumbled open the cufflink on his shirtsleeve and dropped it to the carpet in her shaky state. In a breathless rush, she held his forearm and kissed his inner wrist before biting down. Uncomfortableness quickly turned to exquisite ... bliss! With the heavenly sounds of Valentino leading the orchestra along the baroque tunes, Claudio soared with relief until Selena laved the punctured skin with a motion that was just as profound.

Luminous eyes and fresh red stain on her lips, she embraced Claudio with a surrendering quality. "Your blood is magic."

"And your touch is divine," he whispered in reply as he willed himself not to become too familiar.

"I might only partake of Holy blood from now on."

They were back in their seats before the finale. Even under the dim lights, Claudio could see Selena's warm glow complete with a blush of youth on her cheeks. She appeared pure and whole—virginal even, if it were not for the provocative cut of her gown.

At the close of the performance, Selena clapped and shouted as though reborn. She hastily took his arm and turned for the hall. With the help of an usher, they were brought to a gilt reception room with two dozen other distinguished guests to await Valentino. Selena fingered the floral arrangements and partook of the champagne, all while linked to Claudio's arm. Smiling over his vision from earlier in the evening coming true, he happily obliged her whim of the deception of their relationship.

Several minutes later, the doors opened to the arrival of Valentino with half a dozen female admirers at his heels. He boisterously made his way around the room, shaking the men's hands and kissing all the women while collecting their praise with his ever-expanding head.

Coming at last to Claudio and Selena, Valentino laughed. "I see how it is, *Cogino*. No one at Chateau Rouge would do because you already had your eye on the biggest prize in town!"

With the mention of the brothel, the nearest guests gasped and Selena loosened her arm from Claudio's.

Valentino made use of the change and swept her into his arms for a playful hug and kisses to her cheeks. "If you have a taste for Italians, *Signorina* Prosperie, I will happily provide when Claudio is gone. I assume you will be joining us for tomorrow night's festivities? I have taken the liberty of inviting all of my new friends"—he made a sweeping motion with his hand around the group assembled—"to our party tomorrow night."

When he released her, Selena looked ready to claw his eyes out. But Valentino was already greeting the next guests, his harem trailing along two steps behind.

Claudio clasped her hand in his own. "Have you seen enough?"

"Yes, let's go," she replied.

When her private car pulled to the curb in front of the theater, Claudio escorted her out.

Ready to walk back to the hotel alone, he handed her inside. "Thank you for accompanying me to the orchestra."

"Come." She patted the bench in the enclosed backseat. "We have more to discuss."

He couldn't hide the grin that built from his joy at spending more time with her, but he tapped down the excitement of the thought of her lips on his body once more.

"You may congratulate yourself, Claudio."

Her voice was lighter than anything he had heard from her before and he relaxed into the leather seat.

"I have been swayed by a priest for the first time since I arrived on this soil nearly two hundred years ago."

"And before that?"

She took his challenge, languidly removing her gloves and dropping them beside her. "I worked with one in France. My father was a generous donor to our parish. My childhood memories are of

Mass and church gatherings. One of the priests often took meals with us and became an uncle to me. Father Elijah."

"I am sure he appreciated the family time as much as you."

Her cool skin stroked his cheek. "Are you lonely, Claudio? You are so far from home. Do you ache for companionship?"

"*Sí*. I am human, Selena." He reached into his pocket and retrieved the carved rosary. He kissed the cross, placed it in Selena's chill hands, and closed her fingers around the gift. "For you to remember your faith and your friends—both the old and the new."

"Thank you." She bowed her head over their joined hands a moment. When she raised her head, she hung the rosary from the door handle and projected a composed façade.

"Hold to faith, however you can in your life," he admonished. "You are never alone."

"Do you miss her?" Long fingernails traced his lips as she leaned closer. "Do you still ache for your lover?"

Claudio hugged Selena to his chest, nose buried in her golden hair. "Not typically, though my arms often crave a woman to hold when I am alone."

"Poor, lonely priest." She laid her head on his shoulder.

Out the window, the buildings became smaller, set further apart. He gently set her back and shifted away. "Does your driver not know the way to Chateau Rouge?"

"Of course he does. He's bringing us out River Road. It's the closest location I have around here to feeling like I'm in the French countryside. My father had an estate in the country. I grew up playing in the vineyard every summer."

Hoping to bring the subject back to her pains, he took hold of the changed subject matter. "I too grew up around the vines, but in Tuscany. Their wines are the best."

"I always preferred reds." She ran her tongue over her teeth. "And I as well."

They sat frozen in a charged stare, the roar of the motor the only sound. The tires hit a rut in the road and threw them together. Selena held his biceps, eyes appearing more red than blue in the dark interior.

Claudio inclined his head toward her. "Tell me how you came to work with the church."

"I changed the year I was twenty. The next Christmas I came home, my father found me feeding on one of the stable boys after midnight Mass. The shock of seeing me pressed to the neck of the young man and him squirming in passion was too much. He suffered a stroke. I stayed with him as often as possible as he convalesced, but after several months he physically declined further. When Father Elijah came to perform the last Rites, my father confessed to him what he saw, asking Father Elijah to look out for me, for my soul—if I still had one."

"You do." Claudio kissed her cheek. "I can feel it, Selena."

She smiled as she settled against him once more.

"Father Elijah came to me the following year to tell me about the King's plans to send virtuous young women to the colonists to establish it with families. The church helped select orphans and girls' whose parents could not support them, but Father Elijah was concerned for their welfare. He wanted a chaperone to bring them to the nuns that he could trust. Someone he knew could deal with sailors and pirates without being a threat to the young women themselves."

"A grave responsibility for one so young." Claudio reached his arms about her. She nuzzled into his chest, loosening his bowtie.

"But I did it. I completed the task and was paid handsomely for my efforts. Many of the girls became like sisters to me on the voyage. Angelique especially." Her breath hitched.

"Madame Vivian told me about her. You don't need to speak of it if you do not wish to."

"Even as I set my home here, we kept in touch. I was at her wedding—joyfully happy for her. But on my first visit to see her afterward, I knew she was not happy though she refused to speak ill of the man. I should have taken him out the day I saw the bruise on her cheek."

"We do what we can, but it is not expected of us to prevent all sin."

"But the church! They set the girls up as lambs to the slaughter for those rough men. No, monsters! The nuns should have seen how they treated the working girls and known they would not cherish the flowers sent by the King!" Selena was ashen again, trembling hands grasping at his lapel.

"The Holy Bible tells us to seek the good in others. Do not blame those of us who look forward with hope." He kissed her forehead and followed it with the sign of the cross. "Forgive those who you think wronged the girls through their good intentions and forgive yourself."

Tears wet his shirt and he held her tighter.

"Selena, you did what you could back then. Now there is a new threat to a young woman. You must save Ivy—and the countless others—from Valentino. He will expose you all. Imagine what will happen when he discovers he can make his own immortal harem?"

She nodded but he felt her weakening in his arms.

"And now you need me." Claudio eased himself to lay on the seat, keeping one arm about her.

As though taking power from the dominant stance he gave her, Selena deftly opened his bowtie and collar. Shifting below her enticingly, Claudio gloried in the pleasure of once again offering himself to a beautiful woman.

***

Selena checked her reflection in the mirror one more time before leaving her room. Her blonde hair was perfectly coiffed, a gold barrette holding it in place. She had a black and gold mask she would put in place when she arrived at the Chateau Rouge. Her ivory and black gown swirled around her body with a plunging neckline she couldn't wait for Claudio to see. She longed for the feel of the priest against her again.

Her face flushed as she thought of being in his arms the night before. His lips on hers. Of feeding, and the warmth of his blood as she drank from him. He was exquisite but would be gone after tonight.

She brushed the thought aside. There was no time for such feelings. First, Valentino must be dealt with. Then, Ivy for foolishly bringing such a threat to their world.

With a frustrated sigh, she closed the door to her quarters. *Children!*

A few moments later, her driver pulled to a stop in front of *Enchanteé*. She walked into the store and waited for Madam Vivian to enter the shop area. Shortly, the woman appeared through the beaded curtain, a small vial in hand.

"This will take care of our arrogant violinist?"

Vivian raised an elegantly arched brow, "You doubt me, Selena?"

Selena smiled. "Not at all. In fact, I do believe I owe you."

"The priest paid you a visit, then?"

"That he did. Thank you."

"It was time, Selena. No one should carry around such guilt and be burdened for so long. Angelique would not have wanted that."

"You are right, Madam. As always," she reached out and enveloped the small woman in a hug, "Now, let me go deal with this situation."

"Yes, and come see me soon."

"I will, Madam. Thank you again." Selena slipped the small brown vial into her beaded evening bag.

"Remember, only a few drops. Any more than that will put him to sleep forever."

"I will show him mercy. For his family. And because the disappearance of a famous violinist in New Orleans could bring unwanted attention."

Vivian nodded, "A wise decision."

"Goodnight."

Resigned to her duty and the mess it would leave behind, Selena left the store. Her next stop was the Chateau Rouge for the masquerade.

The normal bawdiness of the Chateau Rouge was replaced with a quiet elegance as people arrived for the masquerade ball. The bordello was closed for the night, the only day it was closed to the general public. An unknowing mortal would never have a chance in a place filled with such bloodlust.

A man dressed in evening gear was waiting to take her hand and escort her from the car. Selena nodded to those she knew, vampires from all over the South. It was one of the two nights of the year they all gathered in one place. The other night being the ball on All Saint's Day, the day after Halloween, and that one was held elsewhere.

As Selena stepped into the lobby, her heart skipped a beat when she saw Claudio dressed in a freshly pressed tuxedo. His face was covered with a mask when he spotted her, but she could feel the passion beating from his heart. It was intoxicating. Had she been there for any other reason, she would have spirited him to a room on the fourth floor and taken her fill of his body and blood.

"*Signorina*," he said in that European accent, and it made her body ache.

"Claudio," she whispered, her voice raspy with need.

He leaned down and placed a warm kiss on her cold cheek. She was distracted for a moment, but then reached into her purse for the vial Vivian had just given her. She pressed it into Claudio's hand.

"Take this. Add only a couple of drops to his drink. Do this, as I do not trust myself to not add more and end this completely."

He cupped it in his hand then slid it into his pocket. He nodded, "Thank you."

She trailed a finger along his jawline, "You may properly thank me later."

His eyes flared with desire. "I will do what I can."

He offered his arm and Selena tucked her gloved hand into the curve. As they walked through the lobby to the ballroom, she could feel Alcide watching them. She turned and looked at him, her eyes sharp. She would deal with him later as well. He had a hand in this too, letting Valentino into their midst and risking all of their safety.

"*Signorina?*" Claudio said as she stopped for a moment. She looked into his kind eyes.

If only Angelique had found such a man.

She exhaled a breath. "It is nothing. Shall we proceed?"

He smiled. "As you wish."

Selena leaned into him for a moment before addressing the reason they were there.

"We have work to do. I trust that you have contacted the nuns? With their healing herbs, they may be the only ones who could save him if the potion takes to his body too strongly."

"They are expecting us."

"If it were any other man, I would kill him and leave him for the alligators to eat in the bayou."

He patted the hand tucked into his elbow, "Thank you for your mercy."

Two white-gloved men opened the double doors as they approached the ballroom.

"So it goes, my priest. Are you ready?"

He leaned down and placed a tender kiss on her lips. "Yes, *signorina.* Are you?"

The ballroom was decked out in hues of white and silver. White fabric streamed from the ceiling to create a cloud-like effect. The tables were adorned with tall centerpieces that featured feathers trimmed with silver and each with a special masquerade mask. A single skeleton key, a Chateau Rouge trademark added to the décor. A band was on the stage playing a Viennese Waltz.

"Perhaps I may talk you into a dance before we foil Valentino's plan?" Claudio asked with an arched eyebrow.

A thrill went through her body as she thought of swaying in his arms to the beat of the music. Unable to speak, she nodded.

Selena stopped at several tables to greet people, some vampire, some human. The party had begun, as vampires and mortals reveled in their freedom. One young vamp had mortal women on both knees, taking turns feeding from each.

Ahhhh, the insatiable appetite of the young, Selena thought.

They reached the table already occupied by Ivy and Valentino. The black suited Valentino had one arm draped around Ivy's shoulder. He leaned in to trail kisses across the exposed skin from her low cut, white evening gown.

Claudio cleared his throat to gain his cousin's attention.

"Cogino!" he exclaimed, jumping up to embrace Claudio. When he approached Selena to do the same, she pasted on a smile and returned the hug, while inwardly shuddering under his kiss. The man was ridiculously forward.

Just one snap, and his neck would break. Just one. She looked to Claudio for patience.

He smiled at her, and like a giddy schoolgirl, she flushed and returned the grin. He pulled out the chair next to Ivy, seating her as far away from Valentino as possible and for that she was grateful. Whether it was out of consideration of her feelings or for the safety of his cousin, Selena did not know.

"I am excited that you are here to witness my glorious transformation!" Valentino held out a glass of champagne.

"Valentino, are you sure you want to do this?" Claudio asked.

"I get to spend eternity with this beautiful creature. I will never grow old. I will be just as handsome as I am at this moment for the whole world to enjoy for centuries to come!"

The band began a new song, a lively ragtime tune that had Valentino jumping out of his seat. "Come, Ivy, let's dance!" He grabbed her hand and led her to the dance floor.

"Now?" Claudio asked.

Selena nodded.

Claudio removed the vial from his pocket, and with a quick motion of his hand, allowed two droplets of the mysterious liquid to drip into Valentino's bubbling champagne.

He slipped the drug back into his jacket and made the sign of the cross. A prayer for luck? Guidance? A miracle?

When the song ended, the couple returned to the table. Flushed and overheated from the dance, Valentino grabbed his glass and finished it off.

Selena squeezed Claudio's hand under the table. Now, they only had to wait for the potion to work its magic on Valentino. It couldn't come quick enough. She took a sip of her own drink.

When the music shifted to another waltz, Claudio stood and offered his hand. "Shall we have that dance now?"

"I would love to."

He held her hand as she followed him to the dance floor then led her in a flowing movement of sensual grace. Selena took in every moment. The feel of his body against her, the smell of him, the way his heart sped up when she ran her hand along his back.

But tomorrow he will be gone.

Ever perceptive, he picked up on her sudden shift in mood. "What is it, Selena?"

"Tomorrow is coming too fast."

He pulled her even closer and time stood still as his lips moved against hers.

"We have this moment," his voice was ragged, hoarse. "Selena, I—"

"Valentino!" Whatever he was about to say was cut off by Ivy's scream.

The music stopped and a hiss sounded throughout the ballroom. Claudio and Selena rushed for the table.

Valentino lay crumbled on the floor unconscious, a gash on his head. Surrounding him were several young vampires, teeth bared, Ivy moved to protect him, her own eyes red with hunger. Valentino's blood was staining her pristine white dress.

"He just stood up," she panted. "He fell. Please, Selena. I don't know what's wrong! He only had a few drinks! You have to get him out of here!"

Claudio moved swiftly, gathering his cousin in his arms. He was quickly surrounded by a pack of young, hungry vampires. Their low growls were echoing throughout the room.

Selena pushed through the crowd, tugging on Claudio's coat, "Come with me!"

Selena led them to the back of the ballroom, to the service hallway. She closed the door, locked it, then leaned her body weight against it. Even through the heavy wood, she could hear the frustrated howls of the hungry.

It was then she spotted the small quiet, Anisette, a blind girl Josey had taken in when she'd been orphaned. She was always exploring the hotel and knew every nook and cranny of the building.

"Anisette! Lead Father Claudio out the back way of the hotel. Then, take him to the nuns. I will pay you handsomely upon your return."

The girl nodded and held out her hand to Claudio, who stood breathing heavily, his cousin and his ever-present flaws a heavy burden.

He took one last look at Selena, as if there was something he wanted to say.

"Go, Claudio. Be safe."

He nodded and said softly, "*Signorina.*" Then he followed Anisette down the hallway.

When she was sure Claudio was safe, she unlocked the door and stepped back into the ballroom. She nodded at Alcide who had stood guard at the door. She addressed the crowd of vampires. "It's all over. Go get yourselves together."

She watched as their eyes returned to their normal colors, breathing slowed, and fangs disappeared.

She went to see about Ivy who still lay on the ground. Blood tears ran down her cheek as she sobbed Valentino's name.

"Valentino De Fiore will not be returning to the Chateau Rouge. His cousin has taken him away. We will discuss this further tomorrow."

This only served to make Ivy cry even harder, her body shaking. Selena leaned down and tucked a strand of hair behind her ear.

"Alcide!" Selena called, the big man by her side in moments, "Please take Ivy up to her room. See that one of the other girls stays with her. She will have a difficult time tonight."

He nodded and cradled Ivy in his arms, carrying her out of the ballroom.

Selena watched them leave through the same doors Claudio had taken Valentino. It was then that she finally allowed the tears to trail down her own cheeks.

***

Twenty-four hours after Claudio rescued Valentino from the masquerade, he still lay unconscious on the narrow cot within the infirmary at the Ursuline Convent. Surrounded by candles, crucifixes, and a strange mix of fragrant herbs, his cousin looked peaceful in his repose though the priest was uneasy. He trusted Selena and Madame Vivian not to murder Valentino, but the use of magic was not ideal. And he had been the one to administer it.

It was the only way to free him from himself.

He had repeated that to himself all day to no avail. It was time to move beyond the suffocating weight of passivity. Standing from the simple cane chair at the foot of the bed, Claudio stopped beside the young nun currently praying over his cousin. Laying a hand on her shoulder, he waited for her prayers to cease.

"Sister Sarah, please tell Reverend Mother I've gone to the cathedral to pray. Have word sent if there is any change before I return."

"Yes, Father De Fiore."

He crossed the room, and paused just outside the door. Looking over his shoulder, he watched the nun place a tentative hand on Valentino's cheek in a caressing motion.

"Sister, you are relieved from your post!"

She jumped to her feet, wide brown eyes filling with tears.

"At once, Sister."

"Father, I—"

He took her hands into his own. Knowing she felt enough guilt, he softened his tone. "You are fatigued. Send Sister Agatha for the next watch. I will stay until she arrives. And be sure to spend time on your knees for yourself tonight, Sister Sarah."

"Yes, Father De Fiore."

"Have faith." Claudio blessed her before she departed.

As soon as the elderly nun arrived, Claudio exited the building into the crisp, midnight air. He passed the Ursuline chapel, crossing the courtyard to the guarded gate. With a humble bow, the gatekeeper opened the spiked fence and Claudio strode onto Chartres Street with one hand gripped around his rosary. Cassock billowing about his legs, he made his way down the cobblestones to avoid the drunken pedestrians on the banquette, but rather dodged piles of horse dung and smelly puddles for three blocks instead.

As soon as he was through the heavy doors of St. Louis Cathedral, he crossed himself and whispered a prayer in his native tongue. After lighting a candle for Valentino and a second for Selena, he made his way down the silent nave. His hands trailed the rounded edges of the pews as his eyes looked heavenward. The arched ceiling reminded him of The Cathedral of the Immaculate Conception in Mobile, and he smiled to think of his friends there.

"*Sanctus. Sanctus. Sanctus,*" he whispered as he approached the altar. "*Dominus. Deus. Sabaoth.*"

Rather than entering the holiest of spaces, he knelt on the steps and clasped his hands in supplication and pled for forgiveness in harming his cousin.

"Help him heal, O Lord. Allow the punishment to be mine for tampering with unholy magic in order to save my cousin from a greater sin."

Twenty minutes? Thirty? Claudio did not know how long he prayed, but his legs were unable to support him once he was done. He fell prostrate onto the altar floor, arms outstretched in complete surrender.

When he at last stood, he did so as a humble servant. Crossing himself, he whispered a final covenant. "In the name of the Father, the Son, and the Holy Ghost, I will always help those you place in my path. Thy will be done—no matter the cost."

As though the city went to sleep while he prayed, Claudio journeyed toward the convent on the deserted banquette with a pace to match the stillness of the night. Two blocks away, a lone figure cloaked in a purple cape stood beneath a gas lamp.

Selena's blond hair shone bright with the yellow illumination. "I thought I'd never see you again."

Smiling, he cupped her cheeks, his olive skin dark against her lily whiteness in the shadowed street. "I will come to you whenever you need me, *signorina,* but Valentino still sleeps. I will not leave town until he awakens."

"Then I shall pray he sleeps through one more night."

He rested his forehead on hers and absorbed the carnal sensation of her breathing him in. "Do you need me, Selena?"

She shifted closer, teeth scraping his chin. "You are a gift from God, Claudio. I need to taste your benevolence once more."

Holding hands, she steered him around the next block and down an alley. Opening a wooden gate, she brought them into a courtyard lush with evergreen bushes. Selena's intent face and the tinkling of a fountain were all Claudio registered until he felt the damp bricks against the back of his cassock. Selena's hands on his shoulders pinned him to the wall.

Claudio unfastened his collar and spread his arms in an imitation of his prone position on the alter floor. "Partake of your sacrament and know that God loves you."

"And the man, Priest?"

"You are in my heart, Selena. I will see to your needs tonight."

"All of them?" She licked his throat and opened more buttons.

"*Sí*, all of them."

Claudio's silent smile twisted into a moan of pleasure as the fangs pierced his neck. Unlike the other times, Selena didn't allow him to float into a sated lull. His body was kept alert to everything—the feel of the cold silk of her dress, her open mouth beneath his jaw, and the loosening of his vestments. Claudio knew life would never be the same, but he mentally thanked Valentino for bringing him to New Orleans. Selena needed him as much as his cousin did. And no matter what she took from him, to Claudio it felt the farthest thing from a sacrifice.

THE END

Author's Note

My circle of those to thank is much the same this time around. My family, as always, had my back during the creation, research, writing, and editing of this book. The Mobile Public Library's Local History and Genealogy department was a wealth of information, once again. I enjoy my hours scrolling through microfilm, digging through the map drawers, and scouring the files and shelves.

Candice Marley Conner and MeLeesa Swann were my critique partners. Candice is always loaded with keen character insight and snarky comments about Alexander. MeLeesa is the reason this book—and the following three in the series—exists, because she told me I couldn't leave Frederick Davenport how I did at the close of *Scarred Memories*. Thank you, once again.

Jennifer Lamont served as a beta reader and helped me feel secure with bringing in my furthest outsider to the series. She assured me Melissa Stone blended in well with this cast of characters, though she was leery of the New Yorker at first. Winning people over—one reader at a time.

Many thanks to the members of Dalby's Darklings for showing your support for this untraditional series. We've made it over halfway through—thanks for journeying with me.

And a special thank you to Jolie St. Amant for my first ever co-writing experience. I'm glad you invited Father Claudio De Fiore to come play with your vampires in the "Revelry's Requiem" short.

About the Author

While experiencing the typical adventures of growing up, Carrie Dalby called several places in California home, but she's lived on the Alabama Gulf Coast since 1996. Serving two terms as president of Mobile Writers' Guild and five years as the Mobile area Local Liaison for the Society of Children's Book Writers and Illustrators are two of the writing-related volunteer positions she's held. When Carrie isn't reading, writing, browsing bookstores/libraries, or homeschooling her children, she can often be found knitting or attending concerts.

Carrie writes for both teens and adults. *Fortitude* is listed as a Best History Book for Kids by Grateful American Foundation. She has also published *Corroded*, a contemporary teen novel about friendship and autism, several short stories that can be found in different anthologies, as well as a multitude of Southern Gothic novels for adults.

For more information, visit Carrie Dalby's website:

carriedalby.com